BURNING DISTANCE

BURNING DISTANCE

A NOVEL

JOANNE
LEEDOM-ACKERMAN

OCEANVIEW ⌀ PUBLISHING
SARASOTA, FLORIDA

ISBN 978-1-60809-533-9

Published in the United States of America by Oceanview Publishing

Sarasota, Florida

www.oceanviewpub.com

10 9 8 7 6 5 4 3 2 1

PRINTED IN THE UNITED STATES OF AMERICA

*With love to my husband, Peter,
and sons, Nate and Elliot, who have
loved me and cheered me on*

The Waking

I wake to sleep, and take my waking slow.
I feel my fate in what I cannot fear.
I learn by going where I have to go.

Theodore Roethke
"The Waking"

ACKNOWLEDGMENTS

Burning Distance was written over decades. Many people touched this book, helping with research, confirming facts, details, and plot points. I thank all the friends, colleagues, and family who have been there for me. A few have passed on, including Carolyn See, Rudy Rousseau, and in particular Judy Appelbaum. Friends who read pages and whole drafts, sometimes more than once, include Mary Locke, Hans Binnendijk, Sheila Weidenfeld, Julia Malone, Julia Wheatley, Gilly Vincent, Eric Lax, Azar Nafisi, Susan Shreve, Lynn Goldberg, Jane Friedman, Amy Berkhower, Kamber Sherrod, Maryann Mac-Donald, Lois Khairallah, Soo Young Kim, Joost Hilterman, and Trudy Rubin.

I thank my agent, Anne-Lise Spitzer, for her friendship and for finding a home for *Burning Distance* with the committed team at Oceanview Publishing—Patricia and Robert Gussin, Lee Randall, and Faith Matson.

Family Judy Tyrer; Beverly Campbell; and my sons, Elliot and Nate, and husband, Peter, read, shared wisdom, and have always encouraged me. To you, my affection and gratitude.

PROLOGUE

Daughter of Jesse West

UMBRELLAS SNAP OPEN like a flock of blackbirds arriving at the grave. Twelve of us stand wing to wing as clouds roll over the green hills and the rain falls harder. Few families endure one murder. I am mourning the second in my lifetime. I'm nineteen years old, and I am beginning to see that life connects.

My father used to say, *"There are no coincidences, only life showing you its patterns."*

As I watch our small gathering on the hillside, I strain to see the pattern. My mother stands slightly apart from the rest of us in her old navy coat and thick-heeled boots, her unruly blonde hair curling wildly in the rain. I wonder if she saw the pattern or if my father figured it out before he was killed nine years ago. His funeral was the first I attended.

Early this morning as we gathered on the steps of our home in London, I caught sight of a small man in a black cap and black raincoat watching our house. He stood under a chestnut tree like an exclamation point at the end of the row of white houses. I recognized him.

Standing now at the graveside, I still feel his menace. His narrow eyes honed onto mine like a cobra sizing up its prey, then he slipped away.

To calm my thoughts, protect myself, I think of my father's other observation. A prodigal prophet with a crew cut, he used to quote from Proverbs. I repeat his words as a prayer: *Keep thy heart with all diligence; for out of it are the issues of life.*

*   *   *

I disappeared the day my father died, but no one noticed. My family thought I was with them because they could see me, but I fell into a hole on the other side of the sky where I couldn't breathe and where darkness swept me away.

Mom spent the day talking in a hushed voice, first on the phone and then with the stream of visitors to our house in Bethesda, MD. My oldest sister, Jane, answered the doorbell. My other sister, Sophie, ran in and out of the kitchen getting food for people or taking food from them, but I hid in the corner on the porch watching insects beat their thin wings against the screen trying to get in while I longed to break out. I wanted to fly faster than time back to the moment before my father left this earth. Occasionally Mom appeared to stroke my hair and ask if I needed anything. *I need my father,* I wanted to scream, but then the phone rang or the doorbell chimed, and my mother went away.

The next morning, Sophie found me with my pillow under my bed, holding onto its leg. I was ten years old. I didn't remember crawling there in the middle of the night, but when I woke, I thought it was the only place I could survive. It took Sophie an hour to get me to come out. She didn't call in Mom or Jane to help. She took responsibility for me herself. She told me we were the daughters of Jesse West and had to be brave. She told me Dad was relying on me to hold the family, especially Mom, together because I was the most like him. I don't know how she came up with her reasoning at thirteen years old, but I believed her, and I finally crawled out from the dark. I still believe her.

* * *

The last morning of my father's life, his twin-engine plane rose over the Persian Gulf, the sunlight catching the tips of the wings, my father behind the controls, the wind rushing, lifting him higher and higher from the earth. He was probably smiling. He always smiled at liftoff.

The day before he died, a man called our house. I heard the phone ringing through the open front door. I dropped my bike in the fallen leaves by the pumpkins on the steps and went into the house, down the dark hall to answer the phone.

"Is your father home yet?" he asked.

I stared out the door at the closing daylight. "He's not here."

"Is your mother home?"

The front door had been opened so I called upstairs, but no one answered. I'd been instructed never to let a stranger know both parents weren't home. "I'm sorry, she can't come to the phone right now."

"It's important I speak with her."

"She can't come to the phone."

"You must tell her to tell your father they've sanded his gas tank. Can you remember that?"

I repeated the message, which made no sense to me, but which I've repeated a hundred times since.

"May I say who's calling?" I had the presence of mind to ask, but the man hung up.

Mother came through the door then carrying bags of groceries from the car. "Who was that?"

When I told her what the man said, her lips drew inwards as though she was sucking the truth from his words. I waited for a signal from her—a smile, a nod, a hand on my shoulder. Jane and Sophie arrived with more bags of groceries, and we all went into the kitchen, where

Mom picked up the phone by the stove and dialed a number. She stared into the tiny blue flame of the pilot light while she waited for someone to answer. Jane handed me paper napkins to set on the table. As I walked by the stove carrying the napkins, Mom reached out and touched the top of my head. I leaned into her skirt.

"Then find him!" Her voice suddenly shouted into the phone. "Someone must know where he is." She left the kitchen and went to the den where we heard her making more phone calls.

Jane fixed hot dogs for dinner that night, splayed and grilled the way we liked them, with mustard and ketchup and applesauce and coleslaw. After dinner we carved our pumpkins and set them back on the steps with candles inside.

In the middle of the night the phone rang. I got up and went to the bathroom down the hall, then went into Mom's room, where she was sitting on the edge of the blue chair by the window in her white cotton nightgown, the telephone receiver in her hand and moonlight tangled in her thick blonde hair.

She was trembling. She drew me into her arms. Jane appeared in the doorway. "Dad's plane crashed . . ." She sucked in air. She inhaled all the air in the room because suddenly there was no more air to breathe. "It exploded over the Persian Gulf at six this morning."

The fluorescent numbers on the bedside clock glowed 4:15. I didn't ask where the Persian Gulf was. I didn't ask how Dad's plane could have already crashed. Instead I cried with Mom and Jane while Sophie slept on in her room next door. As the sun rose through the scarlet and yellow leaves of our maple tree in the backyard Halloween morning, we went in and woke Sophie.

Jane drove us to the funeral two days later. She'd just gotten her license. I don't know if Mom felt too shaky to drive or was giving Jane responsibility, but as I watched Jane take the wheel of our Volvo and back out of the driveway, looking over her shoulder the way Dad did, nodding to me, catching my eye, I felt a tiny jolt of hope, an air pocket where I could breathe.

*   *   *

The last year of my father's life, he clung to me. My mother has told me that. I remember sitting with him on the screened porch in the afternoons when he returned from some faraway place. While Mom was still at her magazine working and Sophie and Jane were at school or at the neighbors' houses and Millie, the housekeeper, was in the kitchen, I would be the one to let him in. He never took a key. He told us if anything happened to him, he didn't want some stranger finding the key to his home.

I remember the last time he returned from a trip, he strode through the door tall and straight with his duffle over his shoulder, a small case in his hand, his face tanned, his gray hair in a brush cut and a new beard on his chin. When he hoisted me into his arms and kissed me, I felt the scratch of the bristles and reached out and touched his cheek with my fingers.

"Lizzy!" He said my name as though it were his reward for a hard journey. "I missed you!"

Together we went out to the porch where he dug through his duffle and brought forth a present wrapped in newspaper. Carefully, I peeled away the Arabic headlines to reveal a wooden jewelry box inlaid with mother of pearl. He showed me a secret compartment on the bottom, where he'd left me a note. *For Lizzy, my peacemaker. Keep your secrets here, but take your courage into the world. Love, Dad.*

When he turned a key, music chimed from the box. He told me a story from where he'd been. His stories were always about animals. He liked to talk to me, I think, because I didn't look into his sunburned face and see the worry that Mom and Jane did, and I didn't argue with him the way Sophie did. Instead, I listened credulously to the tales of Klaus, the cagey tiger who chased monkeys, baboons, and antelopes to the river's edge for Abu, the old crocodile, who lay hiding, barely moving in the sun. When an unsuspecting animal jumped in the water to get away from Klaus, Abu snapped him up in his jaws. Andre, the leopard, also helped from time to time. When drought seared the earth, Abu offered Klaus and Andre free access to the receding river without threat in return for sending him food. One day a giant black bear named Ivan appeared and also claimed the river.

Dad's stories went on and on like this—the politics of the animals growing more intricate each time he came home from a trip. Finally, the smaller animals went for help to Lion, the one beast none of the others hunted.

"So, what happened?" I asked, holding my music box, which I realize now Dad must have bought in Switzerland or Germany on his way home from wherever he had gone. The music had stopped.

"I don't know yet, Lizzy. But when I do, you'll be the first one I tell."

Dad never came home from his next trip. When his plane drove a hole into the sea, I imagined animals around the world lifting their heads and listening to the air rushing out of the universe.

*   *   *

A few weeks after my father died, men in dark suits came to our house. My mother spotted them through the shutters and told us not to let them in, then she locked herself in my father's study. I crouched by the front door, pressing all of my eighty-five pounds against it.

Grandma Sha arrived with other men in dark suits who told the men on the lawn to go away. We all drove across the river to Grandma Sha's house by the light of a rising moon. Mother sat in the front seat wearing dark glasses at night, holding a large box on her lap. I don't remember if I missed school or if it was Thanksgiving vacation, but I remember staying at Grandma Sha's, then finally returning home— also at night, but without the box.

Branches of trees lay in our front yard from a thunderstorm. One large limb had been cracked by lightning. We crept in through the back door and found that someone had been in our house. Someone had gone through our things. My music box still sat on my dresser, but large thumbprints were smudged on the mirror in my room.

PART I

THE AMERICAN SCHOOL

1987–1989

CHAPTER ONE

KA-BOOM! GLASS SHATTERED as a test tube exploded, and the liquid and glass flew in all directions.

Adil Hasan let out a surprised laugh, then apologized as he started cleaning up the mess. Mr. Munger hurried over to see if anyone was hurt.

"What did you do?!" he accused.

"I'm not sure."

Mr. Munger looked around Adil's station then spotted the culprit. "Did you put *this* into the solution?" he demanded. "Where did you get this?" He held up with tongs an innocent looking pellet of metal. "This never goes into water. This is sodium metal," he told the class. "It can never, never mix with water! When it does, it explodes, producing very caustic sodium hydroxide and highly flammable hydrogen gas. You're lucky you weren't hurt!"

"I'm sorry," Adil apologized again. He sounded respectful of what seemed to me Mr. Munger's hyperbolic reaction, but he didn't appear cowed by Mr. Munger, whom we called Mr. Magnesium behind his back because of an impassioned lecture he'd given about the element's uses and dangers.

"Who is your lab partner?" he asked.

"I don't have one."

Mr. Munger looked around the room. "You must have a partner. Elizabeth West, I want you to be his lab partner."

For some reason—I don't know why—I was good in chemistry. I could visualize reactions, and I understood explosions happened if you didn't pay attention. I glanced at Toshiko, my current lab partner, and shrugged. "Now?" I asked.

"Now," Mr. Munger said.

"I can't believe your luck," Toshiko whispered. I gathered my books and moved over to Adil's table.

I was a junior at the American School in London, where my mother had moved us five years before in 1982, the year after my father died. She took a job as editor of *Crisispoint,* a political affairs magazine. Adil had come to the American School from Lebanon last year. He was the star of the soccer team. He had straight black hair that flew behind him like a flutter of crows' wings when he ran down the field, clear tan skin, and large, luminous eyes that made you think he knew life you couldn't imagine. He was aggressive on the field, but off the field he didn't force himself on people, and he was shy around girls. Half the girls I knew wanted to take care of him.

"Hi," I said. I don't think I'd ever spoken to him before.

"Hi." He nodded.

Everyone was still looking at us as I unloaded my books on the table. Adil and I finished the lab without saying much. I assumed it was embarrassing for him to be told in front of everyone he had to have a lab partner and to be given me—a girl and a junior. Adil was a senior. But he didn't seem embarrassed. He just started over on the experiment.

In the labs Adil and I worked quietly together, measuring elements, recording the reactions. Adil wasn't very precise in his measurements. He was also impatient when the solution didn't precipitate the way it was supposed to, but when I made suggestions and took the lead, he didn't object. He listened to what I thought we should do. He began getting Bs and then As on the lab work. One afternoon, he asked if I wanted to study for the test together.

"I don't mind," I said. That was the way my British friends answered questions.

Adil suggested we go up the road to McDonald's to work and eat. He counted that as our first date, but I didn't. He told me later he was trying to ask me out, but I was so dense I didn't understand. I understood, but I was determined not to act silly and flirt with him the way other girls did.

Finally, Adil asked me on a real date, to a movie on Saturday night. As we sat side by side in the deep cushioned chairs in the dark Leicester Square Theater, I waited for him to put his arm around me or take my hand, but we watched the whole movie as chaste friends. Afterwards we walked through the Square where a merry-go-round had set up on the large plaza under the trees. We stopped to watch the prancing horses then walked on, still not touching, down the narrow cobblestone streets to Covent Garden, where we found a small Lebanese restaurant tucked into a basement.

The waiter seated us at a private corner table. Adil ordered us honey-dipped pastry with pistachios and sweet tea. Finally, as we sipped the tea, Adil touched my hand on the table. I covered his fingers with my own. He moved his fingers to cover mine. I felt his touch through my whole body.

"Why did your family move to London?" he asked.

"My father was killed when I was ten. My mother wanted to start again somewhere else, where she didn't have to face so many memories," I said. That was the story I'd settled on though I knew the truth was more complicated.

"How old were you?" Adil asked.

"I was eleven when I started at ASL. I was the tallest person in the sixth grade. Not the tallest girl, the tallest person."

Adil, who was six feet, smiled.

"But eventually I stopped growing, and the boys grew." I smiled back. "My sisters and I wanted to stay in Washington. We wanted the memories; they were all we had of our father, but I've gotten used to London now."

"I don't think I'll ever get used to it."

"Why did you come?"

"My father thought London was safer."

"Safer than what?"

Adil let go of my hand and poured more tea. "My father's an important man. Some people don't like him." Adil watched me with his dark, cautious eyes. "Do you ever wish you didn't have to grow up?"

"I have two older sisters. All I've ever wanted is to be as grown up as they are."

"When I finish school, things are expected of me," he said.

Very little was expected of me, I realized, except to finish school, then take my life and do with it what I could. "What would you do if you could choose your life?" I asked.

Adil smiled at the question, a slow smile that lighted his whole face and made me feel I had caused it, that I had this power. I left my hand on the table hoping he would take it again.

"I'd play soccer. I'd try for a professional team. And I'd study history. My father wants me to study medicine or law, but I think I'd like to be a professor. My mother was a teacher."

"What does she teach?"

"My mother's dead."

"Oh. I'm sorry."

"I have to live with it like you do." Adil glanced around the restaurant. He didn't retake my hand. Instead, he slipped his own hands under his legs on the chair and stared out the basement window where the streetlights flickered between the grillwork. If he didn't want to talk about his mother, that was fine. I didn't like to talk about my father. But he did want to talk.

"One afternoon when I was twelve, I'd just gotten home from school. I was alone in the apartment when my father came in carrying a box. Usually my mother or my aunt was there; my father was never there so I knew something was wrong. My father closed all the shutters and told me to sit on the sofa by him. I remember one of the slats was broken, and a shaft of sunlight fell on the table. My father sat the box in the light. He took my hand and held it tight for a minute. That wasn't like him.

"'Where's Mother?' I asked.

"'I've brought you this not because I'm a cruel man, but because I don't want you to forget. You must never forget what they have done!' he said.

"'Where's Mother?' I asked again.

"He gave me the box. My father has a scar on his cheek where he was slashed once in a fight. The scar turns purple when he gets angry. That day it was throbbing.

"I took the lid off the box. At first, I didn't know what was inside, but when I reached my hand in, I touched flesh. I looked inside. I dropped the box to the floor and looked up at my father. He had given me a human hand. Why would he give me such a thing? A human hand in a box like a present?"

I removed my own hand from the table as Adil rocked on his, wedged under his body like a fulcrum ready to shoot him into space.

"'Your mother came to the office,' my father said. 'She needed the car. I gave her the keys. Then I heard the explosion. They wanted to kill me, but their bomb killed her instead.' I couldn't speak. All I could see was my mother's hand, a turquoise ring still on her finger.

"'They've killed her, Adil! We must not rest until they are killed!' My father started shouting, as though his words could bring my mother back. I ran from the room. I hated my father at that moment. I hated all his speeches and politics that had killed my mother. I ran outside. My father was still shouting oaths to the walls. I don't know where my aunt was, but she found me behind the building digging in the earth. I'm not sure I knew what I was doing, but when she found me, she said the hole was already three feet deep, and I was standing in it. I told her I was burying my mother. There was no body left to bury so we buried her hand in a corner of the yard, four feet beneath the earth."

Adil fell silent. Light fractured in his eyes. "I haven't told anyone at school."

Somehow, I knew that. I also understood that he told me because he needed someone else to know, someone to hold the story for him when he could no longer bear its weight, and he'd judged me capable of this. I didn't ask him any questions that night about why someone would want to kill his father. Instead, I reached out my hand all the way across the table to him. Slowly, he extracted his own and gave it to me.

*　　*　　*

My status at school changed because of Adil. People like Molly Dees and Tracy Malin started talking to me. Molly, who was the most popular girl in our class, told me she was glad Adil had found someone he really liked because he deserved a nice person. Toshiko was worried I would stop being her best friend now that I was getting so popular. "Molly will take you over," she said.

"You and I have been best friends since sixth grade!" I protested.

Sahar, my friend from Lebanon, said, "Be careful," without telling me what to be careful about.

"Ask yourself why you're going out with him and why he's going out with you," Mom advised. She hadn't yet met Adil, and I hadn't met his father because Adil was afraid our parents would get between us.

"I'm going out with him because I like him, because we understand each other," I said. Part of me wanted to tell Mom what I was feeling, how I'd felt the first time Adil kissed me, as though I merged with him and he with me and the borders between us fell away and we became one strong, sure force. But for the moment, I was keeping Adil to myself.

"Well then, good," Mom said. "You're right not to let people get between you, including me." Sometimes my mother surprised me.

*   *   *

Lots of kids knew Adil and would greet him, "Hey, Adil!" in the hall, but he didn't travel in any of the cliques and groups at school. He had one close friend, Fatin, who was also his cousin and who didn't like me because Adil spent so much time with me.

One day I found a box of spiders in my locker, small, harmless-looking spiders. I was sure Fatin had put them there. I took the box, punched holes in the top so the spiders could breathe, taped the lid so they couldn't get out, then carried the box into French class. When I sat beside Fatin, he scooted his chair towards the window. The teacher asked in French what was in the box, and I told him a present given to me by a friend who knew I liked spiders. Some of the girls in class went "oooo." The teacher turned the class into a lesson on *araignes*. Molly Dees asked if I really thought a friend would leave such a present.

"I'm not afraid of spiders," I said.

I don't know where my cool came from, but I thought my father would probably take the box of spiders and hand it back to the person who gave it to him so that's what I did. At the end of class I set the box on Fatin's desk. He leaped out of his chair. He was the one afraid.

Later, Molly told me that she'd heard there was a poisonous spider in the box. When I asked Fatin, he denied responsibility. When Adil heard about what I'd done, he was impressed. The story went around school, and I got a reputation for being tough and coolheaded.

Fatin never bothered me again. At the end of the term, he offered to be my conversation partner for the French exam. Fatin didn't have many friends, but everyone wanted him as a partner at exam time. He was so good, he made you look good.

I never did find out who put the spiders in my locker or whether one of them could have hurt me. I had to live with the possibility and then live beyond it. That's what my father would have done.

CHAPTER TWO

"Put your bags in the closet or take them to your rooms. We're having guests for dinner." Mom was reading manuscripts in the wing chair by the fire when Jane, Sophie, and I returned from shopping. The pale afternoon light diffused through the bay window and cast the room in shadows.

"Dinner guests?" Sophie protested, dropping into the wing chair.

"Winston has a business meeting, and he's invited the man and his son to dinner."

Three years after my father died, two years after we moved to London, Mom married Sir Winston Chatham, one of the more literary members on her magazine's board. Winston, who ran a car company, had donated a lot of money to charity and so on the Queen's honor's list long before Mom met him, he had received a knighthood and the title of "Sir." As Winston's wife, Mother could have used the title "Lady," but she was too American for that. Instead, she kept her own name: Miriam West.

"But this is Jane's last night," I said. Jane was home from Columbia University for Thanksgiving vacation. Sophie, who was at the London School of Economics this year, was also hardly ever home.

"I know, but Winston's associate is bringing his son, and Winston thought you might enjoy meeting him."

Mom released the tasseled cord on the drapes and enclosed the living room in ivory brocade. We lived in Winston's house now. "Consider this house your home," Winston had told me when we moved into the white stone and brick Victorian house on Stafford Terrace in Kensington, two blocks from Holland Park. With Winston had come a son, Dennis, now at university, and a daughter nicknamed Pickles who was Sophie's age. None of us wanted any more sisters or a brother, but we had no choice. We didn't understand why Mom had married Winston. She must love him, we told each other, but it was hard for Jane, Sophie, and me to understand why. He was nice, but boring, not at all like our father. He fell in love with her, he said, because she was so unconventional. Jane and Sophie thought she married him because he was safe after being married to our father. They thought she spent all her passion on our father, but I thought they didn't know what they were talking about.

"So who is this man?" Sophie asked.

"Gerald Wagner. He lives in the neighborhood and says he's related to Winston."

"How old is his son?" she asked.

"Near Jane's age, I think."

"You seem calm to be giving a dinner party," Jane said.

"The chicken's in the oven." That was a family saying. It was also the truth. Whenever Mom had to cook, she put a chicken in the oven.

* * *

Dr. Gerald Rene Wagner slipped into our house like a fox with quick steps, shedding a brown and green tweed overcoat, revealing a matching tweed jacket and vest. His face was suntanned even in late November. I wondered if he'd been South or to the tanning salon that had just opened around the corner. He glanced about as if looking for someone or something.

"Excellent. C'est un plaisir!!!" he said to Winston, who led him into the living room. As he passed Winston's upright piano, he exclaimed, *"Exquis!"* At Mother's early American writing table, he judged, *"Parfait!"*

I looked around the room. The old piano, the writing table, the high-backed sofa, the blue wing chairs, and the half dozen blue and beige pillows Mom had scattered about to tie her and Winston's furniture together were comfortable, but hardly exquisite and perfect.

"C'est un honneur d'etre ici!" he said when Winston lined us up to be introduced. Dr. Wagner shook our hands and repeated our names— "Sophie!" "Lizzy!" "Jane!" "Wilhelmina!" —That was Pickles. *"Et quatre belles jeunes filles!"* he exclaimed.

I wondered why he was speaking French and why he was pretending we were so important.

"What did you do, Winston, to deserve this harem?" he asked in English.

Winston smiled and put his arm around Mother. "I married the boss."

Behind him followed a tall young man with cautious blue eyes and blond hair whom his father introduced as James. I offered him a platter of vegetables and dip. I'd dressed up for dinner in a black knit dress, dangling gold earrings, and makeup. People say Jane and I look alike, both tall with shoulder-length brown hair, though mine is darker and curlier, and I have blue eyes and a thin sharp nose, and Jane's eyes are brown and her nose flat. But people confuse us though Jane is six years older. Sophie, who's short with red hair, no one confuses. And Pickles—pale with a round face and round body—looks like Winston, only as a girl.

I set the tray of carrots and celery and cauliflower on the ottoman and settled on my favorite sofa with the high back and sides that surrounded me like a cocoon. James sat down beside me.

"What do you do?" I asked, trying to sound mature and interested.

"I work in my father's factory." He took a stalk of celery and dunked it into the onion dip. "We manufacture machine tools."

"Machine tools?"

"Machines that make machines. We make engines for anything that moves, from lawn mowers to tanks."

"What kind of tanks?" I pictured water tanks but didn't think they had engines.

He listed a stream of numbers and letters and names that sounded as if they belonged in a jungle like leopards and tigers and T-this and T-that.

"*Was haben Sie eben gesagt?*" Gerald Wagner shot over to us. "You mustn't give away the family secrets!" He smiled at me with his mouth, but not with his eyes. "I see you've picked out the prettiest one," he said to his son.

"Please don't call me that," I said.

"Call you what?" He looked surprised that I'd addressed him.

Before I could answer, Mother announced dinner, and Winston led us all into the dining room. He seated Jane, Sophie, and me on one side of the table and Gerald Wagner, James, and Pickles on the other with James next to Pickles. He and Mom sat at the heads of the table.

"Do you also live in London?" Mother asked James as she passed around a bowl of rice.

"James works in Frankfurt for Wagner Machines and Tools Factory," Gerald Wagner answered for him. "James is my second son. His mother was my German wife; she died four years ago."

"Oh . . . I'm sorry," Mother said.

"Does your older son also work for you?" Winston asked.

"François is dead."

"Oh!" Mother exhaled.

James avoided looking at his father and instead concentrated on cutting his chicken.

"He was killed in a car crash five years ago."

"Miriam's first husband was killed in a plane crash," Winston offered as though needing to match family tragedies.

"The Lord chooses his own," Dr. Wagner answered. The table fell quiet. None of us knew how to respond. "James has had to step into the business," Dr. Wagner added. "He's not as talented as François, who was a natural. James is more of a journeyman."

"Sometimes the journeyman wins the race," Winston offered encouragingly. "My own son is a bit of both, I think."

"You have a son as well as daughters? Winston, you are blessed."

"Yes, I am. Dennis is reading political science and economics at Oxford."

"And your daughters go to the American School?" Dr. Wagner asked Mom.

"Only Lizzy is there now."

"My grandson, Jacques, François's child, also goes there. He's eleven. His mother is American and lives with me. After all, we must understand how the Americans think or they'll own the future, right, Winston? There is money to be made! We Europeans must forge partnerships." He lifted his glass in a toast. *"Aux associations!"*

Winston raised his glass. "To partnerships!" Mother picked up the basket of rolls and passed it to James.

As Winston and Gerald Wagner talked business at one end of the table, I talked to James across the table. His voice was soft, and I had to lean towards him to hear. When he spoke, his long blond lashes fluttered over his blue eyes. I wanted to tell him I was sorry about his mother and his brother.

As Mom passed around a bowl of fruit for dessert, James said he liked riding horses, and I said, "I've always wanted to go horseback riding in Hyde Park."

"I'd be glad to take you," he answered. "How about Tuesday at lunchtime?"

I was in school Tuesday at lunch time and was figuring how I could get Mom to let me go when Winston spoke up. "Oh, Lizzy's only in high school. She's just fifteen, aren't you, Lizzy?" He said *just* as if it were a life sentence. "Or are you sixteen now?"

Gerald Wagner laughed, a hard sound like stones falling on pavement. "So, James, *immer auf die Kleinen!*" I didn't know enough German to understand what he said, but later Pickles translated it as: *So, James, you're robbing the cradle!*

James's expression twisted from a shy smile into quite a dreadful scowl. I don't think I've ever seen anyone change so quickly. I wanted to say I was sixteen, but it didn't matter really. He shifted his attentions to Jane. To her credit, Jane wasn't interested or was being loyal to me. When he asked her out later, she declined. He never did speak to Pickles or Sophie.

*   *   *

As we carried the dishes in at the end of the evening, Mother asked Winston, "How did you meet Dr. Wagner?"

"He introduced himself at the reception at the American School last month. You were away. He said he knew who I was. He knew my mother's name, told me her younger sister's sister-in-law had married his uncle or something like that."

"What relation does that make you?"

"Maybe third cousin if it's true. Nothing by blood. Aunt Rose did marry a Frenchman who I think had a sister who married a German lawyer before the war. He said he'd always heard there was a family connection in London. When he saw my name on the school's roster, he recognized it. He's hoping to establish himself here and asked if I might help."

"Help how? Did he seem a bit full of bluster to you?"

"He gave me an order tonight for 250 transport vehicles." Winston carried in a plate of cookies. "For a ten-million-pound sale, I can put up with a little bluster."

"What does he want to transport?"

"He said he's buying for clients who don't have contacts in Europe."

Jane came into the kitchen with a tray of coffee cups. "I think he's smarter than he lets on."

"I think he was staking us out," Sophie said.

"I thought his son was cute," Pickles spoke up.

I remained silent. As I put away the silver in the drawer, I felt a chill and saw the back door had blown open.

CHAPTER THREE

"DO YOU TRUST him?" Mother asked Winston at dinner the next night when Winston reported Gerald Wagner had asked to be introduced to the German Ambassador. We were at the kitchen table eating a giant omelet and salad with fresh baguettes Mom had brought home. Jane left today for the States; Pickles was at a tutorial, but Sophie was still there.

"I told Gerald I was sure he must already know the German Ambassador and shouldn't need my introduction," Winston said. "I don't know how he knew Gustav and I were friends." Winston's blue eyes, like buttons in his round face, sought Mom's approval. "He said he'd spent so much time in France, he'd lost his German connections."

"So, do you trust him?" Mom repeated.

"He seems to know a good many people in London already, and he's promised us more business." Winston pushed his thin gray hair from his forehead. His broad, shiny forehead made him look intelligent, which he was. "His company is important in Germany, and he's trying to internationalize his markets. His firm has been around for a long time. I don't see the harm. He also asked if Lizzy might take his grandson home from football practice on Wednesdays." Winston turned to me. "He said he'd pay £5 plus the taxi ride home. How would you feel about that, Lizzy?"

"I have cross-country practice Wednesdays. I'll do it for free to get a taxi ride home."

*   *   *

"Do you ever think about Dad?" I asked Mom on Winston's and her fourth wedding anniversary the following week. She was sitting at the vanity table putting on the little bit of makeup she wore. None of us looked like Mom with her blonde hair, broad cheeks, and wide forehead. She looked like our grandfather from Sweden. Mom was the daughter of a Swedish businessman and an American diplomat who'd been trapped in Sweden during World War II. Sophie, with her red hair and sharp features, looked like our diplomat grandmother, Sha. Jane and I looked like Dad. Mom used to tell us stories about the war and about sharing her bedroom with children—Jewish refugees from Denmark—who would arrive in the middle of the night. But she didn't tell us stories anymore, and she never talked about Dad. She didn't seem to remember him. When I asked her questions, I saw the questions caused her pain so mostly I'd stopped asking, but I was worried I was also forgetting him.

Mom met my eyes in the mirror. "I think about him every day of my life," she answered, "but he would want us all to go on living."

"Do you ever think what our lives would have been if he was still here?"

She picked up a brush and drove it through her hair. "I can't live that way, Lizzy. I have to live the life in front of me."

I sat beside her and started brushing my own hair. "Do you ever ask why he died?"

We were looking at each other in the mirror, but now Mom turned, took the brush from my hand, and added a few strokes to my hair the way she used to do when I was a child. She put her arm around me. "He told me he quit hearing the music."

"What did he mean?"

She shut her eyes for a moment. "He was worn down. He knew it was time to quit, but he couldn't help himself. He took one last trip." She went to the closet and took out a jacket.

"Trip to do what?"

"Could we talk about this later? Winston is waiting for me."

*　*　*

That night I told Adil how my father died as we walked along the Thames Embankment. Adil wanted to know where in the Persian Gulf his plane had crashed.

"I don't know."

"What was he doing there?"

"He consulted for the government."

"Doing what?"

"I'm not sure. Studying pipelines, I think." That was what Sophie had told me. I was annoyed by Adil's questions. I wanted him to comfort me, at least to put his arm around me the way Mom had done. "My mother doesn't like to talk about his death so I don't ask too many questions."

"My father's the same."

"Your father never remarried?"

"He says Allah gave him one love, and Satan took her away. He will not give Satan another chance."

"Who does he think Satan is?" I asked.

"My mother said Satan was ignorance of God. My mother was Christian."

"And your father's Muslim?"

Adil nodded. "My mother was from Lebanon. My father's Palestin-ian. They met at the American University of Beirut. On their first date they went out with a group of friends. My father taught my mother how to drive. After three months he asked her to marry him."

"How did your grandparents feel?"

"They never talked until I was born. I didn't see my father much growing up because he traveled so often. I spent most of my time with my mother's family. They used to take me to church until my father found out. That's the one time I remember him getting angry at my mother. He's not very religious, but he didn't want his son raised with beliefs counter to his. He said my mother's ideas couldn't hold up in the world."

Adil and I sat on a bench by the river as a lighted barge full of eve-ning diners pulled away from the dock. The street lamps shimmered in the gathering fog. Adil cradled me in the curve of his arm. I rested my head on his shoulder. "What do you believe?" I asked.

"People believe what they're taught."

The barge moved into the center of the Thames and began cruising towards Greenwich, a lighted party dancing on water. "Do you be-lieve there's one truth?" I asked.

"I think there's one God or Allah. Each person discovers what that means in his life."

"My father told me he was still searching for God," I said.

"My father told me I should pray, give alms, fast, go to Mecca. That's what he was taught."

We were holding hands, and Adil leaned down and kissed me. I kissed him back. I reached up and touched his face with my hand, and he slipped my fingers into his mouth and kissed them. We had no place to be alone together. He wouldn't take me to his home, and he was still reluctant to come to mine so we kissed in the dark by the Thames.

"My mother told me to listen to the love in my heart, and I would hear God talking to me. Do you believe that?" I asked.

"I believe you should find out what your father was doing in the Persian Gulf."

*　　*　　*

"I'd like to meet Adil." Mother said it like a request, but also like an order. Adil and I had been dating four months.

"You mean like dinner, or could he just stop by when he picked me up to go out?"

"Whatever makes you comfortable. I won't embarrass you or him, I promise."

Adil agreed to stop by the house the next night on our way to the Kensington Library where we often met to study.

"I'd love to meet your father too," I suggested, but Adil was keeping his father off limits.

*　　*　　*

When Adil rang the front door, I bounded down the stairs, but stopped when I saw Winston sitting at the writing table in the living room. We had agreed Adil would meet Mom, but not Winston this first time. Mom went over to him. "Winston, remember Pickles wanted to speak with you."

Winston blinked. "Oh, yes, yes. I need to do that." As he passed me in the hall, he winked as if we were aligned in trying to please Mom. In that moment I liked him better.

Adil had dressed up in gray slacks and a light blue sweater. His black hair was slicked back and shining, and he'd shaved so close his tanned skin almost glowed. He handed Mom a bouquet of daisies.

She invited him in to sit by the fire. From the care she took arranging the flowers in a vase, I could tell she liked his gift. She asked me to bring in tea and handed me the vase to fill with water.

By the time I returned with the flowers and the tea, Mom and Adil were deep in conversation about his country. They barely noticed when I came in, except that Adil stood, a gesture Mom found charming, she told me later.

"Everyone uses our country to fight their wars," Adil was saying. "The Israelis, the Palestinians, the Syrians, the Iranians, the Iraqis. We're everyone's battleground."

"And you're fighting each other," Mom said. "How do you feel about that?"

"I don't want to spend my life fighting my neighbors. Neither do my friends. We can't move forward because we're trapped in our past."

"Have you ever thought of writing about that? I'd be interested in an article from the upcoming generation." By his smile I knew Adil was flattered. "I'd be happy to help you."

"We have to go," I interrupted. "The library will close soon." I didn't want Mom soliciting Adil for her magazine. Adil and I were no longer in our own universe if Mom was there too. At least his meeting with her was a success. I wondered if I'd fare as well with Adil's father if I ever had a chance.

*　　*　　*

I got the chance during the finals of the American Schools' international soccer tournament. The American School of London was playing the American School of Paris.

I was sitting with Molly Dees. Adil had scored the first goal, but then the French scored the next two. "Isn't that Adil's father?" Molly asked as the second half got underway. She pointed to a man wearing dark glasses pacing on the other side of the field.

"I don't know. I've never met his father."

"Really?"

"You've met him?"

"His father and my father know each other." Molly's father was with the American Embassy, a fact that boosted her status at school.

As the teams ran up and down the field, the skies darkened and then opened. I pulled out a giant umbrella Winston had loaned me and offered Molly a space, but she ran for cover when the light drizzle turned to heavy rain. The man on the other side of the field kept pacing without an umbrella. Adil scored another goal. When the French scored a fourth time, the man climbed into the stands and sat down at the end of my row. He was short and muscular with graying black hair. His hard face didn't look anything like Adil's. I tried not to stare. I wondered if he knew who I was.

"They would win if it were dry," he said to no one in particular, though I was the only one on the row now. His voice dragged out from the bottom of his throat—deep, rasping, filled with smoke.

"They may still win," I ventured. My voice sounded hopeful and childish.

"They're not used to rain."

I wondered what he meant. Half the games were played in drizzle, then I realized he meant Adil. For him the team was Adil.

"They must learn to win in all conditions," he said. Sitting with his black overcoat collar turned up around his thick neck, he looked like a muscled turtle, not tall and lithe like Adil. The scar on his left cheek flared as if life had fought its battles on his face. I offered to let him share my umbrella. He nodded but turned back to the game. I also turned to watch.

"To the left, take him to the left!" he shouted. I doubted Adil could hear him, but all at once Adil dribbled over to the left and started driving down the field. He passed the ball to a fellow player, who scored. Now we were only down by one goal with a minute to go. The French took the ball and began dribbling towards their goal when their forward slipped in the mud. One of our players drove in, snagged the ball, and passed it halfway down the field to Adil, who caught it with his feet as though he were born with it there. He started running, juggling the ball from foot to foot, as if teasing the other team, all the while gliding towards the goal. He was beautiful to watch.

"Go, Adil!" I leaped up. "Go!"

His father also stood. "To the right! To the right!" He looked at me again. His face seemed to allow hope.

But the defense caught up with Adil and surrounded him. He couldn't get a shot on goal, and the time ran out.

Without a word, Adil's father climbed down from the stands. As I went to the field, I saw him across the street getting into a chauffeured black limousine. He sped away without speaking to Adil.

I waited on the sidelines. Finally, the team broke from their huddle, and Adil came over to me. "You were brilliant!" I said.

"We lost."

"I know, but we came in second in the whole tournament. And you were great."

"We lost, Lizzy!" He cut me off. When Adil lost, he plunged into a dark hole; the light in his eyes dimmed, and the wariness returned as if he wasn't sure the center would hold. "I should have gotten that goal!"

We walked towards the bus in silence. "I met your father," I ventured.

Adil looked over at me. "My father?"

"I sat next to him, or rather he came and sat on the same row as me, but then he disappeared. He never introduced himself. I'm not sure he knew who I was."

Adil took my hand. "If he came to sit by you, he knew who you were."

* * *

Adil lived in Bayswater just a mile from Winston's house. He took me by his home only once, long enough for him to dart upstairs to change clothes. We hadn't planned on going out that night, but I was upset because I'd failed a math test, and Adil wanted to cheer me up. No matter how much I studied, I would never be as smart as my sisters, I thought. That was a feeling I had sometimes—that Mom favored Jane and Sophie—though Mom would dispute it. I carried the notion that, had Dad lived, he would have approved of me unconditionally.

"You're as smart as your sisters," Adil said.

"You don't even know my sisters," I said.

"Well, I think you're smart." Adil ran up the stairs to change, leaving me in a cavernous living room crowded with ornate furniture and fixtures. Heavy gold mirrors framed the room at each end; two crystal chandeliers hung from the ceiling. Gold brocade drapes shrouded the windows, which were protected by metal gates. Adil had explained that the flat belonged to a friend of the family who rented apartments around London for some sultan and stored extra furniture here.

As I waited on a sofa, Adil's aunt came in wearing a long black skirt, loose print blouse, white headscarf and no makeup. She was his father's older sister; Adil was the only child.

"Hello." I stood and put out my hand. "I'm Elizabeth West." She gestured for me to sit. "I'm waiting for Adil." I wasn't sure if she understood English.

Two men dressed in black slacks, white shirts, and black leather jackets came in and spoke quickly to her in Arabic. She barked back at them, and the men withdrew to the side of the room and waited.

Adil's aunt asked me something in Arabic. I had no idea what she said, but I answered, "Adil and I go to school together. We're in the same chemistry class. We're studying for exams together."

Adil came in and kissed his aunt on both cheeks, introduced us, then said we should go. I put out my hand again, and this time she took it in both of hers and said something to Adil in Arabic. As we left the room, the men along the wall stepped forward and nodded deferentially.

"What did your aunt say?" I asked outside.

"She said you were much too pretty and smart to waste the whole evening studying."

"She didn't say that."

"How do you know? You don't speak Arabic."

"My father spoke Arabic."

"You want me to teach you?"

"Na'am." I answered with one of the few words I knew: Yes.

"Jayyed." Adil said. Good.

* * *

"*Wa Howa Ka-zaalek!*" Good!

"*Ma tesh'ghol balak.*" Don't worry!

Adil started teaching me Arabic on the tube home each Thursday.

"*El mara el jay.*" Next time.

"*Aistihdaf!*" Bull's eye!

Not exactly a vocabulary to travel the world with, but when whispered to Latifa, a shy Lebanese girl whom I coached in archery, along with five other girls at a local comprehensive middle school, I won a grin. I had taken archery at their age, and it had made me feel powerful pulling back the bow and hearing the arrow hit the target. In January and February, Adil and I volunteered at the school where fistfights had broken out in the past. Adil's soccer coach was friends with the school's principal who'd set up the after-school program. Adil drilled students in football until even the most uncoordinated began to kick the balls and hit the targets. Afterwards, Adil and his other team members practiced with Coach in the gym. Adil practiced every day, even in off-season, dribbling a ball up and down for hours in Hyde Park, driving it to an imaginary goal. He jogged five miles a day, ten miles on weekends. Sometimes I jogged part of the course with him.

"No one works harder than Adil," Coach told me one afternoon. "Someday he'll be a world-class player."

When I told Adil what Coach said as we rode home on the tube, he answered, "I don't know if I'll ever have that chance."

"Why not? It's what you love, and you have the talent."

As the crowds pressed into our car at Baker Street, his eyes measured the distance between us. It was a distance neither of us really understood, but Adil knew what held the plumb line on the other end.

*   *   *

"You want to go upstairs?" Adil asked.

We were half sitting, half lying in each other's arms on the sofa in Tracy Malin's dim basement by the canals in Maida Vale. Several of our friends had already headed up to the bedrooms. Tracy's parents were away for the weekend, a fact she'd failed to mention, or I wouldn't have been allowed to go to her party.

"I'm not ready to have sex," I said. Where Adil came from, a girl would never talk that way.

"I wouldn't ask you to," Adil said though every kiss, every stroke of his hand was asking me to. "I respect you."

"I'm too young."

"I know." He touched my ears with his tongue, then he kissed me so that I felt he would swallow me with his mouth, and I would melt into him and him into me. We were old enough to marry in Adil's country. I'd just turned seventeen, and Adil was eighteen.

As an old Johnny Mathis tape of Tracy's mother played, I struggled to remember the list Toshiko and I had drawn up about when we would make love to a man. "I have to love the person first . . ." I said.

"I love you," he answered. He'd never said that to me before. As if surprised by his own words, he sat up slightly, then he smiled, the smile he offered only to me. As if concluding an argument with himself, he said, "I'm sorry. You want to leave?"

"You don't have to be sorry. I love you too." I sat up. We stared at each other, and we both smiled. Adil drew me off the couch and wrapped his arms around me, and we started to sway to the crooning voice. For the rest of the evening, Adil and I danced, in love for the first time in Tracy Malin's paneled basement by the Little Venice canal.

CHAPTER FOUR

"You've been to Dr. Wagner's home?" Mother asked, buttoning the jacket of her beige silk suit.

"I've only been inside once," I answered.

Gerald Wagner lived just a few blocks from us in a big white stone house with double black doors and security cameras. I'd been taking his grandson Jacques—everyone called him Jack—home after soccer practice on Wednesdays. Unlike Dr. Wagner, who seemed to me rather full of himself, Jack was funny with a gift of mimicry, especially of his grandfather who intimidated him.

"I've only been in his kitchen. It's pretty bleak," I added, settling on the bed while Mom finished dressing for the reception Winston was giving that night to introduce Dr. Wagner to his friends and business associates. Pickles had begged off for the evening, but Dennis had come down from Oxford for the party.

"Have you met Jack's mother?"

"Once. She's a model from New Orleans."

Mother slipped on her black patent leather pumps, which she wore whenever she dressed up. My mother was not glamorous, but she was pretty, I thought. "Winston said Dr. Wagner is looking for a British partner?" I asked.

"Yes. He's been giving Winston big orders. That's why Winston is hosting this party. But Wagner's slow to pay in full. I'm a bit wary." Mother stood. "We better get downstairs."

*   *   *

In the living room, Winston was pacing, rearranging the table, talking to the caterers. He reached up and straightened the mirror on the wall. Meg Mulroney, the Chatham family housekeeper, paced behind him with her big bosom and heavy oxfords making sure his instructions were carried out. Mother had managed to get Meg on a daytime-only schedule, so she no longer lived in the house with us, but Meg still hovered.

"Relax, Winston," Mother soothed. "These are all your friends. Meg, thank you for staying, but I think we're ready now. You can go." Mother smiled.

"Are you sure, my lady?" Meg never called Mother by her name though Mom encouraged her to.

"Yes, I'm sure. Thank you again."

On the sofa, Dennis was reading and turned towards us.

"Wagner talked me into giving this party," Winston complained. "Now I'm introducing him to Lord Covington and Lord Randall from the bank and to the German Ambassador—I thought surely he'd know him by now—and Jean Pierre Margot, whom I also assumed he'd know, and Rupert Kline . . ."

"I thought you wanted him to meet your friends. I thought you were recommending him for your club." I knew Mother didn't think much of British men's clubs.

"How do you like him, Lizzy?" Winston asked. "He treats his grandson well, doesn't he?"

"I don't really know him. I never see him."

Dennis flashed me an ironic smile as if we shared perceptions about our parents. Our eyes met in the mirror, and I returned the smile.

"It hasn't been too much trouble bringing his grandson home from school, has it?"

"Winston, it's fine," I said. Usually Winston was reserved, a bit officious, but tonight he reminded me of his daughter, Pickles. "I've only met Dr. Wagner twice. I didn't like him very much if you want to know the truth, but I don't know him. Anyway, he's your family, isn't he?"

"He says he is. Why didn't you like him?" But before I could answer, the doorbell rang.

Dr. Wagner entered our house carrying an enormous arrangement of flowers, which he presented to Mother. Still tanned, he was wearing an expensive navy suit with a red silk handkerchief in his pocket. His brown hair was combed back to cover his pink scalp. I guessed he was about Winston's age—late fifties or sixty—but he had a boyish face and appeared younger except for the wrinkles on his neck and hands. Jack, with his mop of curly blond hair, stood awkwardly at his side in a matching suit. Next to Jack towered his mother in a black sheath with a black chiffon halter wrap and high heels that set her four inches above Dr. Wagner. Her dark hair was piled in curls on her head, her green eyes dramatized with frosted green eye shadow and false lashes. She was a woman used to being looked at.

"So, Winston, our evening has arrived!" Dr. Wagner said.

"Thank-you-for-having-us," Serena Wagner added quickly in a Southern accent.

Winston hesitated as though he wasn't sure what she'd said. Dennis rose from the couch and joined his father at the door, both six feet tall with round faces. I could imagine Dennis in ten or fifteen years losing his hair like Winston, but for now a pale halo of light hair fell into his eyes. Dennis shook hands with Dr. Wagner and then with Serena. With a flicker of his mouth, he again smiled at me, then his face reset into the detached look he usually wore.

As I escorted Jack and his mother to the bar in the living room, the German Ambassador arrived. Winston introduced him to Dennis while Gerald Wagner waited at the edge of their circle. I was getting a cherry Coke for Jack and double scotch for Serena when I heard Dr. Wagner exclaim, "It is time that we met!" I noticed the Ambassador's face shift to a formal, slightly pained smile as Winston introduced Dr. Wagner.

"Yes, I know of *Wagner Maschinen und Werkzeugfabrik*," the Ambassador said in a reserved voice. "And I know of your father." I wondered if Dr. Wagner's father was still alive.

As others arrived, Winston and his friends moved into the dining room and were congregated in small groups near the buffet table when Adil appeared. I'd promised Adil we only had to stay half an hour. In his dark suit and tie, he looked older and much more distinguished than a high school senior. He made his way over to where Jack and I were playing chess and pulled up a chair.

"So tell me your strategy," he asked Jack. Adil sometimes drilled Jack on the soccer field after practice. Jack whispered something into his ear. "Ah . . . you're in trouble, Lizzy," Adil said. Jack's normally quiet face beamed.

"So how you guys doing?" Serena Wagner fluttered over to us. Adil offered his chair. "Oh-my-goodness, a gentleman!" she exclaimed. "I came all the way to Europe looking for a gentleman but haven't found many. Jacques has told me all about you. He says you can dribble a ball like a goddamn god. I should come see you play some time."

From the buffet table Gerald Wagner hustled over. "You going to play chess, Serena?" he asked.

"Jacques is playing for me."

"You mustn't let your son do all your work." He patted Jack's shoulder.

"I work plenty," she countered. "You know that."

I stood. "Here, take my place. Adil and I are leaving anyway."

"I don't believe I've met this young man," Dr. Wagner said.

"Adil Hasan . . . Gerald Rene Wagner." I introduced.

"Mr. Wagner." Adil put out his hand.

"Doctor Wagner," Wagner corrected without taking his hand. "Are you also at the American School?"

"Yes."

"Are you related to Ibrahim Hasan, by any chance?"

"Ibrahim Hasan is my father."

"Ah . . . Where is he these days?"

Adil hesitated. "He's away."

"In Egypt?"

"I'm not sure."

"He's not in Iraq, is he? Or Iran? This war between them must be keeping him busy."

I took Adil's hand and felt his muscles tense. "We have to go," I said.

As Adil and I put on our coats to leave, I saw Dennis watching me from the buffet table.

*   *   *

The next day, Serena Wagner called to thank Mother for the party and to tell her I no longer needed to pick up Jack on Wednesdays; she would do that now. The following week, Serena invited Adil for dinner as a thank-you for helping Jack.

"Are Jack and Dr. Wagner going to be there?" I asked as Adil and I ate lunch in the high school commons.

"I assume so."

"You might check."

"I told her you'd come too," Adil said.

"She was all right with that?"

"She said she was planning to ask you. Next Friday night." Adil took a French fry from my plate.

"I have an away track meet next Friday. I don't get home till nine."

"She said Jack has told all his friends I was coming to dinner."

"Then you have to go."

*   *   *

On Friday night, Adil was pacing across from my house under the street lamp when I got home from the track meet. I dropped my bag inside then went to him. "What's wrong?" I asked.

"I walked out of the dinner," he said. "All Dr. Wagner did was ask about my father—where was he, what was he doing, who was he working for. Jack sat across the table from me in this huge dining room that has hardly any furniture, but he wasn't allowed to speak."

"Why did he want to know about your father?" I slipped my arm inside his as we walked down the street. "What does your father do?"

"I told you, he works for governments in exports and imports. I asked Dr. Wagner how he knew my father. He said he and my father had worked on projects together, but now my father competed with him. 'I'll be honest with you, young man,' he said, 'your father owes me money, and I'm losing my patience.' He told me next time I talked to my father I should tell him that since he was unable to reach him. He got a phone call then and left the table. I heard him shouting on the phone. I tried to talk to Jack, but as soon as dinner was over, he sent Jack upstairs."

"So what happened?"

"Jack's mother asked me to help her carry the dishes into the kitchen where she said we could have coffee together, but instead I called upstairs to say goodbye to Jack, and I left."

In Adil's eyes I saw light break apart. I reached up and touched his face and kissed him. I wrapped my arm around his waist. He put his arm around my shoulders, and we walked down the street without any more questions.

*   *   *

"What's the name of that boy you've been seeing?" Winston asked at breakfast a few weeks later. I was buttering an English muffin on the kitchen counter; Mom was scrambling eggs. Pickles was staring into our new full-size refrigerator debating between the grapefruit on her new diet and the eggs and muffins Mom and I were making.

"Shut the door, Pickles," Winston complained. "You're letting all the cold air out." Pickles shut the door without taking the grapefruit. "Isn't his name Hasan?" I'd been dating Adil all year, but Winston never remembered his name.

"Adil Hasan. Why?"

Winston was reading *The Independent.* "It says here that a Hasan is wanted for questioning in deals involving illegal transfers of arms and equipment."

"There are lots of Hasans in London," Mom said.

"It says his son goes to the American School, '*allowing the senior Hasan to move in and out of the country on the pretext of visiting his son.*'" Winston read the story as if he were reporting sports scores.

I moved to the table to look at the article. There was a picture of Adil's father in sunglasses getting into a car.

"It says he's suspected of being the silent partner in a company whose shipment was recently confiscated in Portsmouth by customs agents."

Mom handed a plate of eggs to Winston. She put her arm around my shoulder as I scanned the story to see if Adil's name was mentioned.

"*Sources speaking for Mr. Hasan say he is out of the country and not expected to return any time soon,*" Winston read. "*His son lives with an aunt. According to a spokesperson, Mr. Hasan has not seen his son for months.*"

I knew for a fact Adil had dinner last weekend with his father, who was in from Germany. I pushed away from the table. "I have to call Adil."

*   *   *

In my room I sat on my bed and dialed Adil's number. I wondered if his father really did what the paper said, and I found myself wondering what Molly Dees's father had to do with Adil's father.

"You read the paper?" Adil asked right away.

"*The Independent.*"

"It's in *The Independent* too?"

"Is the story in other papers?"

"I can't talk right now."

"What can I do?"

"You can't do anything."

"I could come over."

"No."

"Is your father there?"

"He's out of the country. My aunt's being deported. She got the notice today that she has to leave Britain. The immigration office has found her an 'undesirable alien.'"

"What! Why?"

"They don't have to tell her why."

"Can't she fight it?"

"She can make a presentation, but there's no appeal."

My throat closed. I could barely ask the next question. "Are you being deported?"

"I didn't receive a notice."

"How can they do this? What about school?" I wanted to say what about me, but the fact that I was in love with Adil held no weight with the immigration office. After all, I was an immigrant too. "Maybe Winston can help."

"No. Don't say anything to him. Don't say anything to anyone. Even if my aunt leaves, I may be able to stay unless they decide to focus on me."

I felt my heart release slightly as if it had been gripped by a fist that now let go long enough to allow it to breathe.

"Where would you stay? Maybe you could stay with us."

"I'm eighteen. I can stay by myself."

"Really?"

"I'll see you tonight. I'll meet you at our place at eight."

Our place was the restaurant where we'd had our first date. The thought of Adil living on his own was suddenly thrilling to me.

*   *   *

Adil arrived at the restaurant with two men who stationed themselves at a table at an angle to the front door and the kitchen. He said they were cousins visiting, but they followed at a distance.

"They're bodyguards, aren't they?" I said.

"Why do I need bodyguards?"

"They are, aren't they?"

"My father's worried."

I looked around the restaurant and suddenly wondered who all these people were, especially a new couple walking down the stairs and pointing to a table near us. I'd been going out with Adil all year. I thought I knew him. He relied on my knowing him and caring about him in a way no one else did. He had no brothers or sisters. He shared with me what he shared with few other people, and yet I knew little of the specifics of his and his family's lives. "Have you talked to your father?"

Adil also glanced at the couple on the stairs. They were laughing too loudly. "It's a big misunderstanding, he says. He's sorting it out, but we have to be cautious until it's cleared up."

The couple sat one table away, between us and Adil's "cousins."

"Does that mean you're staying or leaving?"

"I want to stay," he said, but the way he said it made my heart sink.

"You have another month of school." I tried not to put my own interests first.

"I don't want to go, Lizzy."

"If you leave, where will you go?"

"Wherever my father says. I'm not sure."

We were close to being adults, but we didn't yet have control over our lives. We were still tethered to our parents' worlds. I wondered if Adil would ever be free.

"It's not safe in Britain, my father says. But it's not safe anywhere, I told him. It's all politics! I hate politics!" His "cousins" looked over as his voice rose.

I covered his hand. "If you have to leave, maybe I can come visit you," I said as if his anxiety were focused on leaving me.

"I don't know where we'll be. I'm not sure where my home is anymore."

"Do you want to talk about your father?" I leaned close to him on the table.

His body stiffened. "I can't."

"The paper says your father's involved in illegal arms trade?"

"My father's business is his business. The government knows what he does."

"Which government?" I asked, but Adil didn't answer.

*   *   *

The deportation of Adil's aunt was delayed until June either by the good graces or the inefficiency of the Immigration Office. Instead of distracting Adil, the upheaval concentrated his mind, and he studied for exams as though they were his last link to the life he wanted to live. He ended up getting three As and two B+s and made honor roll. Where he lost concentration was with me. I supposed he knew what I was unwilling to accept, that we were destined to part, so he began distancing himself. When I tried to get him to talk, he would say he needed to study.

"Then let's study together." But he said he couldn't concentrate as well with me. We still met once or twice a week in Hyde Park to run in the early evenings, but Adil increased his distance and his pace so that I saw him for only the first half mile before he pulled away to circle the park and then circle it again.

Though he objected, I finally persuaded Adil to go to the junior-senior prom with me. I arranged for us to go with Toshiko and her date and Sahar and hers. Adil and Sahar didn't get along so from the start Adil was quiet. He'd forgotten to buy me a corsage, an oversight Sahar pointed out. I was the only girl at the prom without flowers, which shouldn't have mattered to me, but for some reason it did. Adil barely talked to me or anyone in the car or at the table. When others went off to dance, Adil just sat. When I tried to get him to tell me what was wrong, he said, "I hate all these people around. Can't we leave?"

"Adil, it's our prom, the only one we might ever have together."

Deep down I knew I should go off with him and say to hell with the corsage and the limousine and the dancing, but I was scared and instead clung to traditions as if they might hold off the dissolution coming upon us.

When Adil went to get us sodas, Fatin cornered me. "I can't believe you made Adil come to this." Fatin was at the prom by himself.

"I didn't make him."

"Do you have any idea what's happening in his life?"

I had to admit that I didn't. That was part of our problem. Adil had closed himself off.

"His aunt's shipping out all their things. His father's on the phone to him two and three times a day."

When Adil returned, I said, "If you really want to leave, we can." But I said it more like a challenge than an offer.

He sat back down at the table with its pink and white roses and gold centerpiece. "I'll stay."

I noticed Molly Dees watching us from the next table. "You want to dance?" I asked.

"I don't feel like dancing."

We sat watching everyone else. From the dance floor I again noticed Molly Dees looking at us. "Is there someone else you want to dance with?" The question was provocative.

"What do you mean?"

"You're ignoring me. I thought maybe there was someone else."

Suddenly Adil exploded. "I can't do this!"

"Do what?" I asked innocently.

"I can't dance. I can't bring you flowers. I can't pretend everything is a rose right now!" He pulled a rose from the centerpiece and tore off its head. "I've got to get out of here!" He stood. "Fatin will take you home." Then, without warning, he plunged across the dance floor.

Rather than follow him, I let embarrassment rule and stayed in my chair. I saw him speak with Fatin, then he disappeared.

Fatin came over. "When do you want to leave?"

"I'll stay with my friends," I answered. "They'll take me home."

The last two hours of the prom were the longest in my life. I felt as if I'd swallowed my heart, and it was expanding to fill my stomach and kept expanding to fill my lungs so that I couldn't breathe and filled my throat so that I couldn't speak and my head so that my eyes teared and my skull ached. Toshiko and Sahar tried to comfort me. Even Molly Dees came over.

"Is everything all right?" she asked.

"Fine," I managed to say. "Adil wasn't feeling well so he left."

When I got home, I cried myself to sleep. I was ashamed at how conventional I'd been and yet was furious with Adil for abandoning me.

Adil left London the following week. He came over to say goodbye. We were both chastened. We knew we'd hurt each other. I was in love. He was in love too, I thought, but he didn't know how to deal with the situation any better than I. Though I didn't understand all the events swirling around him and his family, I understood that they were bigger than either of us and that we were too young and too inexperienced to challenge the hold they had on our lives. As we walked mute through Holland Park, I determined someday I would know what to do. Someday I would not simply yield.

Adil must have been sharing some version of that thought because he said, "Maybe it will be different one day."

"Can't you stay?" I'd promised myself not to make a scene, but I couldn't help myself. I kept thinking there was something I could do or say to turn the course of events.

"Lizzy," Adil rebuked me gently, "I have to go." He kissed me goodbye then, a long, tender kiss that neither of us knew how to end nor how to extend. He left me sitting on a park bench on a secluded path under a chestnut tree. I'd asked him to do that. I didn't want to say goodbye at my house or in the street. I wanted to say goodbye in a beautiful place and remember that place. As he left, I looked up into the branches of the tree and wept. I thought there would never be anyone else again in my life, that I had already lost my father and now I was losing the only other man I would ever love.

CHAPTER FIVE

IN EARLY DECEMBER, Mother found me on my bed with newspapers spread all about. Over the summer and fall, reports of Ibrahim Hasan's alleged dealings had drawn headlines. I read whatever I could find in the hope of discovering some clue to Adil's whereabouts. Adil hadn't given me an address because he said his father didn't have one yet. He wasn't sure where they would be settling, but he said he'd write. Every day I checked the mailbox, but no letters came, only two postcards in envelopes, one in July with the Tower of London on the card, a local stamp, and a three-word message:

Don't forget me.
Always, A.

In September, another envelope with a postcard inside of Big Ben and Parliament, a stamp with the Queen's face, and the message:

Sodium + Water
You + Me
On fire.
Always, A.

Again, no signature, no return address, and no way for me to answer. I assumed someone mailed the cards for him. Their brevity hurt
almost as much as silence. Adil and I had never written each other so
I didn't know what I was expecting, but more than this.

Meanwhile, news stories about his father focused on the transfer of
certain machine tools and technology to nations under embargo.
That day the story alleged Ibrahim Hasan's dealings with a West German tool company that manufactured spinning lathes used to build
centrifuges. I didn't know what spinning lathes were, but according
to the paper, they linked to uranium enrichment, and uranium linked
to nuclear weapons. I wondered if the company could be Dr. Wagner's. I alternated between wanting to save Adil from this life and
wondering how I had fallen in love with the son of an arms dealer.

Mom came over and sat under the canopy on my bed. She'd been
reading the paper too. "What do you think?" she asked.

"What do *you* think?" For a change I wanted my mother's
opinion.

"I think Adil's father is in trouble if he comes back to Britain, but I
doubt he will."

"So you think it's true?"

She pulled her skirt up around her knees and sat cross-legged. She
regarded me seriously. "Perhaps I shouldn't assume, but from what
I've read ..."

"Dr. Wagner makes machine tools, and he knows Adil's father.
And Molly Dee's father knows Adil's father." I wasn't sure what these
facts meant, but I offered them in defense of Adil's father.

Mother squinted at the information as if it were a missile far away,
interesting but not threatening. "They do?" she asked glancing out the
window where it was growing dark. I wondered what she was thinking. Mother had worked so hard to get us through Dad's death years

ago and avoid plunging us into her grief that out of habit she avoided talking about her own feelings. Sitting with her on the bed in the late afternoon light, I was thinking about her secrets and my own and wishing we could share them.

"I'll speak to Winston," she said. "He often asks me what you think about things. He thinks you're very interesting."

"Me?"

"You."

I'd never thought anyone outside of Adil and a few of my friends thought I was interesting, let alone Winston. "Why does he think I'm interesting?"

"Because you stand up for yourself in a quiet way. You don't follow everyone else's ideas. You fell in love with Adil, and you don't let all these newspaper articles and other people's opinions get in your way." Her voice sounded almost wistful.

I was ashamed to tell her I'd been wondering if I should let all these newspaper articles matter and try to forget Adil. "I haven't even gotten a letter from him."

"He may be trying to protect you. These are serious allegations. Winston's worried about you. He wanted to know if you'd heard anything more from Adil."

The light shifted in the room. I began folding up the newspapers. I'd told Mother about the postcards, but I didn't want her sharing my confidences with Winston. He was not my father. I no longer wanted to talk about Adil.

"You understand why these allegations are serious?" she asked.

"Yes, Mother," I said more stiffly. "I understand why nuclear weapons are serious."

*   *   *

At school the next day I asked Fatin where Adil was. Fatin and I still had French together and sometimes lunch. "I can't tell you," he answered.

"You can't tell me because you don't know or because you have to keep a secret?"

"I just can't tell you."

I watched him peel pepperoni off his pizza. "Can you tell me if he's received my letters?" From the school office I'd gotten the postbox address in London from which mail was supposedly forwarded to his family.

"No."

"No, he didn't get them, or no, you can't tell me."

"I'm not Adil's keeper," he protested.

I watched his face to see what he knew. Most people's faces align, but the left side of Fatin's face was a quarter of an inch or so lower than the right so that he looked off balance, as if his face had been through a press and a small wrinkle had set in. His mouth looked as if it were in a permanent sneer. "You miss him too," I said. "I think you won't tell me because you're afraid."

"What am I afraid of?"

Before I could speculate, Molly Dees sat down beside us. "Hey, guys." No one else would call Fatin, "guy." I wondered if she'd also read the news article. "What have you heard from Adil?"

Neither Fatin nor I answered, then finally Fatin said, "Nothing."

"Really? That's surprising."

"Why is it surprising?" I'm glad Fatin answered because I also found it surprising.

"I heard he was on the Isle of Wight," Molly confided.

"Who told you that?" Fatin asked.

Molly must have decided she'd said more than she should have. "It's probably just a rumor. If you do hear from him, tell him I said hello and that we miss him. Tell him to sneak back for graduation."

"What would Adil be doing on the Isle of Wight?" I asked after Molly left. Fatin shrugged. I watched to see if he was hiding information, but Fatin's face deflected emotion. "Molly's father works at the American Embassy," I pointed out. "Maybe Mr. Dees knows something."

"I'm sure he knows a great deal. He's the Commercial Attaché. But that doesn't mean Molly knows anything, though she likes to act as if she knows everything. My observation is that she knows very little."

"I hate to hear what you say about me behind my back."

Fatin smiled. "I never talk about you. I'm much too afraid of you."

* * *

Molly drew up beside me as I hurried towards the tube after school. "I probably shouldn't tell you," she told me, "but I heard Adil's father has been back in the country. Do you know anything about that?"

"How would I know?"

"I thought maybe you'd heard from Adil, that he was here."

"I don't know where he is."

"Have the two of you broken up?"

"His family got deported," I reminded her. "It's a little hard to keep a relationship going."

"You want to get something to eat?"

I was cold and wanted to go home, but I followed Molly into the pub on the corner where we settled at a table away from the students playing darts. I decided that Molly either had a crush on Adil, or she was gathering information for her father. "Do you like Adil?" I asked.

"Everyone likes Adil."

"No, I mean more than that. You're always asking me about him."

She twisted a strand of her blonde hair as she prepared an answer. "I'm worried about him. You should be too. He has no chance to live a normal life."

"What's a normal life?"

"Living in one place with your parents."

"How many places have you lived?"

"Four."

"I've only lived in two, but I've lived in two families."

"But your father doesn't sell illegal arms."

"My father's dead."

"I'm sorry. I forgot."

Actually, most people thought Winston was my father. "No reason you should know."

"My father told me."

"Why would your father know?"

"They used to work together. Your father and my father at the CIA."

All at once my childhood shifted in my head as if I'd been grazed by a car in a hit-and-run. This was the first time I'd ever heard that my father worked for the CIA.

*　*　*

When I got home, I went straight to Mom's study. "Do you know Jonathan Dees?" I dropped into the chair at her table.

She looked up from her desk. "His daughter's in your class, isn't she?"

"Molly told me her father and Dad worked together at the CIA."

"I don't remember where I first met Jonathan."

"You never told me Dad worked for the CIA. You told me he was a government consultant."

"He was." She rose and joined me at the table.

"But he worked for the CIA?"

"Before."

"Before what?"

Mom turned deliberately vague whenever I asked about the past. Sophie said she was stoically locked in the present. I'd had to look up "stoically."

"Before Dad went off on his own, he worked at the CIA."

"Why didn't you tell me?"

"I am telling you."

"I mean earlier."

"You never asked me earlier."

"How would I know to ask you?" I felt angry, though I wasn't sure why.

"Sweetheart, we've been living in England for six years. As a child I didn't think you even knew what the Central Intelligence Agency was. What does it matter?"

She was right. Even now, except for what I read in spy novels or saw at the movies, I wasn't entirely clear what the CIA did. Adil had once challenged the CIA, MI6, BND, SDECE, and the KGB, all of whom he said operated in his country, trying to orchestrate his country's affairs. "So Dad worked as a spy?"

"He was contracted to gather certain information."

"Mother, that's what a spy does."

"He gathered information on weapons systems to try to keep them from going into the wrong hands."

"Wait . . . wait . . ." Past and present suddenly collided in my head like a migraine. "What do you mean wrong hands? Whose weapons?"

"Weapons have been flowing through Adil's area of the world for a long time."

"Was Dad ever in Lebanon?"

"I'm sure he was."

"Did he know Adil's father?"

"I don't know who he knew."

"What exactly did Dad do?"

"He monitored governments and companies and individuals who sold weapons and weapons technology."

"Did Dad ever kill anyone?" I don't know why I asked that.

Mother didn't seem surprised by the question. "That wasn't his job, but I never asked."

I didn't know how to evaluate this new view of my father. I'd always thought of him as helping our government, though I was never sure how. I thought of him taking trips to faraway places, bringing me back treasures like the jewelry box I kept my rings in, rings like the gold and turquoise bird he brought me, which now only fit on my little finger. "How did you feel about Dad in the CIA?"

Mom got up and lit the fire in the fireplace. The sun had set. She turned on the lamp beside the table and switched on a small radio on the window ledge. Brahms tripped gently into the room. I remembered how she and Dad used to listen to music after dinner while they sat at their separate desks in the den working.

"I worried about him every time he went out of town, especially after you all were born. I became an editor, quit working as a journalist because of your father. I didn't think I could report credibly on certain international affairs with a husband in the CIA. I loved your father, but we were different people. Maybe because we were so different, there was a passion between us as we tried to clear common ground. But that didn't mean he was easy to live with or that I was easy to live with."

"Is Winston easier?"

"By the time Winston and I met, we'd lived more of our lives. We didn't expect to walk the same road so we don't fight so hard to align. We accept what pleasures we find."

I tried to understand what Mom was saying, to see if it fit anything I felt about Adil, but what she described with Winston was what I observed of her marriage, that it was comfortable and boring. I vowed never to settle for that. "Did it bother you when I started dating Adil?"

"I saw complications."

"But you liked him?"

"I liked the way he treated you, the little I got to know him. You kept him away from us. But he seemed to be a fine young man who knew how to think. He has a very difficult set of circumstances handed to him right now."

"Did it bother you that he was Arab and we're part Jewish?" Mom, who was half Protestant on her father's side and half Jewish on Grandma Sha's, had raised us as Unitarian.

"Did it bother you?" she asked. When she married Winston, who was Church of England, they married at the Old Marylebone Town Hall in front of a magistrate rather than a minister.

"I thought about it. I asked Adil how his father felt. He said it wasn't his father's business. It was our business to sort out the world our parents hadn't been able to."

"It might have bothered me more if you were older and you stayed together. You'd be in a very complex situation."

"Well, it doesn't matter. I don't think he cares anymore."

"I'm sure he cares, but you may not be his first consideration just now." Mom reached across the table to me. The table was filled with books and magazines and the new—January 1989—cover of *Crisispoint*. Russian President Mikhail Gorbachev smiled from the cover. Mom had interviewed him. I wondered how famous my mother was. Occasionally someone would say to me, "Your mother is Miriam

West?" with a recognition I didn't know how to evaluate. "You must have very interesting dinner conversations," one of my political science teachers said when he found out who my mother was. In fact, we didn't talk much about politics or world affairs except when Sophie was around, and it was Sophie, not Mom, who led the discussion. Mom tried not to impose her views on us the way her mother had on her. Mother tried to keep politics and her opinions out of our lives to the point that sometimes I felt she didn't think I was interesting enough to share ideas with.

"You have many turns left in your life, sweetheart," she said now. "To have fallen in love with another person and cared about him is an important step in growing up."

"Don't patronize me." I stood from the table, suddenly angry again, though at one level I felt Mom was talking to me as an adult for the first time in my life. I wondered if Adil had suspected my father worked for the CIA. I wondered what my father would have said about Adil. Well, it didn't matter. Neither of them was there, and that was why I was angry.

PART II

FAULT LINES

CHAPTER SIX

DAD ONCE PREDICTED: "Jane will be the first woman president. Sophie will be secretary of state, and Lizzy will be a peacemaker."

As I prepared to enter George Washington University that summer of 1989, I found myself thinking about Dad's words. Jane was a full-time reporter for *Newsday* covering state and national politics and hoping to shift to *The New York Times*—not a career path to the presidency, though she watched over government agencies and politicians like a hawk. Sophie was a senior at Brown University, planning to attend graduate school in international relations, a path that could land her at the State Department. I had no idea what I would be good at. I wondered why Dad had given Jane and Sophie job titles and only given me a vocation. What was a peacemaker anyway? I looked at my future like a vast uncharted ocean I had to make my way across.

I spent the summer working for Mom at the magazine, reading books from a college list and sunbathing in Kensington Gardens. The summer was one of the hottest and driest on record in London. It was a summer of change and movement in Europe, particularly for the people in Eastern Europe who were agitating against their Communist regimes and pressing at their borders. At the magazine, everyone was waiting to see what would happen next, whether the Soviets would let their satellite countries open up or whether the military would clamp down.

At dinner, Sophie, Winston, and Dennis, who'd just graduated from Oxford with a first in political science, speculated on the stories coming out of Hungary, Poland, Czechoslovakia, East Germany, and Yugoslavia. Sophie and Dennis competed with each other to offer the most brilliant insights. I read the newspapers so I could participate. Even Mom joined in. We finally had those interesting dinner conversations my political science teacher thought we should have.

In the middle of July, Sophie took off for a study project in the Soviet Union, leaving Dennis to pontificate on his own. Mom and Winston had been married six years now, but I'd spent very little time with Dennis, who came home only occasionally for a weekend or a holiday but who had mostly been off at boarding school or university or at his mother's. He'd always seemed remote and much older than me, but now I was eighteen and he was twenty-two, and he actually spoke to me. I don't think he'd spent much time around girls. He was handsome in a British sort of way, with pale blond hair, rosy cheeks, blue eyes, and a constantly ironic smile. He took my innocence and my ignorance as a personal challenge and started taking me to lectures at Chatham House, which hosted government ministers and writers and members of Parliament. The house's name had no relation to Winston, but that didn't keep people from according Dennis Chatham an extra measure of respect when he introduced himself. Dennis and I were often the youngest members of the audience.

One evening after we'd been to a lecture by an economist, I persuaded Dennis to take me to the Limelight, a nightclub in Soho converted from an old Welsh Presbyterian chapel, to hear music. The club was on three levels with a bar and a staircase in the middle and a dance floor around the bar. The music was so loud it was hard to talk, but Dennis tried, explaining to me why the economist we'd just heard was wrong. I couldn't hear him and didn't really want to hear what he was saying so I asked him to dance.

"I can't dance to this music."

"Come on . . ."

"The rhythm's too erratic."

I took his hand and pulled him in his suit and tie onto the dance floor with its strobe lights and crush of people. He just stood there. "Do what I do," I said.

Finally, he began to swing his arms at his sides to no particular rhythm, rather like a lopsided windmill, all the while talking. ". . . The basic flaw of his premise is . . ." His arms bobbed as if it made no difference to him how they moved. It wasn't just that Dennis didn't like the music; he didn't know how to dance. He must never have been taught. He had no natural instincts, and being Dennis, he wouldn't ask for help.

"Listen to the beat," I said. "Here, give me your hand. Follow my feet . . . just move with me." I led Dennis, who at first resisted, but slowly began to mimic those around us. We danced to one song, then another and another. Finally, Dennis quit talking and began to move in some relation to the music. When we left, he said we should go there again.

On the way home we stopped for hamburgers at Sticky Fingers, a new restaurant that had opened in our neighborhood, owned by one of the Rolling Stones. We slipped into a dark wooden booth in the back where Stones memorabilia—posters, gold records, photographs— were bolted to the walls. Rock and roll music vibrated. "Are you ready for your job interview tomorrow?" I asked, leaning towards him so we could hear each other. Dennis had been going out on interviews but so far had received no offer he liked.

"Even if I get the job, I'll just be trapped in the system."

"What kind of job do you want?"

"Frankly, I want a job where I can make a lot of money." As the waiter set down our burgers and fries, I must have frowned because he added, "There's nothing wrong with that."

"But doing what?"

"It doesn't matter. In interviews I talk about opportunities in Eastern Europe as it opens up, the possibility of privatizing inefficient state assets, building political and economic bridges. That will happen if the systems change, but it won't happen unless people can make money."

"But you don't care what you do? I mean selling cars is different than selling apples."

"Not really. You have to know who needs them and why they should want yours rather than your competitors', but I don't want to go into sales. Dad wants me to work for him." Dennis took a bite of his hamburger.

"Why don't you?"

"Dad has limited imagination, and I'd always be his son, and that is a difficult enough proposition."

"What does Winston say?"

"He's given me till the first of November, then he says I have to start paying rent."

"Rent at home?"

"He's bluffing. He's trying to be tough because he thinks that's good for me. The truth is he's still guilty as hell for leaving me with Mother when I was ten. He sent me to boarding school because that's what all his friends did with their sons."

"Maybe he's trying to help you," I said. "Heaven forbid, maybe he actually loves you."

Dennis smiled his full-of-irony British smile that said how naive and sentimental I was. "This place isn't going to make it in this neighborhood," he pronounced. "The food's good, but it's too noisy."

*   *   *

Dennis invited me to a lecture on "Gorbachev's New Deal." We were to meet Mom for dinner afterwards, but when we got to the restaurant, there was a message that she had an emergency at the office and that we should go ahead without her. Over dinner, Dennis told me his view that Gorbachev was in over his head. "He's trying to change a country and keep it the same at the same time, but once he lets go the totalitarian fist, everyone is going to run as fast as they can to get away. Wouldn't you?" I said I would. "Gorbachev either has to call out his troops or give up and let go. Then it will be interesting to see what the Army does. It's a very interesting chess game."

"Like choosing between your bishop and your knight," I suggested.

"More like choosing between losing your queen or getting checked," Dennis countered.

*   *   *

After dinner we walked home along the river. As Dennis was going on about how a cause of *perestroika* was the lack of economic growth in the Soviet Union rather than the good-heartedness of Gorbachev, I was thinking about the last time I'd been here with Adil. Adil had asked me about my father that night. I realize now he must have suspected my father worked for the CIA. I'd heard from Adil only twice more, both times on my birthday when a sentimental card was dropped into our mailbox, not the kind of card I imagined Adil choosing. There was no stamp or postmark or return address and unlike the postcards, there was no message, just Adil's name, printed in ink. I assumed someone else selected and delivered the cards for him. I asked Fatin, but he denied that he was the messenger.

"This is pure economics," Dennis was saying. "Even your mother agrees." He put his arm around my shoulders and turned me to him. I thought he was going to scold me for not paying attention, but instead he kissed me on the lips, an awkward, sloppy kiss. I was so surprised I didn't resist.

"I've wanted to do that all summer," he said.

He tried to kiss me again, but now I said, "Dennis . . . no!" That's all I said, and I said it rather gently, but he must have been prepared for rejection because he let go.

"You kiss like a teenager," he said. "All summer I've wondered if you were as sophisticated as you look or as immature as you think." He flagged a cab.

On the way home, neither of us spoke. I'd thought Dennis and I were friends. I'd taken our boundaries for granted as brother and sister, not by blood but by circumstance, but he'd crossed the border between us with no understanding of who I was or what I thought on the other side, and I'd missed entirely what he was feeling. The breach unnerved me. At home I went straight to my room. As I mounted the stairs, I saw Dennis go into the den with Winston where the two of them lit up cigars.

*   *   *

At breakfast the next morning Winston asked, "Lizzy, what do you hear from that Arab boyfriend of yours?"

Dennis was sitting at an angle at the end of the table wearing tan shorts, showing his pale knobby knees. My gaze fixed on a mole on his leg to avoid his eyes. I wondered if Dennis had told his father about last night. I wondered if Winston was helping Dennis. I felt trapped.

Mom came to my rescue. "What do you have up today?" she asked.

"I'm going to the library," I improvised, then glanced at my watch. "Oh, and I'm late." I jumped up, took my dishes to the sink. "I have to check out *Brave New World* for the college reading list." I hadn't learned that the central tenant of lying was not to elaborate.

"I have that in my library," Winston offered. "Dennis, go get *Brave New World* for Lizzy."

"No, that's okay. I have other books I have to check out too."

"Which books? I may have them." Winston's library took up a whole room and a loft. He probably did have the books.

"That's okay . . . I can't remember all the titles." I set the dishes in the new dishwasher and hurried into the hall before Winston could be more helpful.

"Why don't you go get Lizzy the book," I heard Winston urge.

Dennis went into the library as I tried to find my backpack in the hall closet and get out the door, but Dennis was quicker. He brought the book and set it on the hall table.

"Thank you," I said.

He looked defiant and pathetic at the same time in his baggy shorts and washed-out blue tee shirt.

"Are you still going with that Arab guy?" he asked. His question was petulant.

"No. He's gone."

"Where?"

That's really not your business, I wanted to say, but we were in a family, and I didn't want to set off tremors. "I've got to go," I said instead, slipping my arms through my backpack and hurrying out the door.

*   *   *

I didn't want to be spending Saturday in the library, but I decided to go there so I wouldn't be lying. I hadn't been to the Kensington

Library since Adil left a year ago. I settled at a table with *Brave New World* and a grim determination to push ideas into my head so I would never again feel as intellectually flimsy as Dennis had made me feel last night.

When Dennis sat down across from me half an hour later, I gave a start, then looked back down and kept reading. He passed me a note: "I'm sorry. I was an ass."

I wrote back, "Yes, you were."

"How do you like Huxley?" he wrote.

"Who?" I wrote.

"The book you're reading."

"He's a little full of himself, but then he's British." I answered in the margin of his question.

At first, he didn't smile, but then a grin broke over his face. "Do you want to have lunch?" he wrote.

I don't know why we were passing notes. There was no one else at the table, and there were only two other people in the whole room. "We just ate breakfast," I answered out loud.

"You didn't. You ate one piece of toast."

"Okay." I shut *Brave New World.*

"Aren't you checking it out?"

"Why? We have it at home."

As Dennis and I headed to the Palms café on the corner, he returned to his brotherly behavior, though he didn't take my arm the way he used to when we crossed the street. We sat at a table outside, where we ordered coffee and waited for the lunch service to begin. We settled into talking about Jane and Sophie and Pickles, who'd decided not to go to university in spite of Winston's protests. She was working as a librarian, dating a fellow librarian, and according to Mom, was likely to be the first of us to get married. "What do you think of Randolph?" I asked about Pickles's boyfriend.

"He's a bit of a bore, but at least he has a job. I've got a job, too, did I tell you? I've decided to work with Dad, at least until I find something better."

"Selling cars?" I couldn't imagine Dennis with his first from Oxford describing the advantages of turbo drive.

"Developing international sales. I'll have to travel." I didn't ask for details. "Dad tells me you know Gerald Wagner. I thought maybe your Arab boyfriend knew him too. Wagner knows a lot of Arabs."

The question surprised me. I hadn't seen or thought about Dr. Wagner since Serena dismissed me as chaperone for Jack.

"His name is Adil," I said, "and he's not *Arab*."

"I thought he was."

"He is, but not the way you say it."

"How do I say it?"

"You say it as if that's all he is, as if he's defined and boxed. I don't like the way you say it so please stop."

Dennis watched me. "I think you're overreacting."

I didn't want to argue. "What does Dr. Wagner have to do with your new job?"

"Dad wants me to get to know him. He's given us orders that Dad wants me to follow up. Dad said you've met him. I wondered what you thought."

"I only met him a few times. Mostly I remember that he dominated his son from Germany," I said pointedly.

Dennis didn't pursue the point. Instead he waved for the waiter and asked how much longer until lunch. Under the table his leg moved against mine.

* * *

I began trying to avoid Dennis. I noticed small changes in his behavior. He started getting up early and was the first one to get the mail each morning. At least once a week he asked me if I'd heard from Adil.

"You should know. You get the mail."

When I complained to Mom about Dennis swooping down for the mail, she said, "Let's be grateful he's doing something around the house." While Mother could figure out global politics, she wasn't very alert to the fault lines in her own family. I didn't tell her about Dennis's advances because she'd tell Winston, and then the situation would be too awkward.

On the other hand, Sophie wasn't home twenty-four hours from Russia before she asked, "What's going on between you and Dennis?"

After dinner, Sophie and I were sitting under the canopy of my bed on the white eyelet bedspread among sweaters and slacks I was packing for college. I'd taken everything out of my closet and drawers to figure out what to take, what to leave, what to give away.

"He tried to kiss me and not like a brother. He tries to touch me. I think Winston's encouraging him."

"Have you told Mom?"

I was relieved Sophie understood why I was upset. "I'm afraid she'll make things worse."

"Hasn't she noticed?"

"She's completely focused on the magazine with everything happening in the Soviet Union and Eastern Europe right now."

"You want me to talk to her?"

"No. I keep thinking Dennis will return to normal or move out."

"Can I come in?" Mom knocked on the door as she came in. "Are you sure you'll be all right while I'm away?" She was heading to Poland to cover the elections for Prime Minister, the first free election for that office in over forty years. Then she was going on to Hungary where East Germans were flooding in, crowding the border in the hope of fleeing to Austria. Next, she was going to Yugoslavia to measure the stress on that country.

"We'll be fine," Sophie answered.

Mom set a stack of sweaters on the chair and joined us on the bed. "You sure you can pack for college by yourself?"

"I'm fine." I was anxious to be on my own, though now that Mom was leaving, part of me wished she'd stay. "Will you be home in time to go to college with me?" I tried to make the question casual.

"Of course. We'll all go, even Winston."

"Not Winston," I said.

"Don't bring Winston," Sophie confirmed. "The four of us, like old times. Jane can come down from New York."

Mother set an article on the bed in front of us. "While I'm away, maybe you can help patch over a bit of a mess."

Sophie picked up the pages. "What's this?"

"Dennis submitted it for the magazine, his view of the changes ahead in the Soviet Union and Eastern Europe. I told him he needed to interview people, get firsthand information, not just give his opinion on everything he's read. He didn't take the criticism very well. I told him I'd be happy to work with him, but he said he'd publish it elsewhere. Maybe you can help smooth it over for me, Lizzy."

"Me?"

"Dennis is fond of you."

"That would be very awkward," I said.

"Why don't you talk to Winston?" Sophie asked.

"Winston would only make matters worse. Frankly, I don't know how he and Dennis are going to work together."

"I've been trying to avoid Dennis," I confessed. "He keeps asking me about Adil."

Mother folded the article back in her pocket. "Have you heard from Adil?"

"No. But what business is it of Dennis's?" I'd continued scanning the papers for news about Adil's father, but the stories had stopped. The newspapers never wrote that charges hadn't been brought. Something not happening wasn't news. "I have no idea where he is. Nobody's writing about his father anymore or the investigation."

"The world is looking in a different direction," Mother said. "Everyone's watching the breakup of the Soviet bloc. I imagine a lot of mischief is hiding behind the smoke of that fire."

After Mother left, Sophie said, "You're right not to tell her about Dennis. She's off in Eastern Europe in her mind. Go to college. Time will sort out Dennis." Sophie and I were still young enough to think time was an ally.

"Winston asked me to have dinner with Dennis and him on Friday night," I said. "They're meeting Gerald Wagner. You remember him? Apparently, he wants to see me. Will you come?"

"I wasn't invited."

"I'm inviting you."

*   *   *

Sophie and I arrived first at Scott's restaurant in Mayfair. Neither of us had dressed up for the evening, and the maître d' was reluctant to seat us until we used Winston's name. I was wearing a loose black jersey dress over a tee shirt, and Sophie had on black slacks and a black cotton V-neck sweater without a shirt. The maître d' led us to a table in the corner. Winston and Dennis and Dr. Wagner arrived in suits with silk ties.

"You remember Dr. Wagner, of course," Winston introduced.

I hadn't seen Dr. Wagner since the reception at our home two years ago. His thinning hair was replaced by a rust-colored toupee, which sat low on his forehead so that he appeared to be scowling. He was still tan, but his skin looked more like a hide, and his hands were not tanned but pasty white. Mom had told me that he had placed millions of pounds' worth of orders for vehicles with Winston but fell further and further behind in payments.

"How's Jack?" I asked. "I haven't seen him."

"Jack and his mother moved to America . . . to Virginia." Dr. Wagner said "Virginia" as if he were tasting a new wine. "You remember my son James? He's married a beautiful girl from Frankfurt and runs our factory there. I'm again about to be a grandfather."

"Congratulations."

"What kind of factory?" Sophie asked.

"Engines and tools. I'm trying to persuade Winston here to partner with us to build an assembly line to manufacture heavy duty cargo trucks for a client of ours." He addressed Sophie as though she might hold influence. "Others are also bidding for the project so we must act quickly. It would be an impressive partnership, your company and ours. Our family business goes back four generations, to 1914."

"Through both world wars," Sophie noted.

Dr. Wagner nodded.

"What are you a doctor of?" Sophie asked.

Dr. Wagner had the kind of complexion that flared with emotion and even through his tan, his face reddened. "My father and grandfather earned their degrees in physics and engineering at Heidelberg University, but I was never much of a student. But everyone was used to Wagner Machines and Tools being run by Dr. Wagner so . . ." He gestured to the air. "When my father stepped down, I took his titles." He laughed, expecting us to join him. Winston and Dennis obliged.

"In academia that would be dishonest." Sophie smiled. Anyone who didn't know Sophie might rush into her smile, but I found it scary.

"In academia," Dr. Wagner said, "but in business, it's just good marketing. It gives your customers confidence."

"Who are your customers?" Sophie asked questions like Mom, as though she were owed the answers.

"You know one of my customers." Dr. Wagner turned to me.

"I do?"

"Ibrahim Hasan. You know his son, if I recall. Now, if Ibrahim Hasan wants to buy my machines, does he care what I'm a doctor of? I suspect you didn't ask his son for credentials before you went out on a date, though perhaps we both should have, since we both seem to have been left empty-handed. For me that means a large hole in my balance sheet, which I'm not about to ignore. I don't know if you were left in the same fashion, but perhaps we can help each other."

I didn't answer. I couldn't answer. I was so taken back by this intrusion and betrayal of my private life. I glanced at Winston to see if he expected this inquiry. He seemed at least to accept the questions. Had he passed on the information? Had Dennis? Sophie didn't see all the possible levels of betrayal, but she stepped in. "Did you commit a crime selling to him?" she asked.

"A crime?" Dr. Wagner bleated. His face again flushed.

"Isn't Ibrahim Hasan under investigation?" Sophie knew only what I'd told her. She was out of her depth. I wished Mother were here.

Dr. Wagner fell silent. His tongue swept across his lips, then he laughed. "You've been watching too many American movies," he said, waving for the waiter. He turned to Winston. "Shall we order?" And he dismissed Sophie and me like a flirtation gone wrong.

*   *   *

"I can't believe your sister," Dennis complained the next evening as he followed me around the kitchen. I was making myself a tuna sandwich for dinner; Sophie was out with friends, and Winston was having dinner at his club.

"She's your sister too," I said. "At least theoretically." I scooped tuna into a bowl. "You want some?"

"If she really were my sister, I'd have boxed her ears. She was incredibly rude to Dr. Wagner."

"Boxed her ears? Isn't that a bit archaic?" I dropped four slices of bread into the toaster. "Hand me the mayonnaise."

"Is Pickles here for dinner?" Dennis looked around as if she might be hiding.

"She's with Randolph. It's you and me." I took the mayonnaise from him and turned back to the counter. I was standing barefoot, in black bermuda shorts, a white tee shirt, my hair pulled up in a ponytail off my neck. It had reached 90° today and was only now starting to cool off. "Can I have some mustard?" When I turned around, I caught Dennis staring at my legs. He fumbled in the refrigerator and passed me a jar of mustard.

"What was Sophie thinking?" he asked. "I was hugely embarrassed. I called and apologized to Gerald today. He was understanding. He said the two of you were just young and immature."

I turned back to the counter. This was the second time Dennis had called me immature. I spread the tuna on bread and set my sandwich on a plate.

"Here . . ." Dennis thrust a box wrapped in silver paper at me.

"What's this?"

"Gerald asked me to give it to you. It's a graduation present."

I hesitated, then I opened the box and lifted out a black and gold silk scarf.

"That's nice," Dennis approved. "Isn't that nice?"

I wondered if Dr. Wagner had Dennis buy it for me. I set the scarf back in the box. "Yes, it's nice." It was a scarf Mother might like.

"He said you should call him."

"Why? I'm not calling him." I wondered if he wanted to press me further about the whereabouts of Adil's father.

"I have a deal pending with him," Dennis said and sat down to wait for his dinner at the new round oak table Mom had bought.

I took a soda from the fridge, picked up my plate, and went out of the kitchen, leaving the scarf, along with the bread and the tuna on the counter. In the den I opened the door to the garden, turned on jazz, and picked up *The Economist*. A few minutes later, Dennis put his head into the room. He held a plate in his hands. "Can I join you?"

I shrugged and ate a bite of my sandwich.

"I don't mean to criticize Sophie," he said, "but she's so damned sure of herself. She's not as smart as she thinks she is."

"Are you?"

"What?"

"As smart as you think you are."

He smiled. "Yes. Actually, I am. But, see, I don't think I'm that smart." I looked back at *The Economist*. "Really. I have a lot to learn. Gerald's teaching me."

"Gerald Wagner is teaching you what?" I asked; I couldn't help myself.

"He misses having his son around, so he's been letting me visit his operations and help him on some of the deals."

"Does Winston know?"

"Not exactly." Dennis sat in the easy chair beside the sofa. "I'm negotiating with Gerald on a deal for Dad, but Gerald has much larger deals pending, and he's asked me to do some research and make contacts for him in Britain. He says he'll give me a percentage if the deals close."

"What sort of deals?"

"I can't discuss that. I'll probably have to travel to Germany and elsewhere," he said importantly. He reached out and touched my knee.

I looked down at his hand, and he removed it. I didn't know how to get back on course with Dennis. I'd liked having a brother . . . or sort of a brother the first part of the summer, but now I felt I had to act cool and annoyed around him to defend myself. I didn't like myself this way. "If we close the deals, and I get paid, I'll make more money on one deal than a year's salary in the City. I'll tell Dad after I've made it."

"I don't trust Dr. Wagner."

Dennis leaned forward and took a bite of his sandwich. He'd taken off his tie and jacket and sat in an open-collared blue shirt with his sleeves rolled up. He'd finally managed to get some sun, and his blue eyes were set off by the color of his shirt. He was actually handsome. "You just don't know Gerald," he said. "I can tell you that the deal has to do with sales in the Middle East. That's why he's interested in your boyfriend's father. He owes Gerald money. Gerald thinks he's double dealing."

"He's not my boyfriend. I haven't heard from him in almost a year, and I have no idea what his father is doing."

"I'm glad because his father's in a lot of trouble. I tell you this confidentially . . . Gerald's hired investigators to find him."

"What do you mean he's *double dealing*?"

"Gerald said he bought equipment under false pretenses and is marking it up and selling it to embargoed nations. In the meantime, Gerald may get in trouble because the authorities think he's been selling to those countries."

"So Sophie wasn't wrong?"

"What do you mean?"

"Dr. Wagner may have committed a crime."

"Sophie didn't know what she was talking about. Gerald's hoping Dad will intervene for him because Dad has credibility. He can explain Gerald was only selling equipment to a man he thought represented a legitimate trading partner, and the investigation can be dropped."

"Investigation?"

"Unofficial investigation." Dennis put his plate on the coffee table. "Wagner Machines and Tools is one of the companies the government has been looking at, but not very seriously. Gerald is trying to persuade Dad to help so it won't become serious."

"What does Winston say?"

"Well, you know Dad."

"No, actually I don't know him very well."

"He takes forever to make a decision. And he's not as open-minded to foreigners. He's friendly but not naturally trusting. And he doesn't much like to mix business with politics. Everyone mixes business and politics, I tell him, but Dad's old-fashioned. He listens to your mother, and I'm sorry, but your mother is very American in certain ways." Dennis stood and shut the door. "Though of course in America everyone mixes business and politics. America is one big business. But your mom's full of this puritanical sureness that this is right and that is wrong. The world's very black and white to her. She's like your sister. How did you turn out so well?" He sat back down on the sofa beside me and looked directly into my eyes. I thought he was going to try to kiss me again.

I stood. "You don't think I know right from wrong?"

"I didn't mean that."

"Let me ask you . . . this summer, have you and Winston been watching my mail to see if Adil wrote me?"

Dennis stood too. He shut the door to the garden. Was he closing us in? "What do you mean?"

"Were you watching to see if I heard from Adil so you could tell Dr. Wagner?" We stood opposite each other. He was only a few inches taller, so we were almost eye to eye.

"No," he said, though he didn't seem to be paying attention to the question or the answer. Instead, he slipped his arm around my waist and placed the other at the back of my neck, and he did kiss me. This time he kissed with urgency as if the kiss might sort out a world that was growing complicated for him. I tried to push him away, but he didn't let me. Instead he kissed me again. "Lizzy, I know you want this too," he said. "I think about you all the time."

If I shut my eyes, I could almost let the kiss exist by itself without the complication of Dennis, but only for a moment. Dennis was trying to take that moment and extend it. Had the front door not opened and Sophie arrived home, I don't know what would have happened.

"Anyone home?" Sophie called out.

"Oh fuck!" Dennis whispered.

"Dennis, please. Let go." Dennis released me. "We're in here," I answered.

Sophie opened the door. Dennis grabbed his plate and passed her in the doorway without speaking. Sophie looked at me. I wondered if the air was as palpable with unresolved desire as it seemed to me. "Is everything all right?" she whispered.

I didn't answer.

"What happened?"

I picked up my plate. What was I doing? I'd let Dennis kiss me. Had I kissed him back? A flirtation with him was dangerous. It would ricochet through the whole family. "Nothing," I said. I couldn't talk to Sophie. I couldn't bring all this into the family domain. I didn't know how to sort out Dennis and Gerald Wagner and Winston. I had no idea where Adil was. The fault lines were proliferating. My home in London no longer felt safe. I was going to college in two weeks. I would make a run for the border, flee across the ocean to America, and leave the ambiguities behind for others to sort out.

CHAPTER SEVEN

SOMEONE HAD PAINTED our yellow clapboard house gray with green shutters and added a second story. We drove by slowly, Jane, Sophie, Mom, and I. I remembered everything—the small rise of our front yard that had seemed like a hill to me, the cul-de-sac where we rode our bicycles, my blue Schwinn bike.

"Look, the Campbells' house is just the same." Sophie pointed out the window.

"I wonder who's living in ours," Jane said.

Jane had come down from New York for a day to help me get ready for college, and now we were visiting our old neighborhood. We hadn't been back to our home since we'd moved to London seven years ago. Jane had come on her own, but none of the rest of us had. We'd been back to Washington, but we'd never driven out Massachusetts Ave. into the leafy suburbs of Bethesda where the District of Columbia met the state of Maryland. Mom had never wanted to visit. Even today we had to persuade her to come.

"What's the point? We've moved on. It's just a house."

"It was our house," I said. "Our childhood."

"We've never been back," Sophie said. "It can't hurt us."

Mom didn't look convinced. "We may see people we know."

"So?" I asked.

"Don't you want to see the Campbells or the Robbinses?" Sophie asked. "Aren't you curious?"

"We send cards each Christmas. I know what they're doing."

"I'm sure they'd like to see you," Jane said. Jane could persuade Mother to do what she didn't want to do better than Sophie or I so we climbed quietly into the back seat of the rental car and left Mom to Jane, who got behind the wheel. Reluctantly, Mother sat herself in the passenger's seat the same way she had the day Jane drove us to Dad's funeral.

"It's awkward," Mother protested as we'd passed the small shops along Massachusetts Ave. "Time has passed. We've all moved on. We'll see the house if you want, but let's not go ringing doorbells."

When we turned the corner to our street, which Jane found as if programmed to home, all of us, except Mom, peered out the windows as though the trees, the hedges, the street contained parts of ourselves. Even Sophie, who was usually as unsentimental as Mom, looked out the back window, then let out a cry. "Stop! Stop the car! My god, that's Jimmy Mann!"

Jane pulled over to the curb a few houses past ours, and Sophie jumped out. She approached a tall, square-jawed man in a George-town University tee shirt who was mowing the lawn. Jimmy Mann had been her junior high school flame. He looked over at her now, cocked his head, then hopped off the lawn mower and came down and shook her hand. I scurried out of the back seat after her. Jane turned off the motor.

"Oh lord," I heard Mother exhale, "we're ringing doorbells."

Jane stayed with Mom, but not for long. Jimmy Mann's mother pushed open the screen door, followed by Rosalie Campbell. The neighbors were still there, behind the same doors and hedges just as I remembered them. In London we knew our neighbors, but the Rum-sons traveled to France three times a year and never seemed to be home, and the Sharifs also lived in Dubai. The Thompson-Joneses sent over sugary candy at Christmas, but they were not neighbors from whom you would borrow a cup of sugar or gather for an impromptu barbecue in the backyard. As I stood on the sidewalk smelling the freshly mowed grass and watching the sprinklers shoot water sparkling into the sun, I felt such a tug backwards that for a moment I felt dizzy. I think this was what Mom feared. Or maybe she feared something more tangible. Reluctantly, she got out of the car. Rosalie Campbell aimed down the lawn towards her. Mrs. Campbell's hair had turned entirely gray in the past seven years, and she'd put on twenty pounds, but she embraced me and then Mom in a quick hug just as I remembered.

"Why didn't you let us know you were coming? We would have given a party."

"We don't want a party," Mom said.

"Look at how big your girls are, Miriam. My goodness! This isn't little Lizzy?" Little Lizzy towered over Rosalie Campbell. "How old are you now, Lizzy?"

"Eighteen."

"Lizzy's starting at George Washington University," Mom said. "We've come to drop her off."

By now Hillary Mann had joined us. "You're going to GW?" she asked. "Why, that's where Nora is. She's a junior. Do you remember Nora?"

"Kind of." Nora had been more Sophie's friend than mine.

"She's at school right now, but if you give me your number, I'll be sure she looks you up. If you need anything, you consider this your home while you're here."

"That goes for us too," Mrs. Campbell said. "Here, I'll give you our phone number, and you call us if you need anything." She pulled a scrap of paper from her blue jeans pocket and asked Mom if she had a pen. Mrs. Campbell scribbled down her number and handed it to me. She looked over at Mom, who was standing back from both women. "Did you hear Paula Robbins died last year?" Mother nodded. I wondered how she'd heard. Maybe from the Christmas cards. A sadness passed over Mrs. Campbell's face. Rosalie Campbell and Mom had been good friends when we lived here, but something had happened between them before we moved. I had only a dim memory, but I remembered Mom telling me not to go over to the Campbells after school anymore because I would be bothering Mrs. Campbell.

"We'll look after Lizzy for you," Rosalie Campbell said.

"Thank you," Mother answered stiffly, "but I'm sure Lizzy will be fine. She's very self-sufficient." With those words the homecoming I was feeling suddenly evaporated like water on the grass in the hot August sun. Mom had announced that I was self-sufficient, and I knew that was what I was supposed to be. I was not to lean on these people who had in some way hurt or betrayed my mother years before. I crumpled the paper with the phone number in my pocket. Sophie and Jimmy were standing off to the side talking, but I could tell they had run out of conversation because Sophie was looking towards us.

"It's time for us to go," Mother announced.

"Would you like to see your old house?" Mrs. Mann asked. She'd never been as close to Mom and therefore may not have been part of the hurt I now saw in my mother's eyes. "General Roland Green and his wife bought it. Did you and Jesse ever know them?"

"I don't think so." Mom turned back towards the car. "We don't want to bother them. The girls just wanted to drive by and look. That's all."

We followed Mom's lead, though the three of us would have liked to have seen our old house. As we climbed into the car, Sophie waved to Jimmy, who got back on the lawn mower. Sophie and I watched the neighborhood through the rear window as we drove away. I saw Jane also watching in the rearview mirror, but Mom kept her eyes straight ahead.

*   *   *

At the hotel, Mom claimed a headache and went up to her room. Jane, Sophie, and I went into the lounge where the hotel was serving afternoon tea. According to the bulletin board at the door, a convention of private security agents was also meeting. We settled at a table by the window.

"What happened with Mom back at the house?" I asked.

"You noticed?" Jane said.

"How could I not notice? Something obviously went on between her and Mrs. Campbell." The waiter arrived, and we ordered "English tea" with cucumber sandwiches, fruit cake, and scones with clotted cream.

"Do you remember?" Sophie asked Jane.

"I don't remember exactly. I was pretty focused on keeping my own life together after Dad died, but Mom has told me what happened, or at least some of what happened."

Sophie and I were sitting on one side of the table with Jane in a chair facing us. It was the way we used to sit when we were children and Jane pretended to conduct school for us in the basement. Jane's school was one of my first memories.

"You know Dad used to work for the CIA . . ." Jane went on. Sophie nodded. I wondered if anyone would have remembered to tell me if Molly Dees hadn't. "After he left the Agency, he still worked for them as a consultant. He followed the trail of uranium thefts and shipments of reprocessing equipment. Iraq and Iran had gone to war, and arms sales into the region were skyrocketing. According to Mom, Dad went to monitor one of the points where cargo came in and was then re-marked with a different country of origin and destination to hide illegal trades. On one of his last trips, he was offered a job and an extravagant salary by one of the men he was investigating. He got on an airplane and flew straight home and reported the offer. He was worried he'd lost his cover. The Agency encouraged him to return. Mom pleaded with him not to go back, but he went."

"Why?" I asked.

"According to Mom, he couldn't walk away. He thought he could nail one of the main players and uncover the source. When he was killed, no one would tell Mom what really happened to him. She was told there was a mechanical failure in his airplane, that there'd been an inexperienced crew on the ground the morning he took off. When she asked how the U.S. government could allow an inexperienced crew to handle his plane, she was told Dad was there as a private citizen and secured his own plane and crew. She argued that Dad was an experienced pilot and scrupulous about safety. Two other people were killed in the crash—an arms dealer and a woman with a record of drug smuggling. No one knew why they were on the same plane as Dad. Mother was told that the circumstances looked suspicious. She was also told that she wasn't owed compensation since Dad was no longer a government employee, but because of his prior service, the government was prepared to offer her $250,000, but required a silence clause and a release. In return, the government would do its best to keep quiet the questionable circumstances of Dad's death."

"What questionable circumstances?" I sat forward on the chair.

"The criminal background of others on the plane, why Dad was with them. The person who offered Mom the deal was Joe Campbell. He was at the Pentagon at the time. 'Is this hush money, Joe?' she asked. 'Was his plane sabotaged?' She told me she could barely stay sitting at the kitchen table, she was so disgusted with the offer.

"'There was no sabotage,' Joe answered.

"'What about the phone call warning Jesse?'

"'It was probably a prank,' Joe said.

"'People don't make prank phone calls warning you that your gas tank is sanded. Mom said she called everyone she knew to find out what was happening and to get the message to Dad. She told Joe he might not know what happened, but she wasn't about to accept a bounty to quit asking questions. She told me she was yelling. Rosalie tried to calm her down, offering her tea and a tranquilizer.

"'I don't want a damn tranquilizer!' she shouted. 'Who was it, Joe?' She said he looked at her helplessly. 'Honestly, I don't know. Take the money.'

"'Was it the Iranians? Iraqis? The Israelis? Our own government?'

"'We don't sabotage our citizens. Our allies don't sabotage our citizens.' He tried one more time to pass her the check and the agreement. 'Think of your children. You're upset right now.'

"'My husband was killed, and my government and our best friends want to buy his life for $250,000, then threaten to smear his name if I don't agree.' She left their kitchen and never went back."

I saw in Jane's eyes the burden of family history she carried for us. "Mom vowed to get to the bottom of what happened, but the more she dug and the more evidence she gathered, the more circular the hunt became, and the more irrational she grew. She isolated herself from her friends and even from us. I remember that time. I remember having to make dinner for everyone because Mom would simply forget."

"I remember," Sophie said. "She'd be in Dad's office for hours in his files, and we couldn't get her to come out."

"I remember the day the men came to our house, and Mom told us not to let them in," I added.

"That was the beginning of the end," Jane explained. "That's when Mom took Dad's files to Grandma's. The next day someone searched our house. We stayed at Grandma's while Mom read Dad's papers.

Grandma thought she was having a nervous breakdown. When *Crisispoint* offered her the editorship in London, she took it for all of us. She said the labyrinth in Washington was too complicated for her to find her way through. In the end she decided to save us. She packed up Dad's files and her own, stored them in Grandma's basement in Alexandria, and moved us to London. She's refused to look back."

"No wonder today was so hard on her," I said.

"I don't think she holds a grudge against the Campbells. I just don't think she wants to deal with them or the past, and I'm not sure she should have to."

"What happened to the files?" I asked.

"They're still in Grandma's basement. Mom told me if we ever wanted to see them, we could. So . . ." Jane looked at me. "I leave you here with the trail of Jesse West. I have to catch the 7:00 p.m. train back to New York."

"Can't you stay till tomorrow?"

"I have to work tomorrow. Mom and Sophie will move you into the dorm. But you'll come up and visit me after you get settled, and I'll come down and see you."

"Excuse me." A man at the next table leaned over. "I couldn't help but overhear you mention the name Jesse West. Did you know Jesse West?" The gentleman was stocky with a flushed face and thick neck. I tried to remember when he'd sat down.

"Why?" Sophie asked. "Do you know him?"

"If we're talking about the same Jesse West, we worked together. I wept like a child when he was killed."

"Jesse West was our father," Jane said.

The man leaped to his feet and extended his hand. "My name is Marvin Penn." He fumbled in his pocket and pulled out three white cards, which he passed around the table. President. Penn Security Systems with an address in Falls Church, Virginia.

Jane led the introductions. Marvin Penn went around the table shaking all of our hands. Jane volunteered that I was going to college here.

"Which university?"

"George Washington," I answered reluctantly, calculating that it was big enough that I would soon be anonymous there.

"Well, that's a fine school. Please, don't let me interrupt you. I remember Jesse had three daughters. I'm so happy to meet you. What a fine, fine legacy Jesse left behind." He bowed like a European, though he looked every bit American, and returned to his table.

Jane, Sophie, and I got up and left the lounge. "That was bizarre," Sophie said.

"Washington is a small town," Jane answered. "Everyone knows everyone."

*   *   *

During my freshman year in college, the whole of Eastern Europe turned away from communism and rushed headlong towards democracy and capitalism as if the West were the promised land, and all people had to do to enter was to reinvent themselves. Whenever I called home, Mom was off in Hungary or Poland or Bulgaria or Yugoslavia. I understood why she went to witness the changes firsthand, but I wished I could talk to her more often that fall. I felt disoriented being back in Washington. Memories kept popping up as if they dwelt just on the other side of consciousness. I'd walk into a restaurant and a smell or a taste would set off an inarticulate feeling as if I'd been there before. I couldn't remember if Dad had been there with me. I don't know why childhood hung on so tightly and replayed itself with such force, as though it were imprinted like an outline underneath the years that followed. I didn't know exactly what I wanted from Mom. I wanted to hold onto an anchor that for me was the sound of her voice.

I started calling Jane or Sophie, who would ask, "What can I do for you?" When I said, "I just called to talk," they'd talk a few minutes, but then they'd say they had a test or a deadline, and we'd promise to talk again soon.

Once when I called London, I got Dennis on the phone, and the roles reversed. He wanted to talk. He told me he'd been promoted by Dr. Wagner and was now meeting with government ministers—he wouldn't say from what country—and he was assisting Dr. Wagner in overseas sales.

"I thought you were working for your father."

"I am, but I'm also working with Gerald."

"Isn't that a conflict of interest? Does Winston know?"

"Gerald wants me to keep my work for him confidential for now so don't say anything. I'll be traveling overseas soon."

I ignored the swagger in his voice. "Won't Winston wonder where you are?"

"I don't have to report my movements to my father."

"But you're working for him, and you live in his house."

"Only temporarily. I'm getting my own place as soon as Gerald and I finish a deal. I hate living at home, just Pickles and me with my father and your mother. Gerald is helping me get started on my own. He says I remind him of his oldest son who died. I help him here in London when he has to travel. Sometimes I take short trips for him on assignments."

I wondered what Dennis could be doing for Gerald Wagner, but I kept his confidence, and I didn't mention his work to anyone, not that anyone I knew would be interested.

The next time I phoned home and got Dennis, he told me he'd just returned from "the center of the ancient world." When I asked where exactly, he said, "Maybe I'll take you there someday. I was watching belly dancers, drinking champagne, and eating masgouf—does that give you a clue?" I had no clue. "Seriously, they're trying to build up their society."

"What are you selling?"

"Engines and tools. Whatever they need. My job is to help expedite the shipping on our end."

"What do you know about engines and tools?" I challenged.

Dennis laughed. "I've learned a great deal. Anyway, there are always two of us. I'm more the front man. Oxford, Eaton, Sir Winston's son . . . that sort of thing impresses some people. I may have just made a twenty-million-pound sale."

"You?" I tried to imagine £20 million worth of engines lined up as far as the eye could see.

"Not only me. The final negotiations are in German and Arabic. I'm also helping on real estate. Our clients want to buy a factory in England. We may also help them build a plant in their country so they can produce their own machines. But don't say anything." I wondered who Dennis thought I'd say anything to. "The Minister of Industry had us to dinner. He invited me to come stay any time."

"Be careful," I warned. I don't know why I warned him, except that Dennis sounded so full of his own importance, I was afraid he might get blindsided.

"I've been thinking about you," he said. "What's your phone number there?"

"You'd be wasting your money. I'm hardly ever in the room."

"I have money to waste."

"Really, I'm never here."

"I may be coming to Washington."

Finally, I gave him my address and phone number but told him not to call. I wished Dennis would meet a girl.

I began calling Mom at the office instead. I was finally starting my own life. No one told me what to do, yet I found myself wanting my father and mother. I think that's why I agreed to meet Marvin Penn when he phoned in early February.

"You may not remember me," he began. I recognized the wide Southern accent of a real Virginian, not a Beltway Virginian. "I was cleaning out my garage, and I came across something that belonged to your father. I thought you might want it."

"What is it?"

"I'd rather show it to you. It will take a little explanation."

I hesitated. I didn't know this man, but he had some artifact of my father's from a time far away. "I'm sorry," he apologized. "I should have called you earlier and welcomed you to Washington."

"How did you get my number?"

He laughed as if I'd asked how he opened a door. "I should also have asked how your mother is doing."

"She's fine. She's remarried."

"Please tell her I asked after her. I've been going through an upheaval myself, which is why I didn't phone earlier."

I must have looked unsettled because my roommate Julie mouthed, "Who is it?" I waved, letting her know I'd tell her in a minute.

"Maybe I could meet you for a cup of coffee near the university and give you Jesse's things. My wife and I are divorcing, and I'm trying to clear out the surplus of thirty-five years."

"Okay . . . I guess."

He suggested a coffee shop near campus Saturday morning. That gave me three days to get in touch with Mom and find out exactly who Marvin Penn was and what he might have of my father's, but it turned out Mother was traveling and wouldn't be home till Sunday. When I told Julie about Marvin's call, she said she'd come with me and suggested she and Mahela, my other roommate, sit in a booth nearby and keep an eye on me just in case.

Julie was a theater major from Los Angeles and dramatized everything. Mahela had grown up in Washington, D.C., with a police captain as a father and a school principal as a mother. She looked straight at you and told you what she thought. She reminded me of Sophie.

"Julie's right," she said. "You've got to be careful, Elizabeth." She insisted on calling me Elizabeth. "Washington is not England." Neither Julie nor Mahela had ever been to England. "Maybe we could get Scott to come too." Mahela was happy for any excuse to talk to Scott, who lived in our dorm and was on the swim team.

At 9:00 a. m. Saturday morning, Julie, Mahela, Scott, and I trooped over to the coffee shop. "This is probably silly," I said. As we crossed 25th Street, I felt grateful that I had three friends who would get up early on Saturday to protect me. "He's probably a very nice man who's bringing me a hat or something."

Mahela, Julie, and Scott sat in a booth in the back while I sat in the front drinking coffee and glancing out the window. I wouldn't have recognized Marvin Penn if he hadn't come up to me. I remembered an overweight, balding man with a reddish face. The man who asked if I was Miss West was much trimmer with a salt and pepper moustache, the beginnings of a beard, an ashen complexion. His divorce must be taking its toll. He still had a thick neck. His hands closed tightly around mine. He was dressed in a brown suit with a thin orange stripe and a paisley tie that didn't match. Under his arm, he carried a wooden box, which he sat on the table.

I glanced over at Mahela and Julie and Scott, who all had their eyes on him and on the box. As he sat down, I asked, "What's in the box?"

He opened the lid and turned it towards me. On a black cloth lay a thick-barreled pistol. "It's a gun," I whispered. He'd walked through the streets carrying a gun, or more particularly, as I was to learn later, a semiautomatic nine-millimeter. "Why did my father have a gun?"

Marvin Penn smiled. "To protect himself. And for target practice."

I leaned closer so Marvin Penn wouldn't talk too loudly. I didn't want my new friends hearing what he was saying. "What kind of targets?"

"Soviets . . . Chinese . . . Libyans . . ."

"Those are people."

"They're not ducks." He smiled wider, showing blackened holes in the recesses of his mouth where his teeth were missing. He patted the pistol as if it were an obedient pet. "We trained for contingencies."

"Did my father ever shoot at live targets?"

"If they shot at him."

"Did he ever kill anyone?" I don't know why I kept asking that question of Mom and now of Marvin Penn except the answer seemed to me defining. It set my father apart in a group of people who'd measured the worth of a life in a moment's action. I'd spent half my life living with his absence—a shadow, an unoccupied space—I couldn't fill. I wondered how he felt.

"I can't tell you that." Marvin Penn shut the lid of the box. "I thought you'd want his weapon."

"Can't you get arrested carrying it?" I asked.

"I have a permit. Jesse had a permit."

"I don't have a permit. I can't have a gun in my dorm." I stated what should have been obvious.

I was leaning across the table on my elbows when a waitress with "Janelle" stitched in pink on her pocket set down water. As Marvin Penn paused to study the menu, I ordered corn flakes and coffee. He ordered two fried eggs, sausage, toast, hash browns, juice, coffee, and a side of grits.

"When and where did my father use this?" I asked when the waitress left.

"You don't know much about your dad, do you?" He rubbed the stubble of his beard as if he wasn't used to having hair on his face. I was struck that he'd worn a suit and tie to meet me on Saturday morning. "Maybe I shouldn't be the one to tell you. What did your mother say when you told her we were meeting?"

"I didn't tell her. She's out of town. But she wouldn't mind. I can know whoever I want."

"Well, maybe I made a mistake bringing this."

"What exactly did my father do?"

Marvin Penn pulled out a tin box and opened it on the table. He began rolling up a small wad of tobacco into a ball, which he tucked into his cheek. I'd never met anyone who chewed tobacco. I watched him massage the wad of leaves in his mouth and wondered if my father chewed tobacco.

"When I first met your daddy, we were both in operations in the Middle East. He tracked down weapons and the people who trafficked in them. Your dad was more an intellectual though. He took all the information, laid it out for the higher-ups, told them what it meant. Then he married your mother, and he moved back to a desk stateside, though he still went to the field. I remember your dad fell for your mom right away. He was about ten years older than she was. She was real pretty and smarter than most men wanted in a woman." Marvin smiled, showing his rotten teeth. "But your dad liked that she could answer him back and knew what she was talking about. She didn't like him working for the CIA, thought it was dangerous, and he couldn't tell her what he was doing and that used to drive her crazy.

"After you girls were born and started growing up, he began thinking about getting out, thought he'd like to have his own firm. I'd been thinking the same thing. Because I was older than your dad, I could retire as soon as I turned fifty. For his own reasons your dad decided to leave early, and we started a company together, called it WestPenn for Jesse West and Marvin Penn, opened a little office in Virginia, and clients found us."

"Who were your clients?"

"Like everyone in this town, our government, or those the government sent to us that they couldn't help directly. We also had industrial clients. I did the security work—anti-terrorist training, physical security, defense, that sort of thing—and your dad, he searched out information people wanted. He loved to get on the trail of some piece of information and hunt it down like an enemy soldier. Mainly he was following proliferation threats: nuclear, chemical, biological weapons."

The waitress set breakfast down on the table, shoving aside Marvin Penn's tobacco. "Nasty stuff," she said. "You should throw that away."

"Are you friends with my ex-wife?" he asked.

"Yeah, she sent me to watch out for you."

I was growing worried about keeping my friends too long and concerned they could hear what Marvin Penn was telling me. "Would you excuse me for a minute. I have to speak to some friends I'm supposed to meet later." I got up from the table, leaving Marvin to the waitress.

Julie and Mahela had already finished their breakfasts. "I'm fine," I said quietly. "You don't need to wait. He's harmless."

"Are you sure?" Mahela asked.

"Yes, really. I'm just going to be a little longer. I'll meet you back at the room."

"What's in the box?" Julie asked.

"I'll tell you later." I returned to the table.

"Sending your security home?" Marvin asked when I sat down.

"Excuse me?"

He chewed on a slice of bacon. "You're Jesse's daughter. He'd be proud of you. But let me give you a little advice. You should have sat them between you and the door, not back in the corner where they couldn't get to you before I got you out of here. I could teach you a few things."

"I don't know what you're talking about."

He mopped the yolk of his eggs with a piece of toast. "Yes, you do. You got instincts, but you're an amateur."

I declined Marvin Penn's invitation for instruction. I wanted to leave with my friends as they went out the door. This man in the mismatched suit with missing teeth and a gun said he'd known my father, had been in business with my father, but what he was telling me bore little relationship to the father I carried in my head. "Do you know how my father died?" I asked.

Marvin Penn stared at me for a long minute. "In a plane crash."

"I know that, but do you know anything more?"

He mixed the grits on his plate with the yolk until they turned a yellowish brown. "What I know won't bring him back."

"What do you know?"

"I know the world is more complicated and fraught than you need to know, at least at this stage of your life. You'll learn what you need when you're ready."

I didn't want to pursue what seemed to me a self-important answer, and I didn't want this man to pursue me. I finished my corn flakes. "I have to go," I said. "I have a meeting . . ." I thanked him for the gun but told him I couldn't take it. He agreed to return it to his house in Falls Church, though he had to be out of the house by the end of the month. In his divorce settlement, his wife got the house and he got the van. I could get in touch with him at his office if I needed him, he said. I couldn't imagine why I would ever need him, but I took his card again to be polite.

"I'll keep the pistol until you have a place for it," he said, "and if I find anything else, I'll call."

"No . . . no," I protested. Marvin Penn was curing me of my nostalgia. Mom was right. The past was the past. I had a future to live that was my own.

*   *   *

However, just when I was ready to set the past aside, it rose up again in the form of Marvin Penn, who phoned at the end of the week and said he'd found more items of my father's.

"You can keep them," I said.

"Don't you want to know what I found?" He was going to tell me anyway. "A key ring and a wallet with a picture of you and your sisters in it."

"You can mail them to me."

"And his other pistol," he added. "He kept it at my house because it made your mother nervous."

"Why did he need two guns?" I whispered. I didn't want a father who carried guns, though I realized part of me was already starting to invent a rugged man who knew how to shoot and who thought enough of his family to keep the guns somewhere else.

"I don't think I should mail you the pistol," Marvin said.

"No, you shouldn't. But his wallet and keys . . . why did he leave those with you?"

Marvin didn't answer right away. "Well, they're not exactly Jesse's, if I recall. They belonged to Calvin Wheat."

"Who's Calvin Wheat?" I was sitting on my bed with my back to my roommates hunched over the phone speaking quietly so they couldn't hear, though I knew Julie was trying.

Marvin sighed. "You know, Jesse was lucky to have died young."

"Excuse me?"

"His wife still loved him. He had three beautiful little girls. He never knew what it was to have everything fall apart." He paused. "I'm sorry. Sixty-five years old and not a single soul I can talk to. That's what this work does to you."

"Don't you have children?"

"My son's turned his back on me. He listens to his mother. But I suppose that's my fault." Suddenly he laughed. "Listen to me, I sound like one of those fools on Oprah."

"I'm sorry," I said. "Who is Calvin Wheat?"

"Your father. Only a few people knew him as Jesse West."

"Did Calvin Wheat have children?" I wondered if I was included in my father's second identity.

"Your picture's in his wallet."

I didn't know how to evaluate this information, but I didn't want to talk about it with Marvin Penn, especially in front of Julie and Mahela. "I'm sorry, I've got to go," I said. "I have to study."

"Of course. I'll mail you the wallet and keys."

"Yes." I gave him my address, then wondered if I should have told him where I lived. So much for having my father's instincts.

"What shall I do with the pistol? It's a Walther PPK .380," he told me as if the name and numbers would have meaning to me.

"You can keep the gun," I said then remembered Julie was listening. "You can have it," I amended. When I hung up, I took my Shakespeare book from my desk and opened it to *Romeo and Juliet*, indicating that I wasn't open to questions.

But Julie asked anyway, "Was that that man?"

"What?"

"Was that that man on the phone?"

"Mr. Penn? Oh . . . yes . . . yes, it was."

"Are you all right?"

I turned halfway around to face her. "Yeah, sure." I could tell she was waiting for me to elaborate.

When I didn't, she asked, "He wanted to give you a gun?"

"Ah . . ." I hesitated.

Mahela looked up from her desk as if also waiting for my answer, but then she said, "It's none of your business, Julie. Anything any of us hears in this room is strictly confidential."

She emphasized con-fi-den-tial in four distinct syllables.

*   *   *

Marvin Penn started sending me things that belonged to my father: a maroon sweater, a leather-bound edition of *Leaves of Grass*, a pair of worn Adidas sneakers, size 11. He also called from time to time, usually late at night when he was slightly drunk. He'd call to talk as if I were his daughter. I wondered if this were the kind of relationship I would have had with my father, if this is how my father would have turned out.

CHAPTER EIGHT

DENNIS SHOWED UP at my apartment unannounced on a Saturday morning in early April and insisted I take him to see the cherry blossoms. "Don't tell Dad or your mother I'm here. I told them I was going to Paris for a long weekend." He smiled a conspiratorial smile. I felt wary but also glad to see him. I missed having family around. I hadn't talked to Dennis in two months.

As we settled on a bench by the Thomas Jefferson Memorial where the cherry blossoms exploded into white and pink clouds along the Potomac River, I asked. "So why are you really here?"

"Spend the day with me, and I'll show you." He put his arm on the back of the bench and stretched out his legs, extending himself full length. He was wearing a tan V-neck sweater, blue shirt, tan slacks, and he looked relaxed and settled into himself. We'd brought fresh bagels, and I was pitching bits to the squirrels and pigeons. "I'll take you to Virginia," he said.

"What's in Virginia?"

I handed Dennis a bagel. He considered it, kept the top half, and broke the bottom in two pieces and dropped them to the ground. The two most aggressive squirrels darted off with their oversized bounty.

"My company."

"What company?"

"The company Gerald is making me a partner in. The parent company is in England. It buys and sells air-conditioning equipment and tools."

"Why would Dr. Wagner make you a partner?"

"He needs a British partner. He can train me, and I can help him." Dennis accepted that someone would give him a company as his natural right to ascension.

"Is Dr. Wagner here?"

"I came on my own. I wanted to see the subsidiary before I signed the papers."

"Dr. Wagner knows you're in Washington, but Winston doesn't?"

"No one knows really. Except you and Gerald's daughter-in-law. She's helping set up the offices."

"Serena?" I hadn't seen Serena since she and Jack moved from London when I was in high school.

"I told Gerald I wanted to do some due diligence of my own. I don't know if he realized I'd be coming here to do it." Dennis stared out at the lacy pink and white flowers that formed a crown in front of the dome of the monument. "It's rather spectacular here, isn't it? Your Thomas Jefferson was a remarkable man, I guess." He looked over at me as if waiting for my judgment, though it wasn't clear what he wanted me to judge.

"Are you telling me everything?" I asked.

He smiled again, his more familiar ironic smile that held the world at a distance. "Gerald made me a partner in this company, drew up the papers in my name without asking me, then told me to sign. He got angry when I told him I wanted to know what kind of company I was being made a partner in. 'You're twenty-three years old!' he shouted. 'This is an opportunity that won't come again.' I thought about asking Dad's advice, but Dad would bring in his solicitors and they'd slow everything down and gum up the whole deal. I told Gerald I'd sign on Monday."

"What exactly are you doing for him?"

"Acquiring equipment and getting export licenses."

"But you're still working for Winston?"

"It is getting to be a bit much." He looked out at the water littered with cherry blossom petals. "Dad's losing patience because Gerald hasn't paid for the last order of heavy trucks. He asked me to find out where the trucks were so he could repossess them. We'd delivered them to Cyprus. I went there, but the receiver on the dock told me they'd been shipped on, only he couldn't tell me where. The next day Gerald arrived at my hotel. I don't know how he found out I was there."

As Dennis talked, he continued looking at the water rather than at me. "Gerald told me not to worry, that there'd been a temporary credit squeeze for his client, but he had other deals pending and as soon as they were finished, he'd pay Dad the £20 million out of his own pocket if he had to, though he thought Dad should be more patient. 'We're family, aren't we?' he said.

"I told him Dad couldn't do that. He was responsible to his company. Besides, if we really were family, Dad had to be even more cautious."

"'You can help,' he told me. He's expecting a large contract—as much as £200 million—and if he gets it, he'll bring part of it to Dad. I can help Dad and myself at the same time." Dennis glanced over his shoulder at me and leaned back on the bench. His features were broken by the tight thin line of his mouth that never completely relaxed.

"Be careful," I said. I felt sympathy for him. I understood he wanted to please his father and at the same time break free.

"Our client's pressing us to find and purchase the equipment he wants. Gerald says it's urgent. He also says this will solve all his financial problems. I want to finish this deal, then I'll tell Dad."

"What's so urgent about air-conditioning equipment?"

"Summer's coming." Dennis grinned. I wasn't sure if he was teasing me.

"Are you sure Dr. Wagner's telling you the truth?"

"You think he's lying?"

"People lie, Dennis. They lie all the time."

"That's a cynical view from you, Lizzy. Well, don't worry, I've been keeping a record." He stood. "Now come with me." Taking my hand, he drew me off the bench. "I'm meeting Serena for lunch."

*　　*　　*

Outside the entrance of Tyson's Corner Mall in Northern Virginia, Gerald's daughter-in-law, Serena, leaned against a display window like a teenager wearing a pink tee shirt with a sequined heart between her breasts, a red sweater looped over her shoulders, and rhinestone-studded blue jeans. She'd cut her hair short, sculpted around her face. Her large green eyes were carefully made up and fluttered as Dennis came towards her. He greeted her with a kiss, and she kissed him back. He dropped his arm over her shoulders, and she slid hers around his waist, then her eyes settled on me.

"Lizzy! I heard you were in Washington," she greeted in her soft Louisiana drawl. "Jack would love to see you again."

"Is Jack here?"

"If I'd known you were coming, I'd have brought him, but he's spending the day . . . and the night . . . with a friend." I watched her with Dennis and wondered what was between them.

"I thought we could show Lizzy the company," Dennis said as we settled into a booth at a restaurant inside the mall. Dennis sat beside Serena. "She won't tell anyone I'm here."

"Why would it matter?" I asked. To me, Dennis's secrecy always seemed designed to make him appear more important.

"You don't know my father-in-law," Serena answered. "He doesn't like anyone to do anything without his knowledge and permission."

"Won't he know Dennis is here when Dennis shows up at the company?"

Serena glanced at Dennis then back at me. "No one works at the company but me."

"What do you mean?"

"Are you sure she's discreet?" Serena asked.

"Are you discreet, Lizzy?"

I wondered where and when Dennis and Serena had met. "How long have you known each other?"

Dennis dropped his arm around her shoulders. Their eyes met in a quick exchange. "Serena came to London a few months ago. She's helping Gerald with the purchase of this company in America."

"Dennis took me dancing," Serena added.

Dennis smiled at me. "We went to the Limelight."

"We've been on the phone every day since. Our conversations have gone on and on. I hate to think of the phone bills."

"Gerald won't notice," Dennis said. "Besides, he owes us both money."

"He notices everything," Serena countered. "That's why I left."

As we ate lunch, Serena filled me in on her and Jack's life since I'd seen them. They'd moved to Virginia two years ago. She packed up and left one day while Dr. Wagner was in Germany. "Don't get me wrong. He's been good to Jack and me since François died. He's paid all our expenses, but I'm afraid of him. You know his father's a Nazi who still tries to run the businesses from Argentina. They argue on the phone every day. They compete with each other. Isn't that crazy? His father's eighty-four years old. Gerald told me his father wanted to keep the business only in Germany and work with his old friends, but Gerald has branched out into other businesses with offices in Europe and now America. His father thinks he's too ambitious and not smart enough to run the business. Gerald is sixty-two years old, and his father's still telling him he's not smart enough! I didn't want Jack growing up in that house."

"You were right to leave," Dennis said.

"His father's a Nazi?" I repeated.

Serena nodded. "He's older than sin, at least in the picture Gerald took when he visited him last year. He's all wrinkled from the sun, but he still tells Gerald what to do. I'm afraid of both of them." Serena leaned into Dennis.

"You shouldn't be dependent on him."

"You'll be dependent on him too if you become his partner," I pointed out.

"I'll just do it to get started. It's not costing me anything. Besides, I'm not afraid of him."

"Maybe you should be," I said.

"I keep telling him that," Serena added.

"Gerald told me he wants to be independent of his father," Dennis said. "I understand. That's why he set up business in England."

"He set it up there because I threatened to leave him in Germany," Serena said. "I didn't like Germany so he leased the house in London and started doing business from there, and he put Jacques in the American School. I used to go with Gerald as his escort to meetings and social events and play up to certain people to help him get what he wanted. But he's jealous. He didn't want me to have any friends, particularly male friends. He has a terrible temper, especially when he's been drinking. One night he threw a whole chest of mine down the stairs because he said I was spending too much on clothes. I was afraid he was going to throw me down next. That's when I decided we had to get out of there. I'm still working for him, but I've been trying to get a job on my own. I have a college degree for Christ's sake, but I can't earn as much."

"When this company gets going, that will all change," Dennis said. I watched them holding hands, Dennis's arm encircling her as if she were a fragile new possession. Maybe Serena had found her English gentleman. She was over a decade older than Dennis, but that didn't seem to matter. Maybe Dennis had finally found his woman.

*   *   *

Off Highway 267 to Dulles Airport, where office buildings lined the road in the glass and steel corridors of Northern Virginia, Serena turned her Peugeot onto a leafy suburban street and into the empty parking lot of a red brick building with casement windows. Serena escorted us into a lobby that looked like my dentist's office.

"It's not much," she apologized, taking us to the third floor. She opened a door with Midland Tools stenciled on a plastic name plate and led us into four small rooms, only two of which were furnished. "I haven't finished. Gerald only gave me a small budget, but I wanted to make it nice." The furniture was sparse but quality blonde wood with bright red and blue and purple cushioned chairs. On the desks were new computers.

"Who works here?" I asked. "Did you buy a company or are you just leasing offices?"

"We're opening a D.C. branch for Midland Tools of California," Dennis called from the farthest room, "only Gerald wants to change our name here to Aladdin Tools—you'll have to get a new sign." He returned. "Serena, this is good." She smiled as if pleased to please him. "We can lobby in Washington here and also purchase out of here and ship from the East as well as the West Coast."

"What are you buying?" I asked.

"Air-conditioning equipment, chemicals, engines, machine tools. We need some specialized tools too." Dennis settled behind one of the desks.

"Does that mean you'll be working in Washington?" I asked.

Dennis looked out the window while Serena and I stood in front of the desk waiting for his answer. In Serena's eyes I saw a calculation as if she were measuring what this man might mean or bring to her. Dennis looked down into the parking lot where a black Mercedes had turned in. He began marking figures on a pad of paper.

The four rooms didn't look like much to me, but I didn't understand Dennis's business or the context for these rooms. Suddenly I wanted to get back to my own life.

"I have to go," I said. As I turned towards the opened door, a man entered the office wearing dark glasses and carrying a briefcase; I hadn't heard the elevator.

"Can I help you?" Dennis asked.

"Who are you?" the man countered. His accent was a studied English.

"I think you're in the wrong office," Dennis said.

Serena turned. "Oh . . ." She inhaled. "Dennis, this is Adnan . . ." She stumbled as if unable to remember or pronounce the last name. "He's Gerald's partner in Midland Tools. This is Dennis Chatham."

"No one told me you were in town," Adnan said, taking off his glasses and staring at Dennis, then at me. "Who's she?"

"Nobody," I answered. "Just a friend, and I'm leaving." I moved towards the door with no idea how I was going to get back to my apartment, but I knew it was time to get out of there.

"We expect this office to be functioning next week," the man addressed Serena.

"Yes, yes. Of course."

He started walking around the room. He had a potbelly and a moustache and wore a black cashmere cardigan, an open-collared black and white striped shirt cuffed with large gold cuff links, black pleated slacks, tasseled loafers, and silver-framed glasses. After he toured the other rooms, he announced, "I'll be back next week."

Serena nodded.

"I'll just take the subway," I said to no one in particular.

"Could you drop her off, Mr. Adnan?" Serena asked sweetly. "That way Dennis and I can keep working."

Adnan did not look pleased.

"That's all right. I can get to the subway on my own." I had no idea where the subway was.

"Come," Adnan addressed me.

I looked to Dennis, expecting he would offer to drive me, but he was lost in the figures on his pad of paper. I followed the man downstairs to the waiting Mercedes with a driver, and he drove me to the East Falls Church subway stop. When he asked my name, I said, "Some friends call me Betsy." The mother of a childhood friend used to call me that. I didn't want to give him my real name. In the one sentence he offered me, answering the one question I asked, he told me he was in from Miami, and was going to Dulles Airport to return to Florida.

*　*　*

Dennis called me at midnight a few weeks later. It must have been early in the morning wherever he was, though he didn't say where he was calling from. He was agitated; he said he was sick. He talked about pools of water and dead dogs he'd seen. "I've made a big mistake," he said.

"What kind of mistake?"

"If anything happens, tell Dad I'm sorry. I've made a terrible misjudgment."

"Maybe your father can help."

"I've got to get out of this myself."

"Dennis, you're scaring me. You want me to tell Winston?"

"Don't do that! You'll put him in danger. You've always been honest with me, Lizzy. I just wanted you to know. Promise you won't say anything."

Against my better judgment, I again promised Dennis I would keep his secret. "Where are you?"

"At the center of hell. I've got to go." The static ate our words.

"Call me, Dennis." Whatever the issues had been between us, Dennis was my family, and I cared what happened to him. "Please call me again."

* * *

A week later I incorporated the ringing phone into my dreams and was startled to find Julie shaking my shoulders. She set the phone on my pillow, then stumbled back to bed. In the dark, Mahela snored. My clock glowed 3:45 a.m.

"Hello," I whispered.

"Lizzy? Is that you?"

"Jane?"

"I'm sorry to wake you."

"What's wrong?"

"Mom just called. She didn't want to wake you, but I thought you'd want to know right away . . . Lizzy, Dennis was found dead."

"What?"

"In Germany, in East Berlin."

"Dennis?"

"Outside East Berlin, shot in the back of the head, found by the river. Police say it looks like an execution. Winston is beside himself."

"Dennis . . . ?" I felt as if someone had slammed me into a wall. My head reeled. "Why? Who?"

"No one knows yet. I'm going to fly home. Mom's really shaken herself. She'll call you in a few hours. She didn't want to wake you in case you had an exam. I told her you might not be able to come home with exams and all."

"I'll come. Is Sophie coming?"

"I haven't called her yet. I called you first." For some reason that mattered to me. "I knew you and Dennis were friends." Jane gave me the flight information and said she'd meet me at Kennedy Airport since there were no early flights to London out of Washington. She'd buy the tickets for both of us.

After we hung up, my head felt light. I thought I was going to be sick. Space dissolved around me as my mind spun with images of Dennis in his bermuda shorts with his pale knees, Dennis dancing, tripping on my feet, Dennis cocky and confident after a lecture he understood and I didn't, Dennis smoking a cigar with Winston. Dennis under the cherry blossoms at the Jefferson Memorial, Dennis holding Serena's hand. Dennis wanted to be an operator. He wanted an adventure to jump-start his life and propel him outside the borders of himself and his family. In my head I heard an engine shrieking, birds screaming, sand grinding through gears, life closing down.

I shut my eyes, but I couldn't go back to sleep. I should have told someone Dennis was in trouble. I got up and pulled my suitcase from under the bed and quietly started to pack. I'd call the dean's office and tell them I had to leave on a family emergency and ask them to tell my teachers. I should call Mom and Winston and Pickles—I'd forgotten to ask about Pickles—but I didn't want to have that conversation in front of Julie and Mahela, so I quit packing and started to dress. I could use the pay phone in the lounge.

"What's happened?" Mahela emerged from under her pink quilt.

Julie switched on her light. "What's going on?"

I stood before them in blue jeans and a nightgown, my suitcase half packed, myself half dressed. I couldn't seem to move in one direction before I started in another. I sank onto my desk chair. "My brother's been killed," I said. That was the first time I'd acknowledged to anyone outside the family that Dennis was my brother. And I cried.

CHAPTER NINE

MOTHER WAS SITTING alone in the dark by the fire when Jane and I arrived home. She looked up startled at the light, then exhaled, "Oh! My girls are home!" She rose from the wing chair and embraced us like young children, though we towered over her. She looked worn out with deep shadows under her eyes and her gray-blonde hair tangled. "I haven't slept in twenty-four hours. Winston just dozed off on the sofa in the den."

She led us to the door of the den to show him to us—a great beached man whose moonlike face floated above a plaid blanket with a surprisingly tranquil expression. Outside, the half moon shone through the garden door casting the room in white light. Mother tucked the blanket around his foot, which hung exposed off the edge of the couch. I realized here was the last place I'd been alone with Dennis in London. Mother shut the door and returned us to the living room, where she kneeled in front of the fireplace and turned up the flame. Jane went into the kitchen to make tea. Sophie hadn't come; she was in the middle of exams and would arrive at the end of the week.

"Do they know what happened yet?" I asked.

"No, sweetheart, not yet." She sat beside me on the sofa, taking both my hands in hers. "They suspect it was a professional killing." She said the words as if she had practiced them, as if they were still alien to her, but she was trying to accept them as part of her vocabulary. "There was just one shot in the back of the head. They found over 10,000 deutschmarks on Dennis, so the motive wasn't robbery. We didn't even know Dennis was in Germany. He told Winston he was going to spend a weekend with friends in the country. Why was he in Berlin? Why didn't he tell us? When the police found out he'd lied to us, they began concocting theories of their own, each one worse than the last."

"What kind of theories?" Jane asked, setting the tray with tea on the ottoman in front of us.

"They say Dennis may have been involved in drugs. That's the latest, the most credible possibility, they say. It explains the large sum of money on him and the violence."

"Is East Berlin a drug route now?" Jane asked.

"It didn't used to be, but everything is breaking down there, and people are looking for ways to make money. Winston is devastated. Did you ever know Dennis to be involved in drugs?" Mother asked me.

"No, I don't think he was," I answered.

"I'm so glad you came." She still gripped my hands. "Winston was relieved when he heard you were coming."

"How is Pickles holding up?" I asked. "Where is she?"

Mother lowered her voice. "Pickles is out with Randolph."

"Who?" Jane asked.

"He's her boyfriend from the library where she works. Winston's not happy about that, but I told him he had to let Pickles cope in her own way. When he told her about Dennis, she didn't cry. She just went up to her room. Maybe she cried there, I told him. Finally, he went to her, and I heard them arguing. When Winston came down, he vomited. Her mother called then, and she and Pickles talked for over an hour. When Pickles came down, she asked if I thought it would be all right for her to go out with Randolph. I said I thought it would be fine and I'd talk to Winston." Mother shook her head. I saw how hard she was trying to hold the family together.

"Before she left, Pickles hugged me. 'The best thing my father's done for me is marry you,' she said. 'Don't let them say Dennis was selling drugs or on drugs. It's a lie. Don't let them off the hook that easy.' 'Let who off the hook?' I asked, but she wouldn't tell me, or she didn't know." Mother looked at Jane and me as if waiting to see whether we might know. "So . . . that has been the last twenty-four hours."

Jane sat on the other side of Mom. "You need to get some rest yourself. Lizzy and I can clean up."

I didn't know whether now was a good time to tell Mother what I did know, but I was afraid I'd waited too long already. "Did Winston know Dennis was doing special projects for Gerald Wagner?" I asked. "Dennis told me he might have to travel to Germany. He told me if certain deals came in, he'd get a percentage and earn more money on one deal than he would in a whole year of working for Winston."

Jane was turning off the gas fire, and she glanced up from the fireplace. On the flight over I'd told Jane all the secrets Dennis had asked me to keep. "What kind of deals?" Mom asked.

"Selling engines and air-conditioning equipment and machine tools. He was also helping Dr. Wagner buy a factory in England which had a subsidiary in the U.S. Dr. Wagner made Dennis a partner in it. Dennis came to Washington to help Serena Wagner open a branch office in Virginia."

"Did you know anything about that?" Jane asked Mom.

"I knew Dennis was helping Winston on a project with Dr. Wagner, but it was in England, not Germany or Virginia, and it had to do with Winston's company."

"Maybe I'd better tell you everything," I said. Jane settled on the footstool by the fireplace, but she didn't re-light the fire. The room grew cold around us as I told my story of how Dennis had made passes at me over the summer, how he and Dr. Wagner had questioned me about Adil's father, how Dennis was working on some secret deals with Dr. Wagner, how Dennis had shown up in Washington.

"Why didn't you tell me this earlier?" Mom asked.

"I didn't want to stir everyone up. This summer I figured what Dennis was feeling about me would pass, then Dennis asked me to keep his business confidential and his visit to Washington a secret. I didn't know it would turn out to be fatal." My voice cracked. I felt suddenly responsible. I stood up to get control. That's when I saw Winston standing like a ghost in the doorway. I must have given a start because Mom turned around.

"Winston, you're awake. How're you feeling?" His face was pale as if he'd lost blood, and his thin gray hair stuck out in all directions. Mom went over to him and smoothed his hair.

"What did Dennis tell you about his business?" Winston demanded. There was no greeting, no acknowledgment that we'd just flown 3000 miles to be here, no mention of our mutual loss.

"He said he was working on projects with Dr. Wagner," I answered. "They were selling engines and other tools, and Dennis was helping with some kind of factory Dr. Wagner was buying. Dr. Wagner was making him a partner in one company."

"What sort of deals?" Winston stood over me like a school principal questioning a wayward student.

"Darling, sit down," Mother urged. "Did you know about his work with Dr. Wagner?"

Winston sank into the wing chair. He covered his face. From deep within him came short high-pitched bleats, as if a small animal had gotten trapped inside and was trying to get out. Mom kneeled by him, pressed his head onto her body. Tears welled in my eyes. I looked over at Jane whose eyes had also filled. Watching the pain of a man who has lost his son was almost too much to bear. Jane nodded that we should go, but Winston recovered. "Please stay," he said. "I need to know what you know."

"I don't know any more," I said. "Dennis wanted to please you; he wanted to help recover some of what Dr. Wagner owed you. He said if they got a large contract, Dr. Wagner was going to share it with you. Dennis wanted you to be proud of him. I'm sure he didn't intend to lie to you."

I tried to render Dennis's world in a way that could make what happened more bearable. "Last week Dennis called me. He said he'd made a terrible misjudgment, but he didn't want to tell you because he was afraid to put you in danger. I don't know more than that."

"Gerald Wagner phoned me tonight when you were upstairs," Winston said to Mother. "He said he was in France. He said he felt obliged to let me know Dennis had been doing some work for him, but he'd fired him last week because he discovered Dennis was doing business with criminals behind his back."

"He called you to tell you that? On the day your son was killed?"

"He claimed he didn't know Dennis had been killed."

The front door opened, and Pickles tiptoed into the hallway. From where I sat, I could see her trying to close the door without making noise.

"We're in here, Wilhelmina," Winston called. The name settled heavily on the room.

Pickles entered, her eyes defiant, her cheeks flushed, and her mousy brown hair tousled as if she'd forgotten to comb it after a passionate evening. When she saw Jane and me, she came over and kissed us. "Thank you for coming."

"Elizabeth has been giving us information about Dennis." I don't know why Winston was using our formal names. He insisted I tell my story again for Pickles. I left out the part about Dennis trying to kiss me.

"Did you know Dennis worked for Gerald Wagner in Germany?" Winston asked as if Pickles were at fault if she knew or if she didn't.

"Dennis and I didn't exactly share our lives, though he did tell me he was going to be rich soon."

"Did he say how?"

"I didn't ask."

"Why not?" Winston asked.

"Actually, what he said was that he was going to be rich so he could move out of this family of ill-bred women. That sort of ends a conversation."

Mom took Winston's hand. "Let's go up to bed. We're all very tired. We don't want to say things we'll regret." Winston yielded and stood. As Mom led him away, she reached out and touched the top of my head.

Pickles sank into the chair where Winston had been sitting. "I shouldn't be so blunt, but I hate the hypocrisy. Dad blames me, you, anyone but Dennis. I can't stand that the police are inventing stories. No one wants to admit the truth."

"What is the truth?" Jane asked.

"Dennis was selling arms and the tools to make arms for Gerald Wagner. I heard him on the phone talking about how the export license was supposed to say 'turbo pumps for petrochemical plant,' but they were really for missiles. When I challenged him, he said, 'They might be for milking cows for all I know. I can't follow every piece of machinery we sell. I'm just helping get the licenses approved.'

"'But I heard you,' I said. I told him Dr. Wagner was using him, but he said he was using Dr. Wagner. He said he'd been keeping notes."

"He had notes?" Jane asked.

"Nothing of much use, just scribblings on scraps of paper. Dennis was full of himself. He's been pretty hard to live with this year."

"Why didn't you tell your father?" Jane asked.

"He knows."

"What do you mean?" I asked.

"He's pretending he doesn't because he didn't want to know. He didn't ask questions. He wanted Dennis to succeed like him, but Dennis wanted to succeed beyond Dad's wildest dreams. He wanted to make enough money to buy Mother a house in France, he told me, and take care of her in a way Father never had. 'But Mother doesn't want a house in France,' I told him. Mother hates to travel. She doesn't even like to come into London, but Dennis had it fixed in his head. He felt Dad had left Mother behind. He had in a way, but Mother didn't want to go where Dad was going. She wanted her garden and her friends. She wanted to live in the village where the two of them had grown up, where she felt comfortable. Dennis was angry when they got divorced. So was I, but I was younger. Dennis and I used to be able to talk, but when I told him this winter that I might marry Randolph, that surprised him. He told me about you and him last summer, Lizzy. He was angry at you, at your whole family, but especially at you."

"When I talked to him, he wasn't angry," I said.

"When did you last talk to him?"

"He was in Washington in April. And he called last week."

"Oh," Pickles said. "Well, he didn't tell me that. I told him your family had nothing to do with Dad and Mom splitting up. Father didn't even know your mother when they divorced. But you were the first girl he'd tried to connect with in a while, and when you rejected him this summer, it hurt him."

"Wait . . . wait . . ." Jane came to my defense. "That's a little unfair, don't you think?"

"I'm just trying to explain some history you don't know, but maybe it is beyond you." Pickles stood.

I touched her arm. "Pickles, Dennis was my brother . . . or sort of my brother. It was very awkward. Anyway, Dennis had moved on. The last time I saw him, he and Serena Wagner were together, and they had definitely connected."

Pickles raised her eyebrows. "Well . . . that's nice."

"That's not really the point, though," I said. "Dennis is dead, and no one seems to be looking in the right direction."

*   *   *

The next morning when Jane and I came downstairs, Pickles was already at the kitchen table. None of us had slept well. Pickles said she'd been on the phone talking to Randolph until two a.m. I wondered what they talked about. Randolph was not everyone's heartthrob. He was already going bald, had bad teeth, but he had an easy laugh, was kind, and he was devoted to Pickles. I envied their closeness. As I lay awake in my bed, I wished I had someone to talk to. I thought about Adil and our walks along the river, our runs around Hyde Park, our Arabic lessons on the subway. I missed his friendship and his arms around me. Almost two years had gone by, and while I dated boys at college, no one touched my heart. Through the open window last night, I listened to the buzz of the weekend crowd down the block at Sticky Fingers, which, contrary to Dennis's prediction, was thriving in our neighborhood. I thought about Dennis reinventing himself, trying to break out of his first from Oxford, his father's name, his awkward foxtrot, of Dennis in Berlin working on secret deals for Gerald Wagner. I wondered what had frightened him. I thought of calling Serena to let her know Dennis had been killed. I wondered if she already knew. But I didn't have her phone number, and I didn't know where she lived in Virginia.

In the kitchen, Pickles sat eating crumpets with blackberry jam. "Randolph asked me again to marry him last night. And I said yes."

Jane looked over from the cabinet. "Congratulations!" She went over and kissed Pickles.

"We've been talking about getting married. Last night he said he wanted to take care of me. I cried all night. I realized Dennis would never be at my wedding. He'd never see my children. He'd never have children of his own." She took another crumpet from the plate. "Father doesn't like Randolph. He says I should marry someone with a future. Randolph has a future. He's a librarian, but Father's a snob. He says marriages don't work when the wife has more money than the husband, but I don't have any money, I told him. 'You will,' he said. Now that Dennis is dead, I guess I'll have even more."

I went over and kissed her too. "Congratulations."

Pickles shrugged. "I imagined it differently. Do you think Dennis knew someone was after him? Do you think he was scared? Or do you think they surprised him from behind? I lay awake wondering if he ever knew what happened. What should we do?"

"I think we should find out about Dr. Wagner's business," I said.

"We should find out what the police know, both here and in Germany," Jane added, "though they may not want to tell us, especially in Germany."

"I speak German," Pickles offered.

"To be honest, I don't know how much we can do," Jane said. "I have to get back to New York on Wednesday, and Lizzy has to go back for exams."

"I'm not going back. The dean said I could take my exams here."

"I could go to Germany," Pickles said. "Randolph and I. Randolph speaks German fluently and French and Spanish."

Mom came into the kitchen, followed by Winston who looked as if he'd aged ten years. His chin was rough with gray stubble. His eyes stared out of focus and red like Pickles's, and his nose was inflamed at the nostrils. His skin sagged at his jowls, as though it had finally given up trying to hold to the bone. I wondered if he'd been drinking.

"Who's going to Germany?" Mom asked.

"We were discussing how to find out what really happened to Dennis," Jane answered. "None of us believes he was selling drugs."

"The police are working on the case," Winston said.

"Yes, but they're looking in the wrong direction," Pickles said. "They think Dennis was involved in drugs so they aren't looking where they should."

"And where is that?" Winston asked.

The edge in his voice would have silenced me, but Pickles plunged ahead. "I think Gerald Wagner is involved and so do Lizzy and Jane."

Jane and I had never said that. "Is that true?" Winston asked. He was dressed in khaki gardening trousers and a gray Oxford tee shirt Dennis had given him.

"None of us believes Dennis was dealing drugs," Jane answered.

"In what way do you think Gerald Wagner is involved?" Mom asked.

"I don't know if he is," Jane conceded, "but from what Lizzy and Pickles say, Dennis was probably working for him in Germany and in the U.S. The fact that he called you the day of Dennis's death to tell you he'd fired Dennis . . . I'm not sure I believe that was a coincidence. I'm speculating of course."

"Yes, you are," Winston said.

"Dennis was helping Dr. Wagner sell machine tools and air-conditioning equipment," I added.

Winston turned to me, and his expression softened. "Did Dennis tell you that?"

"He told me he was selling engines and tools to the center of the ancient world. He said he'd been to Babylon. He asked me not to tell. He also told me Dr. Wagner's company was being investigated for exporting rotors or motors, for centrifuges." I remembered that's what Ibrahim Hasan was being investigated for buying, and that the centrifuges were used to process uranium for nuclear weapons. "Dennis told me Dr. Wagner wanted you to intervene for him in the investigation."

"And so I did," Winston answered with a pathetic finality.

"You did?" Mom asked.

"Gerald said the authorities had been given false information. He asked me to speak up for him on some documentation he was providing. I merely passed it on and said I believed the man was honest and had been misled as to the destination and end use of the equipment. I don't know what came of it." Winston seemed unconcerned.

"I don't think any of you should go to Germany," Mom said. "We don't know who we're dealing with, but let's not be naive as I suspect Dennis was. The police will handle the case."

"I will not let the police malign my brother while the guilty parties go free," Pickles said. "Randolph and I will go to Germany."

"No . . . please don't." Winston's voice broke, and tears welled in his eyes. "I couldn't bear to lose both my children." Until yesterday I'd never seen Winston cry. Pickles got up and went to him. She touched his shoulders. He turned and embraced her. I'd also never seen him hug Pickles.

"You don't know . . . I don't know, but I'm afraid for you if you go meddling around." He wiped his eyes with the napkin. "I'm afraid for you and Jane too. Don't be foolish. This isn't a game. Dennis's murder was a cold, calculated act for what reason we may never know."

It occurred to me that Winston might not want to know.

PART III

WAR

CHAPTER TEN

DENNIS'S FUNERAL IS in the village where he and Pickles spent their childhood. We rose early that morning in London to drive north. Mom, Jane, Pickles, and I gathered on the steps while Winston brought the car around. As we stood in the morning haze, quiet and subdued, I saw at the end of the block a man dressed in a black trench coat standing behind a chestnut tree, watching our house. When he saw me looking at him, his beady eyes locked onto mine, but without expression, then he slinked away.

"There's Dr. Wagner!" I said.

Mother turned. "Where?"

"He was there." I pointed.

As Winston pulled up in the Land Rover, Mother peered down the empty street. "He told Winston he was in France. He'd be a fool to come here."

I didn't think Dr. Wagner was a fool.

As the family gathered at the church cemetery, I couldn't get Dr. Wagner out of my mind. His face had registered no emotion, just fierce observation. I stare now into the hole in the earth where Dennis is about to join eight generations of Markwell-Chathams. We all stand silently in a circle. Minus Sophie, who is arriving Friday, there is Jane, Mom, Winston, Pickles, and me, Dennis's mother, her brother—Dennis's Uncle Patrick—his wife and two grown children, Winston's unmarried brother Trevor, and a smallish, white-haired man named Biddy Jarvis, who I learned is a childhood friend and recent companion of Dennis's mother. I had only met Dennis and Pickles's mother once before.

Lady Sara Chatham, who has kept the title "Lady" which Mom doesn't use, reminds me of what Pickles might grow to look like—soft and rounded with a gentle fleshy face, but edgy around the eyes and lips as though she'd scold you if you tramped on her garden or intruded in her life. She's wearing a black polyester sheath that pinches at her waist. When introduced to her, I mumble, "I'm very sorry." I have trouble looking her in the eye, but when I do, I see her gaze is far steelier than Winston's.

She keeps hold of my hand longer than she does Jane's, and I wonder if Dennis spoke to her about me. "I know you're sorry," she says.

The local vicar, who knew Dennis as a child, conducts the service. "Dennis was a mischievous lad and smart as the dickens," the vicar recalls. "He sang in the choir . . . such a lovely, lyrical voice." I didn't know Dennis sang. I wonder when he stopped. The vicar recounts Dennis's childhood as though it occurred last week. I glance at his mother who also seems to be remembering the child of a short time ago, while Winston squints as if not quite sure who the vicar is talking about. The boy the vicar describes is a stranger to our family as well. We met Dennis on the other side of childhood, after his voice had changed and his parents divorced, and he'd gone off to boarding school.

". . . So, our son Dennis Everett Markwell Chatham goes to his rest with the generations of his family. Ashes to ashes . . . Dust to dust."

As clouds roll over the lush hills and rain begins to fall, umbrellas pop open. When we start back to the vicarage, Lady Sara comes up softly beside me, and we walk silently side by side. Winston joins us. He touches his former wife's hand as if seeking balance. I slow my pace to let them have this moment together, but they slow theirs as if they need a third party with them.

We make our way to the modest Tudor-style house where Dennis and Pickles grew up and where a spread of food—shepherd's pie, baked beans, sausages, salad—has been set out on a pink cloth on the dining room table by neighbors who gather at the edges of the room. The women wear black suits or somber flowered dresses with fussy black straw hats pinned to their heads. They busy themselves around Lady Sara when she arrives, giving her far more attention than I think she wants. From the hard light in her eyes, I expect she wants everyone to leave so she can walk in her garden and say her own goodbye to her son. The men stand stiff and formal behind the women. Respectfully, one by one, they approach Winston, who is one of the success stories from this village.

Jane and I ask the neighbors if we can help, but we're assured, "Everything's taken care of," so we retire to a corner of the living room by the bay window overlooking the garden. "You want to go outside?" I ask. The clouds have blown by, and the sun is shining, at least for the moment, though today is one of those English days when the clouds sweep across the sky at such a rate that it is sunny and rainy, sunny and rainy half a dozen times. The garden stretches a quarter of an acre behind the house, planted with rows of rose bushes and daffodils and tulips. As we slip out the side door, I see Pickles settle on the flowered sofa in the living room, surrounded by young women who look oddly middle aged in their twenties.

Jane and I are walking quietly among the rows of roses—neither of us feels like talking—when Mother and Lady Sara come into the garden. Dennis's mother hands Mother a sheet of paper, which she reads, then returns to Lady Sara. The two of them talk for a moment, and Mother hugs Dennis's mother before they return to the house.

"What do you think that was about?" I ask.

"Mother's trying hard to fill in the gaps in this family," Jane says.

"I don't think she can. I don't think she knows where the sink holes are."

*   *   *

The pale blue airmail envelope must have been sitting in the mailbox a couple of days before anyone remembered to get the mail. Since the funeral, Winston has been living in a state of suspension. Our whole house has. Jane has returned to New York, but neither Winston nor Mom has been back to work, though Mom quietly slips off several times a day to phone the office. Once a day a courier delivers papers for her. It feels almost as if we're on vacation. We sleep late, ignore tasks like making beds or getting mail. Instead, we gather in the kitchen and cook and talk. Winston wanders in and out, sometimes sitting at the table with us, but mostly sitting in the den with the TV on. He wears the same khaki pants and Oxford tee shirt each day. Sometimes he goes into the garden where he digs in the earth. I ask Mother what he's planting.

"He found seeds in Dennis's room," she says. "We don't know what they are. The only way to find out is to plant them and wait."

"Seeds?"

"They may be left over from Dennis's childhood. They may be too old to grow, but Winston wanted to plant them."

I go into the garden to visit with Winston one afternoon where the seeds have been planted.

"Don't overwater," I say.

"You think so?"

"The ground looks pretty wet." Rivulets crisscross in the earth. He aims the hose to another patch of ground.

"Because of his mother or me or maybe because he went away to school so young... I don't know why Dennis didn't know many girls, but he liked you, Lizzy," Winston says. "What I would give to have known him better, to have that time with him when he was a boy. Why did we send him away to school so young? I was standing here trying to remember."

I touch his arm. He covers my hand with his own. Mom steps into the garden carrying the mail. She hands the envelopes one by one to Winston as if to prove to him that people still need him. "This one's for you, Lizzy," he says, handing me the pale blue envelope.

As soon as I see the handwriting, I know whose it is. I tuck the envelope into my pocket.

"Who's it from?" Winston asks.

"Oh, someone from school."

"That didn't look like a U.S. stamp."

In the past week Winston has hardly noticed the people around him. He hasn't appeared to notice what he's wearing or eating, but now he notices the stamp on my envelope. I don't know if this is an encouraging sign or an omen of scrutiny to come. "Oh..." I hesitate. "Shall I go start lunch?"

"That would be helpful," Mother says.

I turn and try to walk casually from the garden, touching the letter now in my pocket to make sure it's real. As soon as I get into the house, I go to the kitchen and put a large pot of water on a low flame for spaghetti, then I hurry up the stairs towards my room. I meet Pickles wandering down.

"Is anyone making lunch?" she asks.

"The water's on." I shut my door. I can hear Pickles still standing on the landing. I go into the bathroom, lock the door, then sit on the floor, leaning against the tub as I carefully open Adil's letter.

Dear Lizzy,

I read about the killing of your stepbrother in the newspaper. I am sorry for your family.

I turn the letter over to see where it's mailed from, where Adil would have read about Dennis. *British Knight's Son Found Dead in Berlin.* A variation of that headline appeared in newspapers in England and probably Germany and possibly France, but I doubt it made news anywhere else. The postmark on the letter is unreadable. The script on the side of the airmail note is Arabic, but the stamp is . . . I have to read carefully the wording on the edge of the stamp. The stamp is German. I turn back to the letter.

I have thought about you more than you know. I am sorry for the way life turns out. You remember how I used to play soccer? I haven't played a real game since I left England. I don't think I will play again. But I have learned other things. I wish I could sit at our restaurant and talk with you. You were my very good friend. I hope this sorrow will not be too heavy for you and your family.

> *Always,*
> *Adil*

P.S. If by good fortune you get this letter, please keep it to yourself. I am not too optimistic about the future these days.

There is no return address, no way for me to answer. Though the handwriting is Adil's, the voice of the letter sounds stiff, only slightly like Adil's. I read the letter again.

Pickles knocks on my door. "Are you making lunch, or do you want me to?" she calls petulantly.

I fold the envelope into a small square. In my room I dump out my rings and earrings from the wooden music box on my dresser, the one Dad bought me, inlaid with mother of pearl. I set the blue square of the letter into the concealed compartment in the bottom. Over the years I've hidden keys and locker codes and other secrets inside. I close the hidden drawer, then set the bits of jewelry, which Dad also brought me, back into the box.

"I'm coming. Sorry, I had to go to the loo." Without further explanation I go downstairs and finish making the spaghetti.

"Who wrote you the letter?" Winston asks at lunch.

The question is casual, yet I feel an interrogation has begun. "A friend who heard about Dennis." I stuff my mouth full of spaghetti so I won't have to say more.

"That's nice," Mother says. "Are you planning to go to the library this afternoon?"

I've been going to the library each afternoon as an excuse to get out of the house and to study for the exams my professors have agreed to let me take here. "Can I get you anything?" I ask.

"If you wouldn't mind. I've made a short list on the counter."

Since the news of Dennis's death a week ago, Winston has let no one, not even our housekeeper, Meg Mulroney, come to the house. I heard Mother on the phone trying to comfort Meg, who's worked for the Chatham family Dennis's entire life. After his parents' divorce, she moved to London with Winston to take care of him and his house. Mother is struggling to keep the pieces of their world together as if they may be able to slip back into their lives once this grief has passed. I'm trying to help Mom—shopping, making meals, indulging Pickles. I will stay in London through the summer and go back to school in the fall. I also think if we can keep daily life going, eventually the hole that Dennis left will fill with our cumulative lives.

I take the grocery list. "Can I get anything for you, Winston?"

"Perhaps you can find out where that stamp came from," he answers. He doesn't look up. He's hunched over his spaghetti, eating in small bites. I stand before him silent, like a guilty teenager caught sneaking out. I don't ask what stamp. We both know what he's talking about.

That afternoon at the post office I persuade the woman behind the counter to pull out a large magnifying glass, call over a colleague, and work out that the smudged postmark on Adil's letter is from Kitzingen, a town in southern Germany.

When I get home, I go to Winston's library to look up Kitzingen in the atlas though I'm afraid Winston will find me there and ask what I'm doing, but I'm not going to hide. I've learned that problems don't go away if you ignore them. In fact, they can get much worse than you can ever imagine. I can't help but wonder what may have happened if I'd spoken up about Dennis. Perhaps nothing, but perhaps one event might have changed that would have altered everything.

*   *   *

When I go to my room to change for dinner the following afternoon, I find my drawers in disarray—sweaters, underwear, tee shirts all jumbled. I wonder if Sophie, who's supposed to arrive soon, has gotten home early and come searching for something, but I don't see her or her luggage when I look through our connecting bathroom.

That night at dinner Winston asks if I've received any more letters. "I mean no disrespect," I answer, "but I don't ask you about your mail."

Sophie, whose bags still sit in the front hall, looks over at me wondering what she's missed.

"Winston is just being cordial," Mother says.

"Someone was in my room," I counter. "Someone went through my drawers."

"It was probably Meg cleaning your room." Meg finally returned today to get the house ready for Sophie's arrival. At least that is the excuse Mother used to get her back.

"Meg doesn't go through my drawers."

"What are you suggesting?" Mother asks.

"Why would anyone go through your drawers?" Pickles asks. "You think someone broke into the house? Are you missing anything?"

"Yes, was anything missing?" Mom looks concerned.

"No. I don't think they found what they were looking for." I meet Winston's eyes. He looks more alert than I've seen him. He glances away.

After dinner, Sophie volunteers to go to the store with me to pick up ice cream. As we walk to High Street, she waits for me to explain the exchange at dinner. When I begin, the emotion of the last week spills over, and I surprise us both by crying. "I know it was Winston in my room. I've been trying to help him, pretend to be a daughter or even a daughter-in-law Dennis has chosen, but when I saw my clothes turned over, I knew someone had been searching my drawers and some barrier in me broke. I wondered for the first time if Winston has an agenda of his own."

Sophie puts her arm around me. "It's not your fault," she says. "Dennis was seriously naive. So, I think, is Winston."

"It was Winston who went through my drawers. I know it was."

"What do you think he was looking for?"

"The letter I got from Adil."

"You heard from Adil?"

"Don't tell anyone. Adil asked me not to say anything."

"How does Winston know?"

"He saw the envelope. For some reason I think he connects Dennis with Adil." I remind Sophie about the incident last summer when I thought Dennis and Winston were checking my mail. "I don't know if it was jealousy or . . ."

"I imagine it's business," she says. "Dr. Wagner did business with Adil's father if I recall. I don't know what Winston has to do with it, but I don't see him going through your drawers for nostalgia, though there is something touching about that—Winston searching for he knows not what . . ."

"Sophie, please! I feel sad for Winston. He's been digging in the garden and planting seeds and sitting for hours in front of the television. Mom's trying to keep everything going, but something terrible has happened, and Mom and Winston don't know what to do. Jane called today. I heard Mom tell her everything was fine, that Winston was going back to work next week. Meanwhile Winston was up in Dennis's room on the floor playing with Dennis's conker and marble collections. I told Mom what Winston was doing, but she said that he was just clearing out Dennis's things, that he needed to do that in his own way. I think he's having a nervous breakdown, but Mom seems to think he's perfectly normal."

"I guess she's been through this with Dad. What did Jane say?" As we have done so often in the past, Sophie and I compare our views of the world, then check with Jane. "Let's call her."

"She'll still be at work. I talked to her earlier. She's been researching Wagner Machines and Tools. It turns out Dr. Wagner has interests in a lot of companies, including one here in London called Advanced Technology Partners. There are over a dozen companies associated with ATP in Britain, Germany, France, the U.S., Belgium, Italy. Jane can give you the list. She said there are layers and layers of paper covering the ownership and the exact kind of technology they deal with. Dr. Wagner also owns another company outside of London called

KBT Engineering, Limited. She was trying to find out exactly what the company did. A friend of hers at *The Financial Times* came across a peculiar document on ATP stationary. Here, she faxed it to me this afternoon . . ." I pull the paper from my pocket.

Street lamps---gas centrifuge pipes
Prosthetic limbs---melted zirconium/skull furnaces
Ink (ball pt pens) ---mustard gas
Discs (car gears) ---discs (spinning lathes)
Milk plant (pumps) ---Scud missile motors
Dental lab electrical equip---speed control centrifuge motors

"What does it mean?" Sophie asks.

"They're not sure. I thought I might go by the address to find out, but Jane asked me not to. She said it could be dangerous. She said her friend at the *FT* will know how to do that."

"Who's the friend?"

"Henry something—I read one of his stories. He's good."

"Does Jane think Dennis was involved?"

"At some level, though she doubted he understood the complexity of the organization. She said she was just starting to peel away the layers."

"Is Winston involved?"

"I didn't ask about him. Someone picked up the phone while we were talking. We thought we were on a private line, but we both definitely heard a click. It spooked us so we changed the subject then got off."

*   *   *

Safeway is about to close when we arrive, so we hurry inside, buy ice cream, then head back into the summer night.

"I've been thinking about going to Germany," I tell Sophie as we walk home. "Adil's letter came from a town called Kitzingen. I thought I could go there and also to Berlin to see what I can find out about Dennis."

"Would you try to see Adil?"

"Maybe . . ." I try to understate the possibility.

"It's been two years. It won't be the same," she says.

"I know."

"You still care for him?"

"I don't know. Maybe he's a figment of my imagination, but I'd like to find out. Winston's afraid for any of us to go to Germany after Dennis's murder."

"It could be dangerous, unless . . ."

"Unless what?"

"Unless I go with you." Sophie smiles. Her small face wrinkles, and her eyes shine.

"I don't know if Mom will even let us go."

"How old are you?"

"Nineteen."

"And I'm twenty-two. I mean no disrespect, but we don't have to ask Mom anymore."

"She'd kill us if something happened to us."

Sophie peels the paper from her ice cream bar and eats the chocolate off the outside first as she always does. Her red hair frizzes around her face like Grandma Sha's. Under the streetlights she looks older, almost like a mother herself. In the fall she's starting at Johns Hopkins School of Advanced International Studies—SAIS—in Washington, and we'll be living less than a mile from each other. Jane is my idol as a sister, but Sophie is my mate.

"Nothing is going to happen to the daughters of Jesse West," she says.

CHAPTER ELEVEN

SOPHIE AND I leave for Germany the next week. I'm glad to be getting away from Mom and Winston and the weight of their grief and to be taking action in the face of that grief. I've been helping Mom, cooking meals, and I've taken my exams, but inside I'm filling sandbags to stave off a flood and plug a hole in the universe. I'm worried Dr. Wagner will return; I'm worried Winston is involved in ways we don't understand. The last time I talked with Dennis, he told me, "Nothing is as it appears. Be careful." I feel life pulling away from its core, and I don't know how to hold it together.

Sophie and I haven't spent much time alone since she went off to college the same summer Adil left. Whenever we get together, we take out the family stories. Everyone carts around an ancestral bag of bones, but some people carry it like an attaché case, quietly and efficiently the way Jane does, or like Mom, who would never dump the contents on the dining room table. But Sophie and I open the bag almost every time we have more than an hour together.

"So, what did Mom say to Winston about Dad?" Sophie asks as we speed along the autobahn in our rented white Toyota Corolla. We may be nineteen and twenty-two, but we aren't so old that we don't still pause in doorways to glean bits of information about our family.

"She said she was afraid Dennis's life had intersected Dad's world. She said it appeared Dennis was involved with Gerald Wagner, who was illegally selling arms and the tools to make arms to embargoed countries. Dennis's mother had showed her a registered letter from Dr. Wagner firing Dennis, accusing him of stealing and falsifying documents. Mother and Lady Sara took the letter to the police. Lady Sara asked Mother, not Winston, to go with her."

"Stealing what?" Sophie asked.

"Company papers. Mom said she thought Dr. Wagner was protecting himself so if documents were missing or falsified, he could blame Dennis. She said it appeared the intelligence services had contacted Dennis, and Dr. Wagner had found out. She speculated Dennis was the kind of person Dad would have leaned on to get information. Winston started to sob then so she backed off."

"Dad would have been a mean son of a bitch with someone like Dennis," Sophie confirms.

"I don't remember him that way."

"You were too young. He could be tough. You never argued with him."

"What would you argue about?"

"Me? Everything. Boys. Clothes. Homework. Dad was away for months, then he'd drop back into our lives and try to run them. Jane was more diplomatic. Usually Mom defended me, but I was a pain, and there was a part of Dad that was a child himself. Instead of realizing he had a teenage daughter on his hands, he treated me like a rebel in the camp, grounding me, taking away phone privileges. I couldn't wait for him to go out of town. Then when he died, I felt guilty for years."

"You never told me that."

"You're lucky you have good memories. I never got to make peace with him."

"I hardly remember him anymore. Sometimes I wish he was here to help keep me in orbit, so I don't fly right out of the universe."

Sophie glances at me as though trying to translate what I'm feeling, then she says, "He couldn't have done that. You have to tether yourself." She flicks the signal, and we shoot off the highway.

For the next hour we drive up and down the streets of Kitzingen looking for Adil and his father. Kitzingen is a town of 20,000 people near the large U.S. Army base in Wurzburg where troops live in a state of readiness as part of the European flank of NATO. I wonder what Adil is doing here. We stop by the post office to see if Adil or his father has a mailbox. We call the telephone company for a phone number, but there are no listings. Finally we split up. Sophie keeps the car, and I set out on foot. It's lunchtime so I seek out Middle Eastern restaurants where Adil might eat, then I check Pizza Hut and McDonald's among the German chalets, but there's no sign of Adil.

When we regroup in the afternoon, Sophie reports, "Adil's in Berlin. I went by the Army base, and someone at the American School there knew him and said he's at university in East Berlin. When his father's in town, they stay at the Grand Hotel."

"That's where Dennis was staying," I say. "That's peculiar."

"What?"

"That someone on a U.S. Army base knows where Adil and his father live."

*   *   *

In Berlin we separate again and agree to meet back at the youth hostel at seven. I set out for the Grand Hotel on Berlin Rail. The Berlin Wall has fallen just six months before, and Germany hasn't yet reunited. I take the train as far as the Wall then get off and walk across

at Checkpoint Charlie. I've grown up reading spy novels. I'm not sure
if the thrill I feel walking across the expanse of gray concrete between
the barbed wire and watchtowers of East and West, where so many
heroes real and imagined have crossed or been double-crossed, is because I understand the history that happened here or because I've
imagined the history. I wonder if my father crossed here where the
division between peoples was at its most dangerous. Here the hole in
the universe was monitored twenty-four hours a day. Thousands have
come over since the wall toppled, yet these are still early days. I can
also imagine the wall suddenly being reconstructed, the barbed wire
rolled out and guns mounted back on their turrets.

On the other side of the Wall, I walk through the dingy streets of
East Berlin, past small shops selling tobacco, candy, and magazines,
past apartment blocks in concrete and steel. I find the Grand Hotel,
which was the luxury hotel of the Communists and a hotel for movie
stars and heads of state before the Communists. I look up at the old
marquee and watch those coming and going through the revolving
glass door. The hotel looks like an aged, beautiful woman who no longer has the means to polish her beauty.

Inside, I make my way across faded carpet, past the sweeping staircase and chandeliers to the front desk to talk with the manager. I've
come to pursue questions about Dennis's death and also to look for
Adil. I have no clear idea what I'll do if I find him. I told Sophie I
simply wanted to say hello, greet him across the years and close off
that episode of my girlhood, but I'm not sure my heart is connected to
this reasoning.

The manager tells me that Dennis stayed here for two nights. He
made several local phone calls and one international call, but the police have taken away the phone records. Dennis's hotel bill was paid by
Wagner Maschinen and Werkzeugfabrik the day Dennis died, he reports when I ask if the bill was settled. Dr. Wagner called Dad that

day and said he'd fired Dennis the week before. Why would he pay Dennis's hotel bill?

At the concierge desk I ask a diminutive man in a gray coat if there's a record of Dennis renting a car or making other reservations. "You're the second one asking questions today," he complains.

"The police are still investigating," I suggest.

"Wasn't the police."

"Who?"

The concierge studies me for a moment then answers as though concluding the information has no relevance to him. "Both Middle Eastern. Tall one with a beard, the other shorter, fatter with a moustache, silver glasses. They waited in the lobby all morning, said they'd come back."

The lobby is so large I can't see all the worn sofas and chairs arranged in seating clusters. I worry I'm pursuing something I don't understand. As the concierge checks his book for car rentals, a stocky man in a black leather jacket strides through the revolving front door, followed by a tall, younger man in a gray sweater, carrying a backpack, glancing left and right as if checking the perimeter. Two heavyset men follow them. I must have given a start because the concierge asks if anything is wrong. The older man goes to the front desk then swings around and walks within twenty feet of me. All four men disappear into the elevator.

The clerk bangs a bell for the porter. "Mr. Abraham Zill has left a piece of his mail." He hands over an envelope. "Deliver it to Room 310."

Abraham Zill! I stare up the grand staircase to the terraced rooms above. Is Ibrahim Hasan also Abraham Zill as my father was also Calvin Wheat? Adil once told me that his father carried three or four credit cards, all with different names. I wonder if Dennis ever met Abraham Zill.

As I lift the receiver on the house phone to call Room 310, a hand touches my shoulder, the thumb on the nape of my neck. I recognize the touch even before I hear the voice or see the large, soft-lashed eyes.

"I can't believe you're here! What are you doing here?" Adil stands over six feet, no longer eye to eye with me. His shoulders spread like a man's.

"Adil . . ." I exhale his name as if I've been holding my breath all this time.

"What are *you* doing here?" he asks.

"What are you doing here?"

"I'm at university. My father's staying at the hotel."

The whole drive to Berlin I've tried to grasp the fact that Adil is living only an hour and a half flight from London, not hiding in some remote place as I imagined.

"Didn't you get my letter?" he asks.

"You didn't tell me where you were. There was no return address. I've hardly heard from you in two years," I start to complain, but I don't want to whine. "What university?"

"Humboldt. I'm studying biology and chemistry." His dark eyes embrace me. His lips part with a smile just for me.

"You hate chemistry, and you don't speak German." I remind him of who he was.

He slips his arm around me. "I love chemistry. That's where I met you." His words slip out so easily. Are they just a line? He draws me into the shelter of his shoulder as if I've never left. I feel the muscles of his chest supporting me. "Let's get out of here." He slings his backpack over his other shoulder and moves us quickly towards the revolving door as the two bodyguards step off the elevator.

We hurry across the street in the late afternoon mist and into a shop. Another man with a moustache follows us inside the shop. I notice him glancing at Adil, who goes up to the counter and returns with a small, wooden music box in the shape of a chalet. "I'll get us a taxi," Adil whispers. "If we get separated, listen to the music." He hands me the box without explaining further.

Outside, Adil flags a cab. As I start towards the door, I see him get into the taxi and speed away as the shop door opens. The two men from the hotel enter. I pretend to examine other wooden toys on the shelves. I wonder if the men from the hotel will recognize me. I wonder if the other man in the shop is one of those who was asking about Dennis and Ibrahim Hasan earlier this morning. I try to stay calm, to rein in my imagination. I pretend to be a tourist. I tell myself if these men were dangerous, Adil wouldn't have left me. The men from the hotel walk around the shop. I go to the counter and buy a small wooden box with a sliding lid and tuck it in my pocket. The men from the hotel exit. I wait a few more minutes then also go outside.

I walk quickly down the gray, wet street, past run-down buildings with chipped paint and soot staining their old European facades. Even the newer structures with functional architecture show signs of neglect and rust on their metal girders. I have no idea where I am or where I'm going. I have the uncomfortable feeling I'm being followed. Paranoia is palpable in East Berlin. But when I glance around, no one is there. Where is Adil? I wonder what frightened him away and if I should go back to the hotel.

Instead, I hail a lone cab driving down the street and give the driver the address of the youth hostel where I'm supposed to meet Sophie. I look through the rear window to see if anyone is in pursuit, but I see only an empty avenue. Staring through the drizzle at East Berlin, I wind the music box and wait for the music, but no sound comes. I open the lid. There, wedged onto the keys is a folded square of paper. When I remove it, "Ode to Joy" rings out. On the paper Adil has written: *Meet me in the gardens of Schlosspark Charlottenburg.*

I show the paper to the driver. "Do you know what this is?" I ask in rudimental German.

"You want go there?" He tells me in broken English it is a palace and a park in West Berlin, built by Prussia's first king, Frederick I, for his wife.

The yellow and white baroque palace spreads over several city blocks. The driver points to the corner of the driveway where he agrees to wait after I pay him for this trip and promise an onward journey and a large tip. I hurry up the stairs into the front rooms, past baroque furniture, lacquered cabinets and tables, tapestried walls. I move from room to room beneath ceilings painted with gold cherubs and laden with mirrors. The contrast between East and West is striking here among the opulence of past monarchies. There is no sign of Adil. I look for the exit to the terrace and stare out the windows to gardens that spread behind the palace, hundreds of acres of green laid out in geometric designs, a wilder English-style garden by the river. From the window I see a solitary figure sitting on a bench looking up at the window.

"I knew you would come." Adil stands. "I drove back by the shop, but you'd gone."

"Why did you leave?"

"My father's men were following us. And that other man who entered right after we did . . ."

"Adil, are you in trouble?"

He guides me off the path. "I'm very glad you've come to Berlin." He puts his arm around my shoulders, and I feel my skin alive under his touch.

The sun is edging through the clouds as the sky shifts into a lacy blue. We stop at a bench hidden by the trees facing the Spree River. Adil takes off his sweater and lays it on the wet bench for me.

"I don't want to ruin your sweater." I'm wearing a light cotton skirt; it doesn't matter if it gets wet. I pick up his sweater, hold it for a moment, then give it back to him. Our fingers touch. The sun breaks among the leaves. The rain has left the air clear and bright, and the grass around us shines with raindrops. The scene is as idyllic as the one in which we said goodbye, and I feel a sad longing as though I know we will say goodbye again.

"I sometimes come here to walk in this garden. I've thought of you in this garden." He turns to face me. He takes my hand and stares out over the river. "You ask if I'm in trouble. I only know certain pieces of a very complicated world that I don't know how to get out of right now."

"Because of your father?"

"My father's trying to protect me. I've been living here, going to university to learn so one day I can protect him."

"Does your father live here?"

"Sometimes he's here. Sometimes Paris. Sometimes Beirut or Amman, or Cairo, but you mustn't tell anyone." I wonder who he thinks I would tell. But after Dennis, I don't want to keep any more secrets. "Why did you come?" he asks.

I stare into his face. His skin is still clear and luminescent, but he has a shadow of a beard, and the slight softness of his face has sharpened into the hard angles of a man's jaw and cheekbones. "I wanted to find out about my stepbrother who was killed. Your father's staying in the same hotel as Dennis."

"Your stepbrother was very foolish."

"You knew him?"

"I know what I've heard. The man he worked for is a criminal. He got my father thrown out of England, though he owed my father." Dr. Wagner has charged that Adil's father owed him. "What he didn't know is that my father is helping the U.S. government."

"What?" I'm confused. "What exactly does your father do? How is he helping the U.S. government?"

Adil takes my hand. He stares out at the river, at the light on the water, then he turns to me. "My father has information on that man. He and his friends are supplying a dangerous partner. What will happen next will shake up your country and all the countries of Europe, but no one wants to see what's happening because it hurts business and politics. My father is caught in the middle right now."

"If he's helping the U.S. government, won't they protect him?"

Adil smiles at me as if I'm a child. "That man your stepbrother worked for gave false information to the British to discredit my father. The shipments the British stopped were that man's, not my father's. But everything has become very complicated. We're leaving Berlin soon, at least for the summer."

Adil's words don't make sense. Exactly who is his father working for? And who is a dangerous partner? "I don't understand what you've said."

"I've said too much." He turns around to see if anyone is near, but we're alone. "If it's ever safe, maybe we'll find each other again."

"Why isn't it safe?" I touch his face. He looks down at me as if disoriented and pained by what he can't say or feel. I lean into his hard, broad shoulders. He touches the top of my head then kisses my hair. Cradling my face with his fingertips, he bends down and kisses my lips. His hand slips around my waist, and I feel his warm palm on my skin and lean into him as he pulls me close. The trees, the river, the city all disappear, and the threats recede as we move back into each other's lives. As we kiss, it occurs to me that everyone else is missing the point, which we alone have found.

Adil takes in air then gasps like a drowning man and throws back his head up to the sky. "Ah, Lizzy, Lizzy, Lizzy . . . how can we do this? There's no space for us." I touch his cheek. He takes my hand and draws it to his chest. "Can you come with me? When must you leave?"

I think about Sophie. I don't know how to call her. Even if I could, she'll want to know where I am, and she'll know that I found Adil, and she'll try to persuade me not to go with him or she'll try to find us. One way or another she'll intrude. I will only be a little late, I tell myself. She may be late herself. "I'll come with you."

We rise from the bench. Adil picks up his backpack, and arm in arm we walk through the gardens, holding to each other, out to the waiting cab. The taxi returns us to East Berlin to a small apartment building near Humboldt University.

"My father's men will be there," Adil says as we near the building.

"Do they follow you everywhere?"

"When my father's in town. I left him at the hotel without explaining where I was going."

"Should you call him?"

"If I call, I'll have to explain. We can go in the back way." Adil instructs the driver how to get to the rear of the building. The taxi stops in the alley, and we hurry in the door, sprinting up the back stairs, all four flights as if they don't exist, as if no one else in the world exists.

CHAPTER TWELVE

ADIL'S ROOM LOOKS like a monk's cell with a dormer window overlooking the street. There's a single bed, a desk cluttered with papers and books, a brown sofa, and an eating table for two also littered with papers and packing boxes half filled. There are no pictures on the walls, but on his desk in a wooden frame is a photograph of a gentle-faced woman with a young boy at her side.

Adil shuts the door to the room and stands watching me. I was never in his room when we were in high school. I try now to memorize the space. The boy in the picture is clearly Adil, standing in a market street with his mother, whose large, searching eyes are like his own. "You look so much like her," I say.

He slips his arms around my waist from behind and kisses my neck. "I've missed you. I didn't write because my father said I'd put us all, including you, in danger, but I sent you postcards and then I had cards sent to you on your birthdays. Did you get them?"

I want to say there was nothing personal written on the birthday cards, but he seems pleased to have managed this much subterfuge so I say, "Yes, I did."

He kisses me again from behind. His hands move from my waist upward, and he holds me against him. He holds me with the confidence of a man, not the teenage boy I knew. "I've wished I had a friend as you to talk to these last two years. I've wished I had a lover such as you to trust." He turns me around, and we kiss again.

"Where have you been?" I ask as he leads me over to the bed. I haven't yet made love to a man, and I wonder if I'm about to do that even as I argue with myself. Adil disappeared in my life, left me to wonder until I lost confidence in my own feelings. Can we just pick up again? I try to let anger stir in order to keep myself from disappearing in his arms. He draws me down, sitting beside him on the bed with his arm around me as if he's protecting me or shielding us both.

"My father kept traveling. I finished high school with teachers in Wurzburg, then I settled here to go to university. My father's world is changing, and I'm part of his world."

"Can't you choose your own?" I remember asking the same question on our first date.

"It's not as easy for me as for you. I'll choose my path some day, though I doubt it will be as a professional soccer player. Right now I have to prepare. My father's afraid for my safety if I move outside his protection. He's afraid his enemies will harm me to get to him. I've thought about you, Lizzy. There were times when I couldn't stop thinking about you."

"Who is he afraid will hurt you?"

"My father's connected to powerful people, but he no longer shares all their goals. He thinks the interests of war have manipulated us. He's known war most of his life. When he was my age, he fled Palestine, lived in Iraq, then Egypt and finally Lebanon, but then Lebanon went to war with itself. After my mother was killed, he moved us to Jordan, but after two of his friends were killed there, he didn't feel safe so he moved us to London."

"Why would someone hurt you?"

"My mother was killed by those trying to get at my father. He fears the same for me, though I think he's too cautious. It's been hard to live when there's no one to trust." Adil's eyes are needy like a young boy's, and yet they are bright and aggressive like a man's. "I've always trusted you." He kisses me on the lips, and I kiss him back. He kisses me again and again, slowly lowering me onto the bed.

"Adil, I haven't seen you in two years. I don't know who you are now . . ."

"Yes, you do. You are the one who knows me." His lips move down my neck.

"We need time together . . ."

"This is the time. Stay with me tonight."

I want to talk and ask him more questions, but his hands caress me, awakening me, and as we kiss, my questions blur like so many stop signs and traffic lights when an airplane lifts into the sky. The confusion of the last weeks—Dennis's death, Winston's peculiarity, Mother's denial, my own guilt—fall away as I shut my eyes to the daylight that slips through the window, and Adil and I travel back to each other in a kiss. Since Dennis's death, I've felt disembodied, as if I'm living outside my skin, but now I feel my skin around me as I hold Adil close, feel his smooth skin next to mine, smell the faint lemon of his soap, the smoke in his hair. The voice in my head warns *Don't! Don't!* even as I feel myself losing touch with my own reasons.

"Adil . . ." My head feels light. "Adil . . ." He gently slips off my blouse and my skirt in the same motion as he disrobes himself. We lie beside each other as I've often imagined, our bodies without barriers or boundaries. I find myself trusting him and ignoring my deeper instinct, yielding to the confidence we have in each other. He doesn't rush. "I've needed you . . ." he whispers into my hair. "I love you . . ."

"I love you too," I say.

"I never quit loving you."

I never quit loving him either, I realize, though I don't know who he's become. I am loving the boy I knew, who I still see in this man.

His lips travel down my neck, to my breasts. His hand runs up my legs. He rolls on top of me, swallowing me with his mouth. "Marry me," he says.

I stare into his pleading, insistent eyes. "How? I can't . . . "

"Marry me." He pauses as we poise on the edge of the world, prepared to jump without protection. "Lizzy . . . ?" he asks.

I know what he's asking, know there is nothing between us to shield us. Neither of us has prepared for this moment. What exactly do I think will catch me on the other side? He's waiting on me. The voice in my head screams *Don't!* as I pull him to me, and gently he lowers himself onto me and then slowly into me. I gasp. I hold him so tight I think we will merge into one person and never let go. I touch the birthmark on his shoulder, like a tiny map of the heart. As we cross the border between each other, part of me knows I am making a huge mistake, pretending there are no consequences when there are consequences, but I want to believe in the possibility of our union so I set aside all my reasons to refrain and grasp at this hope. Somewhere in the room I hear air escaping—is it from the steam pipes along the wall? As we make love in the fading light of the Berlin afternoon, Adil guides me and then I guide him to where we can find ourselves together.

*   *   *

A sharp pounding at the door startles us awake. Adil's father's voice barks out in Arabic. It is dark now outside the window. Adil answers back in Arabic. He holds me as his father shouts at him. Again he answers his father. For a moment there is silence, and then the footsteps fall away. Adil turns and kisses me. He tries to take us back to where we've been, but I am starkly conscious now, conscious of myself naked with his father on the other side of the door.

"I have to go." I start to get up. "Sophie will be worried. What time is it?" Adil sits up beside me and begins kissing me. "Where's your father?" I ask.

"He's waiting."

"Waiting where?" I didn't hear the footsteps go down the stairs. "Is he outside the door?"

"He has a friend down the hall."

"Does he know I'm in here?"

Adil draws me back down to the bed. "Lizzy . . ."

I feel him wanting me again, but I'm not able to block out the world this time. "He's waiting for you, and he knows I'm in here with you." Adil is kissing my neck, my breasts, stroking my legs.

"Adil . . ."

"Don't worry about my father."

"I have to worry about your father." His father defines his world.

He kisses my lips. "I'm not worried about your father."

"Because I don't have a father." I wonder if I did have a father whether he would have tried to stand between Adil and me the way he once did with Jane and Sophie and their boyfriends. But Adil is no longer a boyfriend. We've become lovers, and I know by the pounding on the door that I have wildly underestimated the consequence of this act.

Adil's lips move to my ear. "Lizzy, I want to marry you," he proposes again. He buries his head in my hair like a boy, whispers in my ear as he moves against me. "I love you. I want you. I need you."

"Adil . . ." My breath is coming shorter. I'm thinking about children. What if I get pregnant? Isn't that what all those classes in school were about? Haven't I been taught to wait until marriage because marriage protects the sanctity of children? Adil, too, has been taught. In high school we lived under these strictures and abided by them together, but the world is moving so fast and so hard for both of us right now. All these thoughts flood into my mind, only to be met with Adil beside me, whispering in my ear. "Marry me . . ."

I shut my eyes and hold him tightly. I need him too; I love him. I whisper, "Yes!"

*   *   *

I don't know how much time passes before the next knock on the door, but this time there is an urgency in the voice. Adil sits up quickly. "We have to go," he says. He stands and begins to dress.

"What's happening?" The clock by Adil's bed reads 4:50 a.m. I get up too. I want to shower, but instead I quickly slip on my skirt and top. It is cool now, and Adil reaches out and touches the goose bumps on my bare arms. From a drawer he pulls out a pale blue sweater, which he puts around my shoulders.

"What's happening?" I repeat. His father is whispering outside the door.

"Your sister's contacted the police. They're searching for you. They've called my father."

"Why would they call your father?"

"She told them you were looking for me."

"The police know you?"

"They are not unaware of my father." Adil opens the door.

I'm not prepared to face Ibrahim Hasan, the man whom the press has sought for the past two years. He marches into the room as if he owns it, which I guess he probably does. His scarred, pockmarked face looks agitated. His hair has turned gray. He looks at me as though I am a stranger come to satisfy the pleasure of his son. I feel suddenly conscious of the tumbled sheets behind us, and I feel both anger and shame at this treatment. I wonder how these feelings can follow so quickly on the sweetness of the moments before. Adil puts his arm around me as though he knows what I'm feeling. I wonder if he will tell his father that we plan to marry. Do we plan to marry? Adil has asked me in a moment of passion. I have answered in the same. Am I really prepared to marry Adil? He says, "I'll take her home, Father." *Her*, in the third person. Adil speaks English, but his father answers in Arabic. He's keeping me out of the conversation.

"He says his driver will take us," Adil translates. "Where are you staying?"

I dig into my purse to find the address. Adil gives it to his father and speaks in Arabic. I have no access to Adil's world unless he translates for me. In the hallway Ibrahim Hasan hands the address to another man. Adil takes my hand. As we leave the apartment, I pass his father in the doorway. Ibrahim Hasan looks at me now with an expression that I think contains some recognition, perhaps of that day we sat together in the rain watching Adil play soccer. I nod to him then I put out my hand. He looks uncertain whether he should take it, unsure what the hand means. I don't know exactly what it means either. I'm acknowledging he's Adil's father, and I am asserting myself. I'm also acknowledging my responsibility for being there. Some Arab men will not take the hand of a woman, but Ibrahim Hasan takes mine.

After we turn the corner from the building, Adil leans forward and speaks to the driver, who pulls over to the curb. "Let's walk," he says. We slip out of the back seat and start up the empty street arm in arm. The car follows us. I turn around. A church dome rises behind us as we cross a bridge over the river. "He has to follow," Adil explains. "My father told him to bring me back."

"Doesn't your father trust you?"

"Not entirely. We're supposed to leave this morning."

"Leave where?"

Adil draws me to him. I look up at his face in the streetlight and see the calculation in his eyes. "I told you I had to leave Berlin soon."

"Today? You didn't say today!" My voice rises. Adil doesn't meet my eyes. "Where are you going?"

"To Jordan."

"Why?" I stop on the sidewalk and face him. Suddenly I feel tired and raw and in need of a shower. The car stops at the curb. "Tell me the truth."

Adil puts his arm around my shoulders and moves me forward. "If you don't walk, he'll get out to see if we need help." Reluctantly I walk past large museum-like buildings. "I love you is the truth," Adil answers. "I have a responsibility to my father is the truth. I want to marry you is the truth. If you want to come with us, I'll persuade my father to take you. I'm twenty-one years old. I can marry who I want."

Before I can answer, Adil goes on, "But the killing of your stepbrother has made it very difficult for my father here. The truth about your stepbrother is complicated. I wasn't there. No one except the man who killed him was there, but I can tell you what I know." We pass another couple rushing by under the streetlights. "Your stepbrother came to my father the day before he died. He was representing that man."

"Dr. Wagner?"

Adil nods. "He said he'd been sent to tell my father he owed for certain items. My father said his client's government had made the down payment as contracted but never received delivery. He wasn't paying the rest until the shipment was delivered. That had been the agreement. Your stepbrother said no goods would be delivered until full payment was made. I was in the other room so I could hear them. Your stepbrother was sick. I saw him when he came in. He was very pale. His skin looked almost yellow, and he was sweating. He collapsed in front of my father. My father called me in and was about to send for a doctor when your stepbrother revived. He said he'd be all right. He asked if he could have some water and rest for a minute. He drank two full glasses.

"'I think I was sent here to set you up,' he told my father, 'but I'm not sure how the plan works. Maybe we're both being set up.'

"'By whom?' my father asked.

"'My employer or his employer. I thought you might be able to tell me.'

"'What do you want to know?' my father asked. Your stepbrother was still sweating. My father told him he should see a doctor.

"'I think I've been poisoned,' he said.

"'You must go to a doctor,' my father insisted.

"'I'll go tomorrow. I have work I need to finish before I'm put into a hospital.' Your stepbrother stood. 'I've just returned from hell,' he said. 'The streets are lined with trash cans filled with dead dogs.'"

"Adil, why didn't you tell me this earlier?"

"I'm telling you now. The police know my father is one of the last people to see your stepbrother so they're investigating him."

Suddenly the distance between our lives telescopes. "Was your father involved?"

"No." Adil meets my question directly.

Do I believe him? How can I love a man I don't believe? "My mother thinks Dennis may have been spying or investigating to write a story." These are theories she's offered Winston. We all have trouble imagining Dennis as an arms dealer, though we can imagine him getting in over his head and arrogantly, naïvely persisting.

"Whatever he was doing, he was a fool," Adil says.

I don't argue. Dennis was a highly educated, properly bred fool whom I miss. When we arrive at the hostel, I ask, "Can we keep walking?"

Adil checks his watch, then he goes over to the car and informs the driver. It is perhaps useless to continue walking. Eventually we will have to part, or I will have to run in and tell Sophie I'm flying off with Adil. I know I won't do that. I don't know how to free Adil from his father's world. Instead, I would be caught in that world.

"I'll help you find out whatever I can about your brother," Adil says, drawing me to him.

I want to trust him. I need to trust him. "Would your father tell you more?"

"He doesn't like to talk about his business, but if I ask him. He doesn't want me in his business."

I wonder if Adil knows his father any better than I knew mine. "Exactly what does your father do? Who does he work for?"

"Governments, including your own."

"Selling arms?"

"He facilitates sales that governments want to make but often don't want known. In the past they've used my father as a middleman." I grow still. "It's his life, Lizzy. It isn't mine."

"But it is yours. It defines yours." As we walk, our bodies lean into each other, barely moving down the block. "You have to tell me the truth. Did your father have anything to do with Dennis's death?"

"Only that your stepbrother visited the day before he died, and the police know that. I think Dr. Wagner was trying to implicate my father in the death. Did your family get an autopsy?"

"Dennis was shot."

"He was very sick."

"They didn't think they needed an autopsy. They've already buried him." My voice cracks when I say that, and tears rise in my eyes. Adil puts both arms around me and holds me. "When do you have to go?" I ask.

"Our plane is at eight this morning."

I look at my watch. It is 5:30 a.m. Adil knew all last night that at eight this morning he would leave. Suddenly I feel betrayed. The energy drains out of me. I turn and start back towards the hostel.

"Where are you going?"

"You have to leave."

"Will you come with me?" We both already know the answer.

"You must come to me," I say and start up the steps.

Adil grasps my hand. "I will come to you. I'll be back in August—as early as I can."

I continue up the steps. When I turn around at the door, Adil has already climbed into the black sedan and is speeding away through the early morning streets of Berlin.

CHAPTER THIRTEEN

THE MORNING LIGHT struggles through a high dirty window at the youth hostel where Sophie lies fully dressed on top of a cot. Her head turns as I sink onto the bed next to her. "I'm sorry," I say. "I should have called. I didn't know the number."

She stares at me without expression and without answering. I can't read her face so I slip off my shoes and start to climb under the thin white bedspread.

"I can't believe you!" She sits up as if my need for sleep offends her. "You left me to worry all night after we'd talked about the dangers here. I had to call the police to track you down. I was about to have Mom and Winston fly over if I hadn't heard from you. Can you imagine how Mom would have felt after all she's been through?"

I squint trying to imagine. I would have been frantic if Sophie hadn't turned up, but I want to defend myself against blame for pain that hasn't occurred because of an action Sophie hasn't taken.

"I hope you had a good time," she says. "I assume you found Adil."

"Yes." I don't elaborate. I want to tell Sophie that Adil and I are in love—Sophie has never been in love—though the certainty I felt about Adil just a few hours ago has been complicated by the encounter with his father and the realization that Adil wasn't entirely forthright with me. "He's studying at Humboldt University."

"I don't care what he's doing." She rises from the cot. "I'm flying back today. You can do what you want." She leaves the room.

I would go after her, but I'm exhausted, and I know I can't argue with her. She's right, at least from her point of view, and at the moment that is the only point of view she'll listen to. I'm sorry I made her worry, but I'm not going to explain myself because if I share what happened, Sophie will ruin it. I roll over, away from the window and the gray morning light, and fall asleep.

On the flight back to London, Sophie will barely talk to me. I try to tell her some of what I've learned about Dennis without exposing Adil as my source, but she's been given her own story from the police about Dennis getting caught up in Berlin's underworld, and she's taking that back to Mom and Winston.

"You don't know if that's true," I say. "Be careful what you tell Winston. He's fragile."

"I'll tell him the truth. I won't pretend."

"I'm not suggesting you pretend, but you don't know everything, Sophie. You don't."

*   *   *

In the days we were away, Winston has gotten worse. He still hasn't returned to work, and according to Mom, he spends hours in the garden watering Dennis's seeds and weeding and rearranging the flowers.

"He sits on the garden bench staring at the roses and hydrangeas and tulips, then suddenly rises, digs out a plant, roots and all, and moves it to another section of the garden," Mother says. "He's moved half the plants. Some of them have taken root, but many are dying; their roots aren't reconnecting in the soil. I don't want to leave him alone at home even with Meg so I'm still working out of my study. He blames himself for Dennis. I don't know why."

Sophie, Mother, and I are sitting in the living room after dinner our first night home. Winston has gone into the den, where he's fallen asleep on the sofa in front of the television. "He sleeps half the day and evening," Mother says, "then he's up all night wandering the house."

Sophie and I are perched at opposite ends of the room so that Mom has to turn from one of us to the other as she talks. Neither of us wants to add our dispute to her problems, but she asks, "Is everything all right with you two?"

"Winston blames himself because he introduced Dennis to Dr. Wagner," Sophie says. "And Dr. Wagner is the one who sent Dennis to Berlin."

"It's more complicated than that," I offer, but I don't elaborate. My information won't bring Dennis back and will only darken the picture and expose Adil. Privately, I'll tell Mother what I've learned.

"Dennis got involved with criminals," Sophie goes on. "Maybe he knew they were criminals; maybe he didn't."

"I wish you'd be careful what you tell Winston," Mother says to Sophie.

"He asked me, Mother. If he wants to know, I'll tell him the truth."

"Yes, but do we know the truth? Right now, much of what we think we know is speculation."

Sophie looks over at me who has cautioned the same thing. She stands. "You are all living in a bubble!" she declares and heads upstairs.

Mother raises her eyebrows. "What's wrong with your sister? Did you two have a fight?"

"She'll be all right." I hesitate, then I ask, "Did you ever consider getting an autopsy on Dennis?"

Mother frowns. "No. The coroner said the cause of death was a bullet in the back of the head."

"Someone told me Dennis was very sick the day before he died, that he thought he'd been poisoned."

"Poisoned? Who told you that?"

"Someone who spoke to him." I want to tell Mother I saw Adil in Berlin, but she'll ask questions, and I'll end up telling her about staying with him, or worse I'll end up hedging and not quite telling the truth. "Do you think an autopsy is worth pursuing?"

"Ah, Lizzy . . ." Mother exhales. "That would mean digging up the body. I don't know if Winston could handle that." Her voice wavers. "What would we gain? Why would someone poison him and then shoot him?"

"Maybe they got impatient. Or maybe they wanted to cover up the evidence of the poisoning."

Mother takes my hand. "I'm grateful you're going to stay here to help this summer."

"I'll do whatever I can."

"Let me think about what you've told me."

I nod. "And don't worry about Sophie. We'll sort things out."

*   *   *

The night before Sophie's return to Washington for a State Department internship, I go to her room as she's packing. Her room looks bare, most of her books taken from the shelves. On the bulletin board above her desk are still a few snapshots from high school teams and clubs. Sophie joined more activities in one year than I did in my whole high school career. I always thought of Sophie as popular and smart, but as I watch her stuffing clothes and even more books into her suitcase, I wonder if she joined all the clubs so she wouldn't be lonely.

"Thank you for not saying anything to Mom about that night in Berlin," I say. I look for an opening to talk about Adil. Sophie and I rarely discuss boys, perhaps because she doesn't date much. Once, she told me her most active social life was in junior high school in

Washington when our neighbor Jimmy Mann was her boyfriend, then we moved to London. I pick up a sweater and fold it for her and put it in her suitcase.

She glances at me as if struggling to stay mad. "Mom has enough on her mind without having to think about what might have happened."

*   *   *

I've heard from Adil only once. *I think about you every day*, he wrote. *I'll come back early August. Can you come to Berlin, or should I come to London? I asked my father about your brother. He said Dr. Wagner is in serious debt because his main client can't pay. The client owes billions of dollars to all his creditors. My father predicted the client will soon cause trouble for many people.*

I write Adil right back to the address in Amman, but after two weeks my letter is returned. I send it again, along with another letter, but both letters are returned. I send a postcard next to see if it gets through. It never comes back, but it's never answered. I try one last time, a short letter telling Adil I'm working at a travel agency for the summer and can get low fares and visit him if he thinks that's possible. By now I'm worried I might be pregnant. I want to tell Adil in person, but the letter comes back. It looks opened. On the envelope is written in crude English: NOT LIVE HERE.

In late July, two weeks before I'm to fly back to Washington, Dennis's seeds bloom in Winston's garden, and I find out that I am, in fact, pregnant. Dennis's seeds turn out to be marijuana. Winston's brought the plant into the house and set it in a vase on the front hall table, a scraggly green weed that he's decorated with two yellow roses, also from the garden. I return home from the clinic where I've gone to confirm what I've suspected for the last month. I feel panicked as I stare into the hall mirror wondering if anyone can see the five pounds

I've gained. I smell the musty odor of the plant. I stare at it first in the mirror then lean down and actually smell it. It takes me a minute to figure out what it is. When I realize it's marijuana, I laugh out loud. I laugh so that I won't cry.

I think in a corner of my mind I've known from the night I was with Adil that against odds, or perhaps on the odds, we'd conceived a child. All summer I've waited for evidence that I'm wrong, yet each morning the possibility remains. I feel queasy in the morning. No one has taken note of the dry pieces of toast I stuff down before I go to work. I work all day in a quiet state of panic, hoping the next day will deliver me. At night in my dreams, I hear a sound like wind whistling through a rip in a tent. Through this tear the sand, the insects, the rain, the burning sun all invade. In the early morning hours when I awake, I hear Winston wandering the house.

"What's the matter?" Mother comes up behind me in the hall. I'm not laughing anymore. I'm standing in front of the marijuana and roses weeping.

"It's marijuana," I say. "Winston has been growing marijuana!"

"Is that what it is? Winston didn't know. Why are you crying?"

I meet her eyes in the mirror. How can I tell her? She looks worn down, still with dark circles under her eyes. We are all worn out by the grief from Dennis's death that has not yet loosened its hold. Mom has decided not to ask for an autopsy, judging rightly or wrongly that it is more than Winston can bear. Soon I'll be going back to school and leaving her alone to cope with a husband I want to shake by the shoulders. I want to tell Winston to snap out of his grief and help my mother. How can I hand her another crisis? Is this a crisis? I have no idea how I will take care of a child and no idea where Adil is. But beneath the panic, somewhere near my heart, I want this child. Though I don't know how I will manage, I don't have to know yet. I only have to grow a baby slowly, day by day.

I wipe my eyes with the back of my hand. "We never really knew Dennis," I say. "Think how much we don't know about each other, how much we don't know about everything." Mother puts her arms around me and pauses as if considering all that she doesn't know.

*   *   *

On August 2, 1990, ten days before I'm supposed to return to Washington, the phones start ringing early in the morning; then one by one, I hear televisions switching on in the house—first the BBC, then Sky News, then CNN. Because Mom is in the news business, we're one of the few houses I know that has all the new satellite news channels. As I come down for breakfast, Mother races past me on the stairs to the front door, where a messenger is delivering reports.

"Iraq invaded Kuwait this morning," she announces. "Thousands of soldiers and tanks are pouring across the border. The Kuwait government is about to fall." She follows me into the kitchen, where an American commentator on the television is saying: *Most Americans don't even know where Kuwait is.*

I settle at the table with a bowl of corn flakes and dry toast and stare at the map on the screen. I know where Kuwait is. At the American School I have friends from Kuwait and from Iraq. I change channels. A reporter is telling us: *According to Iraqi president Saddam Hussein, Iraq is responding to an appeal from young revolutionaries to install a new free government, but no members of that government have made themselves known. If the current Kuwait government falls, as now seems inevitable, Iraq will have access to Kuwait's rich oil fields at a time when Iraq is in serious debt, unable to pay billions of dollars to its creditors.*

In that moment, watching a still picture and listening to a voice labeled "Live," I connect the dots, and I understand that Iraq is the client Dr. Wagner and Dennis have been servicing. Babylon is in Iraq. Dennis was watching belly dancers, drinking champagne, and eating masgouf in Iraq. This is the conflagration Adil's father has warned about. Because I don't understand exactly what Ibrahim Hasan does, I don't know where he and Adil may be right now. Adil is supposed to spend the summer helping out at a clinic in Jordan, but I haven't heard from him. Suddenly I fear he will be swept into this conflict, or perhaps already is.

A week after Iraq invades Kuwait, I get my last letter from Adil, scribbled on notepaper from a pad and put into a plain white envelope with no return address and a stamp whose origins I can't read and a postmark that is only a smudge. Adil has written *Airmail* on the envelope.

Dear Lizzy,

I can't come back to Berlin or London, not soon. We have moved twice and will move again. I am hoping we will not all go to war, but I fear we will. I think of you every day. My father would be angry if he knew I was writing you. He says it's too dangerous. I have missed hearing from you this summer, but I know you are busy.
Don't forget me.

Always,
Adil

Adil hasn't heard from me because my letters were returned. Did his father intercept the letters? I don't know how to get in touch with him.

Adil doesn't return to Berlin, and he doesn't write any more letters. Every time I wonder where he might be, my heart flies out the window, and I have to stop and grow very still in order to catch my breath and retrieve my heart.

With the crisis in the Gulf consuming the news, Mother finally goes back to her office full-time. She asks Meg, Pickles, and me to help with Winston, though the truth is Winston needs more help than any of us can give. Pickles turns out to be the most useful. Winston responds to her and comes in for meals when Pickles asks him, but Pickles has a job, too, and is planning her wedding. All summer she's been operating in her own world, shielding herself from us and from Winston's breakdown by her own ensuing life.

An ensuing life. That is what I want. As the world mobilizes towards war, my anxiety steels into a resolution to bear this child. When I wake up now, I talk to the child and tell it about its mother and father. The anxiety I feel each day is met by the life within that holds its own imperative. Though I have little idea of what having a baby entails, I reason everyone has babies. I'm almost twenty years old, only a few years younger than Mom was when she had Jane. Of course, I don't have a father to help, and I don't know what will happen when I tell Adil, but before I can tell him, I have to find him. Surely he'll turn up. Something will turn up. I feel panicked, but I also feel ready to love a child. I am a fool like Dennis, only I am bringing life, not death, into the family with my foolishness.

*   *   *

I return to Washington without telling anyone I'm pregnant. I set out to find a place to live and a part-time job before classes begin. Julie and Mahela insist we share an apartment, so I tell them about the baby before I tell Mom or Sophie or Jane. I practice on them. The three of us move into a two-bedroom, third-floor apartment near campus. I take the small bedroom at the back. On a clear day I can see a sliver of the Potomac River and the trees of Virginia on the other side. When the trees flame red and orange across the river, on the ninth anniversary of my father's death, when I'm five months pregnant, I finally tell my family I'm having a child.

I awaken from a restless night and call Jane first. "I know it's early. I've just been lying here . . ."

"That's all right. I was lying here too . . ." We make a point to talk to each other on this day.

Jane is quiet for a moment after I tell her. "You know you'll be responsible for another person for the next twenty years, really for the rest of your life," she says. "Are you sure you're ready for that?"

"In some ways I've been ready my whole life."

"What if you can't find Adil?"

"This child has its own reason."

She doesn't argue. "Have you told Mom?"

"Any advice?"

"Just tell her. I'll call her later."

Telling Mom is easier than I expected, perhaps because she's still focused on Winston or because she understands I'm not seeking her permission. To her credit, she doesn't drill me with questions for which there are no answers, like how I could have let this happen—a question I've asked myself, one for which any answer is irrelevant to the fact that it is happening.

"This will change your life more than anything you'll ever do," she says. I can't tell if her words are a warning or a benediction. She hesitates as though she wants to say more but doesn't want to risk a breach between us. Finally, she adds, "You'll make a fine mother, sweetheart. I'll do all that I can."

At the time I don't understand that for Mom "all I can" means using all her contacts to try to locate Adil. I'm sure phone calls fly across the Atlantic between my sisters and Mother. There are probably discussions with Winston, but to their credit, my family doesn't bombard me.

Sophie is the holdout. When I go to visit her the next day, she protests, "I don't know what's wrong with my family. This is extremely serious, and everyone is acting like you're giving them a present." We're sitting in her studio apartment near DuPont Circle. "This is going to affect us all."

"How's it going to affect you?"

"The fact is you don't know what you're getting into. You don't have an income. You don't have a husband. The father is from a culture you know nothing about, and while I may love your child . . . I probably will love your child . . ." she says this as though she's weighing the options, "I can't support you."

"Nobody's asking you to support me. Why would you think I'd expect you to support me? I'm doing just fine." That very morning Marvin Penn, Dad's old partner from the CIA, called and offered me a part-time job as a research assistant at a good salary. I'm meeting him next week to get my first assignment. And I still have my job at the Elliot School of International Affairs at the university. I'm not sure how I'm going to juggle two jobs and all my classes, but I'm prepared to work. I've never been afraid to work.

Sophie paces by the window dressed in baggy jeans. She's put on weight and cut her hair short. She has the brains but also the resolute looks of Grandma Sha. Rather than argue with her, I go over and hug her.

"Aren't you afraid?" she asks.

"Yes. Sometimes in the middle of the night I wake up panicked as if every mistake I've ever made has piled on top of me, and I can't breathe. But then morning comes. I love this child already."

"You've got more courage than I do."

"No, I don't."

"Yes, you do. It takes courage to love what you can't even see and commit your life to it."

CHAPTER FOURTEEN

I slip into the turquoise vinyl booth at the coffee shop where Marvin Penn first presented me with my father's gun. Marvin is already there, wearing a yellow and blue Hawaiian shirt and tan leather jacket and eating a piece of lemon meringue pie. He's grown a full beard. Mother told me Marvin was the best investigator my father ever worked with. He used to be a gunnery sergeant in the Marines. My dad had been a captain. "He called your dad 'bulldog squared' since your dad went to Yale whose mascot is also a bulldog, and he was a Marine. There's nothing he wouldn't have done for your father."

When Marvin called me about a researcher job, I told him I was doing research of my own, trying to find out information on Gerald Rene Wagner. "Maybe we can help each other," he said.

As I sit down, he pulls a pad from his pocket. "I did some preliminaries on that Wagner fellow you asked about. Exporter of machine tools from Germany, fell on hard times when his father slipped off to Argentina. Changed his name from Gerhard to Gerald. Wagner Machines and Tools is under investigation in at least three countries for illegal arms shipments. How do you know this guy?"

"My stepbrother worked for him before he was killed. My stepfather did some business with him."

"I wouldn't recommend him as a business partner." Marvin slides a folder of papers across the table to me. "Here's your first assignment. I've set you up with an interview with Deputy Assistant Secretary of Commerce Samuel Huggins on Friday. Here's background and some questions on the Balkans."

"Why don't you interview him?"

"If an old warrior like me starts asking questions, he'll clam right up. He likes helping students."

"What do you want to know?"

"Eventually information like your dad and I used to gather. We followed who bought weapons from whom. We saw enough missiles and tanks and guns pass hands to wipe out several countries. Some of the weapons were sold by our government and our allies to those who, sure as geese fly south in the winter, turned them around and used them on us. Who do you think armed Iran? We did. And Iraq? We did. And the British did, and especially the Germans and the French did, and the Italians, the Russians, the Chinese, the whole god-damned UN Security Council, which now has voted to fight the bastard to get rid of the weapons we sold him. Your dad used to say: Follow the weapons, and you'll find the next war. Huggins may have been involved in certain trades blocked at the last minute to Iraq."

"Then why do you want me to ask him about the Balkans?"

"If you ask about Iraq, his guard will go up. He wants out of Commerce, wants to transfer to State. He did his academic work on the Balkans."

"I'm not that smart about global politics," I say. I don't tell Marvin I'm not entirely sure where the Balkans are and get the Balkans and the Baltic confused.

"Don't worry. He's not expecting you to be smart. He wants to show you how smart he is."

"Can I tell him I'm sharing what he tells me?"

"Tell him you're doing a paper."

"What will you do with the information I give you?"

"Don't worry about that. You'll be helping your government."

"Why would the government spy on itself?"

"You're not a spy." Marvin looks up from his plate. "You'll be asking questions and writing a report. The government is a beast with many minds and many masters. One agency doesn't always know what the other's doing. The goals of Commerce aren't necessarily the goals of the State Department, and the goals of the State Department aren't always the goals of the Defense Department, which doesn't always share goals or information with Congress. The CIA operates in its own universe, reporting to the President and Congress, but often not reporting everything. The longer I live, the more cynical I grow, and the more in awe I am that the government functions at all."

*   *   *

As I walk up G Street, I review the questions I'm supposed to ask regarding U.S. trade policy on arms to Yugoslavia, particularly to a dot on the map called Bosnia and another called Croatia. I have to look up these countries in an atlas. I stay awake till 2:00 a.m. reading articles Marvin has given me so I won't make a fool of myself. Passing the windows of Hecht's department store, I straighten the loose black sweater and slacks I'm wearing. I don't look pregnant so much as fat, though according to Mahela, I look sexy.

When I arrive, Samuel Huggins is already seated along the wall in a green velvet booth of the Old Ebbit Grill. He seems young for a deputy assistant secretary, in his late thirties, I guess, though his hair is thinning on the top. He has a haggard brown moustache, the kind men grow when they start losing their hair.

"Chicken or steak?" he asks before I can even look at the menu.

"Chicken."

He waves over the waitress. "One roasted chicken and one steak medium rare, two salads, one fries, one baked potato . . . set those on separate plates in the middle." He glances at his watch. "I've got a meeting at one thirty," he tells the waitress.

"We'll have you out of here, Mr. Huggins."

I check my watch. I'm on time, but Samuel Huggins is already driving in full gear, or maybe he never shifts gears. "You've shown unusual prescience for a student. The Balkans have the potential to be the next powder keg. It's important we have a policy and stick to it, but frankly everyone is focused on the Middle East right now. Exactly what would you like to know?"

I recite the questions Marvin has given me. "You must be an excellent student. Those are very good questions."

"I'm interested . . ." I demur and write down Samuel Huggins's answers. I eat my chicken breast while he talks. After half an hour he flags the waitress and hands her a credit card. I offer to pay for my lunch, but he says, "I went to GW myself. I like to help students. Someone helped me when I was young." He fishes a business card from his wallet. "If you have any more questions, you may call me."

When I report back to Marvin, he says, "Excellent. Call him next week."

"Why?" I don't want to call him.

"He asked you to call. He's not going to call you. Why don't you really do a paper? Then these interviews can help you at school too."

I consider my courses: French, Shakespeare, Psychology, Art History. A paper on the Balkans doesn't exactly fit.

"Then do one next semester," Marvin says.

Next semester I'm having a baby, but I don't say that.

*   *   *

Before I can call Samuel Huggins, he calls me. Or rather his secretary phones and suggests another lunch, this time at Au Bon Pain on G Street. She doesn't say why he wants to see me.

Marvin gives me another list of questions, this time with soft inquiries on Iraq. I phone Jane. "If I were able to speak to someone senior from the Commerce Department, is there anything you'd like me to ask?"

"Yes. Find out how Midland Tools of California managed to ship high-speed capacitors to Baghdad." Jane's question is not so soft. She doesn't ask who I might meet with or why. She assumes I have the same access to government officials that she does. She assumes I know what high-speed capacitors are.

"Midland Tools? That's the company Dennis was opening offices for. Only in Washington it's called Aladdin International."

"Dennis was in way over his head," Jane says. "I'm lost in all the paper on Wagner's companies. They have so many layers of holding companies, it's hard to find the real owners, but KBT Engineering bought a company called Continental Tools, which then changed its name to Midland Tools, and Midland Tools has a subsidiary in California. Midland Tools in California manufactures and purchases machine tools and equipment in the U.S. for KBT Engineering."

"What do they manufacture and purchase?"

"Nothing that you'd rush out to buy: jig grinders, ring magnets, end caps, capacitors, especially krytons." She says the last with emphasis.

"I don't know what those are."

"Neither did I, but I'm learning. One way or another they all link to nuclear weapons. A kryton trigger detonates a nuclear explosion."

Jane's voice is animated. I can see her with her charts and notes, tracing the web of companies, pursuing Wagner like Dad or Mom would, tracking down truth on a paper trail, hoping to snare it by catching the bad guy. Even if we get evidence on Wagner, that won't bring Dennis back, but it may plug up a small hole in the universe.

"How does Dr. Wagner fit in?"

"He appears to own a part of everything. He's partners in KBT Engineering and Advanced Technology Partners. The other partners are Iraqi. And here's where it gets really interesting. He appears to have set up Dennis as a partner, at least on paper, in Wye Holdings."

"What's Wye Holdings?"

"Another company, another screen. Wye Holdings owns Midland Tools and from what you say, it probably also holds Aladdin International. Its owners are Advanced Technology Partners and a trading company in Baghdad whose owners are relatives of Saddam Hussein. Our guess is that Dennis was to be their British front. I don't know if he understood that. Wye Holdings contacted Midland Tools, which purchased from its U.S. subsidiary, which purchased from other U.S. companies. Cargo was then shipped to Wye Holdings in Portsmouth, England, or sometimes to Wagner Machines and Tools in Frankfurt, or Marseilles, which shipped it on to its real destination directly or through transshipment points such as Jordan. On the shipping manifests the cargo was listed as air-conditioning parts, food processing equipment, etcetera."

"Who is *our*?" I ask. "You said *our guess*."

"My friend on *The Financial Times*. I'm just working on this between other stories."

"What does it mean?"

"At the very least it means Dennis was involved with some ruthless partners, though I don't know if he understood the company he was keeping."

"In the end I think he did."

"The trading company in Baghdad only owns a minority percent, but remember Dad used to say it only takes a few drops of cyanide in the water to poison an elephant."

"Why do you think he said that?"

"I guess he'd come across a few dead elephants in his life."

*　　*　　*

I arrive early at Au Bon Pain, where the tables are filling up with workers from the surrounding law offices and government buildings. When Samuel Huggins arrives, he goes straight to the food counter, then looks around and sees me.

"Is that all you're having?" he asks, nodding to my blueberry yogurt and Diet Coke.

"I'm not very hungry."

He stares at me in my loose gray jumper and large black cardigan. "Are you pregnant?" His question falls somewhere between a prosecutor's and what I imagine as a father's.

"Yes."

"Oh . . . Well . . . that may change things."

I can't imagine how my being pregnant should change anything for him.

"Are you married?"

I want to say that is none of his business, but I say, "No."

"I phoned you because I had a proposition, but . . . well, you see, I have a daughter; she's fourteen. Her mother and I are divorced. Her mother works in New York. She lives with me. I've been thinking if I could find a college student . . . I've been looking for someone to help, someone she would accept. I'm often delayed at the office, and I'd like her to have someone at home when she gets home. I was going to offer you a job."

I came to ask Samuel Huggins how Midland Tools managed to ship capacitors to Iraq and to gather information on arms flows, and he called me to be a babysitter. "That would be difficult in a few months," I agree.

"You seemed the sort of young woman my daughter would like."

I'm not sure how to respond, but I have my own agenda, so I begin asking questions.

Carefully, Samuel Huggins answers. "The capacitors were shipped before any of the current hostility and for commercial, not military, use. We wouldn't have allowed them today." He stares at me as if taking my measure, then in a voice that allows mistakes may have been made, he adds, "Perhaps we didn't pay enough attention."

"You turned a blind eye?"

He considers the question and touches his moustache. I note he's taken off his wedding ring. "We are aware of the companies you mention. Some of our allies, or rather companies close to our allies, are invested in them." He smiles then. "I'm sure my daughter would like you. Would you at least think about the job?"

I don't want to appear rude so I say I will.

*   *   *

"How much will he pay you?" Marvin asks. "Unless he pays well, I don't think that's the best job for you."

"I'm not taking it. I can't work for him and do research for you."

"On the other hand," Marvin calculates, "Samuel Huggins could be helpful to your career."

"I don't have a career."

"Let's think about this . . ." We're sitting in a booth at the coffee shop, and Marvin frowns as though my career and future are a problem he's been given to solve. "You should meet him again. Ask the details before you decide. Ask the salary, the hours. Ask to meet his daughter, see if the two of you get along."

"I can't keep interviewing him for you then."

"Why not?"

"If I'm meeting his family, working in his home, I wouldn't feel right. He thinks I'm interviewing him for a class."

"I thought you were going to take a class."

"Marvin . . ." I protest, "it's not honest."

"You think he's being honest with you?"

I hesitate. "I don't know, but I don't see what one has to do with the other. Who's interested in what Samuel Huggins thinks anyway?"

Marvin opens his tin of tobacco with the raven-haired girl on the lid. "I'm interested. And I'm interested in seeing Jesse's daughter prosper."

The waitress with "Janelle" stitched on her pocket sets down breakfast then sits down in the booth next to Marvin, refilling our coffee cups and confiscating Marvin's tobacco without his protesting. When she leaves, he says, "I don't have anyone to look out for these days. I could help you get started."

"Get started at what?" I consider Marvin in his Hawaiian shirt with his chewing tobacco, his fried eggs and grits. Is he my father's legacy to me? He's hardly what I've fantasized all these years. "Marvin, the only thing I'm getting started right now is a baby."

"You got a long life ahead of you. Life goes on and on with turns you can't see or even imagine because you're not there yet. I wish I could tell you all I know and all that your daddy knew, or maybe it's better I don't so you can make it up yourself and make it better. But you've got to be prepared, Elizabeth. Stay low, dart and weave, watch your front, cover your back."

I laugh. "What are you talking about?"

"And don't take anything at face value. Remember, there's always another story, and usually there's someone who knows the real story sitting in the background watching. You got to find out who that person is. Your daddy used to say, 'Life returns on itself.'"

I don't remember my father saying that. "All right. All right. I'll meet Huggins and ask for details."

"Ask him what he plans to do when he gets out of government, if he's received any job offers."

"Don't you think that's a little personal?"

"I'm sure you can work it in."

* * *

When I call Samuel Huggins for another meeting, he picks up himself and suggests we meet at Morton's in Georgetown for dinner.

"That's a really fancy place," Julie says as she sits on my bed painting her nails and watching me search my closet for something I can fit into. "Exactly who is it you're meeting?"

"It's a job interview."

"At Morton's? Some job."

"Elizabeth, are you being straight with us?" Mahela is standing in the doorway in her gray sweat suit; she's just returned from the gym. "I've been going on job interviews, and no one's taken me to Morton's."

I pull out a black wool dress shaped like a tent. "Yes. It's just a job."

"Then why won't you tell us who you're meeting?" Mahela puts her hand on her hip. She's even taller than me, almost six feet. She rows crew for GW.

"If I get the job, I'll tell you. It's kind of a babysitting job."

"With someone famous?" Julie's large blue eyes widen.

"A little."

"Someone in government?" Mahela guesses.

"Yes."

"How do you know him?"

"He spoke on campus." Samuel Huggins had his secretary invite me to a seminar he addressed.

"Ah-h-h . . ." Mahela steps into the room and settles in my desk chair. She unties her ponytail and her thin corn-rolled braids fall to her shoulders. "So let me get this straight—someone just a little famous from the government spoke on campus and is now taking you to Morton's for dinner to offer you a babysitting job. Is his wife going to be there?"

"He's divorced. His teenage daughter lives with him, and he's looking for a college student to help her."

"U-huh," Mahela says.

"Sure," Julie echoes.

"In fact. For heaven sakes, I'm six months pregnant."

"You never know what turns some men on." Julie stands from the bed. She's half Mahela's size. Together they looked like Tinker Bell and the Giant.

"Elizabeth," Mahela says, "there are honorable men in the world, but not every man is honorable."

"Well, I'm honorable."

However, as the hostess leads me to a corner booth and Samuel Huggins stands smiling to greet me, dressed up in navy blazer, gray slacks, silk tie, I wonder if this really is a job interview. A waiter presents us with an array of raw steaks and fish. The menu at Morton's is not words on paper but meat on a cutting board. I order a vegetable plate.

"I need help." Samuel Huggins smiles. "I have a fourteen-year-old daughter who's not happy that her mother and I have divorced. She didn't want to leave Washington where all her friends are when her mother took a job in New York, so she stays with me during the week. At her school she's always working in the theater. I love her, but I'm afraid I'm making a mess of it, and I thought . . . I thought someone like you who's closer to her age, who knows theater . . . I thought you might help."

"I don't know theater," I say. "I've just taken a few courses in Shakespeare." In fact, I think I might understand a teenage daughter with an absent father and mother. "What she probably needs is her parents, at least one of them, to be around."

The glint in Samuel Huggins' eyes fades. "I wouldn't expect you to be a substitute. I'd just like to have someone there if she needs help with homework or something."

My eyes cloud and suddenly tears start down my cheeks. The reaction surprises us both. Samuel Huggins glances around the restaurant. "Did I say something wrong?"

I drink a glass of water and try to wipe away the tears with my napkin. "I'm sorry." I sip more water. Here is a father caring enough to try to find someone to help his daughter, though not caring enough to be the one to help. He's looking to me to bridge what remains a chasm inside me. He's also looking at me as perhaps more than a babysitter at the same time I'm wishing I had a father for my baby and for myself. In the midst of all these confusions, Marvin Penn is asking me to gather information on this man.

When dinner arrives, I concentrate on eating my vegetables: asparagus, broccoli, squash. I cut each bite with effort, and we eat in silence. Finally, I say, "Maybe I can find someone for you." Mahela is looking for a job. I ask about the hours, the pay, the duties.

"Yes, well, thank you. And I'd be happy to help you on your paper if I can," he says.

Before dinner is over, I manage to ask, "Do you plan to stay in government after the next election?"

"I don't have control over that."

"Do you ever get job offers from the industries you're dealing with?"

"All the time," he says.

*   *   *

After Thanksgiving, before Christmas break, a man comes by our apartment and asks for Betsy. "I told him no one lived here named Betsy," Mahela reports, "but he was sure Betsy did live here. He gave me his card and said Betsy should call him." Mahela opens the drawer of the hall table and produces the gold-embossed business card of Adnan Kamil Houston.

"What did he look like?"

"Heavyset man, black hair, small moustache, gold chain. He never smiled."

"Did he say why he was looking for Betsy?"

"He said Betsy had notes that belonged to him and his partners."

"I don't have any notes."

"Well, if you're Betsy, he seemed to think you did. He said if he didn't hear from you, he'd come back."

I look at the card with a Virginia phone number. I wonder if he was the same man I'd met that day in Dennis's office in Virginia. I wonder if he was the man who'd asked about Dennis and Ibrahim Hasan at the hotel in Berlin. "Did he wear glasses?"

Mahela paused to remember. "Yes . . . silver ones, tinted lenses so you couldn't see his eyes."

"Did he say how he knew me?"

"Are you Betsy?"

"I might be."

I want to ignore the message, but Adnan Kamil Houston knows where I live. I phone the number on the card and get Serena's voice on an answering machine for Aladdin International. I leave a message.

Serena rings me back the following day. I had tried to contact her after Dennis's death, but her phone was unlisted. When I tell her how sorry I am about Dennis, she says, "I can't really talk here." She tells me Adnan Kamil Houston is out of town. She and I arrange to have lunch.

*   *   *

The Pentagon City mall bustles with shoppers, including uniformed Army, Navy, Air Force, and Marines darting in and out of stores on their lunch break from the Pentagon. The three-story mall glitters with Christmas lights. The glass elevator in the middle shoots up and down. Shoppers with bags and packages also cram the escalators that connect the open walkways. Christmas music—*Here comes Santa Claus, here comes Santa Claus right down Santa Claus lane*—blares from a loudspeaker.

At a corner table in Nordstrom's department store restaurant, Serena sits reading a paperback with shopping bags at her feet. She's wearing a navy business suit, less makeup, her hair tucked behind her ears. She still looks glamorous but tailored. She rises when I enter the tearoom.

"Lizzy!" We hug. "You didn't tell me you were pregnant! So . . . ?" she asks the way old girlfriends ask, only we're not old girlfriends.

"I'm due late February." That's all I offer. "How's Jack?"

We settle back at the table, and Serena drops her book into her purse. "He's in high school, can you believe it? I've sent him to boarding school in Connecticut. He loves it, lots of boys his age and male teachers . . . he needs that. He's made the basketball team. But most important, he's safe."

"Safe?"

Serena waves to the waiter to take our order then turns to me and leans closer. "I couldn't watch over him. I'm never home. I have to travel. Starting a new business is hard . . ." Her words tumble out almost before the ideas form.

"At least you get to travel? Where do you go?" I've learned from Marvin not to start with the questions I want to ask, but to circle, sneak up on them casually, inadvertently.

"Geneva. Panama. Once or twice to Jordan. If I don't get on another airplane for a while, I'll be happy."

"What do you do?" I ask like a girlfriend as I butter a roll.

"Deliver documents mostly, to banks or friends of Gerald's or Adnan's. They don't trust the mail or messenger services. They pay me pretty well and give me time off after I've made the deliveries so I can look around. Sometimes I take their clients shopping."

I wonder who their clients are. I wonder what happened to Serena's ambition to be independent of her father-in-law. "What kind of shopping?"

"Clothes, jewelry, electronic goods. They love to shop, especially for designer labels for themselves and their wives. I get them to tell me about their wives, then I shop for them, and they tip me well. I'm making decent money, at least enough to keep Jack in a good school, pay my bills, and save a bit, though lately Gerald's fallen behind again paying me. I'll leave him eventually." She glances at me as if to see whether I believe her.

"What kind of documents do you deliver?" I move in carefully as I keep buttering the roll. I wonder if Adnan Kamil Houston really is out of town, or if Serena is meeting with me for him.

"Contracts and checks. I take them to the bank. Gerald won't like me telling you even that, but honestly, I never talk to anyone about my job. I don't talk to anyone period. When I'm not traveling, I have to be at the office. I'm the only one who works there."

"What about that man Adnan Houston who came to see me?" I take a bite of my salad and try to keep my questions conversational. "He told my roommate he thought I had some notes. I don't know what he's talking about." Serena concentrates on picking out anchovies from her salad. I wonder if I've moved in too quickly. "I don't know how he knew who I was or where I lived."

She looks up. "He asked me who you were last spring. I told him you were an old friend, a student at GW."

"Do you know what notes he's looking for?"

The light in her large green eyes shifts. She glances around the restaurant. She leans towards me and lowers her voice. "He and Gerald say Dennis stole documents and records. They thought he sent them to me. I swore he hadn't given me anything, but they searched my apartment anyway. That's when I decided to send Jack to boarding school. I'm afraid of them. I didn't want Jack around."

"Why don't you quit?"

She blinks at the question as if I've thrown dust in her face. "I can't. They'd be too suspicious. And Gerald's jealous about me. He was furious when he found out Dennis came to visit me."

"Does Dr. Wagner visit you?"

"No, but he doesn't want me to have a life of my own, and he doesn't want any other men in my life. It's sick. It's like he's protecting me for François or himself, only François is dead, and Gerald's impotent."

"He is?"

"For years. He used to live through François. Women lined up for François, who thought it was unmanly to turn them down."

"Why did you marry him?"

She rolls her eyes. "I was young and dumb. I used to laugh at his stories about women, never thinking that could be me he would cheat on. I was innocent enough to believe all his stories of late nights at the office. But then I deceived him, too. I let him think I was from a wealthy American family when, really, I was just a college student from a small Louisiana town on a semester abroad. François was my ticket out so I guess I shouldn't complain. If François hadn't been killed, we'd be divorced by now. It's ironic, isn't it? It would have been easier to divorce François than it's been to leave Gerald."

We're leaning closer and closer to each other on the table. "All I do now is work and shop. I'm afraid to have friends, afraid Gerald will find out. I'm sorry I told Adnan your name and where you went to school, but Gerald had figured it out anyway when Adnan told him there was another woman with Dennis that day."

"I'm so sorry about Dennis," I say.

She lowers her eyes. "He was so young. I wanted that."

"What do you think happened?"

Serena looks me straight in the eyes. "They killed him."

"Who?"

"I don't know who pulled the trigger, but I'm sure Gerald and Adnan were involved, though I don't have proof."

I want to ask how she can keep working for them. "Maybe I can help you," I say.

"No. Don't do anything. Just keep on as you are. That's what I'm doing. I have a child . . . You'll have a child soon to think about."

"The documents you deliver . . . you say they're contracts? Anything else? Are there other files at the office?" I'm no longer circling. I'm eye to eye, trying to figure out how to offer safe passage.

Serena again glances around the restaurant. I wonder who she thinks may be watching us. "Most of the filing I do is for orders of cars and trucks, engines, tools, chemicals. But there are also locked files in the back office. I don't have that key."

Marvin has taught me to take low hanging fruit first. Get the easy answers before you go for the payoff in case reaching for it closes down your source and you're left with nothing.

"Do you know what kind of chemicals?" I ask.

"I don't know one chemical from another. Mostly ATP orders in Europe. We order chemicals from different places, sometimes from

Dutch companies. Most of our orders go to Midland Tools in California, which supplies the tools and engines or buys them from someone else. Aladdin International orders the other materials from other companies. I file the orders and keep track of when they're shipped and delivered. But Adnan files other documents in the locked cabinet when he's in town. He also keeps files in Miami, where Aladdin Investments has offices though it's officially based in Geneva and registered in Panama. We're just a room and an address."

"Who handles the money?" Always follow the money, Marvin has taught me.

"Adnan comes up with financing from banks all over the world, sometimes using U.S. government guarantees. Right now, Adnan has a letter of credit from his customer's national bank, only he's not having any luck exercising it, and he's traveling around frantic to cash it."

The structure of the business sounds as complicated as Jane has warned. I don't entirely follow what Serena says. However, Marvin has taught me not to worry if I don't understand the whole picture while gathering information. Get the facts. Get the evidence. Later you can search for meaning. He also reminded me what my father used to say: *If you study the picture long enough, you'll see all the players.*

To Serena I say, "If you could get copies of papers in the locked files, I know someone who might be able to figure out what they're doing and why they were so upset about Dennis taking documents."

Serena starts shaking her head. "I can't. I shouldn't have talked so much. Look, don't worry about Adnan. I'll tell him you don't know anything and don't have anything."

I've pressed too hard, but I keep on with one last question. "So you think Dr. Wagner had Dennis killed?"

Serena begins gathering her shopping bags from the floor. "I don't know. I really don't. Not directly. He seemed scared himself when he learned Dennis had been killed. But I think he knows who did it. I've got to go now. I've already been away much too long. Gerald always calls in the afternoon."

I try to lower the pressure, to divert her. "I'm going to London for Christmas, but when I get back, you want to go to a movie some time?"

"Yeah, sure." Serena leaves money on the table and stands.

"Do you have a home phone number?" Never leave an interview, even a bad one, without an opening for another chance, Marvin has drilled.

She gives me her home number then kisses me on the cheek. "Good luck with the baby," she says. As she hurries from the restaurant loaded down with shopping bags, she doesn't look back. I'm fairly sure we won't be going to a movie.

That night I tell Jane about my meeting with Serena, and we add Aladdin Investments of Miami, Geneva, and Panama to our list of companies to investigate. I tell Jane I'll call Serena when I get back from London and try to persuade her to copy the files.

"Don't press too hard," Jane says. "You're starting to sound like Dad."

Jane is right, but as I draw closer to giving birth and the world moves closer to war, I'm afraid if I don't act, I'll crawl under the bed and hide.

CHAPTER FIFTEEN

DURING THE HOLIDAYS in London my family hovers around me. First, they worry about my flying at seven months pregnant—the doctor assures me that I can go; then they worry about what's going to happen after I have the baby. I worry that Adnan Kamil Houston knows where I live in Washington and that Adil doesn't know and that I don't know where Adil lives. Adil doesn't even know we're having a baby. I worry about a war I have no control over and a future for my child that might not include his father because of the war and a future for me that is secured by an unborn child.

Sophie wants to know how I'm going to support myself. Mom wants to know who will take care of the baby while I have classes, and Pickles wants to know if I'm going to marry the father. Jane hasn't come home to London for Christmas. She has to work. Only Winston seems unconcerned, so I gravitate to him, though he talks about Dennis and me as if we have some vow between us. It isn't until Christmas Day that I realize Winston thinks I'm pregnant with Dennis's child.

When I confront Mom with this fact, she says, "Winston's still a little confused, sweetheart. It's just taking him longer to recover than we expected."

"He thinks I'm carrying Dennis's baby! That's more than a little confused." Mom and I are in the kitchen, where I'm making a peanut butter sandwich. "Have you explained to him who the father is?"

Mother turns vague. "I've been trying to locate Adil." She hands me a jar of raspberry jam. "I've gotten a few leads."

"Where?"

"I asked our stringers in Baghdad and Beirut to make discreet inquiries. They've only come up with rumors so far."

"What rumors?"

"That Ibrahim Hasan is in Baghdad working undercover for the U.S./Arab coalition. They don't know about Adil."

I haven't told Mother that Adil's father helps the U.S. government, but I've been working for Marvin Penn long enough to realize that if such a rumor is circulating in Baghdad, Ibrahim Hasan is in danger, and therefore Adil may also be in danger. If Iraq doesn't withdraw from Kuwait in two weeks, there is going to be war.

"I'm very worried about Adil," I say.

"Apparently Ibrahim is working under an alias, so Adil may also be using one. I've asked our stringers to listen for any news. I've also put inquiries to the U.S. and British embassies in Amman."

I can't figure my mother out. On the one hand, she's running an important magazine and helping me find the father of my child at high and covert levels. On the other hand, at home her husband is breaking down, and she seems to be doing nothing except making him comfortable and living in the margins of his reality. She gently corrects his misperceptions, but to no effect that I can see. The Christmas visit undermines my confidence that life will turn out all right. My mother, whom I've always relied on to keep us from the brink, no longer seems able to hold off the fraying in her own household. I wonder whether I will be able to create a safe world for my child. I wish

Jane had come home. She can stand in for Mom when Mom's shoulders sag. I call Jane every day.

*   *   *

The incident that sends me flying back over the Atlantic happens the day after Christmas, on what the English call Boxing Day. Winston is in the den napping in front of a football game. Sophie is in her room working on a paper. Pickles is in the attic getting dressed to go out with Randolph, and Mother and I are again sitting at the kitchen table, our hands cupped around mugs of tea. Mother is telling me how important it is that I not strain myself these next two months, that I wear boots with heavy treads if it snows, that I get plenty of sleep and eat protein, that I get ahead in my studies because I will inevitably fall behind. She's passing on helpful tips. She hands me an envelope. "I want you to get someone to help you. I wish I could do it myself."

Inside the envelope is a check for $15,000. "Mother . . ."

"It's the last of your father's insurance money. I know he would have wanted you to have it."

"What about Sophie and Jane—they should have some of it."

"Sophie and Jane aren't having babies." I'm not sure if her comment is an indictment or praise. "You're going to need help with the baby."

"Julie and Mahela will help."

"Ah, sweetheart . . ." She waves her hand as if I have no idea what I'm about to experience. "I'll come for as long as I can, but with Winston . . . I'm worried about leaving him alone. Pickles is here, but to be honest, she isn't very reliable. She'll just as soon get angry at him or run out with Randolph."

"When is Pickles getting married?" I shift the subject. I don't want to hear any more of my mother's anxiety.

"The last I heard it was June so you and Sophie can be here." Mom blinks as if the light from that day in the future is too bright. "You'll be a mother by then," she says. As she reaches out for my hand on the table, the doorbell chimes.

The second time the bell rings, it's accompanied by loud knocking. I stand and go into the hall. "Hold on!" I look out the side window. Standing on our steps are two constables. Behind them, in a camel's hair coat and porkpie hat, stands Gerald Wagner. "Mom!" As she steps into the entry, her face tenses. "It's the police and Dr. Wagner."

Tucking in her blouse and running a hand over her gray-blonde hair, she opens the door. The constable takes off his helmet. "Lady Miriam?" He looks uncomfortable. "It has come to our attention that certain documents which uh . . . documents which Dr. Wagner here claims are his are in your, or rather Sir Winston's, possession, and we have been authorized . . ." His deputy hands him a paper. ". . . We have been authorized here . . ." he holds up the paper ". . . to seek from you these documents which you have failed to turn over."

Mom takes the papers from him, though she doesn't look at them. Instead she glares at Gerald Wagner, who steps forward. His hat perches on his small head so that he looks almost comical, except that his eyes are fixed like some ferocious pit bull's on my mother.

"What documents?" she asks. "There are no documents."

"To the contrary, Mrs. West." Dr. Wagner speaks up. He uses her American name like a demotion. "Your husband was subpoenaed months ago as the executor of his son's estate to turn over all business papers, documentation, and notes which Dennis collected or accumulated or originated in his employment with Wagner Machines and Tools Corporation."

"I know nothing of this," Mother says. "You should be talking to Sir Winston's solicitor, not bothering our home the day after Christmas." She uses Winston's title, which she rarely does.

"We have spoken with his solicitor and been told there are no more papers, only we have reason to believe you are hiding them. The court has complied with a search warrant," Dr. Wagner insists.

"A search warrant! Of our house?" Mother protests.

"I am afraid that is correct, Lady Miriam," the constable apologizes.

Mother looks down at the papers. "I'd like to call our solicitor first to see what he knows."

"Of course," the constable answers.

"There's no provision for that. You must search right away," Dr. Wagner tells the constable, "before they have a chance to hide the papers."

"Excuse me," Mother says. "That is not the spirit of British law."

"It is the letter of British law," Dr. Wagner counters. "And these constables had better follow that letter."

I wonder at Mom, an American, and Dr. Wagner, French/German, arguing over the spirit and letter of British law. I, on the other hand, want to block the door as I did years ago as a child, pressing all my weight against it to keep these intruders out of our home.

"Dr. Wagner," the constable says, "you have been allowed to accompany us over my objection, but I must insist . . ."

At this point Winston emerges from the den in his stockinged feet.

"Sir Winston." The constable deferentially repeats why he's here and indicates that he will have to begin his search. Dr. Wagner is instructed to stay outside. He won't look at Winston, but he has no trouble staring at me.

"The papers have already been sent, Constable," Winston replies. "I'm sorry you had to be troubled on this holiday." That's the most lucid statement I've heard from Winston since I arrived home. Even Mother pauses as if surprised to have him grasp the situation and respond appropriately. Turning from the constable, Winston levels his gaze on Dr. Wagner through the open door.

The constable looks relieved. "I'm sorry to have troubled you, Sir."

"That's a lie!" Dr. Wagner shouts. The fierceness of his eyes frightens me. He appears ready to break through the door and search the house himself, that is, after he first sinks his teeth into Mother's ankle. "The warrant says you must search the house."

"It says I may search the house," the constable corrects. "If Sir Winston assures me the papers have been delivered, then I take him at his word."

Dr. Wagner's face goes florid. "It's a bold-faced lie!" He reaches in the pocket of his coat. I step away, half afraid he's about to pull a gun.

Mother stands her ground. "I must ask you to leave if you're going to raise your voice in our home. We have children around." I'm not sure if I'm the child or represent the child unborn.

The constable steps between Gerald Wagner and the door. Winston shuts the door. He and Mom exchange glances. There is more clarity in Winston's eyes than I've seen since before Dennis's death. I turn and see Pickles at the top of the stairs. Everyone is silent for a moment. Mother looks out the window to confirm the police and Dr. Wagner have gone. She nods.

"What shall we do?" Pickles asks.

"Aren't you leaving tomorrow?" Winston asks me.

I'm surprised he's followed my travel schedule. "Yes."

"We can give the notes to Lizzy," he says.

*   *   *

Mom drives me to the airport the following day. In my backpack I carry a brown envelope with notes Dennis had mailed to Pickles, *personal notes*, Winston emphasizes, that are now his sister's. All other papers Winston sent to his solicitor so he can reply to the courts. When Pickles received the envelope, she glanced at the invoices, shipping manifests, scribblings on scraps of paper and the backs of matchbooks, and concluded there was nothing of importance. She placed the envelope in Dennis's desk drawer under his old A-level papers and forgot about it. Foraging through Dennis's drawers in late November, Winston found the envelope. By then he'd already assured his solicitor there were no other papers to deliver, and the solicitor had replied to the court.

Mother found Winston that late November afternoon, sitting in the dark on Dennis's bed. His head was leaning back against the wall, not moving, as if he were asleep with eyes open. She rushed to him, panicked that he'd had a stroke, but slowly he turned his head. On the bed all around him were scraps of paper and a chemistry textbook from Dennis's shelf.

"My son bargained with the devil," he said in a toneless voice. Mother lowered herself on the edge of the bed. Winston began gathering up the slips of paper. "And he lost. I don't want anyone to see these. I want to burn them."

"Do you want to tell me?" Mother picked up one of the sheets. On a hotel notepad were scrawled chemical symbols and beneath those the words: Akashat/Al Qaim. "What's this?"

"The components for nerve gas," Winston said. "And their destination."

She picked up another handwritten list:

--nitroparafins and nitromethane
--ammonium nitrate
--glycol and ethers
--methylethyl esther

"And these?" she asked.
"The same, I fear."

As they sat in the dark on the bed, Mother listened to the story of Dennis moving into Gerald Wagner's world, working with Wagner Machines and Tools and its aligned companies, selling equipment and chemicals to countries such as Iraq, Iran, Libya, but shipping from England, France, Germany, the Netherlands through Jordan, Cyprus, Egypt, Turkey, where the shipments were then sent to their real destinations. Winston speculated on the advantage for Dr. Wagner of having an employee of Dennis's background paying attention to the ministers, jumping at their every wish. He speculated on the pleasure Dr. Wagner must have gotten from these psychological games.

Mother repeated her small offering of comfort. "Dennis may have been gathering information for the intelligence services or maybe for future writing."

"He accepted money!" Winston declared. "And I used my influence to help Dr. Wagner's shipments get through."

Mother glanced at the papers, at the formulas and quantities and equipment and end user certificates. "These could mean anything." There was no narrative to explain what the notations meant, though each paper was dated.

"I know because Dennis told me, but I didn't understand, or I didn't want to understand. He told me they were sales of equipment that of themselves could do no harm—equipment for phosphate extraction and processing. A few machines and engines, what did it matter? Dennis told me he was helping Dr. Wagner get them approved in order to keep good relations with him. He told me Dr. Wagner might buy a company, and he might be able to help. He was excited; he was learning. Only it wasn't a few machines, and the company Wagner was buying made equipment to transform phosphates and other chemicals into deadly gas, and it procured machines and parts of machines to enrich uranium. It was the equipment of death."

As Mother told me this story, I could see her sitting on Dennis's bed, the room growing dark around her. I imagined her shuddering as the past, which she'd held at bay all these years, crept through a break in the fence, crouched in the yard, then rushed into her home when the door opened.

"Are you sure Dennis knew?" she asked Winston.

"He knew his part. Maybe he didn't ask about the rest. If he asked, he was willing to accept false answers. But I didn't ask, and I should have, and I've paid with the life of my son."

"What do you want to do with these papers?" Mother studied them, searching for a way to keep Winston's heart from breaking.

"Dr. Wagner will claim them and destroy them or hold them against Dennis."

Mother looked at sheet after sheet in her hands. "This doesn't look like Dennis's handwriting." She picked up another scrap. "Is it his?"

Winston studied it. "No . . ." He looked up at her. "No, it's not."

"Maybe I can find out whose it is." She'd located a breach and moved in to make repairs.

I am now carrying these papers back to Washington, where I'm to take a note of condolence we received from Dr. Wagner and give it and the rest of the papers to Marvin Penn for a handwriting analysis. "Marvin will know what to do," Mother says as we drive towards Heathrow. "He may also know what to make of these notes."

As I listen to the story of Dennis, I worry that I don't understand the context I'm working in any more than Dennis did and that what I don't understand can turn against me. I tell my mother about my meeting with Serena.

"Let Marvin handle this," she urges. Small wrinkles cut across her forehead. Her hands, freckled with brown age spots, grip the steering wheel. "Give him the notes. Don't keep them at your house. Don't you try to work this." I haven't told her about Adnan Kamil Houston visiting my apartment. I don't want to alarm her any more than she already is, but I will tell Marvin.

"I hoped to keep you and your sisters from your father's world," she says as she turns off the motorway. "Your father would want that too. He was planning to leave that world, in large part because of you."

"Me?"

"All three of you, but mostly you. Do you remember when you were . . . you must have been around eight . . . and Jane and Sophie had gone away for summer camp, and you and Dad and I went on a vacation together? It was your father's idea because you were so miserable at being left by your sisters."

"We went to Virginia Beach. That's one of my best memories."

"One of his best too. For those few days he left the enemy behind and focused on you . . . building sandcastles and playing in the ocean. You had his full attention. You both smiled for four days. There weren't many times like that for you growing up. I know you've missed him, sweetheart."

"I remember walking on the beach with him. He was whistling. He told me to let my life be a song. Sometimes the noise gets so loud you can't hear the song, he said, or people try to turn life into a sermon—tell you to do this, do that—or a destination—go here, go there—but remember what your dad, who's been all over the world, met all kinds of people, good guys and really nasty guys, is telling you: let your life be a song. I didn't understand what he meant. I wondered if he meant I should keep taking piano lessons, which I wanted to quit. He said if I ever had trouble hearing the music, I should listen harder because life was trying to make one giant song out of the universe rather than the giant explosion some people wanted it to be."

Mom smiles. "That sounds like him. On that trip with you he decided to leave the Agency. The information he was turning up was being ignored. He said he was tired of tracking down an enemy only to find out we were doing business with it. There were many jobs he could have taken, but he always wanted a mission. He was searching out the devil, he used to tell me, in order to find God. When he found God, he said he'd quit chasing down the devil. Sometimes I wondered if he needed an enemy in order to know himself. He didn't imagine himself getting killed. No one does." In Mother's eyes I see the hurt she feels that my father hadn't considered us a mission big enough to stay alive for.

"When Marvin and your father went into business together, Marvin promised he'd make Jesse pull back. He would have given his life for Jesse. He always predicted he, not Jesse, would be the one to step on a land mine. I called Marvin this fall when you told me you were having a baby and asked him to look out for you."

"You did?"

"I didn't tell him why. I said I'd heard he'd met you, and I'd appreciate anything he could do to help."

"I've been doing research for him. Did you arrange that?"

"No."

I told her about the research and my meetings with Samuel Huggins and my confusion about why Marvin wanted the information.

"It sounds as if he's doing a background check on this man. Or maybe he's helping the Congressional investigation getting underway on Iraq."

"Whatever he's doing, I quit. I couldn't keep interviewing Samuel Huggins for him," I say. Then I tell Mom what I've told no one: that I continued seeing Samuel Huggins. "We only went out to dinner a few times. I asked him questions about the companies Dr. Wagner is involved in. He told me to check with the British Board of Trade and Industry. He knew more than he was telling me, but I didn't know enough to ask the right questions. We only talked, but he started touching my arm and taking my hand. I knew I was fooling myself, pretending not to see what he was feeling and wanted, but I wanted Adil, not him. Before Christmas I told Sam I had to stop seeing him. He got angry and tried to persuade me he could help me, but I said no."

Mother reaches across the front seat of the car for my hand. "You're wiser than I realized," she says. I don't remember my mother ever calling me wise.

*   *   *

When I arrive at my apartment in Washington, there's a message on the answering machine from Grandma Sha asking me to tea and one from Jane, who says she'll visit me over New Years. My mother has been at work. When I return to the front hall to gather my luggage, I see a business card slipped under the front door. Julie and Mahela are still on vacation. I'm alone in the apartment. I don't know when the card arrived. I bend down and pick up the cream-colored card embossed in gold: ADNAN KAMIL HOUSTON.

CHAPTER SIXTEEN

"YOU THINK HE'S been inside?" I ask Marvin, who's pacing about my living room between the sagging green sofa with the Indian shawl over the back, the wicker chairs, the dining table spread with books and papers we didn't put away before vacation. He's stalking like an old cat searching for something to pounce on. He moves into the doorway of the large front bedroom Julie and Mahela share. Mahela's side is cordoned off with bookshelves around her bed and desk and Julie's is set off by a paper Japanese screen and posters of Japanese flowers on the wall. He stands in the doorway of my small room with its single bed shoved under the window, a baby crib not yet set up in the opposite corner, and a changing table still in a box. On my bed, stuffed animals gather—bears and monkeys and tigers that friends have already given me for the baby.

"I don't think he's been in, but he knows how to get inside if he wants. Let's get you out of here and get some dinner. Bring the notes."

Mom phoned Marvin this afternoon before I landed and told him about Dennis's notes. I called him as soon as I saw Adnan Kamil Houston's card. Then I called Serena.

* * *

At the coffee shop I slide sideways into the booth. Seven months pregnant, I have trouble fitting in places these days. "I need to get in touch with Serena," I say, "but when I called, I was told her home and office numbers have been disconnected, and the phone company won't give out any information. I've been to the office, but I don't remember exactly where it is."

"You want me to get the addresses for you?"

"How would you do that?"

Marvin smiles, sopping up a plate of baked beans with a slice of white bread while I pick at a tuna salad. "You asking for trade secrets? Give me the phone numbers you got."

When he returns to the table, he hands me a paper napkin with two addresses, both in Falls Church, Virginia. "They're not far from where I used to live. You want me to stop by and see if anyone's there?"

"I'll come with you."

"Your sleuthing days are over for a while."

I hand Marvin the envelope with Dennis's notes. "You think Adnan Kamil Houston was looking for these?"

Marvin puts the envelope in his jacket without opening it. "Could be. I'll get back to you." He takes a toothpick from the tiny glass on the table. "Can you stay with someone for a few days until I make inquiries and until your roommates return?"

*   *   *

I meet Marvin two days later for an early dinner in Alexandria's Old Town where I'm staying with Grandma Sha and Grandpa.

"No one was at either address," he reports. "The superintendent says she moved out of her apartment before the holidays, paid two months' penalty and was gone the next day, left no forwarding address. At the office building, the rent's been paid till February. No one's given notice, but the phone bill wasn't paid so the telephone company turned off the phones. No one's seen anyone come or go since before Christmas. My guess is this war about to break out has set them on the run."

"You think the files are still in the office?" I poke a fork into a chicken potpie to let out steam. "There must be more notes than Dennis sent his sister."

"Those notes show someone was shipping pretty nasty chemicals and equipment to Iraq and Iran and Libya."

"Is there any way to get access to the files in the office?"

"Legally?" Marvin waves over the waitress and orders coffee. "I found out Apex Maintenance cleans the building. I've done a little work for Apex in the past, or rather Melvin Penny has. I can get the lay of the offices and find out what's there, then maybe I can stir up some official interest."

*   *   *

When Julie and Mahela return, we take extra precautions, double-locking our apartment door as we come and go, making sure no one follows us into the building. We feel danger in the air. Maybe we're imagining it, but the feeling is amplified by the war with Iraq, which has finally begun with a thundering of bombs around Baghdad and at air command and control centers, an assault that lights up the sky in color on TV screens around the world. Along with everyone else, we watch the war unfold each day as bombers knock out the air defense systems then blow up the electric grid and send smart bombs into buildings.

In the evening I watch the war with my heart in my throat as explosions light the night halfway around the globe. I wonder if Adil is nearby. There is no good answer to that question. If he isn't there, that means he's chosen not to be in touch with me, and if he is, he is in peril. I don't know where he might be, but I know that casualties on the other side are devastating.

I try to concentrate on my courses to get as far ahead as I can before the baby is born. Mother suggested that maybe I should take the semester off, but I don't want to fall behind in college. I don't want to step off the path I'm on even though I don't know where it's taking me. I wake up most nights, often after dreams about my father. He hovers in the back of my consciousness watching over me, that is until he's eaten by a crocodile, or drowned or blown up. He never stays the course of a dream. Some nights Adil enters my dreams, running across a wide green field—is it Hyde Park?—to get to me. I wake up with such a longing for him, his presence is almost palpable. I feel as if he is standing in the shadows looking at me, but when I turn on the light, no one is there.

*　　*　　*

Marvin calls in late January. "We got a warrant and went into the offices," he tells me. "Everything's been cleared out. There were only empty desks and empty files."

"What can we do?" I ask.

"You can't do anything. I'm running a check on Aladdin Investments in Miami."

"Who is *we*? You said *we* got a warrant."

"The royal we."

"You mean you."

"In the plural. Commerce, Customs, IRS, FBI—they are all interested."

*　　*　　*

At midnight February 26, 1991, while I'm watching a tank in real time roll across the desert of Iraq, I go into labor. The following evening Jesse Adil West is born. I consider naming him Hasan West, but I don't feel I have proprietary rights to the name, and I don't want anyone later claiming proprietary rights to my child. Jad, as I come to call him, is born with a full head of black hair, blue eyes, and a little smile on the last day of the war between Iraq and half the world.

Mother has flown to Washington with Winston a few days before. Because of the Gulf War, people are choosing not to fly for fear of terrorist attacks, but Winston says if they blow up Mom's plane, he wants to be on it. Winston's trip to Washington is his first since Dennis's death. Jane takes the early morning train down from New York. Sophie hurries to the hospital from DuPont Circle. Grandma Sha and Grandpa drive in from Alexandria. Mahela and Julie and Mahela's friend Scott show up after classes. There is no father in attendance, but I'm told my family and friends take up half the waiting room.

Everyone gathers in my hospital room afterwards. Mahela brings me the pale blue sweater Adil put on me that night in Berlin when we walked back to the hostel. She hands me the sweater without a word. As I slip it on, my eyes fill with tears. Mahela hugs me long enough so I can regain my composure. "He's thinking of you right now," she whispers, "even though he doesn't know why."

Julie and Mom go on about how beautiful Jad is. I haven't seen many babies, but I think he's beautiful too, though mostly I think he's soulful. When the nurse places him in my arms and I look into his tiny smoldering face, I understand the struggle he's just been through to come into this world because I've gone through it with him. I have the feeling we understand each other already and always will in some deep and essential way. His birth has instant and unambiguous meaning for me.

Keep thy heart with all diligence; for out of it are the issues of life. For the first time I am dead clear where my heart is.

Mom, Jane, and Sophie stay behind after everyone leaves. Mom takes Jad in her arms, strokes his head, then kisses him on the forehead and passes him gently to Jane, who whispers, "Welcome to our family," and hands him to Sophie, who, to my surprise, has tears in her eyes. Sophie holds him longer than anyone else, then she slips him back into my arms.

It isn't until they're leaving that I see Winston in the corner of the room. Mother has assured me that she's told Winston that Jad is not Dennis's child, and he understands. He approaches tentatively. "I've always thought of you as a daughter, Lizzy," he says. "I hope you'll let me love this child as my own grandchild."

I feel a little unprepared. "Of course. Would you like to hold him?" I hand Jad to Winston. "What would you like him to call you?"

"I always thought of Papa?" he answers uncertainly.

"Papa is good."

When he hands Jad back, he kisses me on the forehead. "We're all going to help you."

*   *   *

"He looks just like your father," Marvin says.

Marvin arrives at my apartment two weeks after Jad is born, wearing his brown suit with the orange pinstripe and his paisley tie. He carries a large stuffed lion under his arm. I'm not sure if he's dressed up for me or for Jad or for my mother, who is leaving the next day but at the moment sits on the sofa in my living room. Mom and Winston have stayed in Washington to help me. Mom has also set up interviews, and even Winston has had a few meetings. The trip to Washington is the beginning of Winston's recovery.

Marvin presents the lion to Jad as if he expects Jad to take it and say thank you. "Don't you think he looks like Jesse?" Marvin calls over my shoulder to Mother as though he's picking up a conversation that has merely been interrupted for a decade.

Mother joins us, and the three of us stand staring down at Jad. To me, Jad looks like Adil, and to the best of my memory Adil and my father don't look alike, though I have only pictures of each to compare. They both have black hair, but Adil's face has high cheekbones and fine, sharp features; whereas my father has a square Midwestern face. In pictures my father looks extremely fit, his hair short like a Marine's, his smile wry and detached like a philosopher's.

"I don't know if he looks like Jesse," Mother answers, "but he certainly eats and sleeps like Jesse. One big meal and he's out. And when he's hungry, he's cranky as a cat, but after he's eaten, he has a smile—" Jad's smile broadens as he drifts now into some pleasant dream—"that could bring on world peace."

"Jesse would have been proud." Marvin sits beside my mother on the sofa. "You've raised a fine daughter, Miriam, and now a grandson. I've tried to get your daughter to keep working for me, but she has too much sense."

"So I hear."

I excuse myself to put Jad down for a nap and let Mom and Marvin have time together. Mom was reluctant to see him, but I persuaded her. "He doesn't have anyone, and he wants to see you. Can it hurt?" I ask.

"Yes," she says, "but I'll see him."

When I return to the living room, Marvin and Mom are shoulder to shoulder bent over the coffee table looking at notes spread on the glass top. "See, the 'As' and 'Ss' here . . . and then here . . . they're a match . . ." Marvin lifts a pile of papers. "These formulas and notes are from the same hand as this letter from Wagner. But these are in your stepson's hand, see . . ." A letter from Dennis lies beside Dr. Wagner's letter. "And here is handwriting we haven't been able to identify." Marvin picks up two slips and shows them to Mother.

"I'm still working through the meaning of some of these. This order here is a cause for concern." He shows us the handwritten list on blue-lined paper that Mother has told me about. "Nitroparafins and nitromethane are propellants that can be used in rocket fuel and explosives. And here—this is a gasoline additive used to increase performance of military aircraft, but the raw chemicals can also be used for low-grade explosives, including the triggering devices for nuclear weapons. And this—ammonium nitrate is used in explosives. Glycol and ethers are raw chemicals that can be converted to explosives and to nerve gas. Methylethyl esther is generic, but could also be isopropyl methylethylphosponoflourodite—known as Sarin GB, highly toxic. The Iraqi Army has used it in the past. I'd like to make copies of everything, Miriam, and turn it all over to investigators here and in Britain." He meets my mother's eyes. He knows what he's asking her. These notes could implicate Dennis and Winston. It isn't just the past Mother wants to avoid with Marvin, it is the present—yet she has brought Marvin in.

"We have Congressional hearings underway looking into the U.S. role in arming Iraq," Marvin says. "Some in Congress are calling for a special prosecutor, but I don't think that will happen. The investigation here is likely to be quick and contained. Britain, however, is only beginning its investigation, and Germany has also launched an investigation."

A frown spreads across my mother's face, starting at her forehead, furrowing into rows of wrinkles. "Excuse me a minute," she says.

I hear her on the telephone. I assume she's talking to Winston. When she returns, she says, "Make the copies. Turn them over to the authorities, but please, as best you can, protect my husband and stepson." Her eyes plead in a way I'm not used to seeing from my mother.

"I will as best I can." Marvin gathers up the papers into the envelope, which he returns to his pocket. He reaches for a cup of tea. "I'm afraid I've had less success in your other request. The young man you're looking for may have been using an alias like his father. I have reason to believe his father, who was working undercover, was captured during the war and probably executed."

"Ibrahim Hasan?" I take in air. Mother hasn't told me that she's asked Marvin to help.

"You know him?" Marvin asks.

"Lizzy and Adil Hasan went to school together. They were very good friends." She turns to me. "I didn't want to get your hopes up."

"I haven't located the son, but if he was anywhere near his father, I don't hold out much hope, I'm afraid. If he was also using an alias, we may never find him. Over 100,000 people have been killed in Iraq and Kuwait during the war. We will probably never know most of their names."

I gasp. For months I've reasoned that Adil will find a way to contact me unless he's been killed, and that possibility is so real I haven't been able to speak of it. In the early morning hours as I rocked Jad back to sleep, his warm body molded into my arms, I've imagined Adil wounded somewhere or captured, struggling against odds to get to me. I haven't acknowledged this fantasy to anyone except Mahela, who has encouraged me. "True love only comes once or twice in a person's life, Elizabeth," she insists as though she knows. "You can't mess with true love." All of a sudden my throat, my eyes, my head ache, and I gulp in air.

Marvin glances at Mother, then at me. "I'm not saying he's dead," he hastens to add. "The truth is I have no way of knowing. It's chaotic there. It will be difficult to locate anyone for a while."

"He may not even be there," Mother suggests.

I can't speak. I can barely breathe.

"We don't know that he's there," Marvin agrees. He looks again at Mother. "I should go." Mother stands with him. "I'm sorry," he says to me. "I didn't know. I had no idea. I should have read better between the lines." Mother walks him to the door. "I'm sorry, Miriam," he whispers.

She puts her hand on his arm. "We are all trying to read between the lines these days."

*　*　*

My life falls apart after Jad is born and Mother and Winston go back to London. At the same time, a place opens inside me that I didn't even know existed where power lies, fueled by my love for my child. I operate on a constant sleep deficit. I study late, fall asleep over my books, then awaken when Jad wakes every night crying between two and four a.m. Jad doesn't whine into consciousness. He moves from sleep to hunger in an instant wail as if he's afraid no one will hear him and he's in danger of starvation. However quick I am, he still wakes up Julie and Mahela, sometimes two or three times a night. I feel guilty and yet powerless to keep my child quiet.

At the end of March, Julie announces she's moving out. "I'm sorry. I'm falling asleep in all my classes. My grades are going down. I have to leave."

I've seen this coming. "No, I'll move instead," I say.

Over Mahela's muted objections, I pack up the playpen and the crib and the changing table and the stuffed ducks and lion and go downstairs to a tiny one-bedroom apartment with half the space, but for me double the rent. I don't want to ask Mother and Winston for more money, and I don't want to use up all the savings Mother has given me so I get another part-time job at a travel agency, which allows me flexible hours. I consider going back to work for Marvin, but my heart isn't in his investigations since he's told me he thinks Adil is dead. I want a job that doesn't require papers and interviews and sub-terfuge. I want a job that allows me to master a function and not have to think too hard outside of school. I want to consider the world through the lens of mountains and beaches and beautiful places and imagine other destinations in my life.

With even less time to study, however, I have to drop two courses, and I become a part-time student. That winter, the only highlight of my academic career comes in my political science class, where I finally write my paper on the Balkans. Marvin was right. Yugoslavia is start-ing to make headlines as it struggles to stay together. I title the paper: "Yugoslavia: A Quagmire Ahead for U.S. Foreign Policy?" I footnote my title as coming from an interview with Samuel Huggins. My pro-fessor is so impressed with the paper that she gives me the first A+ I've ever received in my college life, and she recommends me for an honors seminar the next semester and tells me I should go to graduate school.

For his part, Samuel Huggins resigns from the Commerce Depart-ment after the 1992 elections and moves back to his home in Okla-homa with his daughter. Marvin assures me his leaving is a matter of politics and not the result of any of my interviews.

As I juggle school and work and Jad, I try not to think about Adil, but sometimes alone in my apartment with Jad sleeping in my arms, I'm so lonely I cry myself to sleep just like Jad. Each day my memories of Adil fade, and each day my own needs increase.

*   *   *

The summer of 1991, Pickles gets married. Jane gets a reporting job at *The New York Times*, and Sophie finishes graduate school. Sophie takes a job at the State Department and prepares for the Foreign Ser-vice exams. The police investigations into Dennis's death conclude that Dennis was involved with Russian criminal elements trafficking in used weapons in East Berlin, and one of his contacts shot him. The German police arrest a man, but later release him for lack of evidence. The thought of Dennis initiating business in Russian weapons is implausible to all of us, but we have no convincing evidence to the contrary.

Unanswered questions pile up in a corner of my life like stones in a wall between the past and the future. Though I have no clear idea of what my future will bring, with Jad I glimpse more of myself.

I never hear from Adnan Kamil Houston after the war starts, but I move down the street now alert in a way I haven't been before. I think of Adil in Berlin who moved as if he knew what was to the left and right, in front and even behind him. I take a martial arts class at Marvin's suggestion with the excuse that I need to lose the weight I gained when I was pregnant. Twice a week I take Jad to the studio as I learn karate. Sophie joined me once, but didn't come again.

"I'll do better negotiating with my assailant," she says.

"What if you don't speak the same language?"

"Don't confuse karate class with real life," Sophie answers.

By September I've achieved two stripes on a white belt. However, I have to stop the classes to manage my real life, but I walk more conscious now of my perimeter.

PART IV

BORDER CROSSINGS

CHAPTER SEVENTEEN

WHEN MY FATHER died, the air rushed out of my universe. Ever since, I've stayed alert for sources of air. My mother taught me to move forward and not let the past stop me in my tracks. As I try to build a life for Jad and me, I often feel breathless as though there's a small hole leaking air, but most of the time I'm so busy I don't have time to breathe.

I've had to drop out of half my regular classes at university because I need to work full-time. I take Arabic two evenings a week. On Tuesday and Thursday evenings, I jog from work to the university to get exercise and drop into the back row, where I eat a banana and granola bar for dinner and spend the first quarter of an hour worrying about Jad, who's almost three. He goes to a small preschool nearby, and on Tuesday afternoons Sophie picks him up so I don't worry as much on Tuesdays. I've lost all the weight from when I was pregnant and more because I don't have time to eat.

Also arriving late to class and sitting in the back row is a man in a suit and tie who eats apples for his dinner. Ramsay Coleman is the best in the class, so the discussion often orients to our back row. Ramsay works as a computer consultant for companies that do business in the Middle East. On the first day of class, he announced he wants to learn Arabic because no one in his company, which is headquartered in Austin, Texas, speaks Arabic, and he wants to be the one who understands what the other side says when they think no one understands. Everyone except me is learning Arabic for work. I want to learn so that I can share with Jad some of his heritage, but the class is also helping my business. I've started booking flights and hotels in and out of Saudi Arabia, Kuwait, Bahrain, and Dubai for class members, including Ramsay.

In the fall of Arabic 3, Ramsay took the initiative to host a conversation group at his apartment one night a week. The sessions are more like parties except we all speak Arabic. I usually arrive late, dropping Jad off at Mahela's or Sophie's.

On one of the nights in early December, Ramsay asks me to stay after the session. He says he has something to give me. I'm helping him clean up when he hands me a clear blue stone the size of a half dollar.

"It's beautiful," I say. We're standing by the window that overlooks the Washington Zoo. The lights from the paths through the animals' habitats thread the dark below.

"I want you to have it," he says.

"Why?"

"What am I going to do with it?"

That is the kind of question that has no answer. "I don't know. Where did you get it?" I've noticed Ramsay watching me in class, but he watches everybody. Ramsay is thirty-three; I'm twenty-four. He has intelligent eyes—dark brown and focused—but an innocent face, as though he's spent so much time working, he hasn't taken the time to grow up in other ways. A mop of brown hair falls into his eyes and a dimple appears on his cheek when he smiles. "What do you want me to do with it?" I ask.

"I've been saving it until I met the person I wanted to give it to. I found it when I was excavating on a site last year, and I got it polished."

I'm touched by his awkwardness, this smart man I've looked up to. I can tell he wants to kiss me. "Thank you. I'll keep it for you on loan until you want it back."

He puts the stone in my hand and keeps hold of my hand. "I won't want it back," he says, then he takes me in his arms and kisses me like a man who isn't so young after all.

I begin seeing Ramsay once or twice a week outside of class. I stay after the sessions in his apartment to help him clean up and to talk. I tell him right off that I have a child. I don't know how I feel about him, but however he feels about me, he needs to accept Jad as part of my life.

"How lucky," he says. "When can I meet him?"

"Later."

I try to keep some distance between us, but Ramsay doesn't make that easy. He's accepting of whatever I tell him about myself, as if he's discovering some new and interesting person who is me. "I dropped out of college, or almost," I tell him. In fact, I'm still taking one course and this evening course and slowly accumulating credits to graduate.

"I spent nine years in university, got a PhD, and you're as smart as anyone I ever met," he says.

"Where did you go?" I expect some small university in Texas.

"Stanford," he says.

I worry about complicating my life, but Ramsay is so occupied with his own work that he gives me plenty of space. If I can't see him, he doesn't ask why. We go to movies, to concerts. I find myself looking forward to being with him. When he brings me home, he kisses me good night—a long passionate kiss—but he rarely comes in. I think he's being respectful of Jad or he's uncomfortable around my friends, who are usually the ones babysitting. Mahela gives him a hard time because he's older and he doesn't laugh at her jokes, but mostly Mahela has wedded her imagination to Adil. Ramsay is perhaps also cautious because I've made no secret of the fact that Adil may still be alive, that he may one day show up, though the more time Ramsay and I spend together, the harder it is for me to believe Adil exists, and the more uncomfortable we both become when I mention his name.

One Saturday morning in early fall 1995, Ramsay appears at my door with a soccer ball, ready to meet Jad. He's been pressing to meet my son, but I've put off the encounter. I don't want Jad getting attached to a man who isn't his father, especially since I haven't committed to how I feel about Ramsay. As unlikely and irrational as it is, part of my heart is still held in reserve. Sophie says I have a prodigious capacity to believe in case miracles happen and Adil is found alive with an unassailable excuse for why he hasn't been in touch in five years.

But now here is Ramsay at my door. I worry he and Jad may not like each other, a worry quickly put to rest. Ramsay drives us out to Rock Creek Park. The leaves are turning yellow and red and orange. The air is clear and smells of wood fires. The sun shines in the blue sky. We start kicking the ball around. Jad and I often play catch or football, but I've never played soccer with him. I guess I've been saving that for Adil to teach him. Jad takes to the soccer ball as if he's always known what to do. Ramsay shows him a few moves. His long skinny legs fly after the ball. He catches it with his feet and dribbles it as if his father has coached him in the womb. Ramsay is athletic and a tolerable player for a grown-up computer scientist whose greatest athletic feat was winning the ultimate Frisbee tournament at Stanford. Seeing Jad fly down the field with the ball, I feel exhilarated but also sad for the time when he will long for a father, when he will turn in all directions trying to fill that space inside himself.

"You've got to sign him up for soccer," Ramsay insists when we come home from the park. "You're terrific," he tells Jad, who beams. Ramsay gives Jad his soccer ball. The next day Ramsay brings me back information on a soccer league in my neighborhood. "He can start at five."

"He plays like his dad," I say. "Adil was brilliant."

At the mention of Adil's name, Ramsay's mouth, then his whole body tenses, but he says, "I hope I can see him play one day."

That's what touches me about Ramsay. I see him struggle with the ghost of another man and come out willing to applaud him. "Look, I'm sorry, I won't mention Adil again."

"He's Jad's father. Of course you should mention him."

"He may not even be alive."

"Would you like me to try to find out?" Ramsay asks.

"I've tried. My mother's tried. A family friend has tried." Marvin continued making inquiries after the war, but I haven't talked to Marvin in almost a year. My fear that someday someone will confirm Adil is dead has kept me from pursuing the question, I think. I've been protecting Jad and myself with the possibility of Adil still in our future. But now Ramsay is calling the question. "Adil may have been using an assumed name so it may be hard to trace him," I say.

"I have some contacts."

"You don't have to do this."

"Do what?" he asks. Ramsay's strong-jawed face and inquisitive eyes remind me of those intelligent German shepherds who guide the blind—alert, trusting, stronger, and more competent than those they guide.

"You don't have to be so"—I can't think of the right word—"so decent-."

Ramsay laughs, and Jad, who's running by with his new soccer ball, laughs with him.

* * *

When Ramsay returns from one of his trips in late November, he takes us to the circus. He often travels to the Middle East, installing computer equipment used in oil production and other government systems and training people in their use. He usually calls at least once a week from Riyadh or Manama or Abu Dhabi. We spend half the phone call talking about Jad or Jad gets on the phone and talks to Ramsay directly, mostly about Rain, Ramsay's half sheep dog/half Labrador who stays with us when Ramsay is away.

Jad has never been to the circus, and Ramsay is as excited about taking him as Jad is about going. He lets Jad buy a monkey on a stick and a black plastic eight ball that tells fortunes and a hot dog, cotton candy, Cracker Jacks. We can barely get to our seats with all our loot.

We're watching clowns tumble off the elephants when Ramsay hands me a box. I think it's the prize from the Cracker Jacks. "Let Jad have it," I say.

"No, it's for you."

Ramsay answers so seriously that I look again. When I see the small black velvet box, my heart sinks. Without opening it, I know what is inside, and in that moment I know that I don't want what is inside, at least not yet, but I feel as though I'm in a movie already running, and I can't change the scene about to unfold so I open the box. There on blue velvet sits a diamond ring. Ramsay must read my face because he says, "Don't answer. I've been carrying it around, waiting for the right moment. Obviously, this isn't it, but think about it."

After the circus, at my apartment, Jad goes straight to bed. Ramsay and I settle in my small living room. I sit in the corner of the blue corduroy sofa with Ramsay next to me. "I'm really honored," I start, but Ramsay cuts me off.

"I don't want you to say anything unless it's yes. I love you. I think I've loved you since that first night I sat next to you in class, and you asked me if I knew the Arabic word for *snow*. I want to marry you and share my life with you, but until you want to marry me, don't answer."

"But that's not fair to you."

"Let me worry about what's fair."

"Maybe it's not fair to me. I'll know you're waiting, and I don't think ... don't know ... I don't know that I'll ever say yes."

In fact, I've quit dating the few other men I saw. They weren't as interesting or as kind as Ramsay. I used to picture myself married with children, having a career only if I had time, but now that I have neither time nor a husband, I'm managing, and I see a wider frame where I fit, participating in the world as the world citizen my mother raised me to be. I don't know what my contribution ultimately will be, but I want to marry only when I'm deeply in love.

Ramsay stands. "I have to go."

"Where are you going?"

"I've got some things I need to do." He kisses me without lingering and leaves.

The next day, Ramsay phones to say that he'll be away for a few weeks and will call me when he gets back. Usually I book his flights, but this time he says his client has bought the ticket. When I ask him where, he slips out of the question. "I'll be all over the place."

"In the Middle East?"

"Mostly."

Ramsay stays away for the next three weeks without calling. I'm planning to go home to London for Christmas, which means I won't see him until the new year. I begin to worry that something has happened to him. Finally, I phone his office and ask if there is a way to get in touch, but his assistant says she hasn't heard from him in over a week. "If he calls, will you ask him to please phone Elizabeth West."

* * *

"How do you know if you're in love?" I call Jane.

"Are you in love?"

"I don't know." I've been seeing Ramsay for the last eleven months and have told Jane about him. I've been more cautious about sharing my love life with Sophie after the night in Berlin, but Jane doesn't judge me. She's carrying on a long-distance romance herself with her friend Henry at *The Financial Times*.

"Is he in love with you?" Jane asks.

"He says he is. He asked me to marry him, but I said no, and now he's left."

"You said no?"

"Well, I didn't say yes, and I told him I wasn't sure if I'd ever say yes. The next day he left."

"Where did he go?"

"I don't know. I'm worried something happened to him. What if I've made a mistake and lost him? Do you love Henry?"

"Yes, but neither of us is thinking about getting married right now."

"Why not?"

"We're married to our jobs, though Henry's being assigned to Cairo, and I've put in a request for our Cairo bureau."

"Cairo? You'll be a million miles away."

"More like six thousand. Most days the phones work."

I envy Jane her certainty about Henry and her work and her life. I don't know if she is really as secure as she seems to me, but I'm glad that for me she's grounded. "I don't know what to do. What if Adil is alive somewhere? Or, what if he's not?"

"Don't act out of fear," Jane says. "Fear that you'll be alone or fear that Adil's dead or alive, or fear that Ramsay will leave. That's the wrong reason. Love will wipe out the fear. That's how you'll know it's love."

*   *   *

The day before I'm leaving for London, Ramsay calls from Kuwait City. The phone line is filled with static so we don't talk long, but he says he's coming home via London so we can see each other there. My whole family will be at our home in London for the holidays. Jane and Sophie are making pilgrimages. Even Grandma Sha and Grandpa are coming. Ramsay doesn't know exactly when he'll arrive, but he says he'll be there by Christmas Eve.

Mom wants Ramsay to stay with us, but I say he's staying in a hotel. I don't want my family swarming all over him. I don't want pressure from them or from him. I also want a place where we can be alone together. Counting Pickles and Randolph and their two children—and Pickles is pregnant with a third—there will be thirteen people for Christmas dinner, or maybe fourteen, if Henry's in town and joins us. I offer to stay at the hotel, too, but the offer upsets Mom. "Well, if that's what you want, but leave Jad with us."

Jad loves the holidays in London where there are always people around, unlike in our apartment, and everyone pays attention to him. He and Mom and Winston go to the shops together and to the park nearby, where there are other children. Jad is almost five, and sometimes I worry I'm depriving him by living alone in the space I can afford. Mother has offered to have us live with them, but the thought of moving home depresses me. Besides, my work and all my friends are in Washington.

*   *   *

Ramsay arrives the day before Christmas ready to meet my mother. I greet him at the front door. He's tanned, in need of a haircut, a cautious smile on his face, his dimple showing. "I've missed you," I say.

"Good," he answers. With his palms, he takes my face in his hands and kisses me long and hard. "I love you," he answers, "in case you forgot."

I feel relieved as if fresh air has suddenly blown into my stuffy room. I straighten his brown wool jacket and frayed blue shirt. I sweep my fingers through his disheveled hair. "Why didn't you call while you were away?"

"I was moving around. I had a lot on my mind."

"I was worried something happened to you."

He kisses me again. "I like you worrying about me."

Is worrying about him, missing him, wanting him to come back the same as loving him for the rest of my life? I lead him by the hand into the living room where Mom is waiting by the fire. Ramsay has brought my mother a book. I remember the first time Adil came carrying flowers for Mom. The book is by a friend of his, and the friend has signed it: "For Miriam West, whom I read and respect. Malcolm Dodd." The book makes at least as good an impression as Adil's daisies did.

"Malcolm Dodd was one of my professors in college," Ramsay says. "He had a book signing in Washington before I left. I've just started the book myself."

"*Web of Deceit*. Yes, it's gotten very good reviews," Mother says.

Ramsay also gave me a copy before he left, and I read it while he was away, but I didn't know he bought a copy and had it signed for my mother. I wonder if he planned this visit all along. I sit listening to Mom and Ramsay talk about the book, though I am the only one who's finished it. Here is part of the problem coming home. I watch myself taking my place as the youngest and least informed member of the family. Mom and Ramsay talk for almost an hour before we're interrupted by Winston returning from the park with Jad, who runs to Ramsay when he sees him. Mom smiles. I wonder how Jad will feel if I don't marry Ramsay and Ramsay goes away. How will he feel if I marry Ramsay and then discover that his father is alive and I'm still in love with him? How will I feel? I can tell Mom likes Ramsay, but I think she would like anyone I bring home. She wants me to have a husband and Jad to have a father.

The real test for Ramsay is Sophie, who only met him a few times briefly in Washington when we picked Jad up at her apartment. We never stayed long to talk.

"What exactly is it you sell?" Sophie asks Ramsay at dinner that evening.

We're all sitting at the formal dining room table covered in a white linen and lace cloth with Mom's place settings of bone china rimmed in royal blue and the heavy Georgian silver that has been in Winston's family and crystal water glasses, also Winston's. Candles flicker on silver candle sticks. It is Christmas Eve. We have all dressed up, and Ramsay is the special guest.

"Computer systems," Ramsay answers. He's dressed in his brown wool jacket he wears everywhere.

"What kind of computer systems?" Jane asks. I've made Jane swear not to tell anyone Ramsay has asked me to marry him.

"Systems that operate refining plants or run transportation systems or municipal services. Fairly complex systems."

"You can do all those things?" Grandma Sha asks. Her gray hair is fluffed like a halo around her face and matches her gray silk jacket.

"I oversee the installation of equipment that can do all those things, and I teach people how to run the system they need."

"You must be very smart," Grandpa, who also has a halo of thin gray hair, speaks up from across the table. "What will happen to those

of us who never turned on a computer?" he asks Ramsay. "Are we di-
nosaurs on the way to extinction?"

"Some animals survive extinction," Ramsay says.

"Ah, you're a diplomat too," Grandpa approves. "But tell me, do all
these computers make us better human beings?" The personal computer is still a relatively new phenomenon, barely a decade old. Mom
uses one because she's in the news business, and she's arranged a tutor
to come to the house to teach Winston.

"They make us more efficient," Ramsay says.

"They connect us," Jane adds. She's cut her hair in a blunt bob—
cooler, easier to manage in Cairo, she says. I've never seen her with
short hair. We no longer look alike. "Computers make it easier to find
information and more difficult for villains to hide."

"Villains hide as well as they ever did," Winston says from the head
of the table where he sits in a green velvet jacket.

"What do you consider evil?" Sophie asks no one in particular.

"Torture," Mom proposes, setting bowls of mashed potatoes and
stuffing and salad on the table. "Torturing another person is evil."
Mom's wearing the simple red silk dress she wears every Christmas.

"We read about torture every day in Bosnia, in Rwanda. How do
we stop that?" Winston asks.

"You can't solve every problem in the world," Grandpa says.

"Oh, but you must try!" Grandma Sha insists.

"What do you think?" Sophie asks Ramsay. I glance over at him.

He accepts a roll from the basket Grandpa passes across the table.
"It's difficult to respond in the abstract," he answers.

"Then specifics. Bosnia. How do we solve Bosnia?" It's an unfair
question, a Sophie question.

Ramsay is silent as he butters the roll. "I don't know enough, but if I
were in your position . . ." He implies that he knows what Sophie's position is in the State Department, that we've talked about Sophie when

she wasn't there. "If I were in your position, eventually I might turn the situation over to Lizzy. Bosnia, Croatia, and Serbia were beautiful once before their wars. Maybe the tourists can reclaim them someday."

Grandpa, Mom, Jane, and Grandma Sha smile, but Sophie seems to be considering his answer, which reflects conversations I've had with Ramsay when I've wondered if I were related to the other women in my family. I complained that if you got Mom, Sophie, Jane, and Grandma Sha together, they would race across the political landscape, bumping against each other's views at a speed that gave me a headache. I'm the least political member of my family, and the more I observe wars that ensue from politics, the more I say a hex on politics. My son has lost his father to politics as I lost mine. At university I've taken courses in literature and comparative cultures and now language. As a travel agent, I consider the miles of beautiful beaches and forests and mountains and all the people and cultures and art in the world that have been devastated by the battles for power. I once suggested to Ramsay that the world should be turned over to the travel agents. I don't see myself as a travel agent in the long run. I'm still figuring out where the long run leads. Ramsay is paying tribute to my idea.

"Would you do the same in the Middle East?" Sophie asks. She's leaning forward towards him intently in her brown suit without a touch of the red and green holiday colors the rest of us conform to.

"At least the Syrians and Israelis and Palestinians are talking," Jane says.

"Don't hold your breath," Winston counters.

"There are some signs of hope," Grandma Sha notes as she eats small, careful bites of her salad. I wonder if her teeth are bothering her. "The international community gave away Lebanon for Syria's support in the Gulf War, but at least with the Syrians in Lebanon that civil war is over," she says.

"There's still fighting on the border," Jane observes.

"Not everyone wants peace," Grandpa adds.

"This is all very interesting, but I want to know who's going to carve the turkey," Mother interrupts, setting the bird on the table.

"I'll do it." Randolph stands. As he goes to the head of the table, wearing a holiday tie with wreaths on it, Pickles smiles at him. I watch Pickles in a puffed-sleeved maroon velvet dress feeding Dennis Jr., who is eighteen months old. Beside her, three-year-old Sara sits trying to cut her own vegetables.

"Here, Sara, let me help you," I say, cutting up the turkey and the carrots for this earnest, fair-haired, blue-eyed child who looks like Dennis and who is my niece.

After dinner, Jane and Sophie and Grandma Sha corner Ramsay. Sophie wants to find out exactly what countries Ramsay works in and what he does there and what he thinks of the governments. Sophie is steeped in U.S. policy. She's passed the competitive Foreign Service exams and is being sent somewhere in the Middle East or Northern Africa next year. Jane has been given a temporary nod for an assignment to Cairo. Though Jane, Sophie, and I differ in our aspirations, we all have gravitated in our study and our work to the area of the world where we lost our father.

*   *   *

Ramsay whistles outside my window at dawn on Christmas morning. I hurry downstairs to let him in, but he says, "Let's walk for a while." I leave a note on the hall table telling Mom I've gone for a walk with Ramsay. If Jad wakes up and I'm not there, he'll go into Mom's room. Grabbing my jacket and keys, I slip out of the house. We haven't really had a chance to talk yet. I take his arm and slip my hand into his pocket as we head towards Holland Park. A neighbor walking his dog hails us entering the park.

"Merry Christmas," I answer back. I glance at Ramsay—his clean, literal jaw, his credulous eyes, his curly, uncombed hair. Sometimes he can spend an entire walk without speaking. He's the most self-contained person I know and yet in a way the loneliest.

"So tell me about your trip." I feel a barrier still between us from our last meeting. He takes hold of my hand in his pocket but doesn't answer right away.

"I finished the project in Kuwait," he says finally, "and then I had a project of my own."

"What kind of project?"

"I was installing a monitoring system at an airport," he answers the first question. We stop by the duck pond at the top of the park. A few hearty ducks are out swimming. "In Kuwait I located a man"—he glances at me then looks away—"who knew Adil."

"Adil Hasan?" Suddenly I'm alert.

"The man told me Adil had been in Saudi Arabia during the Gulf War working as a medic's assistant on the Kuwait-Iraq border." Ramsay concentrates as though delivering a message he's promised to bring. "After the war, he said Adil returned to Lebanon." Ramsay pauses. "He told me Adil was married and had a child."

"Adil Hasan? The same Adil Hasan?"

"I believe so."

Adil is alive? He's married? "Where in Lebanon?" I ask.

"Beirut. I thought of going there, but I wasn't sure I could get in. Besides, I didn't want to do that without speaking to you."

I sit down on the edge of the pond, but the stones are cold. I stand back up.

"You want to go see him?" Ramsay asks. He faces me, his eyes narrow. He tucks his chin and whole head into his body as if anticipating a blow.

How did the man know Adil? I want to ask. How could he be sure it was Adil? But I don't ask. Ramsay wouldn't bring me this news casually. All these years I've been waiting for what? For the past to come back to life, to transport Jad and me over five years to the meaning I think the past should have. But the past is the past. My mother has tried to teach me that. You can't bring it back. You can't make it turn out differently. You have to live through it and beyond it.

I suck in the cold air. "Americans aren't allowed to travel to Lebanon," I say.

CHAPTER EIGHTEEN

I CAN'T SLEEP and am up early the next morning. So is Winston. As I pass his study, he calls, "Lizzy, come in a minute." He's sitting behind his desk in a navy cardigan with a knit cap on his head as if he's ready to go outside or has just come in. "I like your young man," he says. "He has gravitas. You don't find that so much these days in young people."

I sink in the chair opposite him. He pushes a leather portfolio across the desk to me. Inside are hundreds of newspaper articles. On top are stories by Jane's friend Henry at *The Financial Times*. Winston is semi-retired now, though he sits on the board of his company. Mother has told me he spends his days searching out information in the library and on the internet, which has burgeoned in the five years since Dennis's death.

"Jane's partner also has gravitas, but then so do you and Jane and Sophie. I credit your mother. I didn't do as good a job with my children."

"Pickles has taken on the most important job of all, raising three children," I say. "She's a wonderful mother."

"Yes . . . yes, you're right, of course. Pickles has turned out all right . . . probably in spite of me." He offers a weak smile.

"What are all these?" I pick up articles from *The Financial Times*, *The London Times*, *The Independent*, *The Telegraph*, *The Guardian*, *The Observer*, *The New York Times*, *The Washington Post*, *The Christian Science Monitor*, *The International Herald Tribune*, *Der Spiegel*, *Le Monde*, *l'Express*, *Le Figaro*, *Stern*, *The Village Voice*, *The Dallas Morning News*, *The Florida Sun-Sentinel*, *The Minneapolis Star Tribune*, *The Wall Street Journal*. All appear to report on illicit weapons flow.

"I've had to face up to the fact that my son, who could have done anything, veered into the underworld seeking I don't know what—money? adventure?"

"He was trying to prove himself," I suggest.

Winston raises his hand. "Don't make excuses. I've made my peace. No, that's not true . . . I'll never be at peace, but I've been following this trade that took him in." Winston touches the small globe that sits on his desk. "Most of those involved pass through London at one time or another or have offices here."

I'm not sure why Winston is telling me this. "How can I help you?" I ask.

"I want you to write a book with me."

"Me?" The request takes me by surprise. "Why not Mom . . . or Jane? That's what they do."

"I thought of them, but your mother has her magazine. She's writing her own articles. I can't do this on my own, but I can get us a contract."

"What about Jane?"

"She has her job. Besides, Jane is a sprinter like your mother, or maybe a relay runner. This project is going to take a long-distance runner. I think you're the marathoner of our family. Your mother tells me your professors have urged you to go to graduate school. She says you've finished your bachelor's degree with high honors."

It's true. It's taken six and a half years, but according to the registrar, with the Arabic classes and the classes I've taken in Middle Eastern literature and history in the summers, I've earned enough credits for my degree, which will be granted summa cum laude. The diploma is being sent in the mail.

"If you want to go to graduate school, I can help you with tuition and expenses. Your father's partner told your mother you're a natural investigator. The book could be your thesis."

"Graduate school means classes for several years, and I'd have to do a thesis on my own."

"Of course. We could discuss what part of the book was your thesis. But the book will be bigger than a thesis. I'm not in a hurry, but I'm also not letting this rest. I've thought carefully about whom I trust the work to."

I have in fact wished I could go on with my studies. At my professors' encouragement, I'd even put in a few graduate school applications with teaching fellowships, but I don't know if it's possible with Jad. I'm touched by Winston's offer, but I'm also wary.

Winston takes off his cap. "Gerald Rene Wagner remains free. I don't know if he was directly responsible for Dennis's death, but I'm fairly certain he was involved. He lied and cheated my company and me. He never paid for at least £20 million worth of equipment. I've found out that the trucks we sent were shipped on and fitted and used as mobile missile launchers in Iraq. In the end, he and his client declared bankruptcy."

"Do you know where he is now?"

"He still lives in his house in London, at least part of the time. Your mother ran into him and his daughter-in-law on High Street Kensington a few weeks ago."

"Serena's here?" I can't believe Serena has come back and is living with Dr. Wagner.

"Your mother was so surprised. She asked about that little boy you used to bring home."

"Serena's son, Jack?"

"She told your mother he's in college in the States and will be here for Christmas. She asked if you were coming to London. Gerald pulled her away then, your mother said. He never spoke to or even acknowledged your mother."

"How can Dr. Wagner keep living in that big house if he's bankrupt?"

"I'm sure he has funds hidden somewhere. I suspect some of his companies are still operating under the radar. I wanted to sue him, but our company wrote off the loss rather than risk the publicity. Our lawyers speculated they wouldn't be able to recover funds for him to pay anyway."

I put Winston's articles back in his folder. "I'll think about your offer. It's very generous, but there are other decisions I have to make first, though whatever I decide, thank you."

Winston slips the folder into his desk drawer. "I've become a more patient man," he says. "I'm willing to work a long time to find the truth and even longer to get justice."

*   *   *

Sophie insists we all go to an American School party for alumni between Christmas and New Years. The reunion at the Café Royal in Piccadilly is featuring a popular new London band, a member of which graduated with Sophie. I don't want to go, but Ramsay wants to meet my friends. It will be peculiar going back to see old friends with another man on my arm and Adil's child at home, though few people from school know I have a child.

Before the party we gather in Mom's room the way we used to, with Sophie sitting at the dressing table fussing with her hair. When I come in, she hands me the brush, and I step behind her and begin to style her frizzy red hair as I had so often when we were growing up.

"I think you should marry Ramsay," she says.

Sophie and Ramsay have spent the last two days talking almost more than he and I have. When I ask Ramsay what they talk about, he answers, "You . . . and the rest of the world."

"He's extremely decent," Sophie says. "That may sound boring, but I'm twenty-eight years old, and I'd love to meet a man that decent."

"He's smart too," Jane says. "And he's wonderful with Jad."

"Most important, he loves you," Mom adds.

"So?" Sophie asks as I pull half her hair up on top of her head.

"So, I'm thinking about it."

"Are you both thinking about it?" Mom asks.

I smile. "Yes."

"I'm so glad. Have you met his family?"

"His mother's been to Washington. She's not much like Ramsay. She's very . . . well, very social. She was nice to me, though she kept asking exactly who my mother and father were in London and who my first husband was. Ramsay hadn't told her anything about Jad's father, so she just assumed."

"What's holding you back?" Sophie asks.

"I've only dated him a little over a year. I don't know where Adil is . . ." I realize that may no longer be true.

"Adil is a dream," Sophie declares. "Ramsay is real, and he won't wait forever. Trust me."

"Did he say anything to you?" I look at Sophie in the mirror. I've transformed her thick wiry hair into a sophisticated twist with curls down her back.

"No, but I know guys that age. When they're finally ready to settle down, they settle. They don't let too much time pass." The doorbell rings as if punctuating Sophie's point, a point I haven't been willing to admit.

Ramsay arrives wearing the navy cashmere blazer I've given him for Christmas. I saved my commissions and went to Harrods and found it in a holiday sale. I figure he'll have the jacket for years, and I'm surprised to realize I'm thinking of myself with him over those years. Henry arrives right behind Ramsay in the tweed jacket he's worn every time I've met him. We all set off in a London black cab.

* * *

In the entry outside the ballroom of the Café Royal, a lanky young man at the welcoming table hands me our tickets for the evening. "You don't recognize me?" he asks in a British/American accent.

I peer through the tangle of his pale blond curls. "Jack?" He stands. "Oh my god . . . Jack!" He towers over me. I give him a hug and introduce Ramsay.

"Oh . . ." Jack says, as in "Oh—I-expected-someone-else."

"How are you? Where are you?"

"Sophomore at Penn. Home for the holidays trying to survive my crazy mother and Nazi grandfather. I came tonight to see if there might be some root here I could cling to."

I haven't seen Jack in eight years. "University of Pennsylvania? That's very good."

"Acceptable for the prep school Serena masterminded me into."

I'm genuinely glad to see him, a small link to my past at the American School. I haven't been back since I graduated. On the surface, at least, Jack appears to have survived his mother and grandfather. "Well . . . tell your mother I said hello."

"Will do."

Ramsay and I wedge our way into the ballroom to the edge of the dance floor with its strobe lights crisscrossing over us.

"Lizzy!" a voice trills, and a hand flutters over the crowd and moves towards me like a flapping bird. "I didn't know you were coming! You weren't on my list." She reaches out and kisses me on both cheeks then stands waiting to be introduced. Her shining black hair streams down her back.

"Sahar Jalil . . . Ramsay Coleman."

"Actually, that's about to change, you know," she says.

"What's about to change?"

"My name."

"Are you getting married?"

"I thought you knew."

"How would I know?"

"So you don't know? I just assumed he'd tell you. I don't know why; but I didn't want to ask him. Last summer I went home to visit my parents who've moved back to Beirut, and we met there after all these years."

Out of the corner of my eye I see a tall dark figure walking towards us through the crowd and the strobe lights and the smoke. The strobe lights move inside my head, and I feel suddenly disoriented and dizzy. I take hold of Ramsay's hand for reference.

After all the years, I'm encountering Adil by accident at a party. When he sees me, he also stops. Then he puts out his hand. "Hello! How are you?" He speaks now as though no more than high school has passed between us. He puts his arm around Sahar. Sahar watches us both. No one speaks.

"Hello. I'm Ramsay Coleman." Ramsay puts out his own hand.

"Adil Hasan."

Ramsay extends his arm around me, as if he knows I need support. "How have you been?" Adil asks.

I can't answer. I literally can't make words form. Ramsay comes to my rescue. "We're living in Washington," he answers. *We?* Is he defending me or staking out territory? "Lizzy is one of the travel czars of the city. Clients stand in line for her. Half the embassies use her." What is Ramsay doing?

I take a breath. "That's an exaggeration," I say.

"I heard you were successful," Sahar says. "I also heard you were a mother. Congratulations. How long have you been married?"

Adil watches me but doesn't wait for an answer. "I was sent over to tell you the band has arrived," he says to Sahar.

"Oh. I'm supposed to get them set up," she apologizes. "We'll see you in a minute." She takes Adil by the hand, claiming him.

As they turn to leave, Adil nods to Ramsay. To me he says, "Take care of yourself." But he doesn't meet my eyes.

I stand for a moment without speaking. I'm afraid if I say anything, I'll scream or burst into tears. How casual Adil was, as if nothing has happened between us, as if my thinking of him every day for five years has had no effect, as if my thoughts have drifted into the atmosphere, diffused, never reaching him or touching him. Is it possible we are that disconnected, that our realities are so far apart? My hope has been only a bubble of air, nothing.

I hold Ramsay's arm. As we move through the crowd, every few moments someone greets me. "How are you? How've you been?" "Fine. Fine." "What are you doing?" "I'm in the travel business." I make my way across the floor. In the travel business. I move between illusion and reality, and at the moment I feel a fool who's spent the last years in a dream. I dreamed of Adil suffering in war or in prison or even dead, dreamed of him crawling his way across a desert, swimming an ocean so we can be together. *I heard you were a mother*, Sahar said. *How long have you been married?* Jad is not a secret in my Washington life, so I suppose I shouldn't be surprised the grapevine works the news back to London. Sahar has always been on the central switchboard. Did she tell Adil I was married? Did he assume the child is someone else's?

Ramsay draws me over to a table. "The man who told me about Adil was a building contractor from Beirut," he says. "He spent the last two years reconstructing the city. He knows the political networks. What I told you is what he told me."

Ramsay's face is so earnest, I lean over and kiss him. "I know you'd never lie to me. That's why I love you."

He blinks. "That is the first time you've said you loved me."

"I'm sorry it's taken me so long. I don't know what I was waiting for."

Sophie is the first one over to tell me Adil is at the party. Jane has never met him, but the year I dated Adil in high school, Sophie met him a couple of times. "Are you going to speak to him?" she asks. We're all sitting at the table now. The music is so loud you can only hear the person shouting in your ear, so Sophie and I can talk while Ramsay talks with Jane and Henry.

"I already did."

Sophie raises her eyebrows. "And?"

"And nothing. He's engaged to Sahar."

Sophie looks out on the dance floor. Adil is dancing in very small rhythmic steps while Sahar—tanned, beautiful, dressed in red chiffon—twirls around him. "Did you happen to mention Jad?" Sophie asks.

"He's getting married," I repeat. "Sahar told him I had a child. He thinks Ramsay and I are married."

"So he thinks Ramsay's the father?"

"I guess."

Sophie doesn't speak for a moment. "When will you tell him?"

I'm wondering if I will, but I can't think here; yet if I don't speak with him here, I may not have another chance.

"You have to tell him," Sophie says. "He has a right to know he has a son. Jad has a right to know his father."

I know Sophie is correct. I just don't know how to do that with Ramsay and Sahar and our whole school in attendance. Molly Dees advances to our table with a book of raffle tickets and the answer. I haven't seen Molly since the summer Sophie and I went to Germany, though we've exchanged holiday cards. I know she's now at graduate school in international relations at Columbia University and her father, who left London for Zurich after we graduated, has recently returned to the embassy here in an even more senior position. I hardly recognize her. She's let her hair go brown, cut it short, gained fifteen pounds. She looks more serious, a woman whose intelligence no longer threatens her.

"Lizzy." She leans over and kisses me on the cheek. "I heard you were here."

"Would you mind if I ask Ramsay to dance?" Sophie asks me as Molly sits down. Sophie leads Ramsay to the dance floor.

"I'm here . . . on a mission." Molly lowers her voice. "I don't want to interfere so tell me if you want me to mind my own business." In my memory Molly never minded her own business. "You've seen Adil and Sahar?" I nod. "Sahar told you they're getting married this summer?" Sahar didn't say when, but again I nod. "I've known Adil ten years," Molly continues. "I haven't seen him in ages, but I spent time with Sahar and him this holiday. I can tell you he's not in love with her, but his father is determined he align with someone of Sahar's family's wealth and position in Lebanon. He wants to see Adil secure. His father's been very sick for the last year—they think from chemicals he was exposed to during the Gulf War or from being in Iraqi prison. You know he was captured during the war? Adil is protective of him, especially now that he may be dying."

Why is Molly telling me this? Did she want to see me cry? I wish she'd leave. I watch Sophie and Ramsay dancing. Sophie is telling him something, and Ramsay is laughing. "What's your mission?" I ask.

"First, to find out if you're married to the man dancing with your sister."

"No."

"I didn't think so."

"Second, and this is where you may want to tell me to mind my own business . . . I hear you have a child. Is that man the father?"

I would have told Molly it was none of her business, but she questions me like a lawyer, not like a high school gossip. "Why do you ask?"

"Because if the answer is no, Adil wants to see you."

"Did he tell you that?" I glance quickly around the room, which is spinning under a silver mirrored globe, or is it my head that is spinning? I want to leave. How can I stay here with all these people? I can't see Adil, and I can't not see him. To Molly I say, "If Adil wants to see me, he can come himself."

Molly studies me for a moment. Sophie and Ramsay return to the table. Molly kisses me on the cheek then stands. "I'll deliver the message."

"What are you selling?" Sophie asks, nodding to the raffle tickets.

"Oh . . . a weekend in Brussels. You want to buy a ticket?"

"Did you buy a ticket?" Ramsay asks me as Molly leaves the table. "What?"

"Shall we go to Brussels?" Ramsay is flirtatious and completely out of sync with how I feel.

"Let's all go," Sophie says.

"You want to dance?" Ramsay suggests. I don't feel like dancing, but I let Ramsay lead me out under the twirling mirrors. I hold him as

I try to stop the mirrors in my mind's eye long enough to see myself in one of them.

*   *   *

When we get home, Mom and Winston and Grandma Sha and Grandpa are still up, sitting by the fire playing bridge, though they seem not to be playing so much as reminiscing about the War. For my generation, "the War" means the Gulf War. For Mom, who got married in 1963, "the War" usually means the Vietnam War, though sometimes it also means the Korean War since that is the war Dad served in. I'm not sure what "the War" means for Winston, who is sixty-three, but for my grandparents it means World War II, the only true war. All the others have been regional conflicts.

Though they spent the war in neutral Sweden, my grandparents worked with the Danish Resistance. As a child I loved listening to Grandma Sha tell me how the little boats ventured forth from Denmark carrying the Jews in the dark of night on the stormy North Sea and how people stood on the Swedish shore only a few miles away and watched and prayed for each boat. The older Grandma Sha gets, the more insistent her memories become of the War. Tonight she's telling Winston about someone she knew whose job it was to interpret reconnaissance photos before the D-day invasion. Ramsay and I settle on the sofa nearby.

"They were looking for troop movements," Grandma Sha explains, "for anything that would help them plan D-day. Thirty times they flew over Auschwitz and Buchenwald. They took pictures of the death camps, of people lined up going into the gas chambers, but they weren't looking for such camps. They couldn't imagine such camps. There had never been anything like those camps. Anytime they got pictures of lines of people waiting outside a building, what do you think they called the building?"

We all knew the answer because Grandma Sha has told us this story before, but Ramsay doesn't know so he asks, "What?"

"They labeled the pictures 'Mess Hall.' Mess Hall! Can you imagine? Every time they saw a line of people, they labeled it 'Mess Hall.'"

"Isn't that something?" Grandpa says.

"What do you say about that?" Grandma Sha asks Ramsay. "Not gas chamber, but mess hall."

Ramsay hasn't yet received tutelage from the Jewish part of my family. He looks impressed. I try to imagine how Adil might respond.

"It must have been impossible to imagine such evil," Ramsay says.

"You didn't have to imagine," Grandma corrects. "There were pictures."

"You did what you could," Grandpa consoles.

"None of us did enough. None of us!"

"Mother . . ." my mother says. "That was over fifty years ago."

"For me it's yesterday."

I take Ramsay's hand.

"Do you remember?" Grandma asks Mother.

"I remember very well," Mother answers. "I remember all the children I shared my room with."

"Good," Grandma declares. "I don't want you ever to forget." Then she looks over at us, her eyes larger than ever, like two searchlights fixing us in her stare. Her frail face seems more skeletal every day, as if she's slowly losing her substance and one day will float away. She and Grandpa are both ninety. Mother thinks they stay as agile and active as they are because they've loved and cared for each other over the years, defying the friction and wear that life extracts from most people. I wonder if I will ever care and sustain love for another person over half a century. As I hold Ramsay's hand, I'm thinking of Adil.

CHAPTER NINETEEN

SERENA CALLS THE next morning and says she heard I was at the party last night and wonders if we can meet. "I know I skipped out on you back in Washington," she apologizes. "I got scared. The FBI came to see me, and people were snooping around our offices. I didn't want to get arrested."

"Why would you get arrested?"

"I didn't stay long enough to find out. I have something I want to give you. When Jack said he saw you, I thought, Lizzy will know what to do. You once told me you knew someone who could help."

"Help with what?" A horn honks. "Where are you?"

"In a phone booth on the street. I've got to get back. Can we meet tomorrow? At Sticky Fingers. Gerald hates that place so there's no chance he'll come there. In the afternoon, around four?"

Fatin calls next. I haven't seen him since graduation six and a half years ago, though a while back I tried to locate him in order to find Adil.

"I hear you were at that party last night," he says.

"Were you there?"

"I hate those parties, but if I'd known you'd be there, I might have come."

"You would have come for me?" I banter.

"Does our friendship mean nothing to you?" he says. "Can you get away for coffee this afternoon? You know the café near Covent Garden?"

I grow quiet. That is Adil's and my restaurant. "Of course." I start to ask if anyone will be with him, but I decide I don't want to know. It's one thing to go out and meet an old friend for coffee. It will be quite another to meet Adil. Ever since the party last night, Ramsay has been more sociable than usual. He misses the still, alert part of me, and I don't want to show it to him. His ease is because I've finally said that I love him, because he heard Adil is getting married, and because my family approves of him so completely.

I tell Ramsay I'm meeting my old French partner for coffee. Sophie offers to go with Ramsay to the Geological Museum for the afternoon. Mother and Winston are taking Jad to Hamleys, the giant toy store on Regent Street, to pick out a birthday present. Jad turns five in February, and they won't be there for his birthday. I don't know why I feel so guilty. I dress more carefully than usual, then out of guilt change into jeans and a sweatshirt. I almost ask Ramsay to come with me to meet Fatin so I can assure myself that I'm not fooling myself by pretending not to know what I know. No one has said Fatin is the go-between for Adil, that Adil, not Fatin, will be sitting in the restaurant waiting to meet me for the first time in five and a half years. A war, a child, a career, a college education have all intervened in those years. No one has said Adil will be there, but I know he will.

When I arrive at the restaurant, no one is there. The pale brown walls, the stick chairs and tables, the smells of garlic and cumin are the same, but the room is empty. I've even arrived a few minutes late. I have imagined coming down the stairs and seeing Adil at the corner table looking up at me. Instead I take the chair in the corner, and when a waiter comes over, I ask, "Are you open? Has anyone been here before me?"

As I ask the question, I hear the flight of feet above, and then I see Adil, his dark, insistent eyes finding mine like radar locking onto home. I feel my breath come short. I begin arguing with myself. Half a decade has passed. I'm not a schoolgirl. I'm a mother. I have a career. I try not to smile too broadly as he comes over to the table. After all, he is about to marry my friend. His own expression is tentative, inquiring. "Fatin couldn't come. He sent me to make his apologies."

"I'm disappointed."

The waiter arrives. Adil nods for him to leave. "You look wonderful," he says.

"No, I don't." How I look is my penance, my hair in a ponytail, no makeup. I won't try to make this meeting work.

"Okay, you don't look wonderful."

"How's Sahar?" The question is a rebuke.

"Sahar says hello."

"She knows you're here?"

"I asked her to come, but she thought we should meet alone."

Now I feel myself rebuked. Adil has been more honest with Sahar than I've been with Ramsay. "I can't stay long," I say. "I have to meet someone."

"I wanted to see you. I felt I owed you an explanation. I want to clear everything up . . . I mean, before I get married. Sahar understands."

"Understands what?" I wonder if Adil has told Sahar about our night together in Berlin.

The waiter reappears at our table. "Tea," Adil orders. "Bring us two mint teas then leave us."

"What is it you want to clear up?" I ask.

Adil ignores the edge in my voice. "I got your postcard—I still have it—but I couldn't write again. The mail wasn't safe, my father said. He feared for anyone to know where we were."

"I wrote you three times."

"I only received the postcard."

"All the letters were returned." I remembered the NOT LIVE HERE printed on the envelope.

"My father was distressed when your card arrived. He said I shouldn't have taken the chance giving you an address. I wanted to see you, but the invasion of Kuwait happened that summer, then the war broke out. We had to leave Jordan. My father went undercover into Iraq where he was captured. It was only because of the chaos at the time that he wasn't executed right away. He was my first concern. It's a very long story, and you have somewhere to go. All I want to tell you . . . well, I wanted to tell you I'm glad you're happy and getting married."

I'd never said I was getting married. I told Molly I wasn't married to Ramsay, but Adil perhaps assumed I was planning to marry him. "I don't know if I'm getting married," I say.

"Sahar says you have a child?"

I nod.

"How old?"

"He turns five in February."

"What's his name?" I wonder if Adil is really so obtuse, if his math has failed him.

"I call him Jad."

"Jad?"

I pause. "His full name is Jesse Adil West."

There are a few moments in life when reality turns on a thin line and never looks the same again. Such a moment for me was the day Jad was born. For Adil that turning came in front of me in the moment that he realized he had a son.

"He's beautiful," I say. "He's the tallest boy in his class, and you should see him play soccer. He leaves everyone behind."

"He's mine?"

"Ours."

Adil's face looks stunned as if life as he's known it stopped, and he's at a loss to know what to do next. I've put too much faith in Molly's comment that Adil wanted to see me if Ramsay was not the father of my child. I see now his own paternity hadn't occurred to him. I see his clear brown eyes start calculating. "Why didn't I know? Did you try to reach me?"

"I wrote to you. I didn't have any phone number. I wanted to come see you to tell you. All my letters were returned. I called the school for your address, but their mail to you was also returned. My mother tried her contacts. I tried everyone that first year. Then I heard your father was in Basra during the Gulf War and had been captured and probably killed. I was afraid you were there too. I thought you'd been killed." Tears start down my cheeks.

Adil gets up and comes over to me. He stands before me as if he doesn't know what to do. I shake my head. "I'm all right. I don't know why I'm crying. Really . . . that's just left over." I take the napkin and wipe my eyes. "Really . . ."

Adil pulls his chair near me so we're sitting knee to knee. "Lizzy, I didn't know. I had no idea. I wanted to see you too, but so much happened. I didn't hear from you, and then I heard you were married. Sahar told me you were married. Can I see him?"

Adil's leaning towards me, his face like a child's himself, uncertain. I reach into my purse and pull out my wallet. I show him a picture of Jad with Rain, Ramsay's dog. Adil stares at it for a long time.

"Is he here in London?"

I nod. "Mom is taking him toy shopping today for his birthday. He turns five in February. He gets completely spoiled here."

"Does he know about me?"

"I didn't know what to tell him. I said you were a scientist, and you may have been hurt in a war and weren't able to get home."

"What must he think?" Adil says. "Doesn't he wonder?"

"He's starting to now that he's in school and the other children talk about their fathers. His teacher had the class draw pictures of their parents and talk about them. Jad told everyone I sent people on trips, but when it came to you, she couldn't make him answer. The other children started to laugh at him. We'd practiced over and over that you were a scientist who'd gotten hurt in a war, but Jad's smart. Even at four, he recognized a phony story. Finally, he blurted, 'My father sells computers all over the world.' Then he sat down. That's what Ramsay does."

I've been carrying this story with me ever since Jad's teacher told it to me before Christmas. I feel relieved to have Jad's real father here to talk to. I hope he'll know what to do and how to help his son. I haven't told Ramsay the story, though when the teacher told me, I felt like marrying Ramsay on the spot just to make Jad's words true.

"I'd like to meet him," Adil says.

"We're leaving day after tomorrow."

"Leaving where?"

"We go back to Washington."

Adil stands up. He begins to pace beside the table. "You can't leave."

"I have a job. Jad has school."

Adil stares at me, trying to comprehend the life I'm living outside of his own. "Please . . ." He sits down again. "Please don't go so quickly. Promise me you won't go yet. Lizzy, we can't do this again."

"Do what?"

"Walk out of each other's lives." He drops money on the table. "Let's get out of here. When do you have to be back?" For a minute I think he means to Washington. "You said you have to meet someone."

I glance at my watch. "Oh, yes. Well . . . I have time."

We walk side by side through Covent Garden without touching, like two platonic friends who don't know how to travel the road back to each other though we're bound on the same road because we have a child. I remembered walking through this open-air market with its stalls and shops and restaurants on our first date, wishing Adil would take my hand, wondering how all the other couples strolling by found each other. On this winter afternoon there are few people in the square and even fewer couples. It is a day to be indoors, but Adil and I walk towards the river. The flowing water, even the brown water of the Thames, holds a promise of motion, of destination, of times past when we walked here before.

"Let me make a phone call," I say. I stop at a booth on the Strand and call home. Jane answers. "Is anyone back?" I ask.

"Not yet. Where are you?"

"I'll tell you later. Listen, I may be a while. If Ramsay comes back, would you tell him I'll pick him up at his hotel for dinner at seven."

"Sophie said he's eating here."

"Is Sophie back?"

"No, but when they left, she said they'd be back home for dinner."

"Okay. Well, I'll be home by seven. Tell Mom."

I return to Adil. "I'm fine until six thirty." We turn onto the embankment.

"I'm supposed to meet Sahar then." Adil drives a hand through his thick black hair. "What do I tell Sahar?"

I've lived without worrying about what to tell Sahar. I don't answer. We start across the Waterloo Bridge, then pause and stare over the edge. The tide is unusually low, baring refuse along the shore. I can feel Adil watching me.

"I don't think you'd like Beirut right now," he says. "They're starting to build it back after fifteen years of war, but it's not much of a place for a child right now."

"What are you talking about?"

"That's where I live."

"So?"

"What about . . . Jad?" He says his son's name for the first time.

"What about him?" I can't figure out what's going through Adil's mind. "Jad lives in Washington with me."

"But how will I see him?"

"Come and visit us."

"My father's dying."

"I'm sorry. But your son is alive, and he and I have a life in Washington. You're welcome to visit."

"You've changed," Adil says.

"I've grown up. My parents don't run my life anymore."

"My father's dying," he repeats. "I'd like him to see my son, his only grandson, before he dies. Can I take Jad to Beirut?"

The question is outrageous and at the same time reasonable, but I'm not about to let Adil, whom I haven't seen in five years, take my son to Beirut to meet his dying grandfather, the arms dealer. "You can come with him," he adds.

We turn onto the promenade by the National Theatre. The sun has slipped from the sky. It's not yet five o'clock, but the lights are already starting to blink on along the riverfront. "Exactly who is your father?"

"What do you mean?"

"He's my son's grandfather, but I don't know who he is. I've only met him twice. I've never spoken more than a few words to him. I've read about him in the newspapers. He's an arms dealer? Is he also in politics? I'm told he worked for the Arab-U.S. coalition in the Gulf War."

"He's my father," Adil answers. "Since he was young, he's been involved in political struggle. His family's home and businesses were lost in the war over Palestine. His family lived there for hundreds of years. They were one of the largest landowners in their region. They lost everything when Israel was formed. From the time my father was my age until I was born when he was forty, he worked with other Palestinians to try to regain their homeland. He studied in Cairo, then at the American University of Beirut, where he met my mother. He speaks six languages—Arabic, Hebrew, Farsi, English, French, and German. When I was young, he was hardly ever home. He traveled all over the Middle East and in Europe."

"Is he with the PLO?"

"One way or another, everyone working for the return of Palestine is with the PLO. He helped governments, including Egypt and Jordan and Iraq, in arms sales and negotiations. He was trusted because he didn't cheat people, and he used his money not just for himself but for education of other Palestinians. But he opposed terrorism, and he opposed the sale of chemical and biological and nuclear weapons. That's where he fell out with certain people."

I wonder if Adil is inventing his father as he wants him to be. I'm beginning to suspect I've been inventing mine. "You mean he's a *good* arms dealer?"

Adil frowns. "I'm not apologizing or defending what my father does. You asked me so I'm telling you. I am not my father, Lizzy. Until my mother was killed, the struggle for my father was political, and arms were a means to an end. After my mother's murder, my father spent the next years plotting revenge, only he found there was no one enemy or rather each enemy led to another. Then he discovered it wasn't his enemies, but one of his associates who set the bomb that was meant for him but killed my mother. Some people thought my father was becoming too independent, too willing to seek peace. When we got to London, he contacted the U.S. embassy."

"Was it Molly Dees's father he contacted?"

"Mr. Dees is one of the first people I met here. My father told him about certain sales possibly linked to weapons of mass destruction. Though he distrusted the U.S., he distrusted it less than others. He also felt we needed protection. He thought the U.S. would try to stop these sales too, but that didn't happen, at least not right away. One of the suppliers to both Iraq and Iran was the man your brother worked for."

"Dr. Wagner?"

"He was afraid of my father because my father knew what he was selling and to whom, so he got my father thrown out of Britain."

"Why didn't the U.S. intervene?"

"My father's arrangements were kept informal. Anything else was too dangerous for him. He spoke only to Mr. Dees. Often they met as parents at school events. My father was worried about being exposed. He knew the British and the Americans would believe a fellow European over a Palestinian. He also came to realize that the U.S. didn't speak with one voice. Just because Mr. Dees believed him, that didn't mean others did, or even had an interest in believing him."

"Why did you go to Germany?" I ask.

"My father wanted me to finish my education. He had contacts who could protect me in East Germany. When I saw you in Berlin, investigators of your brother's death were focusing on my father. He thought he'd been set up so we had to leave. I didn't know I'd be seeing you. Everything was already arranged. My father worried that if his enemies couldn't get him, they'd get me. We went back to Jordan, but then Iraq invaded Kuwait that summer. My father's position was very unpopular in Jordan, so we had to leave there too. That's why I didn't get your letters."

I suspect he didn't get my letters because his father intercepted them.

"My father agreed to help the coalition against Iraq for the same reasons other Arabs helped, because Saddam Hussein was ruthless to everyone. My father sent me to Saudi Arabia, where I helped with refugees. I also worked as a medic's assistant on the Iraqi border. My father went into Iraq. Because he'd lived there, he knew how to get around."

"What did he do?"

"He helped set up clandestine radio and monitoring stations and gathered information. If he survived, he said he wanted to retire and spend the rest of his life living in a beautiful place with his family nearby. He wanted to see me with children he could enjoy before he died."

"Is that why you're marrying Sahar?"

"I'm ready to settle down."

"Is Sahar ready to have children?"

"She says she is."

"Well then, I guess Jad will have half brothers and sisters in Beirut."

Adil stops walking and stares over the river. We still haven't touched. He puts his hand on my shoulder, and I feel his touch like a finger running softly down my spine. "Do you think he'd ever have full brothers and sisters?" he asks.

I stare into his face, the clean, hard face of a man I hardly know anymore. "I don't know, Adil. I really don't know." I ignore the shiver in my soul. He removes his hand.

"I guess the next step is mine. Can you give me a few days . . . Please don't leave on Friday."

"I suppose we can wait until Sunday."

"Can I kiss you . . . just for old times as one of my oldest friends?" I hesitate. He cups my face in his hands. His fingertips caress my cheeks, and he kisses me gently on the lips as a friend and then as more than a friend.

* * *

When the first shot fires, I think it is a car backfiring, even though there are no cars on the embankment. Adil, however, recognizes the crack of gunfire and grabs my hand, pulling me to the ground, shielding me with his body. There are two more shots. Other pedestrians duck nearby. Adil draws us behind a bench, where we have slightly more protection between us and whoever is shooting. The shots seem to be coming from the outside stairway of the Queen Elizabeth Concert Hall.

"What's happening?" I whisper. I hold Adil's hand as we crouch on the cold pavement. Every nerve in my body is suddenly alert.

"Can you jump over that wall?" He points to the wall by the river.

I nod. "What's on the other side?"

"A small ledge. After I go, count to ten then come over at the same place. I'll be there to catch you."

Before I can ask more questions, Adil vaults over the wall. I watch him disappear, wait ten seconds, then jump myself. Before my feet hit the ground, I feel Adil's hands catch my waist and guide my landing to a narrow ledge, which at normal tides would be under water. I wonder how Adil knew the ledge was there. He must have noticed as we crossed the bridge. He's been trained to take in the details of his surroundings. He takes my hand and hugs the wall. We hurry towards the lights of the Waterloo Bridge. Beside us laps the cold, dark water of the Thames. I wonder if the shots were aimed at us. At any moment will someone lean over the wall and shoot us? Or hurrying along the slimy ridge, will we slip into the freezing water with no one to pull us out? When we reach the bridge, Adil whispers, "Can you go further?"

"Why?"

"Whoever it is may be up there."

"Were they shooting at you?" I want to protest that we're in London, not Beirut. People don't shoot at you in the streets here.

Instead of looking frightened, Adil looks alert, almost energized. "I don't know. There are a few things I haven't told you."

That seems an understatement of historic proportions. What instinct am I following to go with this man? Adil clearly isn't going to settle into a secure home with me and Jad. We stop a quarter mile farther down the river where stone steps lead to the road. Adil sprints up the stairs to see if the road is safe. He waves for me to follow. A light drizzle has turned into steady rain. As I reach the street, I'm shivering. Adil takes off his jacket and puts it around my shoulders.

"You'll freeze," I protest. But he holds his coat around me as we start down the street in a dark, industrial neighborhood where few cars pass. "Tell me what's happening. Is someone trying to kill you?" Adil's expression has turned inwards. "You must tell me!"

"I don't know. My father told me that if they kill him, they'll come after me for fear I'll take revenge. I didn't want to come to London, but Sahar wanted me to meet her college friends and family during the holidays. My father insisted I go."

"You think they were following us? We should go to the police."

"I don't want to do that until I know what's happened."

We're moving up the road in the shadows of the buildings. Every time a car passes, we step into a doorway. All I can think about is Jad. If something happens to me, what will happen to Jad? If I marry Ramsay, Jad will be safe. We'll live in a safe house on a safe street in Washington or the suburbs, and Jad can go to school nearby and play soccer and have friends. I can't allow Jad to be in danger. In that moment I understand why Mom married Winston.

On the corner Adil spots a pub, and we duck inside to get out of the rain. The streets are empty, but the pub is crowded with workers from a nearby factory. We manage to find a table near the telephone and the slot machine. Adil goes to get us coffee while I call a cab and then phone home. No one has noticed I'm not there. Sophie and Ramsay are on their way and will pick up Chinese food for dinner, according to Jane. Mom is giving Jad a bath. Jane and Henry are working on their separate stories in Winston's office.

"Don't worry," Jane answers. "Everyone's fine." I want to tell her I am not fine, but I see Adil returning to our table.

"I'll be home soon," I say. As I sit back down, I ask Adil, "Where are you staying?"

"At Sahar's." He scans the room.

"You think it's safe there? How did they find you? Who do you think it is?"

"I don't know. I better call Sahar."

I watch Adil as he goes to phone the woman who was my friend, who now has a claim on him, though if someone is trying to kill him, I suppose all claims are off. The only claim I understand is Jad's on me and mine on him, but even Jad will grow up and try as I may to protect him, he'll set out on his own road and fight his own battles, which may well be the battles his father leaves him.

"That's odd . . ." Adil looks at his watch as he sits down. "No one answers."

"You shouldn't go back there until you find out if it's safe."

A stout bald man opens the door of the pub. He pauses in the doorway and looks around. Adil's body tenses. The man goes to the bar and speaks to the bartender.

"Anyone order a taxi?" the bartender calls out.

"You better come with me," I say.

"I don't want to involve you."

"I'm involved. You can't help that." I assume whoever was shooting doesn't know me and doesn't know where I live, though the possibility that someone will follow us gives me pause. It may be dangerous for my family, but I can't leave Adil, not again. I don't know how I will explain bringing him home, but I can't think about that right now. It isn't until we are driving back over the Waterloo Bridge that I realize I'm also bringing Adil to meet his son.

*　　*　　*

Winston greets us in the hallway. I'm not sure if he knows who Adil is. We're both soaked, and he urges us to come in and sit by the fire. "Do you think my friend could borrow a sweater?"

Winston goes off to find a sweater. From the speed with which Mother appears, I realize Winston knows more than I give him credit for. Adil stands when Mother enters the room. She holds out her hand to him, but is reserved. Winston returns with a navy turtleneck and leads Adil to a bathroom where he can change.

"You need to change yourself," Mother says. "You're shivering."

Upstairs in my room, Jad is sprawled in the middle of the floor building with giant tinker toys Mom and Winston have bought him. "Jad, go get your mother the books we bought," Mother says. "They're on the table in my study." Jad pads off in his socks and pajamas to do his grandmother's bidding.

"What's Adil doing here?" Mother demands as soon as Jad leaves.

I can't tell her everything, so I start at the end. I tell her someone has shot at Adil. At least we think Adil is the target. I've brought him here to be safe.

"How do you know you weren't followed? Have you called the police?"

"We weren't followed. Adil thinks something may have happened to his father."

Jad returns with three books and a report that Sophie is in the living room.

"Did you go downstairs?" I pick him up and hold his warm, freshly bathed body close to me.

"No, but I heard her talking."

"She's probably talking to the person I want you to meet." Jad's blue eyes widen beneath thick black lashes. His large doe-like eyes, his straight dark hair, his clear olive skin remind me of Adil's in the picture with his mother. He wiggles out of my arms and runs to the stairs where he slides down on his bottom. Instead of answering the accusations buried in Mom's questions, I follow Jad. Mom follows me.

When Jad comes to a thud at the last stair, he plunges into the living room and the gathering of people as if they've all come together to see him. Everyone is silenced by his entry. Even I'm taken aback seeing him in the same room as Adil. To any adult eye he is clearly Adil's child, but Jad has no such eye. He goes over and climbs into Ramsay's lap. Ramsay holds him, though he glances at me with a question. I go over and lift Jad into my arms.

Sophie interrupts. "Ramsay, shall we go unpack the Chinese food?"

"Yes," Winston says, "I'll help you."

"Will you be staying for dinner?" Mother asks Adil. She seems unwilling to leave the room and instead sits down in the wing chair by the window.

But Adil doesn't answer the question. His whole being focuses on Jad, who is now looking over my shoulder at him. I nod for Mother to leave. I sit on the sofa beside Adil with Jad on my lap.

"Jad, this is Adil Hasan," I say.

Jad looks up at me then at Adil. "Adil is like my name," he says.

I nod.

Adil puts out his hand, and Jad shakes it with a kid's quick jerk.

"I hear you like to play soccer," Adil says.

Jad nods.

"Your mother can tell you, I used to love soccer."

"Don't you like it anymore?"

Adil smiles for the first time since he's come into the house. "Yes, I do still like it very much, but I haven't played for a while."

"I'll play with you," Jad offers.

"I'd like that."

Jad looks up at me. "Can we play now?"

"It's a little late tonight."

"Ramsay plays too," Jad offers. And then out of the blue that is childhood, he asks, "Are you my father?"

A quiver runs through me as that cosmic question locks into place. Adil reaches for him and transfers Jad to his lap. "Yes, I am, and I am very sorry I haven't met you until now."

"That's okay," Jad says. "Ramsay says he'll be my father."

I wait to see how Adil will react. "Would you like two fathers?"

Jad thinks about the proposition then shakes his head. "No." He wiggles to get off Adil's lap. Finally, Adil lets him go. Jad turns to leave the room.

"Where are you going?" I ask.

"To see Ramsay."

"Can we still play soccer?" Adil asks.

Jad thinks for a minute. "I'll play with you tomorrow."

Mother returns as Jad scurries by her in his blue flannel train pajamas. "I called Reuters," she says. "Fighting has broken out again in the South on the border. There's no word about your father. Where's he living?"

"Beirut." Adil stands to meet Mother.

"He should be fine. Today may have nothing to do with that fighting. Your father is in more danger from Iraq's Mukhabarat, I would think." I realize Mother knows more about Ibrahim Hasan than I do. "I wouldn't return to where you were staying until you confirm it's safe. You must contact the police. I don't know the level of intelligence we're dealing with, but someone could know about Lizzy and Jad. I'm surprised you brought him here," she rebukes me. "Fortunately, you're returning to Washington."

"Adil asked if we could stay until Sunday."

Mom's eyes flash to Adil. "For what purpose?"

"Your mother's right," Adil concedes. "It may be dangerous."

I want to protest, yet my first concern is for Jad, who is running now through the door. "Dinner's ready," he announces. Mother doesn't move. Jad takes her hand and begins pulling her towards the door.

"We'll be in in a minute," I say.

Mother glances over her shoulder. Her eyes contain a lecture I choose to ignore.

"He's very smart," Adil says, also choosing to ignore my mother's lecture. "I'd like to see him again before you go?"

"I think you have a soccer date tomorrow."

Adil begins to pace in front of the fireplace. "I'd like to see him without Ramsay. He's *my* son."

"Ramsay knows you're his father. He's never tried to pretend otherwise. He even tried to find you for Jad and me. Someone told him you were married with a child of your own."

Adil stops in the middle of the floor. "That was a mistake."

Suddenly reality shifts again, this time for me. "What was a mistake?" Adil doesn't answer. I stand to face him. "You mean it's true?"

"After the war, I went home. I wanted to have a life. I married someone I'd known since childhood. It was a mistake."

"You have another child?" I step backwards as though Adil has struck me. I touch the mantle above the fireplace for balance.

"My daughter wasn't a mistake."

"You said Jad was your father's only grandchild."

"I said, *only grandson*."

"Does Sahar know about this?"

"She understands."

"Understands?" How can Sahar understand so much? She understands about me? She understands about another wife? I remembered Sahar from school. She was not this understanding. "Well, I don't understand!"

Adil looks pained. "I have to call my father. Can I use a phone?"

I hesitate. We can't have an argument right now, but this revelation is clarifying my choice. I show him the phone in Winston's office. As I turn to leave, he grabs my hand. I pull it away. He takes it again. He doesn't say anything. He just holds it for a moment, then lets go and dials the operator.

*   *   *

Jane and Henry are making plans to meet Sophie and possibly Ramsay in Cairo when I come into the dining room. Jad is sitting between Ramsay and Sophie, who is helping him cut up pieces of chicken. Henry is leaving in two weeks for his posting, and Jane has just confirmed she's leaving the following month. Sophie is leaving in March for a posting in either Egypt or Morocco. By spring I'll be the only one of us left in America. When I enter the room, the conversation stops. "Adil's using the phone," I say.

"Where's he calling?" Winston asks.

"Beirut, I think."

"Where in the house?"

"I let him use the phone in your office. He's using a credit card," I add as if Winston's concern is who pays for the call.

"I don't want him in my office." Winston has let Jane and Henry use his office. Ramsay has used his office. "There are papers in my office."

"Adil's not going to look through your papers."

"If Winston doesn't want him there, he shouldn't be there," Mother says.

Winston stands.

"Where are you going?" I ask. "He's trying to reach his father."

"He can reach his father in the den."

I glance around the table. Only in Jane's and Grandma Sha's eyes do I see any sympathy. Henry and Grandpa aren't aware of what's going on, but everyone else looks at me as though I've broken a family trust by bringing Adil home now that Ramsay is the presumed intended. Ramsay doesn't meet my eyes. "I'll go tell him," I say.

Adil's head is buried in his hands. Rather than scanning Winston's desk for stray papers, his eyes focus on a small circle he's spiraling inwards with a pen on a Post-it as he listens. He doesn't hear me enter.

"So what's left? Where's Raja? Can you get out?" Suddenly he gives a start. "What was that? Hello...hello!" He taps the phone. "Hello..." He sees me in the doorway.

"Is everything all right?"

"The phone went dead." He picks it back up.

"I'll show you another phone." He's already dialing. I step over to him. "Adil, I have to show you another phone. Winston needs to use his office." Adil's body strains as if he's poised to sprint to wherever he's calling if he can't get through. As we head downstairs to the small den off the garden, I ask what happened.

"My family's not there."

I wonder which family. His father? His wife and child? "Who were you talking to?" I show him the phone by the sofa in the den.

"The housekeeper, but then there was an explosion and the phone went dead." He begins to redial. This time the operator says all the lines are down, and he will have to try later.

"Did you reach your father?" I'm standing over him.

"No one answers there either. The phone just rings and rings."

"What did the housekeeper say?"

"My wife—my former wife," he emphasizes as if answering my charge, "lives near Tyre and went to her parents' home. The house-keeper was about to go too. There's mortar fire all along the border." He stands from the couch as if going somewhere himself, then stops as though uncertain where to go.

"Do you want to stay here?"

"Your mother wouldn't like that. She's right; it could be dangerous."

I don't imagine anyone tracking Adil here, but there's much about Adil's life I can't imagine. We've shared one year of our youth and one night of our young adulthood. Is that enough to build a life on? As if reading my thoughts, he reaches out and touches my shoulder, then gently draws me to him without trying to explain or answer any of the questions racing through my mind. The situation is impossible. There is no space for us. Adil will have to go back to Lebanon; I have to go back to Washington. Only Jad offers hope that the space exists if we have the imagination to create it. Yet Adil and I haven't been together long enough to know how to occupy the same space. Adil is holding me with his chin on top of my head and my cheek against his chest when Mother opens the door.

"I'm sorry to intrude," she intrudes. "I wanted to know if you're staying for dinner."

We move apart. "I'm very sorry to be inconveniencing you, Mrs. West." Mother waves aside the apology. "I should probably be leaving."

"I'll get your clothes from the dryer," Mother agrees. "I can call the police for you if you like or just a cab?"

"A cab, please."

"Where will you go?" I ask after Mother leaves.

"To Fatin's. I'll be safe there."

"When will we see you?"

"Jad and I have a soccer date tomorrow, I believe."

* * *

The next morning, I tell Jad only that we're going to my old school to play soccer. I don't tell him we're meeting Adil. I don't want him to mention that fact to anyone. Ramsay and Sophie are flying back to Washington at noon. Ramsay has moved his departure forward because he says he has to get back for business. Mother urges me to go with them, but I tell her I can't change my tickets, and I need another day.

As Ramsay and I say goodbye, I choose not to explain myself, and he chooses not to ask. I don't know what will happen between Adil and me, and I don't want to lie to Ramsay. Anything I say might end up hurting him, so we say goodbye in a state of painful ambiguity. Sophie, however, tells me in no uncertain terms that I'm a fool or worse if I turn away from Ramsay for Adil.

As I hug Ramsay that morning, I whisper, "I love you. I'm sorry." I do love him in many ways, and I am sorry, though Sophie would argue that if I am truly sorry and I truly love him, I wouldn't behave the way I am.

Ramsay kneels down to take a long hug from Jad. "You playing soccer today?" He ties the laces on Jad's soccer shoes. His eyes travel up to mine.

"We'll play a little," I answer. Ramsay's eyes hold me in their gaze, and I know that he knows I'm meeting Adil.

At the American School the security guard lets us in after I present an ID and explain that I want to show my child where I went to school. It's still Christmas vacation, but the school is open. Adil and I have decided the gym will be safer than meeting outside in a park. The wrestling team is practicing in the upper gym. Jad and I watch for a while then go down to the basketball court and begin kicking around the soccer ball I've brought. We run up and down the court for half an hour while I keep my eyes on the door. Every time a student comes in, I stop, but Adil doesn't show.

Finally at the pay phone in the hall, I call home for messages. Jane reports, "Serena Wagner just phoned. She said she can't meet you today after all. She's been called out of town. And Adil called right after you left." My heart sinks. "He was on his way to the airport. He said to tell you that he has to go home, that his father's been taken to the hospital. He says to tell you that he's no longer engaged to Sahar, to tell you that he wishes he could play soccer with you and Jad all day long."

"Is that all?"

"That seems quite a lot," Jane says.

"Did he leave a number or address?"

"No. But I gave him yours."

PART V

CATCHING HISTORY

CHAPTER TWENTY

It's been snowing all night and all day, and the snow is still coming down. The blizzard of 1996 is being called one of the worst in Washington's history. The news is predicting another foot before morning. Residents of our building have shoveled the sidewalk three times already and finally given up. The snow will reach the windowsills of the first-floor apartments by evening, but since it's Sunday, no one minds. The city looks magical in its white dress. No cars move on the streets, and neighbors venture outside to cross-country ski in the middle of the road. The snow is so dry you can't make snowmen or snowballs, but we play in it. Jad has already been out twice. Ramsay is on his way over with Rain, so the next excursion promises to be the best. Sophie is hiking over from DuPont Circle.

Ramsay hasn't mentioned marriage again. He hasn't asked me to explain Adil or myself. Instead, we've settled into an almost comfortable friendship. I've heard from Adil four times already, once in a phone call from Paris on his way home and then in a letter mailed from Paris, and again briefly in a bad connection by phone from Lebanon, where he told me fighting in the South has intensified as the peace process has resumed between Israel and Syria. The explosion he'd heard over the phone that evening in our home was part of a missile attack launched by Hezbollah from Tyre, which has been followed by Israeli shelling on the border. His ex-wife, who works for an international aid agency nearby, has gone to her parents with their daughter, and he is now arranging housing for them farther north where they'll be safer.

I also heard from Adil again two days ago by fax. I've only started to use email, and the internet is still problematic in Beirut where his father has been released from the hospital and moved in with a cousin. Beirut is rebuilding, he says, but the south of the country remains un-settled. *"I'm not sure where my home is in the world,"* Adil wrote. *"I have been asking myself if you and I could ever make a home together?"*

I've been asking myself the same question. I don't know what is compelling me towards this man whose future is anything but set-tled, who's disappeared from my life for years at a time. I can't talk to Sophie or Mom about my feelings because they are so sure I should marry Ramsay, but Jane listens.

"I think you're too much like Dad," she says.

"What do you mean?"

"Dad used to say, don't live a small life. He said when he fell in love with Mom, he thought their love could change the course of nations. Under all his toughness, Dad was a romantic and an idealist."

"That got him killed."

"Or he was killed when he quit believing," Jane suggests.

"What do you think he would have advised?"

"I don't know. Maybe you can find out. His papers are still at Grandma's."

Jane had sent me the key Mom gave her to the storage cabinet in Grandma's basement. Yesterday I went over and picked up three boxes of Dad's papers, which now sit in the corner of my bedroom.

As Jad and I wait for Ramsay and Rain to arrive, I'm writing out birthday invitations for his preschool class. Jad is looking out on the street, sitting on the window seat of our new three-bedroom apartment I'm finally earning enough money to afford. When I finish the invitations, I start a letter to Adil. I can't answer his question. Instead I tell him about the birthday party and wonder if Power Rangers and four- and five-year-old preschoolers have any link to the life he's living. I'm writing in Arabic, at least the opening, telling him about the blizzard. I now know the word for *snow*, which I once asked Ramsay in Arabic class. Back then I wondered if there was a word, or if it had been constructed from existing concepts by the first Europeans arriving in Arabia. *Cold white sand* was the bridge I constructed. But, of course, there was a word, *thalj*, for there is snow in Arabia. There is snow in the mountains of Lebanon.

"It is snowing so hard it looks as if the sky has merged with the earth and day has folded into night."

The doorbell rings, and Jad runs to the door. Sophie stands in the hallway like an abominable snow woman. As she stamps her feet, the snow falls away. "Tea. I need hot tea." She sheds parka and boots and gloves. As I put on a pot of water, she calls into the kitchen, "I got it. Morocco in March."

"When did you hear?"

"Roger phoned this morning. He planned to tell me tomorrow, but the office will be closed because of the blizzard. I'm assigned as first secretary doing political analysis."

"What does that mean?" I step into the doorway.

"I gather information, read all the papers, write reports. I'll probably work with intelligence units on occasion. Speaking of which, Jane says she sent you the key for Dad's files."

"I was going to tell you. I picked them up yesterday. I haven't opened them."

"What do you want them for?"

"To learn about Dad." I state the obvious. What isn't so obvious is that I hope to learn something that will help me make this major decision about my own life.

Jad points out the window. "Ramsay!"

At the front door Ramsay and Rain both shake violently, shedding snow. Jad chases Rain inside as Ramsay kisses first me, then Sophie.

"Morocco in March," Sophie announces.

"Great! That's what you wanted." Sophie told me she didn't have a preference. "I'm in Morocco in June," Ramsay says.

"You are?" He hasn't mentioned that to me.

"You can stay with me," Sophie offers.

"Maybe we'll all come visit," I suggest.

"Sure," Sophie and Ramsay answer at the same time like a couple who echo each other. For a moment I feel the bottom shifting under me.

"Can I take Rain outside?" Jad interrupts.

"Let's all go." I pull the bottom back under us. We bundle up again and plunge into the whiteness where definition and boundaries no longer exist, where the snow obliterates the sky and the trees and leaves us with only its relentless beauty.

*   *   *

On a shelf in my closet, I keep Dad's size eleven Adidas sneakers, along with his early edition of Walt Whitman's *Leaves of Grass* Marvin Penn sent me. The sneakers are worn down on the outside of the left foot as if Dad used his foot as a rudder or a brake, dragging it behind him. In the drawer by my nightstand I keep his wallet Marvin Penn also sent me with the American Express card issued to Calvin Wheat. I've framed the picture that was in it of Sophie, Jane, and me at the beach around ages eight, five, and two and have set it on my dresser. His maroon sweater I've folded in the same drawer as Adil's sweater. The guns I let Marvin Penn keep. Such are the mementos I have of my father.

Now sitting on the floor of my bedroom are three boxes of papers that belonged to both Mom and Dad. My first task is to separate them. Sophie has volunteered to stay the night and help since she doesn't have to go to work tomorrow and doesn't feel like hiking back to DuPont Circle in the snow. The difficulty is that neither of us has the discipline simply to sort. We pause and read almost every page. We're sitting cross-legged on my double bed with papers stacked on the comforter. We're placing Mom's papers in a box on the floor with a blue sticker, Dad's papers with a red sticker, and combinations or papers of unknown origin in a plain box. Two hours have passed, and we've only sorted about ten inches of documents.

"Listen to this . . ." Sophie reads out another discovery. We're keeping notes on yellow pads, writing down facts and details. "In February 1969, Dad got a letter from an Arthur Baldwin telling him to follow the shipping manifests if he wanted to find the uranium. I wonder who Arthur Baldwin is. And what uranium?"

I keep track of the questions. Eventually I'll ask these questions of Marvin Penn and Mom and anyone who knew my father. It is past midnight. Most of Dad's notes and letters and memos concentrate on weapons transfers in the Middle East and uranium shipments that disappeared, the first from a nuclear enriching company in the U.S. in 1965, the next from a Belgium shipment in 1968 en route to a chemical company in Italy, but never received. That is the shipment Arthur Baldwin refers to. There are also logs of uranium shipments from South Africa and Brazil in the late 1960s, and in 1980 several hundred tons of "yellowcake"—uranium ore—disappear out of Portugal. Someone or someones are secretly buying or hijacking these shipments. Uranium flows link to nuclear buildup. As Sophie and I read and separate letters and documents, we see our father at work tracking the raw uranium and the equipment used to process it.

Also among Dad's papers are sketches and handwritten notes about satellite photographs of some structure growing in the desert. Dad has circled an area on his sketches in red and drawn an arrow off the page. Whatever seems to be growing under the arrow, Dad is following it.

"These photos are just copies; the originals would have been classified," Sophie says. "Dad must have brought home his notes one day and never taken them back. You couldn't do that today."

"Here . . . *IS* and *IQ*." I point out small, precise letters in the corner of two copies in our father's handwriting. "What do you think that stands for?"

"Some code?" Sophie suggests.

There are half a dozen sketches. Sophie digs through the pages she's already filed and pulls out a memo. "*Note grass cover. Something's fishy.*" Dad's land and sea metaphor. On the back of the sketch is: *IS, 1965*, the year Jane was born. Another more defined sketch shows a beehive structure and on the back: *IQ, JNE, 1981*, the year Dad was killed.

* * *

Around two a.m. Sophie goes to the kitchen to make coffee. I'm in a reclining position, barely keeping my eyes open, when the phone rings. I snatch the receiver so it won't wake Jad.

"Are you awake?" Even through the static I recognize the voice.

"Yes."

"Will you fly here and marry me?"

"What?"

"I can't get to you. I can't get a visa." Adil's voice drives through the phone line as if he's trying to deliver himself into the room. "I'm afraid if we don't get married now, we'll be separated for good this time."

"What's happened?"

"My father's upset I've broken my engagement and plan to marry you. He wants to stop us. He's discovered who your father was. He knew your father."

"He knew my father?" I sit up on the bed. All around me lay papers I'm searching through to find my father. "How did he know my father?"

"Your father was a man named Calvin Wheat?"

"He sometimes used that name."

"He said your father was one of the reasons my mother was killed. He tried to recruit my father to work for the U.S. government."

"But your father worked with the U.S. government."

"Much later, after he learned who killed my mother. My father is old and dying. He's angry and blaming everyone right now."

"Why did you tell him we were marrying? You haven't even asked me."

"Yes, I did. I asked you in Berlin. You said yes."

"That was years ago."

"Lizzy, will you marry me? I love you."

Sophie returns with the coffee. "Who's on the phone?"

I wave her away. Her eyebrows rise. I push my hand towards her, urging her to leave and shut the door. She backs out of the room. I'm not prepared to answer Adil's question so I say, "I can't get a visa either. They don't want Americans going to Lebanon."

"How long does it take to get married in London? I'll meet you in London."

"All the airports are closed on the East Coast." I don't know why I think he should know that. "There's a giant blizzard. Besides, I can't leave Jad."

"Bring Jad. Bring everything, your whole life."

"I can't."

"Then bring Jad and yourself. I'll wait for you in London. I'll stay with Fatin. Call Fatin and tell him when you're coming. We should have married in Berlin. With you and Jad I know how to live my life. With you and Jad I'm not afraid."

I've never thought of Adil as afraid. I think of Jane's advice that love will dispel the fear. I have no idea what my life will be if I marry Adil. I suppose I've been in love with him for almost half my life, though maybe I'm only loving an idea of him. Maybe I love him because I think he needs me. Maybe he is only loving an idea of me. Or maybe we are meant to shape a life together. I'm concerned about Jad's safety if I marry Adil. On the other hand, I'm concerned about my son's sense of himself if I turn away from his father. Sitting among my own father's papers, I long to know what he might have advised. *Keep your heart with all diligence, for out of it are the issues of life,* he counseled. Is this the life my diligent heart is seeking? I know Mother will oppose the marriage. She told me before I left, "Adil is a mistake. Don't make a second mistake."

"What was my first mistake?" I challenged. She didn't answer. She can't say Jad was a mistake.

When Sophie finally returns to the room, I try to act as if nothing has happened. "That was Adil?" She both asks and answers the question. "Are you leaving Ramsay for him?"

I wonder if she's been listening at the door. "I think Ramsay may be falling for you," I say. I haven't acknowledged this possibility until I speak it.

"Me?"

"Yes."

Sophie doesn't argue. "What do you want me to say?"

"There's nothing to say." I know Sophie likes Ramsay, though she won't allow herself to admit more than friendship. I pick up the photos from the bed. "I think I know what IS and IQ are." Adil gave me the clue when he said his father knew mine. "Dad was tracking the building of the atomic bomb in Israel and then in Iraq. Somewhere in this story I think Calvin Wheat met Abraham Zill."

"Who are Calvin Wheat and Abraham Zill?"

"Poles of history that seem to have come together in my life."

*   *   *

My mother would argue that history is not coincidental. In her articles, she traces economic and political relationships, declining growth rates, military spending, social spending, political instability, war. History has patterns that can be traced and events that can be sourced in economic and political theory. History has a DNA that runs through world events, she believes. As I read my father's papers, especially his memos to himself, I see that he has less faith in the information he's spent his life pursuing and instead considers intuition as a guide, and character as a determinant of history.

"We are blind to the future. We don't understand the present because we recognize only what we've seen before. We don't see what we don't want to see." My father scribbled this note in August 1980 in the back of a small, green spiral notebook in which he recorded a meeting with "a young man on vacation." It isn't clear if the young man or Dad was on vacation. They met late one night when neither could sleep, at an outside hotel lounge overlooking the Mediterranean. According to his notes, they talked as one talks to a stranger in the moonlight, as if what passes between will have no consequence in the morning. Dad refers to the young man only by the initial V. It isn't clear from his

notes if Dad has put himself in V.'s path or if he has met him by accident. Sophie says the meeting must have been a setup by Dad, who must have found out from a contact that V. was unhappy and was going on vacation.

"Why do you say that?" I ask.

"Because that's how agents work."

When Dad asks the young man what he does, V. answers, "You don't want to know what I do." Finally, he tells Dad that he works in a place called Dimona, the facility my father has studied in satellite photographs and intelligence data. Dad has left the CIA by this meeting, and it isn't clear from his notes if he's on an assignment from the Agency or working on his own project. He mentions "my project" in his later notebooks. Whatever his reasons, he can't resist pursuing a firsthand report on all the secondhand data he's studied. The man offers incomplete information, but it is enough to confirm what Dad and others have long ago concluded: that beneath the ground cover of the arid earth, behind the barbed wire fences in the desert, nuclear bombs and warheads are being produced in Israel.

Dad wrote a memo after that meeting to the head of the CIA's Office of Science and Technology. A copy of the memo is in his files. *"We all know what's happening at Dimona, but have not pressed to set it under international controls because we're afraid to look the beast in the eye. Does the President really believe there are good atomic bombs and bad ones? The same deception, the same suppliers are now building in Iraq with a far more dangerous partner. The Osirak reactor there will soon go critical. Perhaps it's time I go critical?"*

Dad's threat would not have been taken lightly. Dad left the CIA in 1976 shortly after Senate hearings exposing bribes by American corporations to foreign officials to encourage arms deals, some of which linked to CIA activities. Dad's written testimony is in his files though some of the testimony, which had to be cleared by the Agency, has been redacted. His handwritten scribbles in the margins are hard to read, but may have been part of his actual testimony. He doesn't name names, but he breaks ranks by talking at all. The committee hearings on arms sales led to public hearings on the CIA itself. Before those were over, Dad had resigned.

V. told me he's thinking of quitting, Dad wrote in his notebook. *He talked about disappearing into another time and place and starting all over. We talked about how lives are determined by choices, sometimes small decisions we hardly realize we're making which shape the rest of our days. Do I go to a movie or to a party? At the party, do I speak to the woman talking to my college roommate? Do I ask her to a movie? Do I ask her to marry me, this woman from the party who was speaking to my college roommate, the woman I took to the movie who looked me in the eye and listened as most women I've met don't know how to listen and challenged what I said with experience of her own? If I spend the rest of my life with this woman, will I grow tired of her and she of me, or will I spend the rest of my life trying to prove myself worthy of her? I told V. his was not a life, living under the earth building an atomic bomb. The love of a woman, the smile of a child—that is a life worth choosing.*

I couldn't sleep and returned to the patio and the moon. I fear I'm losing the love of that woman I asked to the movies, and I see too rarely the smiles of my children because I too have gone to live underground with an atomic bomb and its fear of the future. I look up at the moon that shines on my family, who are perhaps looking up at the moon and thinking of me.

"Sophie . . ." I shake her shoulders. "Sophie . . ." Outside the snow is still falling, illumined by the yellow streetlight.

"What . . . What time is it?"

"It's almost four." I hand her Dad's notebook. "Do you think something was wrong between Mom and Dad?" She sits up and reads the entry. "You think Mom would tell us?"

Sophie rolls her eyes. "You can ask, but knowing Mom . . . What else have you found?" She heads into the bathroom.

"Nothing as personal." When she returns, I show her a stack of memos about a nuclear buildup in Iraq and Dad's notes of frustration. *Our allies France and Germany are key providers. Israel has the bomb so why shouldn't the Arabs, they reason. Iraq will contain Iran, they argue. The truth is everyone is making money hand over fist.*

I show Sophie all the notebooks except one dated October 1981, when Dad jotted notes about someone he called A.Z. *Can't convince A.Z. his friends are his enemies. He told me if I come again, he will kill me, but he looked me in the eye so I know he will not slip behind my back.* I reason that A.Z. could be Abraham Zill, the name Adil's father used in East Berlin. I slip this notebook under my pillow. It has the most recent date and must have been among Dad's final effects found in his hotel room and shipped to Mom after his death.

* * *

"Was something wrong between your father and me? Is that what you're asking?" Mother protests when I call.

I'm talking to her on the phone from my bedroom as I watch the snow coming down. It has been snowing for thirty-six hours. The bushes and cars are just gentle curves on the landscape now. It is hard to remember what the street looked like before. It's hard to remember when it wasn't snowing. Sophie left around nine. I told her that I was going to tell Ramsay I can't marry him and that Ramsay might want to talk to her. "I think you're dreaming," she says.

"Having looked through all your father's papers, that's what you want to know?" Mother asks.

"Why do you sound angry?" The censure in my mother's voice is her way of diverting me. That she feels the need to divert makes me wonder if I've struck a truth. Was she angry at my father when he left? How hard that must have been for her when he never came back.

"I also want to know what project Dad was working on. He writes about *my project* in his last notebooks."

"He was writing a book, though he doubted he would ever be able to publish it, but he wanted to write it anyway. No one knows where these files are. I should never have given Jane the key."

"They're almost twenty years old. They can't hurt us now." I remember the men who came to our house, remember my mother riding to Grandma Sha's house with the box of papers, remember her returning home without the box. "What are you afraid of?" I ask.

"The past doesn't fade in twenty years, Elizabeth. You understand that, don't you?"

"You always told me the past was the past, not to dwell there but to go forward with my life."

"I also taught you to choose what you took forward with you and what you left behind."

That was true. When I was eleven, I had to sort through all my clothes and toys and books when we moved to London and bring only two suitcases and three boxes and one piece of furniture. I chose the bed I'd picked out with Dad and Mom for my tenth birthday, the bed whose canopied sky has sheltered me in London half my life.

"I knew a politician once," Mother says, "in many ways a decent man, but he was involved in a terrible deed. Neither he nor his advisors would admit what they'd done, even the parts of the story I could confirm. Instead he told half-truths and twisted the story. Over time I watched this man forget other things until finally his mind shut down, and he could remember nothing, not even his own family. I always thought he couldn't bear the responsibility that went with memory, so he lost his memory, and history crushed him. I wanted you and your sisters to be able to live on top of history, not under it."

I hear a sigh on the other end of the phone as though my mother has been holding her breath for years.

"I'll bring the files with me," I say. "They'll be safer in England." I'm turning into a courier, whisking Dennis's notes out of harm's way to America and Dad's to England. I realize I've never gotten the file of Dennis's notes back from Marvin Penn. I add Marvin to the list of people to call today.

"Are you coming here?" Mother asks. "Is Jad coming?"

"I'm bringing Jad and a large suitcase."

"Is anything wrong?"

"No, but nothing is simple either." I don't tell Mother about Adil. I don't know what will happen between Adil and me, but I need to see him and spend time with him before I can know if he is the love I will set the course of my life with. "I'll come as soon as the snow clears."

*   *   *

Ramsay walks over for lunch. The city is still shut down. Snow plows haven't reached our street. After lunch, Jad and Rain go into the living room, and Ramsay and I stay at the kitchen table. All through lunch Ramsay seems to be waiting to hear what I will say. I don't know exactly what I will say. As I pour the coffee and set a plate of fruit and cheese on the table, I know my time is up.

But before I can speak, Ramsay says, "Why don't you and Jad come with me to Morocco in June? We can visit Sophie, and we can get married."

"Married?"

"Or we can marry in London on the way so your family will be there."

I didn't see this new proposal coming. What has he been thinking these weeks? Did he assume because I haven't talked about Adil that Adil isn't in my thoughts? "Ramsay . . ." He is trying by sheer logic and will to move me. I'm thrown off my plan. "I still have a lot unsettled from the past."

"I'm in the present, Lizzy. I want to be in your future and in Jad's future." He takes my hands on the table and holds them firmly as if he can settle all the confusion and ambiguity with a strong grip.

"But Jad's real father is alive, and he wants that too."

Ramsay keeps hold of my hands. He stares at me from deep inside himself as if trying to find what is deep inside me. I want to hide from his stare. Slowly he releases my hands. "If I thought I could fight for your heart, I would."

My fingers are flushed from his grip. "I'm sorry." I touch his hand, then stand and go into the bedroom. From the same drawer where I keep my father's wallet, I take out the large blue stone Ramsay gave me a year ago. I set it on the kitchen table. "Did you know aquamarine is Sophie's birthstone?"

Ramsay doesn't answer.

"Sophie told me you are one of the most decent people she's met, and I agree."

Still, Ramsay doesn't answer.

"But, Ramsay, I can't marry you. I love you, but not in the way I want to love a husband if I ever have a husband. Maybe life brought us together for other reasons."

"What other reasons?" He hasn't taken his eyes off me. His focus is so intense that suddenly I worry I've misread his feelings for Sophie. I glance into the living room where Jad and Rain are playing tug-of-war with a sock.

"I didn't know I'd see Adil. I didn't know how I'd feel."

"How do you feel?"

"I still don't know entirely, but I have to allow the possibility that I'm still in love with him and the possibility of giving Jad his real father as his family."

"I see."

I look down into the cold coffee in my cup. I feel ill. I don't know how not to hurt this man I care about. "I wish you'd stay part of our lives . . . the way we've been these last few weeks. I thought you . . . I thought you'd stepped back because . . ." Still, Ramsay remains silent. "I thought with Sophie . . . I mean she's terrific, and you and she have become such good friends . . ." I'm on difficult ground here, and Ramsay isn't helping. "My whole family likes you. And, of course, Jad . . ."

Ramsay fingers the blue stone. "Are you giving this back to me?"

"I told you I'd keep it until you found someone else you wanted to give it to."

"And I told you I wouldn't."

I wonder if I'm making a mistake, but I feel dishonest holding onto Ramsay while I pursue the possibility of a life with another man. "I don't want to keep someone else from coming into your life. I know Sophie also considers you a friend . . ."

Ramsay puts the stone in his pocket. "I have to go."

"Will you call me?" He doesn't answer. "Jad and I are going to London as soon as the airport clears. I wanted to tell you."

Ramsay doesn't ask why we're going or how long we'll be gone. As he leaves, he touches Jad on top of the head.

I feel ashamed that I've been so sure with Sophie about how Ramsay feels, as if his feelings are mine to direct. After he leaves, I call Sophie. I tell her that Jad and I are going to London and that I've hurt Ramsay, and I wish she'd call him. Hurting him is the last thing I want to do.

"You want me to make things better for you, Lizzy?" she asks. "I can't do that."

CHAPTER TWENTY-ONE

IT'S BEEN ALMOST a year since I've talked with Marvin Penn. Each February he sends Jad a birthday present. I'm surprised when I'm told his phone is disconnected and there's no listing for Penn Security Systems or for Marvin Penn in the Northern Virginia, D.C., or southern Maryland directories. I feel a momentary panic that I have let this problematic link to my father slip away. I track down the phone number of his ex-wife in Falls Church, VA, and phone her, explaining that I'm a business friend of her former husband and am trying to locate him.

"At least have the courtesy to conduct your liaison out from under my nose," Noreen Penn answers.

"Liaison? No . . . no . . . I'm the daughter of one of his old partners. He has some papers of mine."

"What partner?"

"My father was Jesse West."

"Jesse West?" She repeats the name as if she recognizes it but is trying to summon up a specific memory. "You're Jesse West's daughter?"

"Yes." I explain that Marvin's phone and businesses are no longer listed in the directory.

"He probably owes someone money," she says. "Wait a while. He'll resurface under a new name and new business."

I wonder if Mother would ever have sounded so bitter about my father or if I would ever sound that way about anyone. "Do you have any idea how I might reach him?"

Noreen Penn hesitates then gives me the name of a bar in McLean, Virginia. "He sometimes goes there to meet old friends." I call the bar and leave my name in case Marvin comes in.

Marvin phones the next day. We agree to meet at a restaurant near the DuPont Circle Metro early that evening. For reasons he doesn't elaborate, he doesn't want to meet at our old coffee shop.

Marvin is sitting in the far corner with his back against the wall when I arrive at Kramerbooks, a café on a glassed-in porch attached to a bookstore. His beard has grown past his chin. He wears wire glasses, has lost more weight. He looks like a wizened old professor rather than the beefy, ruddy-cheeked man who introduced himself to my sisters and me seven years ago. He resembles a picture in one of my textbooks of Lenin in his last years, though I doubt Lenin ever wore a Hawaiian shirt. I wonder if this is Marvin in old age or in disguise.

I slide into the chair opposite him and set my notebook of questions between us. It's only five in the afternoon, but outside the streetlights have switched on.

"It's damn pretty out there, isn't it?" Marvin says. "Few more days it'll all be brown slush, but right now it's damn pretty."

I look out the window. The city is brilliant under the snow, which continues to fall as a light dust from the sky and the trees. It covers the park benches and the shrubs of DuPont Circle. The landscape has turned into one white rolling snowbank. Unless you know what lies beneath, you can't distinguish a bench from a shrub from a car parked at the curb. It is for just such definition beneath the cover of years that I've come to Marvin Penn.

We are blind to the future. We don't understand the present because we recognize only what we've seen before. We don't see what we don't want to see. I think of my father's words. I know what I don't want to see. I'm pursuing my fear in the hope it will recede and dissolve if I get close enough. I will set my box of spiders on the table and see who flinches. Was Ibrahim Hasan the "A.Z." who threatened to kill my father? Did he kill my father? It is difficult to believe such a coincidence. But my father would have said it only appears as coincidence because I don't yet understand the pattern. Grandma Sha once told me that children bring your lives back to you. Jad has done that for me as I am bringing Mother's past back to her, not because I want to make her face what she doesn't want to face, but because her past intersects my future. Life, it seems to me, is a giant helix where everything intersects and comes back on itself with variation.

Marvin slides an envelope across the table. "Here's the report I sent to your mother and to the British Commission investigating arms sales to Iraq."

"Did you figure out what Dennis's notes meant?"

"Most of them. They include specifications for machine tools and processing equipment and the components for nerve gas and other chemical and biological compounds delivered to military installations, mostly in Iraq, but also to Libya and Iran. They include false end-user certificates and documents classifying military goods for civilian use. Most of the orders were processed out of Europe, especially France and Germany, then routed through points of entry in the Middle East like Jordan or Lebanon. Some of the certificates are signed by British officials and violate UN sanctions. Some have gone through U.S. Customs, approved by the Commerce Department."

He hands me a second envelope. "Here are the original notes. I sent the copies to the Commission. I'm afraid your stepbrother was caught up in an illicit network I doubt he fully understood, but he understood enough to keep these papers. His notes indicate he was keeping track of equipment and goods being shipped via Wye Holdings in

England, a company Dr. Wagner made him a partner in, at least on paper. It's the holding entity set up to shield other companies, including Advanced Technology Partners, KBT Engineering, Aladdin International, Aladdin Investments, and Midland Tools."

Marvin takes a paper napkin and sketches a diagram of companies in a maze of boxes and lines. "The structure looks something like this as best I can make out . . ." One box spawns baby boxes—or companies—which spawn other companies, most dangling on separate lines, but a few are connected to each other with double lines. "Dennis's partnership wasn't worth much financially. The value was in these companies, though most are now bankrupt. Dr. Wagner told investigators the equipment shipped was for a pesticide plant or for a car factory or a phosphate refinery, but these notes"—Marvin touches the envelope—"in what I'm certain is Dr. Wagner's handwriting, suggest otherwise. The pesticide plant produced nerve gas and the car factory and the phosphate refinery were covers for uranium enrichment facilities. These notes aren't a smoking gun, but they're ammunition and will be considered evidence."

"Who do you think killed Dennis?"

"My guess—his Iraqi partner. British intelligence had started to lean on Dennis regarding Wye Holdings, and Dennis was poking around to get information for them. I doubt he did that undetected. Dr. Wagner has nasty friends. He also sent your stepbrother to meet with Russian arms traders. I don't know why. The Russian mafia could have made the hit. Dr. Wagner may have been setting Dennis up since I suspect your stepbrother had discovered more about his business than he intended."

I remember Adil telling me that his father thought Dr. Wagner had set both of them up, though I also remember Serena saying Dr. Wagner was afraid after Dennis was killed. Dennis perhaps turned a blind eye, and by the time he opened his eyes, he'd ventured too far into the dark.

"Did my father's work link to any of this?" I ask.

Outside the window, a lone pedestrian trudges by carrying a small bag of groceries. Marvin pauses to watch him move up the street before he answers. "I don't have evidence that Wagner got involved until 1982. That was a year after your father died. That's when the Iraqis began writing large orders in the West as the war with Iran escalated. But your mother thinks she encountered Wagner once with your father in Buenos Aires. She remembers a short, dapper man meeting with your father at the hotel, friendly, yet menacing, offering services your father didn't want."

"Why does she think it was Dr. Wagner?"

"She can't confirm. But the insistent tan, the clothes . . . and she remembers the man spoke French though he was in Argentina and your dad was an American. Your father had gotten wind of a project with Argentine generals and ex-Nazis and other exiled German scientists. The intelligence was that they were working to produce a ballistic missile that could deliver nuclear warheads. After your father died, that project, called Condor, expanded with Iraqis secretly sponsoring the research. No doubt there were overlapping clients and suppliers, including Gerald Wagner's father who lives in Argentina. He's the one who first connected Wagner Machines and Tools to that supply train. But I don't have hard evidence that your father met the junior or senior Wagner, though I've wondered if Wagner remembers your mother."

I try to imagine what my father would have done if he'd lived and how he would have related to me. I want to understand the continuity of our lives, but at the same time I want to live on top of history, as my mother counsels, not under my father's history.

"Your father didn't trust anyone when it came to nuclear weapons," Marvin adds. "They were all weapons from hell as far as he was concerned. A dark vision of the future took over in his head as he watched us and our allies selling hundreds of millions of dollars in all kinds of weapons into the Middle East. He watched France and Germany building laboratories that would produce chemical weapons for other countries. He suspected correctly that France was building a nuclear reactor for Iraq, just as it had for Israel. Given the amount of yellow-cake uranium and hot cells the Iraqis were purchasing on the black market, he warned that Iraq was working to manufacture a nuclear bomb in a few years, but no one really listened. The politicians had other agendas. The Israelis were watching the same thing, however, and they blew up two reactor cores in 1979 while the cores sat on a dock in France waiting to be shipped out to Iraq. But the French and Iraqis just started all over again and eventually installed the cores, one of which the Israelis blew up in 1981, shortly before your father was killed."

"Was that the one at Osirak?" I've been reading the history. Marvin nods. "What happened to my father, Marvin? I have a memory of that day, of a phone call the afternoon before he died." I remember staring out the open front door as the shadows fell in the yard.

Marvin's face grimaces as if bearing down on his own pain. "You must have been what . . . nine or ten?"

"I was ten."

"I told your father not to go on that trip. They'd figured out who he was, but he said he needed information. This would be his last trip, then he'd sell out his partnership in West Penn to me. He was going to write a book and teach."

"Are you the one who called our house that afternoon?"

Marvin nods.

"I remember you said, 'They've sanded the gas tank.' How did you know if you weren't there?"

"There were other agents on the ground. I was nearby, and one of them contacted me. He couldn't find your father to tell him. Calling your home was a desperate attempt to reach him."

I remember Mother frantically making phone calls that night. "Did Mother call you back? Did she know it was you?"

"She tried, but she never reached me or your father."

I wonder if Mother carried that failure with her. I see that Marvin has carried it. "Who killed him?" I ask.

"I don't think they ever officially found out."

"Unofficially."

Marvin meets my eyes. "Some questions are best left unanswered."

"Do you know the answer?"

"I could come up with a short list."

"Who would be on the list?"

"The arms exporters he was closing in on, the governments who were selling and buying the arms."

"If you were a betting man?"

"The buyer. Your father was turning into a real threat."

"Who was the buyer?"

Marvin shifts in his seat. "Don't dig up what's been laid to rest."

"Are you afraid?" I ask.

Marvin bends over the bowl of chili that has just been set before him and starts eating. "Not a day goes by I'm not afraid of something. That's the business I'm in. But I know the rules. I know how to get through the day. You don't."

"You won't help me?"

"I don't know how to help you."

"Tell me if you've ever heard of someone called A.Z."

"A.Z. what?"

"I don't know. Just A.Z. Maybe Abraham Zill."

Marvin looks up from his bowl, a wedge of bread in his hand. "I remember an Abraham Zill. He was an Arab, but sometimes used the name of a Jew, spoke Hebrew and Arabic, moved in and out of Israel and Egypt, Iraq, Lebanon, Jordan, and other Arab countries, even Iran."

"Did my father know him?"

"Probably."

"Do you think that's who Dad was meeting with?"

"Where did you hear of him?"

"I've got sources too."

"This all happened over fifteen years ago. I didn't know Abraham Zill, but I recall your dad felt you could rely on what he said, that he wouldn't cheat you."

I watch Marvin hunched over his chili, summarizing his and my father's career in a dry, hard voice. On the phone, Marvin has told me that he's gone undercover, not into debt as his wife suggests. "What are you working on now?" I ask.

He smiles, showing his stained teeth with the gaps in the rear. "Nothing I can tell you about. I'd recruit you if you weren't Jesse's daughter, but your daddy would rise up from his grave and shoot me. He'd be very proud of you, but he'd fight like hell to keep you out of this business. I think about you and your son, especially on his birthday each year."

"I know. Thank you for the presents. Where are you living these days?"

"I'm on the road, at least since your son's second birthday."

"What happened on his second birthday?"

Marvin rubs his beard and stares at me over his glasses. "Maybe it was the day before his birthday."

"What . . . ?"

"You don't remember? Well, why should you? His birthday is what you should remember. I hope you're teaching your son to keep his eyes open. These are dangerous times. Here . . . I've got an email address now. You can reach me in cyberspace if you need." He hands it to me: mpmp2@aol.com.

He isn't going to tell me where he lives or what he's investigating so I ask him one last question about the past. "If you were trying to find out how my father's plane crashed, who would you ask?"

He thinks for a moment. "Seems I remember you had a General for a neighbor back then."

*   *   *

At home that night I look up the *New York Times* on the internet for February 27, 1993, Jad's second birthday:

EXPLOSION AT THE TWIN TOWERS
BLAST HITS TRADE CENTER
BOMB SUSPECTED
5 KILLED, THOUSANDS FLEE SMOKE IN TOWERS

I'd forgotten that the explosion in New York was the day before Jad's birthday and the anniversary of the end of the Gulf War. I read late into the night the articles that followed the detonation of a 1500-lb car bomb in the parking garage of Tower One of the World Trade Center. If the truck had been parked just slightly nearer the foundation supports, the whole tower would have fallen, speculated experts, and in the process knocked down Tower Two. The investigation to find the perpetrators was massive and global.

*   *   *

Rosalie Campbell invites Jad and me over for dinner. She says Joe will pick us up in his four-wheel drive. He's going into town anyway— Washington is still "town" to her—and then he'll bring us home afterwards. Rosalie greets my call as if no time has passed, as if our visit seven years ago is last week and nothing is odd about the fact that I haven't phoned before today. Do I know Joshua had a two-year-old son and is living in Alexandria and Nora Mann is pregnant and living in Baltimore? If the weather weren't so bad, wouldn't it be fun for all of us to get together, maybe when I get back from visiting Mom in London—please pass on her love to my mother. She doesn't seem curious to know why I want to see her and Joe. I say only that I have a few questions about my father I want to ask them. Beneath the surface of her friendliness, however, I hear a tremor in her voice as we say goodbye. But then she adds, "I'll make chicken fricassee. I remember how much you always liked my chicken fricassee." Rosalie Campbell knows parts of my childhood better than I do. She remembers the details.

Joe Campbell rolls up at 6:00 p.m. in his Jeep Cherokee and packs us in. He sets off down our block, which still hasn't been plowed, as if he is a teenager on a racetrack. By 6:40 we are at the Campbells' home in Bethesda. As soon as I enter, I remember everything: the dried flowers on the hall table, the painted coat hooks behind the door, even the red metal umbrella stand spread out like an umbrella, now chipped and in need of paint. I tell Jad we're going to visit neighbors I grew up next to, the same way Mahela is our neighbor, but I haven't been prepared for this time warp. Even the smell of onions and garlic, cloves and carrots-chicken fricassee. It's as though life hasn't changed here. A golden retriever comes bounding around the corner.

"Daisy . . . Daisy . . ." Rosalie cautions. "This is Daisy III," she introduces. "You remember Daisy I?" Instantly, Jad bonds with Daisy, who starts chasing him. "Your son looks like you and your father," Rosalie says. "And look, he's not a bit afraid."

"Oh, he loves dogs."

"Just like you did." Joe settles into the brown velveteen recliner in the living room. His 6'3" frame that I remember bearing down on me as a child is now thick around the middle and stooped, his white hair wispy, and he has a beard. He looks more like Santa Claus than the Superman I once confused him with as a child. "You used to spend hours over here with Daisy. Sometimes we weren't sure if we should feed you at the table or on the floor." He laughs at his own joke.

I ask if I can help with dinner, and Rosalie lets me join her in the kitchen where she's draining rice and buttering garlic bread. The kitchen now has a center island with a butcher block top and pots hanging overhead. It feels safe, though I can't imagine myself living in it or cooking in it. I equate Rosalie Campbell, who's always had a soft, maternal plumpness, with a kind of settled domesticity I've idealized but never lived.

"Now tell me, what is it you want to know?" I hear an edge in her voice.

"I want to know what happened to my father."

"Don't you know?" She stares at me with a less than motherly look, as if my curiosity may threaten her home.

"I know what I've been told, but I don't think I've been told everything."

"Why do you come here and not to your mother?" She dumps the rice into a serving bowl.

"I've asked her over the years. There's only so much she'll tell me."

"Why do you assume we know more?"

"I don't, but I thought it was worth asking. You were his friends." I watch her broad, lined face and decide to press a little harder. "Joe may have been in a position to know more . . . he worked at the Penta-gon, didn't he?"

"He worked for the Pentagon his whole career. He valued loyalty to his country even above his family. He wouldn't have done anything to hurt his country."

She answers more than I've asked. "I'm not suggesting that."

"Joe would never have revealed information even if he disagreed with our policy. He understood he was only one player in a very big game."

"Is that what people think my father did?"

"Joe said the U.S. government was the United States of America, and if it wasn't always right, even if we didn't always agree . . ."

"What kind of information?" I ask. I'm helping her set the kitchen table and concentrate on setting down the wood-handled forks and spoons so I won't appear too anxious.

"You don't mind that we eat in the kitchen, do you?" she asks. "We've got the silver in the dining room, but we hardly ever bring out the silver anymore."

"What kind of information?" I repeat.

"Your mother was stubborn. She hurt you girls in my opinion. Don't tell her I said that, though I said it to her before she left. By not accepting the money the government offered at your father's death, by taking you all the way over to England . . . I don't know what I would have done in her place, but I told her I thought she was hurting you."

"What was her place?"

"She loved your father." Rosalie keeps answering questions I hav-en't asked. I'm trying to understand what reference is in her head. "But she had trouble accepting her place."

"What place? As my father's wife?"

Rosalie Campbell's soft hazel eyes lose focus. "Honey, I wouldn't be the one to tell you that. You have to ask your mother those things."

"Did they fight, my mother and father?" I try to leap to the territory she's speaking from.

"Your mother and father were two strong-willed people. Joe and I used to say that. How did two such strong-willed people end up together? But they loved each other. They just had different drumbeats going on in their heads. I don't think I'd be saying anything against your mother to say she wasn't cut out to be the wife of someone in your father's business." She says *my father's business* as if it were still a secret.

"Do you know how my father died?"

"His plane crashed into the ocean."

"How did it crash? I understand two other people were killed?"

"That was a long time ago. To tell you the truth, I don't remember many of the details." Rosalie takes a spoonful of the fricassee sauce and tastes it. "I think we're about ready. Can you call Joe? He's probably on the floor with your son and Daisy. You should see him with his own grandson. He may not have spent that much time with his own children growing up, but he's making up for it as a granddad."

Joe and Jad come in with Daisy between them. Joe Campbell moves deliberately, his hands reaching out to touch the counter and then the table as he walks. I used to be a little afraid of him as a child, but now he reminds me of my grandfather, and he wears wrinkled chinos like Winston and a flannel shirt and work boots. "This kid of yours is going to run an army some day," he says.

Mom predicts Jad will be a journalist because he's so curious; Winston thinks he'll make a great salesman because he gets along so well with people. Adil wants to train him as a soccer player, and I . . . well, I don't see him as a travel agent—I don't see myself as a travel agent over time in the long run—but he does travel well. "I'm sure he'll find his own path."

*   *   *

On the way home, Joe Campbell tells me what I want to know, at least as much as he knows. As soon as we turn onto Wisconsin Avenue and Jad drifts off to sleep in the back, he says, "I understand you still got some questions about your dad. I told Rosalie I'd tell you what I can. I see you're trying to make your own life. I know that's hard to do if you don't settle up with the past." He speaks to me as an adult, and I'm grateful.

"Your mother always thought I knew more than I did, though I did know more than I told her. I've thought about your father time and again over the years. Your parents were among our closest friends, but there comes a time when even friendship . . . maybe that time will never come in your life. Your father should have gotten out of the CIA long before he did. When the Senate hearings started on corporations offering bribes for arms sales . . . well, we all knew that was going on—people saw it as the cost of doing business—but your mother didn't. She was assigned to write about the hearings. Your father warned her that she was in his backyard. She told him he should help clean up the yard. I don't believe he leaked confidential information to her, but there are some people who to this day think he violated security. And there's more than one who think he shouldn't have told Congress what he knew.

"Finally, the pressure got too much for both of them. He quit and she quit. That was their deal, but you know they couldn't quit being who they were. He became a consultant, and the Agency used him for certain projects because he was so good and knew so much, and your mother moved to editing a magazine. They loved each other—I can attest to that—but there were times when they were struggling hard to stay together. Makes me wonder why life throws some people together the way it does."

I think of Adil and me. It seems in our family the heart is determined to fight battles for love rather than ease gently into union. Perhaps it is the struggle that produces the spark that ignites the fuel that fires the engines that changes the course of history.

"Do you think Dad's plane crash was an accident?" I ask.

"I don't have evidence to the contrary. Your mother thought I did, and I guess I understand why. Two other people were killed in that crash, people of questionable background."

"I heard that. Did Dad know them?"

"We can only assume. It was a private flight. One was an arms dealer and the other a woman . . ." Joe hesitates.

"I've heard she had a record for drug smuggling."

"Yes . . . well, that too." I wonder what he meant by *too*. "You can see that the circumstances raised questions."

"What kind of questions?"

"You want me to be honest . . . ?"

For a moment I'm not sure if I do. Maybe my version is easier to live with. But how can I make decisions about my life if I don't face the truth? "Please," I say.

"People wondered . . . I mean since your father was in business for himself . . . whether he was in business for himself doing his own deals with them. Some people even questioned whether your father was spying for another government—some of his files went missing when he left the Agency. And . . ." Here he grows visibly nervous, then plunges ahead. "Whether Marie Serge was his mistress."

"Who's Marie Serge?"

"The woman. A very beautiful woman. There was no record of your father working with those individuals or trying to recruit them, so people wondered what he was doing with them."

"People thought my father was a traitor, with a mistress? Did they know my father, or were they inventing him?" I feel angry, though I don't really know my father either; but my invention doesn't include a mistress, and *my* father wouldn't have betrayed his country or his wife or his children. "Do you believe that?" I ask.

"I defended him. I don't believe he was lining his own pockets or spying for another government. But there's no way any of us can know for certain about another person. Your father had his faults—he was too much of a maverick—but I'd put money on the fact that he was true to your mother, and I couldn't say that about most men."

"What did Mother think?"

"She fought like hell after he died to find out what happened and clear his name, partly I'm sure for you girls."

"If someone did sabotage his plane, who would have done it?"

"We can't rule out that sabotage was directed at the others rather than, or as well as, your father. Your father had uncovered certain transactions. One of our allies was selling arms to one of our enemies, supplying weapons we had sold to them. We knew about it, secretly condoned it, but your father didn't know. Your father said the law was being circumvented for political ends and threatened to take the information to Congress. The government receiving the arms had a lot at stake. The U.S. government was in an awkward position. Your mother wanted us to call an investigation, but we couldn't risk it at that time."

"So the government tried to pay Mother off?"

At the question, Joe Campbell slams on the brakes. I don't know if he's reacting to what I said or to some hazard in the road. The car skids into the next lane jarring Jad awake and throwing me forward. Joe turns off the engine. He sits flushed over the steering wheel. He seems unconcerned that cars behind him are honking. "I didn't try to pay anyone off," he declares. "I risked my career to clear your father's name and get your mother a settlement to help your family."

"I'm sorry. I didn't mean you."

He leans forward and restarts the engine. I reach back and pat Jad, who has returned his head to the armrest.

"The government is bigger than any one person," Joe says.

"But it answers to the people," I suggest.

Joe drives the rest of the way in silence. On my street the yellow headlights of a snowplow glare down the block, moving slowly towards us like a giant prehistoric animal. Joe pulls up onto a snowbank, and Jad and I get out. "Thank you for dinner," I say.

"I told your mother and I tell you: the government is bigger than any one person."

I don't argue this time, but I am sure my mother did.

*   *   *

I recognize the lilting Southern voice on the phone the next morning. "I've run away!" Serena announces. "Gerald doesn't know. I told him Jack and I were taking a holiday in Switzerland. We arrived in D.C. Saturday night, the last plane to land before the blizzard. I'm not going back."

I left a message yesterday with Serena's housekeeper telling her I was coming to London and asking to see her. "Where are you?"

"At a small hotel—the Lombardy near George Washington University."

"I'll meet you in an hour."

Serena and I settle by the lighted fireplace in the Victorian lounge. At the far end of the room, a birthday party of ten-year-olds provides noise to shield our conversation. Serena has aged considerably in the last five years, her hair gray above her ears and in a swatch over her eyes, a premature gray she's allowing to show. "Where's Jack?" I ask.

"He took the train back to college this morning."

"I was so surprised to see him in London. He looks wonderful."

"He is wonderful. He's entirely too wonderful for Gerald and me. He deserves so much more." Serena lowers her voice. "But I'm afraid for him. Because of his grandfather and I suppose because of me . . . if something happens to us . . ."

"What's going to happen?"

"I've stayed with Gerald all these years to protect Jack. At least that's what I told myself. I've been putting on an act for so long, going to meetings with Gerald, pretending I wasn't paying attention, pretending I was just his escort, his trusted family member who could deliver documents and take his friends shopping . . . I've been pretending for so long I'm not sure who I am anymore." She leans closer to me on the table. "I thought I could watch what was happening and not be part of it and keep Jack safe. Gerald told me he'd protect Jack, but I'm not sure he can anymore. I'm afraid of his new partners. It was a mistake to think I could work safely inside."

"Inside what?" I ask.

Serena hands me a sheet of paper with a list of numbers. "These are the numbers of bank accounts in Switzerland, the Bahamas, Lichtenstein . . . That's where the money is."

I remember Marvin Penn telling me to follow the money. He also told me there was usually someone who knew the real story sitting in the background watching. From inside her sweater Serena pulls out another folded piece of paper and hands it to me. She glances around at the table of children in paper hats with noisemakers. The boys are having a burping contest while the girls dance by their chairs and whisper to each other.

As I open the letter, she says, "Dennis mailed it to me from Berlin before he was killed. I've carried the letter on me every day for the last five years to protect it."

"Why are you showing it to me now?"

"Because I need someone else to know, and you called me yesterday. I got your message when I phoned our housekeeper in London today. I phone each day so Gerald won't get suspicious and will think we're just on vacation. He's getting crazier every day. The investigation into illegal arms shipments is closing in on him. James, his youngest son, was arrested in Germany last week."

"James was arrested?" That would unnerve Dr. Wagner. It unnerves me. I open the letter:

Dearest Serena—

I've seen the refuse from the death machines being built here, alleys of dead dogs from the experiments. I think I've been poisoned, just as you told me you suspected your husband was poisoned. They will not want me to be walking proof of their work if they find out where I've been. You must leave Gerald now.

Yours,
Dennis

P.S. The factory in Florida is shipping out deadly gas as byproduct at night. I don't think the owner knows, but now you know. What will you do?

I look up at Serena, who is reading the letter with me for what I assume by the frayed edges is the umpteenth time. "I was going to leave Gerald, but when Dennis was killed, I got scared. Scared to stay and scared to leave, and then I just pretended that nothing had happened."

How could she do that, I wanted to ask, but Marvin has taught me to suspend judgment while I gather information. Instead, I ask, "This was all before the Gulf War?"

She nods. "During the war, Gerald shut down most of his operations because business stopped. The money stopped entirely. Gerald's father blamed him for the collapse of Wagner Machines and Tools and all the other bankruptcies. Gerald and his father had terrible fights over the phone. My German's not that good, but I understood his father was accusing Gerald of using the family's friends, then not paying them. 'I hear all over your credit is no good!' his father shouted. 'You've ruined us!' If they lived in the same city, I think his father would have shot him. That's terrible to say, but it's true." As Serena speaks, she chips the red nail polish from one of her nails.

"What is Gerald doing now?" I ask.

"He has new customers, even more frightening customers. Some are Arab. Some are Russian. They don't like women, so Gerald stopped taking me to his meetings and sending me to deliver for him, and I don't take them shopping. He's scared himself. I can tell. The other night he got drunk and tried to take away my passport. He pulled out a gun. Jack stopped him. He managed to get his grandfather to bed, but he told me he wasn't ever coming back to visit me as long as I lived with Gerald. That's when I knew we had to leave. We flew out the next morning. Jack wants to go into law enforcement. Can you believe that? I want him to have a future, but I wonder if he has a chance. He doesn't know all that his grandfather does."

"How did your husband die?" I ask.

"In a car crash on the Amalfi coast, driving much too fast, but he called the night before and told me he was sick. He was working on something for Gerald. Whenever I ask Gerald about what happened, all he'll say is, 'The Lord takes His own.' François's death took the life out of Gerald, at least for a time. That's one reason I think he's held on so hard to me, and through me, to Jack. But now the investigations in Britain and Germany are closing around him, and I'm afraid we may all end up in prison. When I called our housekeeper and got your message yesterday, I remembered you said you knew someone who might know what all the files meant. I thought maybe you could help. I copied the files like you suggested years ago and hid them."

I lean forward in my chair. "You have the files?" I can't believe Serena listened to me.

"I've thought of them as my insurance policy."

I think of them as a smoking gun. "Yes. There is someone you should meet."

CHAPTER TWENTY-TWO

I PANIC SOMEWHERE over Greenland. At least it looks like Greenland when I wake in the dark plane and lift the window shade to see a full moon over an expanse of ice and snow. By the window, Jad sleeps curled into himself with his head on my lap. I'm racing back to London to pursue an illusion. I'm old enough to understand that I don't know Adil well enough to commit to spending the rest of my life with him. Before I left, I called Grandma Sha. I told her Jad and I were going to London, and then I asked, "How did you know to marry Grandpa?"

She drifted back over the decades and answered, "On our first date your grandfather asked me who I was. He listened to the answer. He cared about the answer our whole lives."

"So you knew from the start?"

"I didn't know we'd marry, but I knew I could trust him. He was like a tall strong tree where I could land, but also take flight. He didn't try to hold me down, so I wanted to come back and settle there. Perhaps you've found such a tree?"

"You mean Ramsay?"

"Is it Ramsay?"

"You mean Adil?"

"I don't know. You must tell me."

I sit now staring out of the plane's window 30,000 feet above the earth, looking for trees in the cold white sand.

*   *   *

An announcement echoes through Heathrow Terminal 4: "Elizabeth West, go to the nearest courtesy phone for a message." It's six a.m. I've told Mom not to bother to pick us up. We'll get a taxi and see her at home for breakfast, but the driver who follows us to the phone insists he's been hired to take us. He recites our address and my mother's name, then he gathers up our luggage and guides us outside to a Mercedes limousine. If Mother hired a car, I doubt it would be a limousine.

"Are you sure you have the right Elizabeth West?" He reconfirms my address and phone number. I don't want to call and wake Mother. Jad and I are exhausted so I yield, and we climb into the comfort of the deep leather seats, dropping our backpacks on the floor. If I were less tired, perhaps I'd be more suspicious. Jad comes awake when he finds a box of donuts on the seat.

"I thought you might be hungry," the driver says, "so I picked these up."

Jad lies down in my lap eating a jelly roll. I rest my head against the window and close my eyes.

As we drive, I drift between sleep and consciousness, thinking about Grandma Sha, wondering how she and Grandpa envisioned their lives when they started out. Did they see themselves living in two countries? Did they suspect what the war would bring, suspect they would provide refuge for children and families fleeing its evil, suspect that their lives would offer refuge for so many people over so many years? I wonder if my father had been given the photographs of Auschwitz and Buchenwald whether he would have seen mess halls or gas chambers in the grainy black-and-white images. As I rock in the car in an uneasy sleep, I think of the list Jane gave me years ago. I came across it as I gathered papers to take to London. I brought it with me to give to Winston.

Street lamps---gas centrifuge pipes
Prosthetic limbs---melted zirconium/skull furnaces
Ink (ball pt pens)---mustard gas
Discs (car gears)---discs (spinning lathes)
Milk plant (pumps)---Scud missile motors
Dental lab electrical equip---speed control centrifuge motors

A bizarre equation of deception. Henry untangled the dual uses of these machines and chemicals in his articles in *The Financial Times*. The materials can be used for street lamps, for dental labs, for cars, for milk production, but instead they were used for centrifuge pipes and spinning lathes in the equipment that enriches uranium for nuclear warheads. They were used in factories to turn phosphates not into fertilizer as claimed, but into Sarin and Tabun nerve gas. This is the machinery of gas chambers, not mess halls. And Gerald Rene Wagner, whom our family knows, whom we've had over for dinner, with whom we've gone out to dinner, who has given me a silk scarf for graduation, is one of the alchemists. I wonder what Serena's files will yield. Before I flew to London, I introduced her to Marvin Penn in the lounge of the Lombardy Hotel and left the two of them to sort out her options for the future.

I don't know how long we've been driving when I feel the car turn off the highway and pull to a stop. I open my eyes. We're not in London, but on the outskirts in the parking lot of a factory. The car door opens. A tweed suit blocks the light. Smokestacks loom behind the figure in the door. The suit strains around the shoulders and flaps open over the now expansive girth of Gerald Wagner, who climbs into the limousine as if conjured from my half-waking dreams. A shudder runs through me. I haven't seen Dr. Wagner since Boxing Day when he showed up on our doorstep with the police demanding Dennis's notes. His rust-colored toupee butts in first, looking dull and worn like a carpet too often tread upon. His once tanned face, now sallow with liver spots on sagging jowls, bears down on me. He shoves into the back seat, forcing Jad to sit up. He orders the driver to go on.

"I want you to deliver a message," he says without extending a greeting. I wonder if he knows I've just seen Serena in Washington. Has Serena told him I'm coming? "I want you to tell your father I have no intention of going to jail. I want you to tell him I will use all my power to make certain that I don't."

He reaches out and touches Jad's head. I want to push his hand away. Jad leans into me, and I put my arm around him and sit very still. "How are the donuts?" he asks Jad, retrieving a chocolate one for himself. "Do you understand what I'm saying? Tell your father I know what is going on, and I will not hesitate to interfere in your lives should my own be disrupted."

I focus on the chocolate crumbs falling on his pale-yellow shirt. I wonder how he knew I was arriving in London. Does he know I'm coming to see Adil? He assumes Winston is my father, assumes Winston can keep him out of jail. But Winston has no say in the government investigation into illegal arms sales. In fact, Winston is trying to stay as far away from it as possible, Mother has told me, lest he and Dennis be implicated. I know Dr. Wagner is trying to frighten me, and he's succeeding at one level. I reach for common ground. "How is your son, Dr. Wagner?" I ask.

He blinks as if a speck of dust momentarily irritates his eye. "James? James has been arrested in Germany. That will not happen to me."

The driver pulls off the highway and speeds onto a single lane with no traffic. Fields lie on either side of the road. We are well out of London now. "Where are we going?" I try to keep my voice calm.

"Did I ever tell you I was once kidnapped? They kept me blindfolded in a basement for three days. They didn't want freedom or justice or release of prisoners the way they do today. They wanted money. Most people want money, including your father and your brother, and they will rationalize all sorts of deeds to get it, but I won't be the scapegoat for hypocritical British businessmen and politicians who knew exactly what was going on until it became politically inconvenient to know."

I want to say that Winston is not my father, but I remain silent.

"I persuaded one of my kidnappers to let me go. I told him if he released me I'd take care of his family for the rest of their lives. He was sent to prison for twenty years, and I did take care of his family until they were tragically killed in a car crash."

He says *tragically killed* in a flat, monotone voice that lets me know he had them killed. I pull Jad closer. I remember one of my father's stories of a man trapped in a cave with a beast guarding the exit. The man feeds the beast to appease it, but that only strengthens it and it wants more. The man tries to run around the beast, but the beast drives the man farther into the cave until finally the man is completely in the dark.

"What did he do?" I asked my father.

"Finally, he took out his flashlight, and he shined it in the beast's eyes. The beast started to back away from the light. As it retreated, the man ran out of the cave into the daylight. The beast followed but was afraid of the light and quickly went back to the cave."

The story calms me. "Dr. Wagner, do you know what happened to my stepbrother, Dennis?" I ask in a level voice.

Dr. Wagner looks amused by my attempt at poise. "You are a mother since I've seen you," he says. "I hope you are raising your son to respect his elders and do what he's told."

"I'm raising him to think and ask questions."

"Then you must be prepared to pay for the answers."

"You haven't given me an answer." I hold my voice and my gaze steady so I don't show fear.

"The police reported that your brother was shot by the criminal element," Dr. Wagner says.

"They never found the criminal."

"That is the nature of the criminal element. They exist in the shadows of the rest of us. They use our shadows for protection."

"Do they use your shadow?"

Dr. Wagner smiles as though he's weary of these games, but he will run one more lap around the track to show me that he can. "They try, but I move quickly. No one can stay in my shadow for long."

"Was Dennis in your shadow?" I meet his small, hard eyes that assert but don't see.

"Dennis wanted to cast his own shadow."

"Is that why he was shot?"

"Your brother confused shadow for substance." Dr. Wagner's tongue flicks across his lips. He is enjoying this wordplay. I remember Sophie's attempt to pin him down at our dinner years ago. I want to ask if his substance had to do with Advanced Technology Partners or KBT Engineering or Wye Holdings, all of which are now bankrupt, according to Jane, but Jad's warm body against my side restrains me from treading any closer to the edge.

Dr. Wagner reaches for another donut and offers one to Jad, who shakes his head. "You must eat," he says, pressing a glazed donut in Jad's hand.

"How are your grandchildren?" I ask.

Dr. Wagner again blinks, then he calls into the front seat, "Pull over here."

The driver stops the car and gets out at the edge of a field. He takes our luggage from the trunk and sets it on the side of the road. There is nothing in any direction. Suddenly I'm afraid I've shined the light too directly, miscalculated the distance to the truth and smashed into it. Is he going to kill us? The thought flashes through my mind like lightning, illumining unreal scenes from the past—my father plunging into the Gulf, Dennis shot in the back of the head. Yet my imagination refuses to include my own death. How can I deliver a message if I'm dead?

"Get out," Dr. Wagner says.

I take Jad's hand. We pull our backpacks from the car. I calculate how close I need to be to use the karate I studied years ago. I set Jad beside the car door, measure the distance to the driver, note the keys still in the ignition.

"Where are we?" I keep my voice calm. I glance up and down the road. There's no sign of life, only brown fields. Rain is soaking through the cloth of our luggage. In the largest bag are all of Mom's and Dad's notebooks, which I'm bringing to England for safekeeping. In the smaller bag are Dennis's notes, the notes Gerald Wagner has been seeking that establish his intent and remove ambiguity from his action. But Dr. Wagner isn't looking for these right now, so they remain lodged between my sweaters and Jad's socks in the red canvas suitcase on the country road.

My eyes lock on Dr. Wagner's flaccid and undisciplined face, yet his eyes are frighteningly disciplined. Every nerve in my body is ready to spring to defend my child, but Marvin has taught me not to act too early lest I precipitate the crisis. Dr. Wagner gets back into the car.

"How will we get home?" I ask.

"You are the travel agent," he says. I wonder how he knows that. He shuts the door and rolls down the window. He takes out a donut for himself then hands the box to Jad. The limousine turns on the narrow lane and speeds back towards the highway.

*   *   *

Fortunately, Britain is not America where wide-open spaces can go on for hundreds of miles. I shove our suitcases under a bush to keep them dry then start to walk with Jad in the opposite direction from where we came and from where the car returned. I am betting on the landscape ahead of us.

Within a mile, a small village rises on the horizon, along with a red phone booth on the side of the road. I call home collect. Winston answers. "Your mother is already on her way," he says. "An anonymous caller telephoned and told her where she could pick you up. She should be there within the hour."

I tell Winston if she calls again to tell her we'll wait at the Catherine Wheel pub, whose owner I see opening up.

When Mother arrives at the pub, she's furious. At first, I think she's angry at me. In a way, she is. She clutches Jad and me in a grip that makes Jad look to me for relief. "He said, '*You can pick up your daughter and grandson on the side of the road.*' I didn't know if you were alive or dead. After Dennis . . ." I let her hug me, but I free Jad by moving him onto my lap. In the car I wrap Jad in a blanket, and he falls asleep as Mother drives us back to London. We stop on the way to retrieve our luggage.

"Are you sure he's all right?" Mother keeps asking.

"He's fine. A little wet, but we had jackets. It could have been much worse." I'm comforting her rather than her comforting me. "Really. He didn't hurt us. He even fed Jad donuts."

"Donuts?" Mother says with disdain, as if one of her fears has been confirmed.

"He wanted to scare us."

"Well, he succeeded. But he's not finished. Much more is going on, isn't it?"

"What do you mean?"

"Why are you here?" She accelerates onto the highway, already annoyed by my answer.

I decide not to evade the question. "To see Adil."

"Yes," she affirms. "He's called twice."

"Adil called?"

"Why didn't you tell me?"

"What did he say?" Surely, he wouldn't tell my mother we're thinking of getting married.

"He told me he hoped I'd give him the opportunity to meet so he could assure me how much he loves you and wants to care for you and Jad and will never do anything to allow harm to come to you." She glances at me. Her face is without makeup and her hair is more gray than blonde. For a moment she looks helpless as if conceding that my life is mine to live and she no longer has the power to protect or direct me. "What is he thinking?" she demands. "What are you thinking?"

"I think he'd like you to trust him."

"Trust him? Trust him how? Look what happened today."

"Adil had nothing to do with today."

"Oh?"

"Gerald Wagner picked us up, not Adil. You don't even know Adil."

"Gerald Wagner and Adil's father do business together."

"That was years ago."

"You have no idea the world Adil is coming from," Mother says. "No idea."

"That may be, but he doesn't want to do what his father did. He isn't his father. He wants to live his own life, have a family."

"Doing what?"

"What do you mean?"

"Live a life doing what? Live a life where?"

"I don't know. That's why I'm here. We need to spend time together to find those answers."

Mother runs her hand through her hair as though she will pull it out. "Where's Ramsay?"

"In Washington."

"Does he know?"

"I told him. I've got to find out if Adil and I . . . I know it's not what you imagined for me. Maybe he's not who I imagined either, but . . ." I falter. "I can't explain it to you."

"You don't have to," she answers. "I understand better than you think."

"Will you see him then?"

"If you want me to."

"Yes, I'd like you to. I think you'll like him."

"It doesn't matter if I *like* him. I'm worried sick about what he'll need from you, and about how far you and Jad will go from us." I stare at her. Her skin sags at her cheeks and around her eyes. I've never thought of my mother needing me in the way that I've needed her. I never thought of her growing old, but there is nothing I can do to relieve her fears. I watch the road and the tidy British countryside sweeping by.

"I love him," I say.

*   *   *

"We must call the police," Mother declares as soon as she gets in the front door. "Gerald Wagner abducted them!"

Winston is sitting in the living room by the fire with Pickles, whom he's called, and with Dennis Jr. and newborn Liza, whom I haven't yet met. Sara is drawing at Mother's desk in the corner.

Winston stands up. "Did he hurt you?"

"No." I lay Jad, who's still sleeping, on the sofa and cover him with the blanket. "Unless you consider leaving us on the roadside in the rain hurting us."

"Did he threaten you?" Winston persists.

"Not directly. He gave me a message for you. He said he had no intention of going to jail. He seems to think you have some control over that. He said he will do whatever is necessary to keep that from happening. I guess you could consider that a threat."

"We must call the police," Mother repeats, but she doesn't reach for the phone. I wonder why she hasn't called the police earlier.

"I'm not so sure," Winston says. I watch his eyes calculating. "He expects us to do that."

"What do you mean?" Mother asks.

"The press will find out and want to know why he would abduct our daughter. The story of Dennis will come out again. Gerald may be planning to use Dennis as his scapegoat, to say Dennis was responsible for the crimes committed. You can be certain he'll contradict Lizzy's version of what happened. He's expecting us to react."

For Winston everything leads back to Dennis. I don't say anything.

"Then you must at least speak privately to Covington and tell him what has happened." "Covington" is Lord Covington, who met Gerald Wagner at our house years ago at the party Winston gave and is now on the Commission investigating illegal arms and technology transfers. Dr. Wagner tried to sell him shares in one of his companies,

Mother has told me. Several of Winston's friends lost money with Dr. Wagner, but Lord Covington kept him at arm's length.

"I can't interfere," Winston says.

"But Covington is a friend."

"Exactly. I can't risk compromising him. Maybe that's what Gerald is hoping I'll do. Then he can discredit the whole Commission."

"Lizzy and Jad were abducted!" Mother repeats. "If we don't speak to someone, we'll have no credibility later."

Neither Mother nor Winston think to ask my opinion. The event has instantly assumed a political context for them; whereas I think about Dr. Wagner touching Jad's head, handing him the box of donuts.

"He could have hurt them," Mother says, sinking into the other chair by the fire. "He could have done anything to them."

"But he didn't," I say. Mother assumes I did nothing to protect us.

Winston reaches out from his chair. "Your mother's right. He's capable of anything."

I don't know what Dr. Wagner is capable of, but I don't have to imagine all the possibilities in order to act. "Why don't you call him?" I suggest. Mother and Winston look at me as if I'm unbalanced. "Tell him Winston is not involved in the investigation and that if he comes near your family again . . ." I can't think of an appropriate action. "He told me today about the time he was kidnapped. I had the feeling he wanted to tell me his whole life story, even the terrible parts like when he killed the family of the man who kidnapped him. His own son is in prison. He may be facing prison. He's alone; I think he's scared. He might talk to you, Mother."

Mother seems to be considering what I'm saying when the phone rings. Winston picks up. He listens for a moment, then answers. "Yes, they're back . . . Yes. You tell Gerald Wagner that if he ever comes near my family again, I'll guarantee he goes to prison for the rest of his life!" Winston knows how to finish the sentence. I wonder if Winston has that power. He slams the phone down. His face is flushed, and his hands are trembling. Pickles gives Liza to me and goes over to him.

I hold Liza's small, soft body in my arms. She grips my finger and stares up at me.

"That man took my son from me!" Winston wails. "And I let him!"

Mother joins Pickles and holds Winston's shoulders. "I think we must tell someone what has happened," she insists. Sara also comes over to her grandfather and takes his hand. Winston lifts her onto his lap. Pickles moves back to the sofa beside me, but she leaves Liza in my arms.

"She's so alert," I say. "She must be very smart."

"Randolph and I think so too." Pickles touches Jad's forehead as he sleeps. "You must have been terrified."

"At the end . . . but it's odd. I think he was the one who was afraid."

"You always were the brave one, Lizzy," Pickles says.

*　　*　　*

When the phone rings just before lunch, Winston answers and passes the receiver to me. He and Mother watch as I turn my back to them. "Let me change phones." I go to the kitchen. "Where are you?" I ask.

"At a restaurant on the corner. Can you come? I'd come there, but your mother . . ."

"No, don't come here. I'll meet you. It'll take a few minutes."

When I return to the living room, my jury awaits—Winston, Pickles, Mother, even Jad, who is sitting up now. I haven't told Jad why we've come to London. Jad thinks Ramsay is going to be his father.

"I'll take Jad up to bed," I say.

"I don't want to go to bed." Jad scrambles off the couch to make his point.

"Let him stay up," Mother says.

"He can play with Sara," Pickles adds. "We can only stay another hour."

"An hour?" I can't wait an hour to meet Adil.

"Is there a problem?" Pickles asks.

"It's just that I . . . I didn't know you'd be here. There's someone I promised to meet. I thought Jad would nap, and I'd slip out . . ." I decide not to hedge further. "I have to see Adil. I'm sorry. He's waiting for me."

"I don't think that's safe," Winston says.

"Of course it's not safe," Mother declares. "Pickles, would you mind taking the children into the den. I need to speak with Elizabeth alone." Winston rises to help her.

"Have you been following what's happening in Adil's country?" Mother asks after they leave.

"Yes, I read the newspapers." In fact, I've read only one article about mortar attacks and shelling on the border in South Lebanon. Most of the stories now are about peace talks between Israel and Syria and by extension Lebanon. "Mostly people are talking about peace."

"There's continued fighting in the South."

"I don't see what these events have to do with my safety on the streets of London. Adil and his father live in Beirut. According to Adil, his father wants to live his last years in peace."

"That may be, but I don't know if it's possible. I understand why Adil wants out. I admire his instincts for survival, but I don't admire his grasping at my daughter as his exit."

"Mother, you don't know what you're talking about! You don't even know Adil! Adil is Jad's father. He asked me to marry him five years ago, before I even had Jad. And I said yes. I don't know if I'm going to marry him now, but if I do, it won't be because of some political scheme. The whole world isn't driven by politics!" I hardly ever raise my voice to my mother, but right now I feel like shouting at everyone. I stand. "I'm going to see Adil, and I'd be very grateful if you'd look after Jad." I don't wait for an answer. I grab my coat from the back of the chair and head for the door.

"Be careful," Mother says. She stays seated in her chair by the fire, and her calm challenges my passion and makes me wonder if she's right.

CHAPTER TWENTY-THREE

I HURRY DOWN High Street, checking both sides, looking behind me, but don't see anyone following. At the restaurant I spot Adil in a back booth. He's wearing a black turtleneck, his dark hair over his ears. I feel my breath quicken. I envisioned this meeting as a passionate, clandestine reunion, but propped beside him, drinking milk through a straw, a black-haired child with shiny brown eyes occupies his attention. He's buttering her bread and holding her glass so it doesn't spill. As Adil bends down to retrieve a spoon she's knocked to the floor, he sees me.

"Lizzy!"

I walk quickly towards him. He stands, cups his hand gently on my cheek, and kisses me, a kiss I've been longing for, but his eyes stay on the child. He glances behind me. "Where's Jad?" The danger Mother and Winston warned of doesn't appear to be on Adil's mind.

"Is this Raja?" I ask.

Adil speaks in Arabic to the child, who looks up with large doe eyes like Adil's.

"Ahlan, Raja," I greet in Arabic. *Hello.* "Itsharrafna." *I'm glad to meet you.* I slide into the booth opposite her. Adil touches my hand on the table, then he reaches over to balance the glass of milk. "You need a cup with a lid," I say.

"I thought you'd bring Jad."

"We had a hard trip." I planned to tell Adil about Wagner's abduction of us, but Raja says she has to go to the bathroom. She speaks in Arabic, and I reply also in Arabic that I'll take her.

"When did you learn Arabic?"

"I've been studying for years."

Adil smiles, the smile he offers only to me. In it I see Jad, and I see a life we might live together. He explains to Raja in Arabic that I'm the good friend he's told her about.

When we return to the table, I ask, still in Arabic, where her mother is. Adil's expression darkens. He cuts Raja's sandwich into smaller squares and hands her a section, then in English he answers, "After the fighting she drove from her parents' home back to her house. The road was mined. Raja was visiting me. She doesn't know. She's only two and a half. I don't know if she'll even understand." He touches the top of Raja's head.

"She was killed?" He nods and strokes his child's hair. I grow quiet. I try to imagine this woman I never met—where she was, what road, what point of history? The violence I only glimpsed with Dr. Wagner this morning has shoved its head through the fence—bare teeth, ham fist, sightless eyes—and taken this woman. I reach across the table to Adil as I've done before. Adil's eyes meet mine, and I see in them the boy who lost his own mother. He puts his arm around his daughter, who is up on her knees, precariously holding the open glass of milk as Adil tries to steady them both. He smoothes Raja's hair and hands her another piece of sandwich. All at once I understand Adil's call to me. His appeal is not the political scheme my mother imagines, but a much older story of a man left to raise a child on his own, seeking a woman to help. This story is less callow than my mother's, though perhaps no less manipulative. All the way to the restaurant, I wondered if I'd be able to discern the truth about Adil, if the truth was something I could define and draw a line around. I planned to look deep into his eyes, but he hasn't sat still long enough, he is so absorbed by the needs of his child.

"Do you want to go to the zoo?" he asks.

"The zoo?" The question seems a non sequitur.

"We can pick up Jad. I want him to meet Raja."

"Is it safe? Do you feel safe?"

His eyes finally settle on me. "I feel safer with you, Lizzy, than with anyone I know." He reaches now for my hand.

I tell him about Dr. Wagner and about what happened to us on the way from the airport. "Mother's concerned Dr. Wagner's threat is related to you and your father. I don't know how he knew I'd be flying in or knew why I was here, but he may know you're here."

"Are you and Jad all right?" Adil sits forward, his whole body suddenly alert.

"We're fine."

"What did he want?"

"I think he wanted to scare my stepfather. He thinks Winston can keep him out of prison. But Mother thinks it's also connected to you and your father."

"My father knows Dr. Wagner's business. Dr. Wagner has always been suspicious of my father. I told you he got us thrown out of Britain by telling customs agents my father ordered the contraband shipment that was in fact his. He knew they'd believe him, not my father."

"That sounds complicated."

"It's even more complicated, but it is my father's world, Lizzy, not mine. It won't be my world. I promise." He reaches down to pack up Raja's things. "Let's go."

I help Raja on with a tiny pink jacket that is not warm enough for the damp London winter. "You need to get her a proper coat," I say.

"I know. And one of those cups with a lid." He smiles, and his smile reduces the complications of our world to the essentials of taking care of a child.

"I know a place nearby."

As we start down High Street Kensington with Raja in a stroller in front of us, Adil's eyes scan the road. I notice two large men get up and leave the restaurant when we do. They're still behind us. I flag a cab and quickly lift Raja from her stroller. "There's a better store in Chelsea," I say, getting in.

"Where are you going?" Adil climbs in after us.

"We're being followed." The two men are waving for a taxi.

Adil looks around. "I know. By my bodyguards. Slow down," he tells the driver.

"Your bodyguards?"

"My father sent them." Adil puts his arm around Raja, who folds her tiny legs under her and burrows into him. He reaches out and touches my shoulder. "They're only a precaution," he says.

I stare into his deep brown eyes that absorb and reflect the life around him, and I try, but cannot see, the future.

* * *

At Fatin's apartment, Adil and I settle on a white satin sofa facing Bryanston Square. In the corner a fake coal fire flutters in a small marble fireplace while outside the windows snowflakes float in the sky. Raja is taking a nap; Fatin is at work. We're finally alone, but instead of the passionate embrace I've imagined like the one that swept us into our lives in Berlin, Adil and I sit holding hands. "I'm sorry about your wife," I say.

He kisses my hand. "Do you ever feel old?"

"I'm not sure you were ever allowed to be young."

"We were young one night," he says.

"Yes, we were."

He touches the side of my face as though reminding himself of the feel of my skin. I stir under his touch. "That ended your youth, didn't it?" he says.

"Jad changed my life."

"My father changed mine. I was always afraid for him ever since my mother was killed. I believed in the danger that he said followed us."

"Has that changed?"

Adil pulls me closer. His arm encircles me, and I rest my head on his shoulder. He kisses me softly on the lips. "Yes, it has. I've told my father I must choose my life. He told me to prepare for medical school, so I studied science at the university in Berlin, and when the Gulf War broke out, I worked as a medic's assistant along the border in Saudi Arabia." He sits forward slightly, looking at me as he talks.

"I worked with doctors of real courage, Lizzy, but I've seen enough to know I'm not meant to be a doctor. At the end of the days, in the early evenings, I used to go out and kick a soccer ball around just to relax. Children in the camp started following me. I began playing with them. They'd lost everything, but for an hour each evening, they could still be children."

He stands and turns up the gas fire to take the chill out of the room. He begins to pace in front of the bay window. I worry that he's visible from outside. "When my father was captured in Iraq, I was told I might be in danger, so I returned to Lebanon, where I worked with my family and others to get my father released. I thought about you, but you seemed a million miles away. One of those who helped me was a girl I'd known since I was a child. Her uncle had contacts in Baghdad. He owned hotels there and in Damascus and Beirut. Her family helped free my father." Adil is answering questions I haven't asked, setting forth his case, urging me to see the world the way he sees it.

"I was twenty-three years old, and I wanted to start my life. She and I decided to get married. Our two families celebrated. I went to work for her uncle in his hotels, but she and I weren't in love. I was in love with you, and she'd married me on the rebound from a man who was already married in Syria. We realized we'd made a mistake, but by then Raja was on the way."

Adil keeps pacing. He seems unable to settle until he tells me his story. "Sit down," I suggest. He hesitates then sits beside me but continues explaining.

"Maybe because we were also friends, the separation for us wasn't as hard as it was for our families. She wanted to divorce because the man in Syria had finally gotten a divorce from his wife. We agreed Raja would live with me during the summer months. I also visited her every other weekend, and I sent money. I continued managing hotels in Beirut while she got a job with an international aid agency farther south. In the evenings and on weekends I worked at a youth center I helped start, and I set up a soccer camp for kids in the summer."

Finally, Adil takes my hand. Outside, black London cabs circle the square in snow-diffused light. "In Beirut I ran into Sahar, who told me you were married. That's what she'd been told or had concluded because you had a child. I was planning to write your home in London as soon as I got back to Beirut, but when I heard you were married, I felt a door of my life close. Then when I saw you at New Years and learned you weren't married after all, it was as if life had opened a narrow passage and shot a light through. Lizzy, I'm twenty-seven years old. I don't know what I'll make of my life. I don't know where my home will be in the world, but I know the people I love. I'm Raja's father, and I'm Jad's father. I want to be with them and with you. I want us to have time to see if we should be together, though we may not have much time . . ."

I reach up and take Adil's face in my hands and silence him with a
kiss. I'm not certain truth resides in a kiss, but I think I could discern
a lie, and there is no lie there. We kiss in the white afternoon light
while his child sleeps. His hand moves to my breast, and I hold it there
close to my heart. "How much time do we have?" I ask.

"Fatin's gone all afternoon."

I smile. "No, I mean to find out about each other. I can stay three
weeks."

"Three weeks is a lifetime for us," Adil says.

I move slightly away from him, so I can see his face. "Then let's start
now while Raja's asleep. Three weeks will pass faster than you think
with children to take care of."

"How do we start?"

"Let's begin with your father."

Adil laughs. "My father. Which part?"

"You and your father. Then we'll try me and my mother. Your father is opposed to your marrying me because I'm not Arab?"

"Because he says I have no idea what's ahead for me. He wants me
to be a leader in our country, but I say, what country? He says my life
will be difficult enough even with a wife who understands my history
and my people. But to take a wife whose own father was once his
enemy . . ."

"Is he sure he knew my father?"

"Yes. But I don't care. That's his history."

"Will he listen to you?"

"He's developed the ability to remain quiet while I speak, but that's
not the same as listening. He already knows the answers. He says he
wants me to be happy, but he defines happiness the way he and my
mother were happy, though I wonder if they were. My mother made a
life for herself and for me, which he visited. I have few memories of
my father before my mother was killed. Even after that, I lived with

my aunt most of the time. She and my mother are the ones who had raised me until . . . well, until that year when you and I met. That's the year my father came back into my life."

"Does your father know why you've come to London?"

"Before I left, he told me if I was determined to ruin my life, I was on my own."

On our first date when Adil told me the story of his mother's death, I'd understood he was choosing me to help him bear the weight of his history, and I'd accepted the task as I understood it. "You mustn't give up your father," I say.

"I haven't given up my father; he's given up me. He's ill. He's left Beirut. He says he wants peace, but he sees enemies everywhere. I don't want my son and daughter to live surrounded by enemies. I saw too many maimed and killed in the war."

"But you don't want to be a doctor?"

"I want to be a teacher, maybe a professor. My father says a teacher is no future for a man. I told him I'd begin there. How can I know where I'll end? I want to live a life I care about." Adil's eyes hold me and will not let go as he struggles with the two voices in his head, one of his father and the other, I assume, of his mother. "I don't care what your father said to my father."

I lean back into his arms and kiss him. I feel my heart racing, sprinting to find the door to its home. Adil's fingers gently stroke my face, my arms, my breasts as I hold him close and kiss him. I wonder if we can really build a life ignoring the history of our parents and of everyone around us. I sit up and take a breath. I look out the window at the bare trees and the circling flakes of snow, contemplating this *cold white sand* and the imagination it will take to bridge worlds.

* * *

Fatin's apartment is a haven for us over the next weeks. Fatin works at a bank often into the evening, so Adil, Jad, Raja, and I stage our days out of his flat rather than my house. There is nothing Mother can do to stop me except withhold her approval, so my response is to withhold our lives from her.

Adil and I plan our days as if we are camp counselors. Each morning we take the children somewhere—to Madame Tussaud's Wax Museum, the Planetarium, the Natural History Museum, Pollock's Toy Museum—then to lunch, then to the park to play soccer when it isn't raining, and finally back to Fatin's apartment, where Raja and Jad take long afternoon naps, and Adil and I settle in front of the fire to plan our lives. We lie in each other's arms and kiss and hold each other and touch each other, but we don't make love. I want to, but I also want to wait until after we're married, if we marry. We need to decide that first. We already know the passion between us, but more than passion has to guide us now. I think of what Grandma Sha told me, and I wonder if Adil is the strong tree where I might settle but also take flight. And if I am such a tree for him. Each day I return to his arms.

As for Raja and Jad, they're getting along fairly well for a five-year-old boy and a two-and-a-half-year-old girl. Jad has learned a few words of Arabic, mostly "Leave my ball alone!" Raja likes to chase his soccer ball and fall on top of it and laugh when Jad gets exasperated as if his purpose is to entertain her. They are already acting like brother and sister, I tell Adil.

A reminder that our lives are not as normal as they appear is the constant presence of the two bodyguards. When we're in the apartment, they stay outside. When we're outside, they follow at a distance, but I can never forget they're there. Adil assures me they speak no English, so our conversations are private, but I'm not so sure. Omar, the smaller of the two, who is missing a finger on his left hand, always looks alert when we talk.

"Where are they from?" I ask one afternoon as we're sitting by the fire. "They flew here with you?"

"They live here. My father sent them to watch out for me."

"So he does know where you are? I thought you said he'd disowned you."

"Yes, financially, but he doesn't want me killed. I told my father we thought we'd been shot at so he's taking no chances."

"Does he know who it might be?"

"Hamas, Hezbollah, Iraq's Mukhabarat—none have any friendship for my father, but whether they would target me in London, that we don't know. He's on several death lists, and I am his son."

I wonder if we are being followed. Twice on the edge of the park I've seen a large man with a moustache and glasses. I think of Adnan Kamil Houston, but I don't entirely remember what he looks like. When I tell Adil, he alerts Omar and Jawad, who tell us not to play soccer in Hyde Park anymore. This restriction closes down the space around us, and I wonder about submitting Jad to such a bounded world.

"What would your bodyguards say if they knew we were thinking of getting married?" I ask the following afternoon. "Would they be at the wedding?"

"I think they should be."

"Then your father will know we're married."

"Yes, I suppose he will."

For the rest of the afternoon Adil seems preoccupied, unable to concentrate on the mundane questions before us, like whether he's heard about his visa application to the United States, or questions like how he feels about my telling my sisters we might get married. So far we've been operating in the subjunctive, but in less than two weeks I have to return to Washington. We're trying not to rush into a wedding; on the other hand, we're taking the steps necessary so that if we decide to marry, we can do so. It isn't the most romantic approach, but neither of us wants to make a mistake. We find out where we can go for a license. We reserve a day in February at the Old Marylebone Town Hall, where Mother and Winston married. Adil applies for a visa to the United States and explains he's marrying a U.S. citizen. I apply for a visa to Lebanon, though Americans are discouraged from going there. We talk about another country in addition to Britain, where we might live—Canada, France, Switzerland, Germany, but I don't speak much German. We decide we will only go to a country where we both speak the language. That leaves the English, French, and Arabic-speaking worlds.

* * *

As we put the children down for naps one afternoon, Marvin Penn calls. Mother has given him Fatin's number, which I've given her in case of an emergency. "Guess where all the files of Wagner's dealings are?" he asks.

"Where are you?" I ask.

"With Serena in Washington. The files are in Wagner's house in London."

"What?" I sink onto the sofa. Adil is still in the bedroom with the children. "They're here?"

"In Serena's closet, behind one of those false walls the British love. We've been trying to figure how to get them. Serena can't go back."

"Why don't you subpoena them?"

"That takes time. If Wagner hears about it, he'll find them and get rid of them. He doesn't know she has them."

I watch Adil in the kitchen now pouring coffee. "What are you suggesting?"

"You could get into her closet."

"You want me to steal the files?" Adil looks up.

"You wouldn't be stealing," Serena interrupts. She must be on the extension or listening at Marvin's ear. "You have my permission."

"But, Serena, you stole them."

"No, I didn't. The originals are wherever Adnan and Gerald hid them. I found the key to the cabinet and made copies one long, boring week when they were figuring out what to do with everything. I took the copies out each night and shipped them to London with my clothes when we left."

"What is it you want me to do?" I ask.

Adil comes into the living room with mugs of coffee and hands me one as he sits down. I drop my legs over his and raise my eyebrows to indicate the extraordinary conversation.

"My bedroom's the first one at the top of the stairs," Serena says. "In the closet, under the shelf where I keep my purses, there's a latch. If you unlock it, you can push the wall, which opens into a tiny room. I used to hide there when Gerald got drunk. There's a chaise and a lamp and a trunk. The files are in the trunk."

"You want me to sneak a trunk out of your house? What about all the security cameras?"

"They haven't worked for years. I'll tell Claudia, the housekeeper, you're picking up some things for me but not to tell. I'll call in the morning after Gerald goes out. You can go in before he gets back. He usually leaves around ten, then comes home for lunch around one. You'll need to have someone help you though. You won't be able to carry everything by yourself."

"Could you put Marvin back on?" I ask. "Marvin, this is crazy."

"I know, but I don't have a better idea. I'm worried Wagner will leave London by the time we work through the courts. Wagner set up

Serena as an officer in the American company, at least on paper, so technically she has the authority to hand over files."

I tell Marvin about Dr. Wagner abducting us from the airport and Mother's worry that he's dangerous. "Your mother's right. Perhaps I shouldn't be asking you . . ."

"What's in the files?"

"A twenty- to thirty-year jail term on both continents from what Serena's told me—bank records, double-entry ledgers, lists of what equipment was bought and where it was sent and Wagner's handwritten notes from meetings with other arms dealers. Also notes on a business selling used Russian and Serbian small arms into Africa. Oh, and documents from an arms manufacturing plant he bought in Slovakia. He moved the files to Virginia, Serena said, because he thought they were safer there since he's not known in the U.S. He talked of one day settling in Florida. Serena's also copied all the files she could find in London."

"How many files are we talking about? It might be less conspicuous if I could take them out in backpacks."

"Big backpacks," Serena inserts. "I'll tell Claudia you're going into my closet to borrow some clothes. While you're there, could you bring me some of my sweaters in the top left drawer? I hate leaving everything behind."

"Serena . . ." I protest. "Marvin, let me think about this."

"Of course. But time is short." Marvin gives me the number to contact him in Serena's room at the Hotel Lombardy.

"We can go tomorrow," Adil says when I explain the proposal.

"If Dr. Wagner catches us breaking and entering, I don't know what he might do."

"You're not breaking and entering if Serena tells the housekeeper to let you in. You're not stealing if you take something Serena has asked you to take."

"I doubt he'd see it that way. How do we avoid Dr. Wagner?"

"Omar and Jawad can watch outside." Adil stands and begins pacing. "Dr. Wagner should be in jail. If your friend knows how to get him there, we have to help."

* * *

The following morning, Winston takes care of the children while we go to a café down the road from Dr. Wagner's house. Adil and I settle at a table by the window drinking coffee. The housekeeper is expecting us at ten thirty. At ten fifteen, Dr. Wagner in a camel's hair coat and black cap steps onto the sidewalk in front of his house and heads towards us.

"That's him!" I say.

Quickly we turn our chairs so that our backs are to the café door as he enters. In the window glass I see Dr. Wagner peering into the display case. He orders two croissants, orange juice, and coffee then sits at a table in front of us near the door and opens his newspaper. I've assumed he went to an office or to his factory, but he appears in no particular hurry to go anywhere. It is ten twenty-five.

Adil passes me a note. *I'll distract him while you slip out.*

He might recognize you, I write back.

He hasn't seen me in nine years.

I pull the hood of my jacket over my head and gather the mountaineering backpack I've bought. Adil stands up with his own backpack. A few blocks away in Holland Park, a youth hostel gives nightly shelter to young people so Adil and I fit in with the transient student population the neighborhood is used to. Because Dr. Wagner won't be expecting to see me, we count on his not seeing me.

"Excuse me, could you tell me how to get to Oxford Street." Adil approaches Dr. Wagner's table with a map, blocking his view of the front door.

Dr. Wagner blinks as if uncertain what is being asked of him as I slip out. "Where are you from, young man?" I hear him ask. I don't hear Adil's answer.

A few minutes later, Adil catches up with me. "He was actually friendly. He told me he'd been a student himself once, traveling through Europe with a backpack, staying at youth hostels."

"That's a lie," I say. "The son of a prominent Nazi after World War II—I doubt he was wandering Europe going to youth hostels."

*   *   *

A ponderous woman in a gray and white uniform opens the door to Dr. Wagner's house. Claudia looks more like a prison guard than a housekeeper as she leads us into the front hall. Serena has reached her, and she points up the stairs. Outside the white stone mansion, Omar and Jawad take up positions across the street with instructions to ring the doorbell three times if they see Dr. Wagner approaching.

As Adil follows Claudia to Serena's room, I lag behind. Only Adil has been inside the house beyond the kitchen when he had dinner here years ago. He reported hardly any furniture, but the rooms now bulge with heavy dark woods—an oversized entry table flanked by carved chairs, a grandfather clock, a heavy dining table with eight large chairs with carved backs and four additional chairs along the wall. Serena has told me Dr. Wagner suddenly moved everything out of Germany and sold his house there.

Serena's room by contrast is pure French with a pink-flowered organdy vanity table and stool, pink satin chaise lounge, a French provincial double bed with a blue satin headboard and bedspread, and a display of dolls from different countries and different historical periods. All I know about Serena is that she's from New Orleans, one of three sisters like me, but she's spent most of her adult life in Europe in the company of men. On her dressing table is a silver-framed photograph of a handsome, dark-haired man slightly shorter than she with his arm around her. They're standing by a bookstall along the Seine. He gazes out with a squint in his brow as though he's trying to recognize who's taking the picture. Serena herself is very young, strikingly pretty with dark curls and bangs and a bright college smile. I imagine Gerald proud of such a dashing son conquering the women and the political life in Paris. I wonder if Serena keeps the picture for Jack's sake, or for Gerald's, or for her own memory.

Adil goes directly to the closet, which is the size of Jad's and my bedroom in our first apartment. Inside, rack upon rack of clothes and shelves of shoes and bags are lined up. "She said the latch was under the shelf with the purses," I say.

"There are three shelves of purses!" Adil protests. In rows are blue, red, green, yellow, and black purses, lizard and alligator and ostrich purses, sequined purses, large and small, heart-shaped and box-shaped purses. "Who uses all these? Do you have this many purses?" he asks.

I step into the closet. Shoes in all colors and heel heights line up on another wall of shelves. "I have three purses and a backpack," I answer. "And five pairs of shoes, seven if you count sneakers and boots. Here . . ." I feel the latch and flip it.

The wall opens inwards revealing a small room with ceiling and walls wrapped in pale yellow fabric with tiny vines of blue flowers, a chaise lounge covered in the same fabric, and next to it a honey-colored wooden trunk inset with the fabric. A small, arched window lets in light. The trail of evidence to the criminal world of Dr. Wagner leads to this boudoir of a lonely woman.

Adil lifts the trunk lid and starts loading files into his backpack without looking at them. "We've got to hurry."

I check my watch. "It's just eleven." I also stuff files into my pack. I'm not sure what we'll find in these, but I feel the thrill of a hunter catching his prey.

"I have a bad feeling. Dr. Wagner was just passing time at that café. He may come home early."

I hurry filling my pack. Whatever Serena said about inviting us, whatever Marvin said about Serena having the authority to hand over files, I can as easily imagine Dr. Wagner going to his room, getting his pistol, and shooting us, then reporting that we were breaking and entering.

"Are you finding what you need?" Claudia calls into the bedroom.

"Yes . . . yes, fine," I answer. "We're almost done." There are over two hundred files in our backpacks. I jam in the last of the folders then draw the string at the top of the bag and shut the trunk. We pull the shelf closed behind us, re-latching the wall. "You have room for a sweater or two?" I'm ferreting through the drawer of sweaters, which we can use to camouflage the files, trying to guess which ones Serena might want, when the doorbell rings three times.

"Lizzy!" Adil warns. "We have to go!" I grab three sweaters for each of us and stuff them on top of the files in the backpacks. As we step onto the landing, the front door opens.

"Dr. Wagner!" Claudia announces.

"I'm tired," he complains. "Did Serena call?"

"Not yet."

He sinks into the chair by the door. "Where is she? I told her to come home."

"I'm sure she'll be here soon."

"She is defying me! I'll take her passport when she comes back this time. She is ungrateful!"

"Come into the kitchen, and I'll make you a cup of tea."

"I don't want a cup of tea. I want Serena to return now!" He settles in the chair as though he plans to stay until Serena appears.

"Let me at least take your coat."

Dr. Wagner yields his coat but doesn't get up. "Every day she doesn't come back, I'm going to give away her clothes. Tell her that when she calls! Every day I'll take an armful of her clothes down to the Oxfam store on the corner. That should bring her back!" He stands. "I'll begin right now." He starts towards the stairs.

I motion for Adil to follow me. We hurry up to the third floor. Sahar lived in a house like this. Most of these grand old homes have a second set of stairs for the servants. Adil and I hurry along the hallway. Sure enough, near what would have been the nanny's room is a back staircase. We slip down just as Dr. Wagner reaches the top of the main stairs and heads into Serena's room for his pillage. Claudia lets us out the kitchen door with our backpacks full of files, and we slip into the garden and out the back gate.

* * *

At Marvin's urging and in consultation with Mother and Winston, we turn the files over to the British and U.S. authorities, but not until Winston makes copies of everything. Each day in his office at home Winston searches through the files, looking for clues to what happened to Dennis and to his dealings with Dr. Wagner. Upstairs on my desk and on the floor of my room are the less orderly papers of Dad's and Mom's and a copy of Dennis's notes. Our house is turning into a repository of documents as Winston points out one morning when we meet to review the information he'd uncovered the day before.

"There's a wealth of material here for a prosecutor," he says, "and also for an ambitious graduate student."

"I'm still thinking about your proposal," I answer. In a week I have to return to Washington. "But I have to figure out other parts of my life first."

"That young man loves you," he says.

"And I love him. But Mother's upset. She doesn't want me to marry him."

"The world looks different from her point of view."

I sit in the chair on the other side of his desk. "What's your point of view?" I ask.

"My point of view doesn't matter. Yours and Adil's and the children's are what matter. The mistake I made with Dennis was . . ." He stops as if realizing all his conversations lead back to Dennis. ". . . Too many mistakes. I wish I'd loved him better, without all the judgment."

"You love us. Thank you for that."

He nods and picks up today's set of folders. "A pattern's emerging, don't you think? It appears Dr. Wagner overcharged clients for years and took a percent of the contracts as a 'finder's fee' as well as 'legal and accounting fees' for himself. He booked only part of the income from sales to his companies." Winston picks up another folder. "That behavior extended to his suppliers whom he also charged finder's fees. That's the way he behaved with his legitimate businesses. No wonder his father was threatening him."

"Would he have made profits if he hadn't cheated?"

"Probably. From what you tell me, I'd bet Wagner Sr. had the brains, but Gerald wanted to outdo his father. He set up separate companies his father had no control over. It appears he lost money on almost every venture he started, or maybe he just siphoned off so much cash that the companies never had a chance. Judging from the bank statements, he's been hoarding away money for years."

Winston hands me a timeline he's made of Wagner's business acquisitions. Winston has also charted all the transactions he's found.

"Along the way, he started dealing in contraband, shipping out machine tools and weapons to embargoed countries. Here were even larger profit margins. During the early years of the Iran–Iraq War, there was lots of money to be made, but then the state agencies quit paying their bills, and Wagner was left holding huge debts. At least his companies were. He managed to shield his own wealth."

"But there were always new suppliers who gave him credit," I note.

"Yes. When the Iran–Iraq War was over, he got new contracts in that window when the West was allowing credit. That's when we got lured in. We wanted the business, but he was in a serious credit squeeze before the Gulf War and used one revenue stream to partially pay off his debts to keep creditors at bay. He owed not just us, but less tolerant suppliers." Winston hands me a folder. "You think Adil could translate these for us?"

I open the file. There are letters in Arabic and in German. "What are they?"

"I can only read a bit of the German . . ." Winston's voice catches in his throat. He hesitates. "I think Dr. Wagner offered Dennis as a sacrificial lamb. See what Adil says. You sure he doesn't mind?"

"Dr. Wagner cheated his father, got him thrown out of Britain, and tried to implicate his father in Dennis's death. Adil wants to help."

* * *

Adil stops by the café where Dr. Wagner has breakfast each morning just to confirm that he's still in London. As the deadline for the Arms Commission report approaches and prosecutors close in, we are all afraid Dr. Wagner will skip the country before a case can be brought against him.

"You're sure he doesn't know who you are?" I ask as we walk with the children into Kensington Gardens.

"I have to keep myself from telling him. Every morning he gives me advice and tells me what to see that day." Adil kicks the soccer ball to Jad who runs ahead with Raja racing after him.

"What kind of advice?"

"'Save your money. If you jump on a bus and jump off before the ticket taker comes, you can ride for free. Be careful who you travel with. Your companion can rob you blind. If you travel to the continent, get a Euro rail pass, but don't go to Amsterdam, Naples, or Barcelona. The immigrants have taken over there. Remember, you can trust only yourself. Remember, the Lord helps those who help themselves.'"

"What do you say to him?"

"I write down what he tells me. He likes that. He wants to have someone listen to him."

"That's what I told Mother. I told her she should interview him."

Adil puts his arm around me as we settle on a park bench by the pond. "That's a conversation I'd like to hear. Today he told me he thought I was brave, and he asked me if I was. When I asked him why he thought I was brave, he just stared at me with his tiny bloodshot eyes. For a moment I thought he recognized me. He looked as if he'd just as soon kill me, then he said, 'Sometimes that will save you.'"

"What did he mean?"

"I don't know."

"Be careful." I remember saying the same thing to Dennis, and I feel a sudden shiver. I watch Jad and Raja follow two swans around the rim of the pond. "Winston asked if you'd translate these. He thinks they may be about Dennis."

I hand Adil the letters and go to retrieve the children. I give them each a small bag of bread and tell them to try to get the ducks and swans to follow them onto the grass. Omar follows at a distance as we lay a trail of breadcrumbs away from the water's edge.

When I return, Adil hands me one of the letters written in Arabic. "I'm not sure who it's from, but he knows who Dennis is, and he says Dennis is working for British intelligence. He's arranged to take Dennis around in Iraq and fill him with the information they want reported back to the British . . ." Adil pauses and frowns. "Then they plan to kill him."

I sink onto the bench and take the letter. I hold it limp in my hands. "Dennis went to Berlin after that trip to Iraq. I don't think he ever came back to Britain."

"MI6 may have met him in Berlin before he was killed," Adil says. "Dennis was killed in May 1990. In March of that year there were major arrests in London relating to arms sales to Iraq. This person is complaining about those."

"Who's the letter to?"

Adil turns it over. "Adnan Kamil . . ."

"Houston?"

"Yes. According to this letter, they are suspicious of all operations out of London now. They told Kamil Houston to inform Dr. Wagner that he must demonstrate his loyalty to his client, or he would be considered an enemy since he had a spy working for him."

I look at the children on the grass with a crowd of ducks at their feet. If it is Adnan Kamil Houston I've seen in the park, we could be in danger. "Let's get the children home," I say. "Jad . . . Raja . . ." They come running towards me dropping breadcrumbs with Omar and the ducks in pursuit. As we move out of the park, I ask Adil, "Do you think Dennis was a spy?"

"If he was working for MI6, he was either a spy or an informer."

CHAPTER TWENTY-FOUR

I MAKE MY decision to marry Adil the afternoon he tells his daughter that her mother has been killed. As I make lunch in the kitchen, which opens onto the living room, I watch Adil draw Raja up on the couch beside him. She holds a small, dark-haired doll Adil has bought her at a Bayswater Road stall. He's reading her favorite story about a prince and princess who disappear on a flying carpet. The whole time he reads, Raja watches him with credulous eyes.

When he finishes, he strokes her hair. "Raja, do you know how you used to live with Mommy and visit me?" She nods. "From now on you are going to live with me because Mommy was killed. Mommy loves you, but she can't see you anymore." He speaks in Arabic.

"What is *killed*?" Raja asks. Raja has lived amidst fighting, but that doesn't mean she understands the concept of death. I wonder how well Jad understands.

"Killed means you are no longer living here," Adil answers.

"Mommy has gone to Damascus," Raja interprets. "She won't be back."

"No, she won't be back."

I come in with sandwiches. During lunch I ask Raja if she has ever been to Damascus.

"Children can't go there," she explains. "It's only for grown-ups."

As I watch Adil cradle his daughter in the well of his arm, I make my decision to pair my life with his. I love and care for who he is, for what's happened to him, and for who he wants to be. I believe he loves and cares for me. For the rest, I will have to trust.

*   *   *

I tell Adil that he doesn't have to ask my mother's permission for us to get married, and he certainly doesn't have to ask Winston's, but he insists. "My father won't come. It will be bad for the children if no family is there."

I ask Mother if she'll see Adil. "You're getting married," she asks and charges at the same time.

"Yes." I sit down in the chair across from her by the fire in the living room. She shuts her eyes, and her hand reaches for her forehead as if she's suddenly in pain. "I love him," I defend. My marriage undermines her in a way I don't understand. I want to ease her pain, but I resent her making me feel guilty. She didn't object to Adil when I was younger. She even tried to help me find him when I was first pregnant. "What are you afraid of?" I ask.

She opens her eyes as if surprised I see her fear. "I'm afraid you'll find yourself trapped in a family and a culture over which you have no control. You won't be able to get out because, to do so, you'll have to leave your son behind. I'm afraid the powers that govern Adil's world, at least his father's, are relentless. You tell me Adil wants to break from his father, but that's easier to say than to do. You tell me Ibrahim Hasan has worked for the U.S. government in the past. That makes his world all the more dangerous. I married a man who worked for the U.S. government. When the government's political interests and your father's no longer aligned, your father lost his protection."

"Are you saying the government sabotaged my father?"

"I'm saying he was working independently, and they didn't protect him. Given the assignment, that had the same result."

"But Adil doesn't work for any government. He wants to be a teacher."

Mother goes over to the bookcase in the corner, where she removes several volumes to reveal a safe I never knew existed. She brings forth not jewels or money, but a plastic sheaf of news clippings and two green spiral notebooks, which I recognize as the kind my father used. She sets them on the ottoman between us. The news articles are dated November 1, 1981, the day after my father died. There are only three of them, small stories from the inside pages of the *Washington Post*, the *New York Times,* and the *Baltimore Sun*. I pick them up, expecting to read an account of my father's death or at least his obituary. Instead, they contain wire service reports on the crash of a private airplane in the Persian Gulf carrying an international arms dealer, an American citizen, and a Lebanese-French woman whom investigators suggest may have been the mistress of the American. *"Investigators suspect a faulty fuel pump as cause of the crash."* My father's name is never mentioned.

I look up at Mother. "Your father's work added up to that," she says without acknowledging the reference to a mistress. "No one's ever acknowledged his work for the Agency or listed him on the Honor Roll of those who died in service." Mother takes the articles and refolds them.

"What's in the notebooks?" I ask.

"Notes and the outline of the book he wanted to write. Except for these notebooks and the clippings, I left your father's story behind when we moved here." I wonder what notes of my father's she's chosen to take. "I couldn't pursue his story and raise the three of you. I thought you had a right to live out from under his shadow and have space to make your own lives; but now here you are, racing into the darkness I've tried your whole life to protect you from, as though how I raised you made no difference."

"Mother . . ." I protest gently. I don't understand why she's so upset. "My marrying Adil isn't about you or Dad. I'm not *racing into the darkness*. I'm marrying a kind man who's struggling to find his own life and is the father of my child, your grandson."

Mother slips the news clippings back into their plastic envelope. "When do you want me to meet him? I want to see him alone."

*   *   *

Mother and Adil spend two hours together. Adil presents her with his *excruciatingly*—Mother's word—honest proposal, explaining that his father is opposed to the marriage and has cut him off, but that he wants to marry me anyway, though he doesn't want me to be cut off from my family. "It's important to Lizzy, though she may not say it, that her family approves of her, and therefore it's important to me," he tells Mother. He says he'll get a job as soon as we figure out where we will live, but at the moment he's living on the charity of his friends and a modest bank account he's saved on his own. We'll have to depend on my salary for a while. "But I'll work like a horse for my family," he tells my mother, who tells me.

"Lizzy's capable of working," Mother answers. "I'm sure she prefers your company to that of a horse. But are you prepared to have a wife who's an equal partner?"

"I'm marrying her so that I may have an equal partner. But it's bad for the children if no family supports our marriage."

That is the argument that wins Mother over. She tells Adil she'll be there for us and the children. If Adil becomes my husband, she says she accepts him. "You must understand that my reservations are not personal."

"I wonder what she thinks they are," Adil asks me later, but he knows he's won over my mother.

*   *   *

Adil has not entirely won Jad, however. They've become friends, but Jad resists Adil when he tries to get too close or tries to hold him, and he argues that Raja is not his sister when Adil says that she is. Jad likes playing soccer with Adil, but yesterday Adil raised his voice when Jad hit Raja, who took his ball, and Jad told Adil that he didn't want him as a father because Ramsay was going to be his father. Then this morning Jad declared he didn't want to go play with Raja and Adil anymore. "I don't like them."

"Why don't you like them?" I should have seen this coming. I urged Adil not to press Jad, but he seems unable to back off. He plays with Jad, then he tries to take Jad on his lap with his sister.

"Children don't like change," I tell him. "You have to give him time."

"We don't have time."

"We have our lifetime."

"Raja's taken to you."

"Raja's two years old. Jad's almost five. Ramsay is the first man who cared for him."

"What can I do? He's *my* son," Adil says with a proprietary air I don't like.

"He's a person. He's not *yours*. He's not *mine*. You can't make him feel the way you want, but if you give him space, just love him, I promise he'll come around."

Adil keeps trying, but he's not very good at giving Jad his own time. Yesterday I said, "You're acting like your father!" The comment just popped out. Adil's face went rigid. He walked out of the room then out of the apartment. From the window I saw Omar follow him; Jawad stayed with us. I realized I'd never seen Adil really angry, except once in high school. I'm not sure if I should marry a man whose anger I don't know. I wonder where that criterion has come from. Adil has never really seen me angry either, but I know my anger. It's rarely deep, and I don't hold grudges.

When Adil finally returned, he stood at the foot of the sofa. "Don't speak to me that way."

"What way?" I bristled.

"Without respect. I respect you. I don't tell you you're like your mother. How can you say I'm like my father? You don't even know my father."

"I'm sorry. I don't know him. But I know you, or I'm beginning to. I certainly know our son. He's kindhearted. You have to trust who he is, even if he's only five."

"How can we get married if he doesn't love me."

"Just love *him*."

But now here is Jad telling me he doesn't want to see Adil. While I told Adil we have a lifetime, I'm also concerned. I haven't told Jad I'm marrying Adil. When I suggested the possibility a few days ago, Jad threw such a fit that I backed off. It wasn't the kind of tantrum he sometimes had when he was younger and I cut his sandwich on the wrong diagonal or insisted he go to bed when he was overly tired, or when he couldn't fit a piece of a puzzle together. With those I could distract him and talk him back to calm. When I told him I might marry Adil and not Ramsay, he started shaking his head violently. "No . . . No . . . No. I forbid you!"

"*Forbid me?*" It is not a word I ever remember using.

"I forbid you! I forbid you! I forbid you!" he screamed and broke down in tears.

I drew his lanky body into my arms, pressed his heaving chest onto mine, encircled his flailing arms and legs until my hold contracted his world back into a frame he could deal with. I tried to explain to him that I loved Adil in a different way than Ramsay, but most of all I loved him. I told him nothing was decided. Finally, he fell asleep in my arms.

I quit trying to convince Jad by telling him Adil is his father. That fact threatens him as if the freedom to choose his father has been taken from him. Though the decision on whether I marry Adil is mine, I want Jad's blessing.

"Do you know I've known Adil almost half my life?" I say as Jad and I sit on the floor of the room among his books and toys and the clothes he refuses to put on. "He's one of my oldest friends. It will make me very sad if you don't like my oldest friend because I love you more than I love anyone in the world."

"More than Adil?" Jad asks.

"I love you differently, but yes, more than Adil."

"More than Raja?"

"I'm just learning to love Raja. I've loved you before you were even born."

Jad watches me carefully to make sure I'm telling the truth. Slowly he begins putting on his socks. "Okay, I'll go," he says.

As he dresses, I pick up the children's atlas he loves with its pictures of different countries and people. I open to the page showing the Middle East, which we often look at together. "Here's where Adil was born." I point to a small yellow arc against the blue Mediterranean. "And where Raja was born." I turn the page. "And here is where you and I were born."

"Washington, D.C.!" he affirms.

I turn more pages. "And here's where we all met."

"London!" he declares.

"The four of us have lived in this much of the world." I show him on the larger map. "So together we know a few things."

*   *   *

When we arrive at Fatin's apartment, it turns out Adil has also been worrying over Jad. He tells Jad he has a place he wants to take him, just the two of them. Jad looks over at me, wary but curious. "There's something I want to buy, and I need you to help me pick it out and share it with me."

Adil and Jad go off together, and Raja and I stay in the apartment playing. Around noon a commotion of feet come up the stairs, then all at once Jad and a brown and white puppy bolt through the door. Raja runs into my arms. Adil has never owned a dog, but he's watched Jad run after every dog in the park and listened to Jad talk about Ramsay's dog. Adil and Jad explain together that they have chosen this puppy from the pound, where he was going to be killed that very day if they hadn't taken him. Jad not only has a dog of his own now, but the knowledge that he's saved the dog's life. This appeals to his very large heart, which it seems is finally letting Adil in.

"How will we take care of it?" I ask. We don't even know where we'll be living. Now there will be four of us and a dog.

"I'll take care of it," Adil says. "Jad and I together. It will be ours." Adil and Jad name the half shepherd/half retriever Pelé after the great soccer star. Pelé draws the two of them together faster than any reasoning I could come up with. It turns out Pelé loves to play soccer.

*   *   *

Jane flies over for the wedding. Sophie can't come. Or won't. When I asked if she'd heard from Ramsay or called Ramsay, she cuts me off. "You can't just arrange people's feelings, Lizzy." I understand that means she hasn't heard, or he hasn't responded. I don't press her.

For my family this wedding is sudden, though for me it is six years overdue. Because of Adil's visa application, which came to the attention of Jonathan Dees, Molly found out we were getting married and phoned me. She is still home on semester break.

"I feel like a matchmaker," she says. "I don't want to intrude, but can I come?"

I can't say no. The only other friend from school will be Fatin.

"I always thought the two of you belonged together," Molly insists. "You were so independent, Lizzy. I admired you for that." I think of the energy I wasted in high school being suspicious of Molly Dees.

For a small wedding, ours is growing quickly. We're scheduled for two p.m. Thursday, February 1 at the Old Marylebone Town Hall. Adil and I finally confirm January 27 that we are getting married. Adil arranges with my mother to take care of the children so he can take me out to dinner alone. We go to a new restaurant by the river. As we sit looking out at the lighted boats passing by and the lights on the bridge across the water, he asks me to step outside while we wait for our food. We huddle in the chilled air at the rail overlooking the Thames. He puts his arms around me and kisses me and then he gives me a small velvet pouch. Inside is a ring with tiny pearls framing a diamond.

"It was my mother's," he says. "My aunt saved it all these years. She didn't give it to me when I married before, but when I was home this time, I told her I knew the woman I wanted to spend the rest of my life with. She went to her dresser and brought out this ring that my mother had left on the counter the day she died." Adil slips the ring onto my finger, then he asks me to marry him for the third time.

We have four days to put together a wedding. Mother, who's in the middle of writing a major article for her magazine, commits to the wedding preparations with the same energy she gives to all her work. She wants to know what I will wear, do I want a reception at our home or at Winston's club or at a restaurant, what will Jad and Raja wear, does Jad even own a suit, who's ordering the flowers? When Jane arrives two days early, she helps absorb some of Mother's energy. When I tell Adil my mother is driving me crazy, he asks why I don't just let her do everything, then I won't have to be bothered.

"But I want to be bothered. It's my wedding."

"I thought you said you didn't want to have to worry about all the details."

"I didn't want to worry about them alone. I wanted to worry about them with you."

One detail Adil takes the initiative on is choosing our wedding bands. It is his idea to take Jad and Raja with us and buy them each a ring too. He suggests we all exchange our rings at the ceremony to show we are a family. Jad and Raja try on their rings in the store with solemnity as if they understand the importance of the act. When it comes time to take the rings off, neither wants to so we let them wear the rings out of the store and spend the afternoon making sure they don't lose them.

*   *   *

The day before the wedding, an enormous arrangement of lilies arrives at the house addressed to me. Jane brings them to my room where Jad is trying on the gray slacks and navy blazer I bought him that morning, along with a red and blue tie that matches the tie I bought Adil for the wedding.

I take the lilies as a hopeful sign until I read the card: *Consider the lilies. They toil not, neither do they spin. But partnerships and unions toil and spin and then EXPLODE!* The card is unsigned. I show it to Jane.

"You think it's a threat?" she asks.

"It sounds like one." I phone Adil.

Adil, Winston, two police officers, Jane, and I are gathered in the living room when Mother arrives from work. Outside the house, Adil's bodyguards stand watch.

"Let me see the card," Mother says.

The officer hands it to her. "The clerk in the shop wrote the card," the older officer tells us. "She said the order came in by phone."

"How was it paid for?" Mother asks.

"Cash. Someone dropped an envelope through the mail slot."

"It may not be a threat," the older officer says. "Maybe it's just a warning about life."

I wonder if he has any idea what has happened to our family, if he knows about Dennis's death. He is not the local constable.

"I think you should take this card very seriously," Mother says.

"Any angry girlfriends or boyfriends out there?" the young officer asks.

Adil and I look at each other. Sahar and Ramsay would not send threats. "No."

For half an hour the police question us with no clear direction, as if they have no idea what they're looking for and no belief they will find it. Mother tells the officers about Gerald Wagner abducting us at the airport. They take down his name and address and say they'll check all leads and get back to us. After they leave, Mother suggests we postpone the wedding.

"No," Adil and I answer at the same time.

"What about changing the location?"

"No one knows the location," I point out. "This isn't a public event."

"Does Gerald Wagner know you're getting married?" Jane asks.

"How would he know?"

"Does he know you were in his house?" Mother asks. "That you took out files? Do we know if the authorities have contacted him yet? Is Serena Wagner trustworthy?" Mother fires questions. She doesn't approve of our excursion into Dr. Wagner's home no matter the legal rationalization Marvin provided or the payoff Winston has confirmed. We put ourselves and by extension Jad and Raja at risk, she says. This reprimand is from a mother who's spent part of her life traveling to war zones to cover stories.

"I don't know if Serena's trustworthy, but I can't imagine her telling Dr. Wagner. And Serena doesn't know we're getting married." I sent Serena's sweaters to Marvin, who told me she got scared and left Washington the day before. The box with sweaters remains on the floor of his closet.

"Maybe the message has nothing to do with the wedding," Jane suggests. "The card doesn't mention a marriage."

I reread the card. "It says, *partnerships and unions.*"

"A business partnership?" Jane suggests.

"Perhaps I'm the target," Winston says. "Investigators have contacted Dr. Wagner's solicitors and subpoenaed documents here and in Germany. We've turned over our company files that relate to him."

"The flowers were sent to Lizzy," Mother points out.

"Maybe he's still trying to scare us," I say. "Maybe..." I look at Adil, "... maybe he knows who you are."

Everyone sits for a moment contemplating the possibilities, searching our memories for clues to construct a scenario that makes sense.

"I for one am uncomfortable with the wedding going on as planned," Mother says.

"The wedding is tomorrow," I remind her.

"We must at least ask for protection."

*   *   *

That night I lie in bed staring up at the white canopy that has arched above me since I was a child. I remember the day before my tenth birthday when Dad and Mom took me to the basement of Hecht's department store to choose this bed with the lacy white eyelet ceiling. When the bed arrived, I felt transformed, elevated to equal status with my sisters, neither of whom had such a bed, but both of whom wanted to sit beneath its protective sky. I stare up in the dark now at the worn cloth, listening to my own breathing. In twelve hours I'm marrying Adil. I wonder who sent the note today. I try to hear where this shrill warning comes from, like a high-speed projectile up in the atmosphere. Is it aimed at my world, or will it burn up before it hits the earth?

It's still dark outside when I hear the front door open and footsteps on the stairs. Scrambling into a robe, I tiptoe to the edge of the doorway and open my door a crack. I'm ready to react when Sophie turns the corner. I scream. "Sophie! Oh my god, Sophie!"

I scare her. Sophie screams too. The two of us hug each other, trying to calm ourselves. Mother comes to the doorway of her study, where she's already up working. She smiles. Jane emerges. Jad races into Sophie's arms. "Did you know she was coming?" I ask Mother.

"She called yesterday. She wanted to surprise you."

"Well, you did!" Tears come to my eyes, and I start laughing. I haven't realized how much I missed Sophie not being here until she is here. Suddenly threats seem insignificant. Everything will be all right. Sophie has come. We are together as a family.

"So when do I get to talk to Adil?" she asks.

*   *   *

At 8:00 a.m. Adil calls. I was going to tell him about Sophie, but the tone of his voice silences me. He says a slight complication has arisen.

"Complication?"

"My father's arrived."

"Your father?" Suddenly I'm alert. "Well, good."

"He came in the middle of the night."

"So did my sister. She decided to surprise me. She wants to talk to you."

"Yes, well, I'd like to talk to her too, but my father's asked us to postpone the wedding."

"What?"

"He says he wants to speak with you. If we are to marry, he wants us to marry properly, not in some London city hall."

"I have to be back at work Monday. Today is Thursday." Mine is the only job we have.

"My father's relented. He's giving us a sizeable wedding gift. You won't have to work."

"But I want to work."

"Well, you don't have to return on Monday."

"Adil . . ." My heart sinks. Part of me is glad his father isn't turning his back on him. I've seen how hard it is for Adil with only my family as reference, but I don't trust his father. "Are you sure he's not just trying to buy you off?" Instantly I regret my choice of words.

"Is that what you think? Is that all you think my word is worth?"

"I'm not marrying you because of your word. Or even because I'm the mother of your son."

"Then why?"

"If you don't know that, we have a bigger complication than your father."

"I told my father about the flowers and the note. He's worried. He thinks it's dangerous for us to go ahead with the wedding."

I wonder if Ibrahim Hasan sent the note to delay the wedding, though I don't imagine him quoting from the New Testament. "How did your father know we were getting married today?"

"Omar told him."

"I didn't think Omar knew. I didn't think he spoke English."

"Omar's invited to the wedding. You knew that."

I grow silent. Doesn't Adil understand what his father is doing? First he'll get Adil to postpone the wedding and then cancel it.

"My father would like to meet Jad. And he wants to speak with you."

"My whole family's here. They came at expense of time and money because we're getting married today."

"I know. My father came for the same reason, but he'd like his sister, my aunt, to be at my wedding and my other relatives as well. He's just asking us to wait for a month or so to prepare a proper wedding."

"We've prepared a proper wedding. We can have a reception later. Or maybe we can marry twice."

Adil is silent for a moment, then he says, "I'll do whatever you want."

"That's not good enough!" I hang up. Now Adil is seeing my anger. I feel numb and at the same time confused. The phone rings. I don't answer. Jane steps into the den. When she sees I'm not going to answer, she picks up the receiver. She passes it to me. I shake my head.

"It's Adil."

"Tell him I'm not here."

"He can hear that you're here."

I take the phone, but I don't speak. "Lizzy?" Adil asks. I make a small noise. "I'm coming over. I'm bringing my father." I don't answer. "Do you hear me?"

Finally, I say, "Yes," and hang up. I sit there with Jane watching me. I don't know how to begin to explain what's happening or what I'm feeling. If Adil can't stand up to his father now on this important issue, how can I expect him to later and for the rest of our lives? How can I marry him if we're going to live in his father's orbit? I love him. I know that now. I don't want to break off the wedding. After all the years, we've finally committed to each other, and I don't want to lose him.

"Do you want to talk?" Jane sits beside me on the plaid sofa in her blue wool robe. She sips coffee from a mug, her short chestnut hair framing her face. I remember her with a ponytail in high school when we first moved to London, when I thought she was all that I wanted to be.

"Do you think Dad had a mistress?" I ask.

She stares at me hard. "Where's that coming from?"

"Mom showed me the clippings about Dad's plane crash. The paper said the woman on the plane was thought to be Dad's mistress. Joe Campbell told me people wondered."

"I don't know."

"Mother never said anything to you?"

"No, and I never asked. Whether Dad did or didn't, his story is not your story."

"How do you know for certain about another person?" I ask. "Can you ever know?"

"I suppose we're lucky if we know ourselves."

I consider my sister, who's just turned thirty-one, and I wonder why she hasn't yet married, and why Sophie hasn't married. Have their careers filled all the space in their lives, or is our father's ghost circling them too? I tell Jane what has happened with Adil, about Ibrahim Hasan's request that we postpone the wedding.

"Ibrahim Hasan is coming here?"

I nod.

"Shouldn't you tell Mom?"

"What would you do?"

"To be honest with you, Lizzy, you are way out there in some place I can't imagine myself. You'll have to make it up as you go along, but don't get caught in conventions when you're inventing a new world. Hear what Adil and his father have to say. Give Adil some credit. He's out there with you trying to create a new life for himself and you."

I hug her. "I guess I'd better get everyone up," I say. "Ibrahim Hasan is coming to our home."

CHAPTER TWENTY-FIVE

WHEN I ENTER Mother's study, she raises her hand in a greeting and a signal to let her finish the sentence she's writing. Glancing up, she asks, "Did you know the gun that killed Dennis was the same kind used by the old Yugoslav Army?" She has that intense look in her eyes I've seen so often as she drives through papers and facts to shape her story. "A Czechoslovak-made Skorpion. Those same guns have been shipped out to civil wars in Africa."

"Good morning," I say.

"I'm sorry. Good morning, darling." She's sitting cross-legged in her chair wearing sweatpants and a blue turtleneck sweater. "This deadline is on top of me."

"Is this the story you and Winston were arguing about?" I heard them behind closed doors.

She uncurls her legs. On the floor lie interview notes and folders and books, the storm of papers that precede most of her articles. "Winston's afraid the press will focus on him and Dennis if I write about the arms investigation, but the Commission Report is coming out this month whether I write about it or not. Frankly, I'm more concerned Winston will be hurt because of your marriage."

"My marriage?"

She gestures to a chair. "Sit down."

"I came to tell you Adil's father is on his way over to see us."

"Ibrahim?" She calls him by his first name, though I don't think they've ever met.

"He arrived last night. He wants us to postpone the wedding."

"Then we are agreed." She closes her laptop and joins me.

"Who?"

"Ibrahim and I."

"I don't know. Are you agreed?" I don't want to argue with my mother on my wedding day. "Why do you say my marriage threatens Winston?"

Mother's blue eyes, which I once thought saw everything, focus now on me. Her face is without makeup, her skin slightly discolored and heavy around her chin. "You know the investigation going on . . . ?" I nod. "Among others, the Arms Commission is investigating Dr. Wagner and Ibrahim Hasan. Winston accommodated Dr. Wagner on several occasions at Dennis's request. He wrote letters attesting that equipment Dr. Wagner was exporting was for general use rather than for military purposes. Winston's also being investigated. We provided the Commission with Serena's files and with Dennis's notes, along with the handwriting analysis of Dr. Wagner's, to show that Wagner knew the purpose of the equipment he was shipping even though Winston insists he did not know."

Mother speaks slowly as if presenting evidence in a case she's building. "Many of the exports went through Jordan, where Ibrahim Hasan was based and where a company, KEY Imports, was based. Both Ibrahim Hasan and Gerald Wagner have shipped arms through KEY Imports. The company re-labeled cargo and shipped it on. Until now there's been no link between Winston and Ibrahim Hasan, but once you marry his son, it will be a plausible defense for Dr. Wagner to argue that he was the one duped by them."

I stare at my mother. She is spinning her fears, creating scenarios that don't exist. With my father she saw events get woven into a story that was presented as fact and used in the agendas of others. A lie took on the shape of truth, and truth disappeared from view. How safe Winston must have seemed to her when she married him, a man who sold cars to a nation, was knighted by the Queen for his charitable work. Now history seems determined to circle back on her. "Then why are you writing an article?" I ask.

"Whether I write an article or not, the Commission report will make headlines. I'm thorough. The truth won't hurt Winston if it can be uncovered." From the tremor in her voice I understand the fragile thread upon which this proposition hangs. I wonder if she used the same logic when trying to defend my father.

"Who owns KEY Imports?" I ask.

"A consortium, including ex-government and military officials from a number of countries. The company gets a fee for services but never takes possession of the goods."

There is a part of my mother I've never been able to bridge to—this professional person who's able to keep at a distance the emotions around the stories she writes, even today on my wedding day. I know she feels emotions, but sometimes I think they threaten her. They threaten to complicate the world she needs to report clearly. They threaten to open up a pain she's long since buried. Maybe she fears the devastation from that pain could unhinge us all.

"So you don't want me to marry Adil because my marriage may hurt Winston with the Arms Commission? Why didn't you say anything about this before?"

"I only figured it out when I heard Ibrahim was testifying before the Commission."

"When did you hear that?"

Mother glances out the window. The sun is shining in a rare London winter's day. I wonder if it will hold until two o'clock. "He called me yesterday."

"Ibrahim Hasan called you? From where?" I can't believe Mother has talked to Adil's father and hasn't mentioned that to me.

"He's in London. He wanted to know how I felt about the wedding. I told him I thought the two of you were taking on more than either of you understood. I wasn't certain love was strong enough to buoy you up under so much baggage. On the other hand, you had a child between you. I told him I wasn't wise enough to know the right answer. Then Ibrahim told me he'd agreed to testify before the Commission. He didn't tell me what he'd say, but I assume it's at least partly against Dr. Wagner. He told me I might be interested in knowing that the gun that killed Dennis had been made by a state company in the former Czechoslovakia. That company was bought by Dr. Wagner in 1990 as part of a network of arms factories in Eastern Europe. The evidence against Dr. Wagner is still documentary and circumstantial. A good solicitor might be able to exonerate him. Ibrahim's testimony will be critical. He can connect and explain the documents, but I'm afraid he'll be suspect as soon as he becomes your father-in-law." Mother opens her hands on the table as if delivering her case to me and seeking my approval.

I do not approve. I stand. "So you want me to cancel my wedding so the British Arms Commission can do its job?"

"I can't tell you what to do."

"Adil said his father wanted the wedding postponed so he could have his relatives there. He didn't mention any political reasons."

"I don't know how much his father's told him."

"Is everything driven by politics, Mother?" I ask and protest at the same time.

"I'm just telling you what I see. The timing is difficult."

"The timing is always difficult! It's been difficult ever since I've known Adil." I sink back into the chair opposite her. I'm in jeans and a sweatshirt and need to get ready if Adil and his father are coming over. Mother has made appointments for us all at the hairdressers this morning. I'm supposed to be getting married in five hours.

"Maybe that tells you something," she says.

"What?" I challenge. Over the years I've backed away from confronting my mother about my father and her own marriage, but now I plunge ahead. "Was the timing perfect for you and Dad? You had problems. I know you had problems."

"Yes, we did."

"So what did you do?"

"I suppose we took them one at a time."

"And so are we. But we have to start, and we have to start with what we know about ourselves, not what everyone else thinks." I look about her room where papers and books spill off her shelves. She's also supposed to go to the beauty salon with us, but I suspect she'll cancel because of her deadline. My mother has never lived her life worried about what she looked like or what other people thought. She never had the time.

"And what do you know about yourselves?" she asks.

"That we've loved each other for over a decade. That there are large areas we don't know about each other, but we want to spend our lives finding out."

Mother sighs the way she does from time to time over my life. "You can't see from my perspective, and I can only dimly remember yours," she says. "Your dad used to say you'd be the peacemaker. I don't know whether this marriage is putting you into a position to accomplish that, or if you're marrying the wrong man to fill the space your father left in your life."

"Mother!" I protest. "Adil is a person, not a political space. He's the person I want to share my life with. The answer depends on what I do with my life." I shift the agenda then or rather broaden it. "I went to see the Campbells while I was home." Mother's hands, now freckled with tiny brown age spots, tense on the table and fold on top of themselves. "I wanted to find out what they knew about Dad's death."

"And what did they tell you?"

"Joe told me about the other two people in the plane when Dad died."

"What is it you want to know, Elizabeth?" Mother asks with the edge in her voice that often causes me to retreat, but I push ahead.

"I want to know if what happened to Dad relates to me. I want to know how my life connects to his. How can I have the perspective you want me to have if I don't understand the past?"

"Of course what happened relates to you. He was your father."

"Adil's father told him he knew Dad."

"They could have met." Mother takes the coincidence matter-of-factly. "You know, you're more like your father than either of your sisters." Her tone softens. "I see him in you, and I think how much you both missed. That stirs me, Lizzy, and sometimes it puts distance between us. You challenge the powers that be not by words and arguments, but by your life. Your father would have understood you, I think; whereas I want to ask you quite conventional questions like how you plan to raise the children—as Christians or Jews or Muslims?"

"The same way you raised us, as human beings. You never talked about dividing lines between religions and people. You told us God was universal. You said that was what held us all together."

"When did I say that?"

"After Dad died. I asked you if Dad was dead in the ground the way Grandma Sha said, or if he was in heaven the way Grandma West said, and you told me he was right where he'd always been, in my heart. You told me people had different ideas about what happened after you died, but there was one idea that held us all together."

"What was that?" Mother asks as if she's forgotten and wants to know.

"You told me life kept going on. You told me love would keep going on, that those we loved stayed in our hearts." I remember walking across the cemetery at Mother's side after we buried my father. She took the long journey back to the car with me. Jane and Sophie were ahead of us surrounded by their friends, and Grandma Sha and Grandpa and Grandma West were behind us. Mother and I walked slowly over a hill. She held my hand tight as though she needed me to guide her as much as I needed her. "You said God was Love, and the more we loved, the closer we were to God and to them. You said that was universal."

"I don't remember being so wise."

"I remember because I've tried to do that with my life. I think that's what I'm doing now, following the love and sorting out the rest."

"Ah, Lizzy . . ." Mother sighs again. "I can't argue with you."

"Good, because Adil and his father are due any minute, and no one's ready." Mother stands. "Can I ask you one more question? If you don't want to answer . . ."

"Go on."

"What did you think when you heard about the other people on Dad's plane?"

"I thought how sad for their families."

"I mean about who they were, what they did, why Dad was with them?"

"I probably wondered how many stories would be invented to accommodate the circumstances."

"But you didn't worry about the circumstances?"

"I knew the truth would be long in coming if it ever came. I defended the man I knew."

"What about the woman? The one mentioned in the article as Dad's mistress." I don't want to upset my mother. I still want to protect her as I wanted to the day of the funeral, but I need to know.

"That was the government's story. Did Joe tell you about the proposal he offered me?"

"No, but Jane did."

"Some people were threatening to smear Dad's name. That article was a not-so-subtle warning of how that might happen."

"But the article came out the day after the crash, before you even talked to Joe. It was written by a reporter, not the government."

Mother just looks at me. "Where do you think the wire service reporter got his information? He wasn't sent to the crash site. He made and received a few phone calls."

"So you think it was planted, that it wasn't true?"

"Are you asking me if your father had a mistress?"

"I'm not sure what I'm asking you." At one level I want to know my parents' lives and the context I've been missing, but I don't want to be bound by their lives and mistakes. I want room to imagine and make my own life. "Were you sure you knew Dad? Sometimes I wonder if I've invented who I want him to be. I wonder if I'll feel the same way about Adil someday."

"At our best your father and I loved the best in each other," Mother says. "To that extent we knew each other."

"Was that enough?"

"It would have been."

* * *

Adil kisses me at the front door. He's wearing the tie I bought him for the wedding, a navy blazer, and gray slacks, just like Jad will wear in a few hours, though at the moment Jad is sitting at the top of the stairs in his superhero pajamas. Behind Adil on the sidewalk, between Omar and Jawad, Ibrahim Hasan paces in a dark blue suit and sunglasses. He moves up onto the first step. Omar and Jawad stay on the sidewalk. Anyone watching our house will know *someone* is inside.

"Where's Raja?" I ask.

"Fatin will bring her. Father . . ." On the threshold, Adil presents his father. "You remember Lizzy."

I remember the night in Berlin when I extended my hand, and he reluctantly accepted it. This time he holds it for a moment, as if determining what he might do with it, and then he touches it to his lips in European fashion. "Benti," he says as though he concedes in that moment, or wants me to believe that he's conceded. *My daughter.* My eyes seek Adil's, but Adil is already heading inside. Speculatively I think, "Abi," *My father,* but I can't say the word. "Marhaba," I say instead. *Welcome to our home.*

"Heyyei b'tehki arabi?" he asks Adil. *Does she speak Arabic?*

"Kalil," I answer for myself. *A little.* "Lakin ana ata'alm." *But I'm learning.*

He proceeds to talk to me in Arabic. "Adil needs a wife who can speak our language."

"Father, please," Adil protests.

I lead them both into the living room, where Ibrahim Hasan sits beside me on the sofa. His gray hair has thinned on top so that his scalp shows through, making him look more vulnerable. His scar has sunk into his cheek, a rift across his face. His face has grown thin. "I have come to talk with the woman you tell me you are to marry. Let me speak."

Adil stands above us. "It's all right," I say. "Jad's waiting for you on the stairs. I don't know why he hasn't come down." Adil leaves to find Jad.

"Your children will need to know our language," Ibrahim Hasan continues in Arabic. "Does my grandson speak Arabic?"

"He's learning."

"Good, otherwise he will not make friends."

"We live in Washington," I point out. "He has friends."

"You live there now, but the time will come when Adil will return. You must support him in his role."

"I have my own work."

"I know. When the conflicts are over, we will need tourists to come back. You can help us."

Jad shyly turns the corner of the living room. "Ah . . . here . . . Jad." I shift to English. "I want you to meet Adil's father." For some reason I can't say, "your grandfather." The relationship feels as strange to me as it does to Jad, who hangs back in the doorway. I don't know if it's the scar on Ibrahim Hasan's face or the reserve in my own voice, but Jad comes over reluctantly. "This is Mr. Hasan," I say.

"You can call him Jiddu," Adil says to Jad. "That's what Raja calls him." Ibrahim Hasan touches Jad on the shoulders as if measuring him. "Adil Adil Ibrahim Hasan," he says to me in Arabic.

"His name is Jesse Adil West," I answer in English. "We call him Jad." I look to Adil for help, but it is my mother who steps in.

"*Salaam aleikum.*" She holds out her hand to Ibrahim Hasan, who stands up. Mother has assured me they've never met, but they talked more on the phone yesterday than she's revealed, for Adil's father asks her if she finished her story, and she asks him if he'd be willing to confirm some of it from his point of view. This is to be my wedding day, and my mother and father-in-law are doing business. She adds, "After the wedding, of course." Jad scampers onto the couch next to me.

"Has anyone offered you coffee or tea?" Mother asks. "Or breakfast?"

"We've eaten," Adil answers, watching me.

"I'll go get tea," I say.

"I'll get it," Mother offers.

"No, I will."

"I'll help you," Adil says. Jad scrambles off the couch to join us. "What's the matter?" Adil asks as soon as the kitchen door shuts.

I fill a pot with water. Suddenly I feel far away from his life. "Your father is laying out our lives for us."

"Ignore him. I told you that."

"Part of me is afraid you're going to look up one day and say that he's right."

"About what?"

"You'll want to go back, go into politics and run the country or something."

"What country? I don't even know what my country is. I wouldn't go anywhere without you and Jad and Raja."

"What if we don't want to go?"

"Lizzy, I can't worry about what might happen. We have enough to worry about." Sometimes Adil seems much older than me.

"I don't want to limit you," I say, "but . . ."

"I know that."

"But I also don't want to live in a country as a stranger, booking tour packages with your father. I wish I loved him."

"You love me. I don't love your mother. And I certainly don't want to live with your mother."

"Neither do I."

"So . . ."

Jad is sitting at the kitchen table trying to follow the conversation. "I want to live with Pelé," he inserts.

Adil laughs. "Yes, we all want to live with Pelé. We must ask Pelé where he wants to live."

"Do you want to postpone the wedding?" I ask.

"No. I want to marry you today. I told my father that." He kisses me, then puts his arm around Jad and kisses him too.

"Mother's concerned our getting married will hurt Winston with the Arms Commission."

Adil just smiles. "Maybe my father and your mother were meant for each other. Whatever they say, we're getting married today."

*　*　*

When we return to the living room, Mother and Adil's father are sitting on the sofa together looking at a photo album.

Ibrahim Hasan is studying a picture carefully. "Yes, that is Calvin Wheat, though he is younger than when we met."

In the picture, Dad is standing beside a prop plane with me in his arms. Jane and Sophie, dressed in identical plaid dresses with white collars, stand on either side of him. This is one of my favorite pictures because Dad is talking to me in it. According to Mom, it was taken just before we all flew with him to North Carolina for one of his four-day vacations. Dad made vacations special when he flew us there himself.

"So you did know Lizzy's father?" Adil asks. He stands behind the sofa looking at the album.

Ibrahim Hasan's pockmarked face inclines towards me, but his voice remains matter-of-fact. "The last time I saw your father, he tried to get me to work for your government. He had tried before in Beirut and in Amman. I told him if he continued to pursue me, I'd kill him." He keeps his eyes fixed on me like an old crocodile sizing up his prey.

I don't flinch. I've read my father's journals. I know he didn't think Ibrahim Hasan would kill him. He had a begrudging respect for this man. "Who did kill him?" I ask.

"You threatened to kill Lizzy's father?" Adil reacts.

"Most likely Hamid Jaafari," my father-in-law answers. "Though some say Avi Sher."

This is the first time I've ever heard a name attached to the act, an actual person rather than a political force or a set of events. I sit down in the chair opposite Mother. "Who are they?"

"Hamid Jaafari is an arms dealer. Avi Sher was an agent for Mossad. Avi Sher died in Beirut in 1984."

"Why was my father killed?"

Ibrahim Hasan shifts to Arabic. He looks directly at me as he speaks. "Your father spent too much time looking at the sun. You can't stare straight into the sun; you must divert your gaze."

I struggle to translate for my mother. I'm not sure I hear the words correctly and am not sure what he means.

"For different reasons, with different partners, your government... *sahhal*..."

"What is *sahhal?*" I ask Adil.

"Facilitated..."

"... facilitated certain arms sales to Iran and Iraq during their war, though U.S. law... *ma samaht*..."

"What is *ma samaht?*" I ask.

"Forbade..."

"... forbade such transfers."

I wonder why he's speaking in Arabic rather than English. Perhaps history is complicated enough in one's own language. Adil takes over the translation. "Your father discovered the Israelis were selling missiles and military equipment to Iran. He also discovered Washington secretly approved the sales, though publicly it urged an arms embargo. American hostages had been released earlier that year, in January 1981, from the embassy in Tehran. Many assumed the release was delayed until after the American election so Iran could get more arms from the new U.S. administration. But if the world found out America was allowing arms sales to Iran through Israel to pay for hostages, it would be disastrous for all three governments." Adil watches my mother as he explains his father's story. So do I, but I can't read her face.

"My father was involved in some of the sales because he operated in both countries," Adil translates, "but your father wasn't involved. The Israelis were suspicious of your father for reasons my father never learned, and the Iranians didn't trust him because he couldn't be bought.

"At the same time many in your government also wanted to keep Iraq armed so it could continue the war with Iran. They worked through nations like Jordan and Egypt and through men like my father and through ex-CIA like your father. They sold these nations missiles and arms, then those governments turned around and sold to Iraq." My father-in-law pauses, letting these facts sink in. I glance again at Mother. Her expression remains intent but unsurprised, and I realize that none of this information is new to her.

"Your father understood these deceptions. 'We are letting scorpions loose on the nape of our necks,' he said. 'Eventually they will sting us.' One of the arms dealers was a man named Hamid Jaafari—one of the few who managed to sell to both Iran and Iraq. Jaafari was also part of a network trying to acquire nuclear technology. Your father was pursuing him, though my father wasn't certain on whose behalf. He got the impression your father was acting on his own, though the CIA knew Jaafari. Hamid Jaafari offered your father a job with a very high price tag. Your father knew if he turned Jaafari down, he would be a marked man." Adil's translation presses on, a steady cadence over the harsher voice of his father.

"My father says your father was chasing Jaafari down . . . how do you say in English . . . down a viper's hole, but your father didn't know all the tunnels. It was a time in history . . ." Adil hesitates again, seeking another comparison. "Nothing was as it appeared. The political forces had sucked truth to the bottom. In English you would say it was a Bermuda triangle of history.

"The last time my father saw your father, they were in Baghdad, where your father was to meet Jaafari the next day. That summer the Israelis had blown up the Iraqi nuclear reactor Osirak, and the Iraqis were rebuilding. Rumor was that Iraq was trying to make an atomic bomb. There were rumors about the scientist who'd signed the contract with the French for the Osirak reactor, rumors that he'd been tortured and was now lost in an Iraqi prison because he'd refused to turn his work to building an atom bomb.

"'Can a man of courage survive here?' your father asked my father. They were standing in a hotel room in Baghdad with the curtains drawn behind them looking out the window at the blacked-out city at war. Your father had turned the radio up loud so they wouldn't be heard. 'Courage like that whistles in the dark,' your father said, 'bound to a higher power.' Your father started to whistle then, but he made only a high, thin sound, more like air escaping through a hole. My father began to whistle. They stood looking out on the dark city, trying to out-whistle each other."

"I would not have killed Calvin Wheat," my father-in-law says in English. "He was an honorable man. That night he told me his family was the music in his life." Ibrahim Hasan reaches for the tea on the table. I glance at Mother, who's shut her eyes. Her eyelids flutter as though she's reviewing scenes on the membrane of her mind.

Ibrahim Hasan resumes in Arabic. "The next day, instead of meeting Jaafari, your father flew to Kuwait," Adil translates. "He picked up two passengers in his airplane. One of the passengers was a competitor of Hamid Jaafari's, a young Frenchman connected in high places; the other passenger was the man's Lebanese mistress."

"You knew them?" I ask in Arabic. I wonder if that meant the woman was not my father's mistress or if my father-in-law was shielding us with another version of the story.

"We all knew each other. We were like a family of scorpions."

I try to absorb this story, to link it to the father I've carried in my head all these years, but the only link is my father-in-law. I've never heard of these other people. Who was the Frenchman? I think of Serena's husband who died that same year, but he died on the Amalfi coast, Gerald, her father-in-law, had told her. Gerald Wagner hadn't featured in my father's world, according to Marvin Penn, but I wonder now if he was on the periphery of this world after all. The networks my father was investigating were not Advanced Technology Partners or KBT Engineering. Those companies were set up after my father's death, but they sold into the same insatiable markets.

"Did the woman on the plane have anything to do with my father's death?" I ask, avoiding my mother's gaze.

Ibrahim Hasan reaches for the sugar and dumps three spoonfuls into his tea. He sits, stirring his cup. "I've become an old man," he answers in English. "I remember some years like yesterday. Others I don't remember at all, and what once seemed important to me is no longer important. The past is as unpredictable as the future. When Calvin Wheat's plane crashed, I remember thinking he'd flown himself up into the sun and then crashed to the bottom of the viper's hole. Your father—how do you say in English—was playing a deep game, setting one arms dealer against the other for information. What he discovered didn't show your government or other governments in such good light. But I think he lost the game because of an even older game. You see, the woman you ask about on the plane, the beautiful woman with the Frenchman, she was, in fact, Hamid Jaafari's wife, and Hamid Jaafari would never allow such a betrayal."

Without transition my father-in-law now states what he requires of me for this memory. "I would like to see my son married in Beirut," he says in English. "If you will wait, we will fly your whole family there. You can use the time to get ready. You can buy your trousseau. We will give you a proper wedding, one your father would have been proud of."

"Father, we are getting married today," Adil says.

"The children wanted to keep the wedding small—" my mother starts to explain.

"Mother," I interrupt. I turn to my father-in-law. In Arabic I say, "I will be glad to come to Beirut for another wedding, but today I would like to marry your son. We have waited a very long time."

"We are getting married, Father," Adil repeats. "You told me you would not press this."

Ibrahim Hasan sets down his cup and turns to my mother. "So, what are we to do?"

I wonder if he and my mother scripted his request, but as Mom closes the photo album, I see in her eyes that she's not thinking about Ibrahim Hasan's entreaty. She is thinking perhaps as I am about how much my father would have wanted to be at my wedding. Perhaps she is also thinking about the blessing delivered from my father over all the years on my wedding day. In his final hours he told this stranger that *we were the music in his life.*

*   *   *

Adil and I get married at two p.m. in the Old Marylebone Town Hall, a building that looks like a grand home with wide steps and columns. The ceremony takes less than twenty minutes. Before a British magistrate in a blue and white parlor, I stand at Adil's side wearing a white wool and crepe suit with white satin ribbon braided in my hair. Behind me, Jane and Sophie stand in pale blue wool suits, and behind Adil, Fatin attends in his banker's pinstripe. Jad in his gray slacks and blue blazer and Raja in her new yellow organdy dress hang onto the edge of the magistrate's desk with our rings between them, along with Pickles's daughter Sara holding a bouquet of baby orchids. Mom and Winston and Ibrahim Hasan sit in the front row. Behind them, Pickles cradles a sleeping Liza, and Dennis Jr. wiggles uncomfortably in his new suit while Randolph tries to quiet him. Molly Dees and Henry, who is shipping out for Cairo in a few days, sit in the third row next to Meg Mulroney, who clutches a handkerchief. Meg has all but retired as our housekeeper. She comes to work only on Monday and Thursday mornings to shop for us at Marks and Spencers where she meets up with her friends. In the back against the wall, Omar and Jawad stand as solemn as if they are at a funeral. Outside the door, two police officers have been persuaded to keep watch.

As the magistrate reads the service—a mixture of governmental and Anglican sentiment—I realize how uncomfortable it must be for Adil's father to see the British, who intervened in his country years ago and who've thrown him out of Britain, marry his son. I half regret that I haven't let him have the wedding he wants. At least Adil and I have written our vows so the promises we make to each other are our own. *We will keep our hearts with all diligence . . . we will love and be loving . . . seek and give space to each other to seek . . . We will be faithful.* We hold hands during the proceedings, which are an anti-climax after all the years that have gone before. That twenty minutes of words, officiated by a stranger, constitutes our being married and committed to love and support each other for the rest of our lives seems an improbable threshold.

At 2:20 p.m. February 1, 1996, I, Elizabeth West, daughter of Miriam Weiss Hansson and Jesse Samuel West, and Adil Ibrahim Hasan, son of Ibrahim Hasan and Janan Abd al Karim, join as husband and wife and family for Jesse Adil West and Raja Adil Ibrahim Hasan. In those twenty minutes we merge three religions of the world and half a dozen nationalities, and we, the children and our own children, will have to figure out how to make peace among them all.

After the wedding we plan to return to the house where caterers have set up a lunch. Mother has offered to keep the children for a few days afterwards so that Adil and I can have a brief honeymoon. We're going to Paris. My father-in-law has arranged rooms for us at the Plaza Athenee Hotel. We planned a much more modest accommodation, but when Adil's father heard where we were staying, he asked if he could at least help with the wedding trip. Adil and I let him, though I had reservations about his getting even this involved. I asked if we had to have bodyguards go with us. His father persuaded me that Jawad, who is the most pleasant and at the same time the more remote of the two, should accompany us, though always at a distance.

"What's the point of a bodyguard if he's at a distance?" I asked Adil in private.

"He watches the perimeter," Adil said.

I've come to realize that Ibrahim Hasan is a master negotiator. He began by objecting to our marriage, withholding his blessing, then he urged us to postpone the wedding, all positions he must have been prepared to lose, so that when we got to the details and he had already conceded the larger issues, we felt obliged to allow him some say in our lives. Thus, Ibrahim Hasan scheduled our honeymoon and was sending his man to accompany us. If I hadn't been so focused on keeping him from taking control, I might have learned something from him, but I never got the chance.

*   *   *

Gunfire cracks against the blue afternoon sky like thunder and hits like lightning. We are walking down the steps of the Town Hall after the ceremony when the first shot bursts. This time I recognize the sound instantly. I grab Jad and Raja while Adil literally throws us back up the stairs towards the building. I glimpse a purple skirt falling beside me. As I turn, I see Ibrahim Hasan throw his body across my mother in what I think is an effort to shield her, but I realize now was only the trajectory of his fall. There are screams—maybe they are mine—and a round of rapid shots—more screaming and children crying, and another body falls to the steps. I can't see whose it is. In a corner of my vision as I turn, I see a red double-decker bus whizzing by. We plunge inside the foyer of the building just as the police come running out. I try to run with them back to my mother, but a policeman restrains Adil and me until the police have cleared the steps. Within moments sirens pierce the air.

I finally rush down to where my mother is lying with her head at an angle and her eyes open. Ibrahim Hasan still lies across her. I shout, "No!" Then I see her blink. I sink beside her. "Are you hit?"

She blinks again. "I don't know. Is he dead?" Ibrahim Hasan is pinning her with his chest pressed on hers as in a wrestling match. Blood seeps onto her lilac crepe suit.

By now Adil has reached his father. I glance up the stairs where Pickles is keeping the children as Jane, Sophie, and Winston run towards us. Adil feels his father's neck and turns his head. Adil's eyes cloud over. He lifts his father's body into his arms. My mother drags herself from under it. "Is he dead?" she asks again.

Adil cradles his father. I put my arm under Mother's shoulders. "Can you stand?"

"I don't know."

"Stay still." Jane reaches us.

"An ambulance is on the way," Winston says.

"I think I'm fine." Mother attempts to stand and then slowly sinks back down. "I tripped is all." She looks at Adil, who holds his father's head in his lap. The bodyguards appear on either side of him. Omar speaks in Arabic. He tells Adil it isn't safe for him to remain there.

"I'm staying with my father," Adil says.

I leave Jane and Sophie and Winston with Mother and move beside Adil. I put my arms around his broad shoulders. I don't have to ask. Ibrahim Hasan is dead. "I'll stay with you," I say.

"No. You must take the children home. Make sure they're all right. They'll be frightened. I'll come as soon as I can."

It isn't until I stand and turn towards the street that I see who else has been shot. Off to the side of the steps, an attendant is lifting Molly Dees onto a stretcher. She's sitting up. I go over to her.

"Someone shot me in the leg!" she protests as the attendant wheels her away.

The press is already arriving. I wonder how the word has spread so quickly. The police are roping the area with yellow plastic tape. We're turning into a cordoned-off event, a story to be told. One of the journalists tries to get my attention. "Excuse me . . . excuse me . . . What's happened?"

I hurry up the steps to the children. "Mom is all right," I tell Pickles.

"Is he dead?" she asks.

I nod.

"Who's dead?" Jad asks full of urgency as though he understands what the question means.

I put my arms around him and take him in my lap, trying already to protect him from what this might mean in his life. I draw Raja over to me. "Adil's father, your grandfather . . . Jiddu, whom you met this morning . . . he's been shot."

"Who shot him?" Jad asks.

"I don't know." I haven't paused to ask that question. Is it his own people spilling the fighting onto the streets of London? We've never confirmed who shot at us on the Embankment, though my father-in-law thinks it was the Iraqi Mukhabarat who also tried to kill him in Beirut. Is it Dr. Wagner trying to keep my father-in-law from testifying? In that moment I realize Adil won't be able to walk away from his father's murder. We can't go off so easily to some neutral place to begin as a family—one wife, one husband, one son, one daughter—living as everyone else lives. As the member of my family who's eschewed politics, I have in the very personal act of marrying Adil made a profoundly political decision. Adil and I won't be going on a honeymoon to Paris, but to a funeral in Beirut, one from which we may or may not return. In his death Ibrahim Hasan may have succeeded in getting the political life he wanted for his son better than he ever could have with his life. So it is, I fear, that history holds on.

CHAPTER TWENTY-SIX

"You're sure you're not hurt?" I ask again as Mother peels off her lilac crepe suit stained with blood.

I've been hovering ever since she returned from the police station. I sit on her bed where Raja sleeps clutching the doll Adil has given her and Jad lies half asleep watching television. I stroke their foreheads. Since we've come home, I've kept them close, changed their clothes, held them in my arms. Raja is subdued, but Jad has been on high alert, talking rapidly about the gunshots, talking about them over and over as he circles the room.

From her closet Mom pulls out a pair of tan slacks and draws a white turtleneck over her head. "Where's Adil?" she asks.

I slip off the bed and follow her into the bathroom, where she tries to wash the blood from the suit's skirt then hangs the suit over the shower stall and washes her face. "He's still with the police," I say. I strain to keep control, but my voice breaks. "I'm sorry . . . I'm so sorry. I didn't understand."

She puts her arm around me, drawing me into her space the way I do with Jad. "It's not your fault."

"I didn't imagine . . ."

She puts her hands on my shoulders and looks at me straight on. "This afternoon Ibrahim told me that he accepted you as his daughter-in-law.

He said you showed the courage he wanted his son to have in a wife. You stood up to him as his wife stood up to her family. You gave him the pleasure of seeing his son marry."

I try to find in her words release from the terrible responsibility I feel that by insisting we go ahead with our wedding, I set up my father-in-law's death.

Mother runs cold water on a washcloth and hands it to me. "Your father would have told you to live your life with courage," she says. "I'm sure of that. The choice you've made marrying Adil and the choice Adil has made marrying you is going to take courage and considerable humanity."

"Humanity?" I sit on the edge of the bathtub and put the cold cloth on my face.

Mother begins reapplying her makeup. Her hands tremble slightly as she harmonizes the shadows and stains of age with a beige foundation, a dust of powder, and a swipe of peach blush on her cheeks. I remember when she rarely put on more than lipstick. She looks up at me in the mirror.

"You'll have to see through the debris people will throw your way. See their humanity, often in spite of them. Grandma Sha told your father in order to fight a fire he didn't have to rush into the flames. He needed to figure out how to keep a safe distance but cut off the oxygen. She told him not to lose sight of the good as he pursued the plots of evil in the world. In the end, I think that's what happened to him, Lizzy. He plunged down . . . what did Ibrahim call it . . . down the viper's hole, and he lost his way out."

*　　*　　*

Jane, Sophie, and I fold up the tables and chairs in the living room where we'd planned to have the reception after the wedding. We put away the catered food—the lamb, the grilled chicken breasts, the penne pasta with sun-dried tomatoes, the vegetables with goat cheese. We call the hospital to check on Molly Dees, who has already been released.

We're sitting around the kitchen table when Adil lets himself in with the key I've given him. The blue and red tie I bought him hangs loose around his neck. His white shirt is spotted with blood. His dark hair falls in his eyes. He embraces me and the children, then he turns to my mother, who stands and touches his hair, clearing it from his forehead. They both have spent time at the police station.

"I went by Gerald Wagner's house after I left the station," he tells her. "I pounded on his door, but no one answered."

"I also told the police they should question him," Mother says.

"The house was dark. As I started down the steps, the housekeeper opened the door and told me he was gone, that he'd taken off this afternoon."

"I told the police to check the airports for him," Mother says.

"We will not let this pass," Winston declares without saying what can be done. He then rises from the table, along with Sophie, who touches Adil's hand. Mother and Jane embrace him, and they all excuse themselves.

I wrap my arms around Adil and lean into his hard, broad chest as he leans into me. At our feet, Jad and Raja look up at us, uncertain what they are supposed to do.

"I'm sorry your father is dead," Jad offers.

Adil sinks to his knees and folds both children into his arms. "I am very sorry too."

"Where did he go?" Jad asks.

Adil hesitates, unsure of the question, but Raja answers, "Damascus," which means she's understood both the English and the question.

"Oh," Jad says. He seems satisfied with the answer. He perhaps pictures the blue dot on the yellow triangle in our atlas with the basket of olives in the margin.

"I'm so sorry," I say.

Adil rises and draws me back into his arms. We stand together, breathing, letting the air rise and fall between us and inside us, filling the space around our hearts. "I'm glad he got to see me marry," Adil says. He sits down at the table and takes Raja onto his lap. "I need to use the phone."

I nod and hand it to him. "I'll get you some dinner."

As Jad and I gather dinner for Adil from the containers piled up in the refrigerator, Adil makes phone calls to prepare for his father's return to Lebanon. "He's gone now," I hear him say in Arabic. Jad carries over a platter of lamb and vegetables and stands at his father's side until Adil also lifts him onto his lap. Adil eats dinner with his arms around both children.

*   *   *

After dinner we tuck Jad and Raja into beds in Sophie's room, then retire to my room next door, where Adil hands me two small boxes wrapped in gold paper. "They were in his pocket."

Carefully I unwrap the first box. On white Harrods tissue lie two keys. I hand Adil the note written in Arabic. *The brass key is from our home in Palestine 48 years ago. The silver key you must cut for yourself.*

Without comment Adil unwraps the second box and lifts out two burgundy-colored Lebanese passports, his and Raja's. He begins flipping through the pages. Stamped in red and blue ink are visas for the United States. Also in the box is a letter on official Lebanese government letterhead: *This is to certify entry for Elizabeth Adil Ibrahim Hasan (ne: Elizabeth West) and Adil Adil Ibrahim Hasan (ne: Jesse*

Adil West) to Lebanon without restriction. I wonder if Adil's father has withheld these gifts until after the wedding in the hope we may not get married. But in the end, he chose to connect.

Adil sets the passports and the keys on the nightstand, and we lie back on the bed with my head on his shoulder. He rolls over and kisses me as if he will swallow me. I hold his head in my hands, draw him to my breast, then I pull him into my heart and will not let go. We make love three times before we finally fall back to sleep in the bed I've grown up in as though the years apart have only been an interlude.

*   *   *

In the distance a clock chimes three times. I lift my head from Adil's chest. He is also awake. "I love you," I say, resting my chin on my hand so I can look into his eyes.

"I love you too." He strokes my hair. His dark lashed eyes search my face. "I have to take my father back to Lebanon. I don't know if it's safe for you and the children to come right now."

Ever since Ibrahim Hasan was shot, I've known we will be pulled apart again. I want to protest, but I can't risk going with the children, and I can't leave them behind after what's happened. "How long will you be gone?"

"Only as long as I have to. I need to sort out his things and see my family. Are you all right here if I go?"

I look around the room, at the canopy over the bed, the white-painted dresser with the music box Dad brought me. I've been all right here for more than half my life.

"I figured something out today, Lizzy. As I was moving from office to office filling out forms, I wanted to find who killed my father and kill him, but I kept thinking what you would say and think if I did that. And if I killed him, his son would come to kill me. Then Jad would want to kill his son and on and on. I don't want Jad to have to kill anyone for me." His dark eyes bear down on me with a light in them that I haven't seen before. "I want to study law and teach the law and perhaps someday even write the laws we live by." He runs his hand gently down my bare back as if he's feeling the path ahead of him on my spine.

I rise on my elbows and kiss him. "What would you have done if Dr. Wagner had been at home tonight?"

"I would have told him who I was. I would have asked if he had my father killed. He is arrogant enough, he might have told me. Then I would have had him arrested."

"He's good at slipping away from the law," I say. Next door I hear Jad get up and stumble towards the bathroom that connects Sophie's and my rooms.

"I am not yet trained, but one day I will be."

*   *   *

Adil leaves for Lebanon today. Before he goes, he takes Jad to Holland Park with a soccer ball, and the two of them dribble the ball on the frozen field for an hour while Omar and Jawad pace up and down on either side.

After I take Adil to the airport, I go to Dr. Wagner's house. I don't call; I just ring the bell.

"I was wondering when you'd come back," Claudia says. She stands in the doorway blocking the entrance like a bouncer, dressed not in a uniform but in baggy gray slacks and a loose white shirt that I can't imagine Dr. Wagner allowing her to wear. I have the impression she is now mistress of the house.

"Have the police been here?" I ask.

"They've come around twice." She steps aside, letting me into the dim front hall. It is late afternoon, but there are no lights on.

"What did you tell them?" She leads me back into the kitchen, where Adil and I snuck out just a few weeks before. The painted cabinets are a dingy white and the tiles are beige, and the appliances are at least thirty years old. Setting a saucepan of water on a gas flame, she brings out two white china cups and a tin of shortbread to the Formica table in the corner. "Do you know where Dr. Wagner went?" I ask. "Do you know where Serena is?"

"Don't know where either of them are." Claudia pours tea.

"Has Serena called?"

"She used to call every day, but not anymore. She always called when he was out. She wanted me to give him the message that she'd called and was coming home so he wouldn't go after her. Then he'd get mad at me when she didn't come back. She told me she'd take care of me when she returned." Claudia eats a cookie and then another cookie. "But she's not coming back. I told her that he was taking out her clothes every day and giving them away to the shop down the road. She asked me to pack up her best clothes and send them to her, but leave the old ones so he wouldn't notice."

I lean forward in my chair. "Did she tell you where to send them?" Serena still hasn't retrieved her sweaters from Marvin.

Claudia goes to the kitchen drawer and hands me a piece of paper:

Pam Fields
c/o PO Box 753
Baton Rouge, LA 70821-0753

"Who's Pam Fields?"

"'Send them to me,' she said, and she gave me that name and address. She told me to send the clothes, but she didn't tell me what I'm supposed to use for money, so I haven't sent them. Nobody's bothered to tell me what I'm supposed to use for money."

"When is the last time you saw Dr. Wagner?"

"The morning he gave me an envelope to deliver for him. When I got back, he was gone." Her thick fingers bob up and down dipping pieces of shortbread into her tea.

I reach for a cookie to slow myself down so I won't push too hard. I'm not sure where Claudia's loyalties lie. *Circle, don't rush*, Marvin always told me. *Point to the sky when you ask people to step into a mine field*. I ask, "What envelope? Deliver it where?"

"To a hotel in Bayswater."

"You remember the name?"

Claudia squints. Her eyes disappear into her heavy cheeks. "The name made me think of birds and thieves . . . Craven Gardens Hotel."

"Who did you deliver it to?"

"'Drop it at the front desk,' he said so that's what I did, then I went to have lunch with a friend who was in the city for a wedding. When I got home, he was gone. He left me a note, told me to take care of everything, but he didn't leave me any more money. I've almost gone through all the money."

"What friend? What wedding?" The dots suddenly connect as Marvin told me they would when I got enough of them and could start drawing lines between them. I press. I can't help myself. "Was your friend Meg Mulroney?"

Claudia's flat face sharpens into a frown. "Maybe I shouldn't be talking to you."

"But you know Meg. Was it my wedding?"

"I don't want to get no one in trouble."

"Did Meg tell you when and where I was getting married?" The connections fall into place. "Did you mention that to Dr. Wagner?"

She stands and begins clearing the cups. "I don't want trouble. They left me here, no money, nothing. Just this big house full of stuff. I been looking everywhere to find the money. What am I supposed to do?"

*   *   *

Claudia calls Meg after I leave, and Meg calls Winston and comes over. Winston and Meg spend an hour together in his office. Meg emerges in tears. She tells Winston that over the years she and Claudia have met in the food hall at Marks and Spencer's and talked about their families. She's told Claudia that I'm a travel agent, told her when I was coming to London, told her I was getting married to an Arab. Claudia was curious about the wedding, and so Meg shared the details, including where and when the ceremony would take place.

Winston phones the police, who take down Meg's statement and then go again to interview Claudia, who confirms that Dr. Wagner often asked her about our family and instructed her to find out the time and location of the wedding. On that morning he asked her to deliver an envelope to two men registered at the Craven Gardens Hotel, where the police have already determined the assassins stayed. The police caught one of the men, who looked in the wrong direction when fleeing across Marylebone Road and was grazed by a double-decker bus. In the hospital he confessed, allowing the police to arrest his colleague at Gatwick Airport. The two men don't know who hired them. They know only an anonymous middleman in Goma, Zaire, where they come from. They say a note was delivered that morning to their hotel, telling them the time and place and providing photographs of their targets—a man and his son. How, I wonder, did Dr. Wagner have a photograph of Adil? If he had a picture, then he knew what Adil looked like. At some point he must have realized who Adil was when he met him each morning. Is that why he told Adil he was brave?

The police find Claudia's information provocative enough to set up a watch on Dr. Wagner's house, though Claudia says she doesn't know when he's returning. Sometimes he stays away for months, though usually he leaves her money to take care of expenses. The police instruct her to contact them immediately if she hears from him. They alert authorities in Germany and France. They also alert Interpol and United Kingdom immigration offices so that if Dr. Wagner tries to leave or return to Britain, he will be arrested.

*　*　*

Mother writes the story about the death of Ibrahim Hasan for the arms issue of *Crisispoint*. She rushes to press the sidebar article, which starts with the bullet, tracking it on its journey through the history of the arms trade after World War II to the end of the life of one of the smaller actors in that post-war drama. She uses Dad's notes to assist her.

It turns out that the bullet that killed Ibrahim Hasan comes from the same type of gun as the one that killed Dennis, manufactured by Gerald Wagner's company located in Slovakia. The company has shipped guns to Yugoslavia and then to Serbia as Yugoslavia broke apart so that the guns are widely used in the Balkans War. As the war in Bosnia draws to a reluctant truce, surplus arms are now shipped by the Serbs to Iraq and also to refugee camps in Eastern Zaire and the Great Lakes region in Africa, where two mercenaries were recruited for a furlough to London. Their only job was to assassinate an Arab man and his son. Because they have no record or prior contacts in London, if they had succeeded in getting away, there would be little to trace them. One, dressed as a street cleaner, was sweeping the streets below the Town Hall before he fired the bullet that traveled upwards from the sidewalk into the heart of Ibrahim Hasan. The other assassin, dressed as a beggar, shot Molly

Dees in the leg, though for what reason or by accident still is not clear. Adil Hasan got away by bolting back up the steps with his wife and children, the article says.

Mother notes that Molly and Jonathan Dees, who has served off and on in the American Embassy in London over the last fourteen years, departed suddenly and cannot be reached for comment. Mother cannot confirm in time for her deadline her own suspicions that Jonathan Dees is conducting surveillance out of the Embassy and collecting information on black market arms merchants operating in London. Mother does confirm, but does not write, that Jonathan Dees has had contacts with Ibrahim Hasan.

Why the assassins chose such a public place puzzles the police and MI5, who are investigating the murder. They finally conclude that the men, both in their early twenties, never traveled to Europe and had insufficiently imagined the venue.

In that same arms issue of *Crisispoint*, Mother also publishes the article she'd been researching that tracked arms flows into the Middle East after the oil crisis of 1973 when the West began making sizeable weapons sales partly to recover the money it had to pay out for oil. In 1980 when Iraq and Iran went to war, sales into the region escalated into a bonanza for the arms trade, she notes, allowing governments to offset research and development costs for their own new weapons. Over the years there are those who warned against this proliferation, she writes, but like the biblical Jeremiah, they cried in the wilderness. One of those Jeremiahs, I've come to understand, was my father.

*   *   *

The arms issue of *Crisispoint* appears on the newsstand the day before the Arms Commission report, which criticizes Winston in two paragraphs for not investigating the materials he vouched for in Dr.

Wagner's shipments. The Commission has turned over its files on Gerald Rene Wagner to the prosecutor's office.

The day after the Commission Report, Mother comes into Winston's study and lays several newspapers on the desk as Winston and I are working. I'm cataloguing Dr. Wagner's invoices, and Winston is studying news clippings with a magnifying glass at the library table. The children are visiting Pickles's children, their cousins, all day.

Mother reads out loud from one of the papers: *A private airplane crashed into the Baltic Sea last night carrying industrialist Dr. Gerald Rene Wagner, former President of Wagner Machines and Tools and a resident of Frankfurt, Marseilles, and London.*

I look up. She hands me the newspaper. I skim the small article on the inside page: The plane was traveling from Hamburg to Bratislava when the pilot called in a May Day that his left engine had exploded. A witness on a fishing boat below reported seeing a single parachute open over the water just before the plane dove into the ocean. It was an uncorroborated sighting but means that the pilot may have bailed out, the article says. None of the passengers are thought to have survived.

"You think it's true?" I ask. I pass the article to Winston.

"He was on the plane. I checked," Mother says.

"I got a call yesterday from Marvin," I say. "I was going to tell you. British and U.S. Treasury officials discovered two accounts on Serena's list were closed and the funds withdrawn two days ago. Do you think Dr. Wagner could have faked his death?"

Mother sits down at the table. She's working from home today. In her sweat pants and sweatshirt without makeup, she looks tired. She told me she's thinking of retiring as editor at the end of the year. "He would have killed four people to do so," she answers, "though that is not beyond him. The Interpol warrant for him has circled the globe. I think it's more likely his partners decided to cut their loss and took him out."

I shift in my chair. An uncomfortable feeling of *déjà vu* stirs me like a tiny electric shock. Mother looks at me over the top of her reading glasses and nods as though she too feels the jolt. That Dr. Wagner and my father, men of such different character, could have the same end leaves me staring out the window into the garden. By the wall I see a small animal crouched at the base of a tree. I squint. Is it a squirrel? Or a rat? I can't tell. As if sensing it is being watched, it scurries away.

"So who took the money from the bank accounts?" Winston asks. "Dr. Wagner?"

"Maybe Serena?" Mother suggests.

"Or Dr. Wagner Sr.?" Winston says.

"Or Adnan Kamil Houston?" I offer. And then more dots connect. "Or Claudia, the housekeeper." I can see her moving through the dark house at will, looking for the money, negotiating the craziness of Dr. Wagner and Serena at war with each other, both taking her loyalty for granted. "She has access to everything." I can see her standing in the doorway of the grand home in her bedroom slippers and baggy pants. "She was the one left in charge."

* * *

As I wait in London for Adil to return, I'm reading my father's papers and have come to some conclusions, though I can't yet prove them. I don't believe my father was having an affair, though I understand that interpretation exists. I think he knew how dangerous his liaison was with the other passengers on his plane, but he took the risk because he wanted one last triumph of intelligence before he ended his career. I think he wanted to confirm who was shipping the most dangerous of arms to the enemy, or perhaps he was trying to determine exactly who was the enemy. *We are all deep in the cave with the beast,* he wrote in the back of his last notebook. After all, he too had facilitated these trades.

I've wondered if he grew afraid on his last trip. He may often have
been afraid as Marvin told me he was, but he was a professional and
knew how to look the beast in the eye. I don't know exactly what my
father was pursuing when he flew his passengers out over the Persian
Gulf that morning, but he failed to calculate the burning distance—
that distance it is necessary to keep from the sun.

Adil calculates this distance daily. Before Adil left, he and I fantasized about moving to a place where no one knew us, where we could
invent ourselves, to Canada or to California, though we would be
very far from our families there. Or to Paris. Or Cairo, where Jane
would be. Perhaps someday to Beirut. As we talked, we knew we were
planning a fantasy, and yet life has roads and directions that are quite
fantastic, patterns we don't see when we're in the midst of them, a
sense of humor, and strange harmonies few of us hear. After all, hadn't
the daughter of Jesse West, alias Calvin Wheat, and the son of Ibrahim Hasan, alias Abraham Zill, met at the American School in London and been drawn together by their mutual loss?

Adil has been gone nine days now. So far, our relationship has been
defined more by our absences than by time together. I woke up this
morning to the thought: *I am a mender of the fabric.* Not that *I* am
the mender of the fabric ripped and torn but that the fabric of life
mends. I received a call this afternoon from a reporter at BBC World
Service who saw Adil just yesterday. The phone service is still problematic in the south of the country where Adil is. Adil asked him to
phone me when he got to London and let me know he's coming home.
Jad, Raja, and I are now his home.

As I wait for Adil, I feel hopeful. I can't say why except that hope
too is a threshold of history. Life is a song, as my father said, though
at times the music plays in a register almost beyond the human ear.

AUTHOR'S NOTE

During the first Gulf War with Iraq in 1991, I lived in London where my children attended the American School. At the time my youngest son, Elliot, age ten, was friends with the son of the Kuwaiti ambassador and with an Iraqi student. When I picked him up from summer camp, I told him that the previous week Iraq had invaded Kuwait. He immediately asked: "What will happen to Talal and Alec?" He understood instantly the invasion would have consequences for his two friends.

Burning Distance began germinating as I watched the Gulf War while living in Europe with my family. At the American School, children of diplomats, businessmen, journalists, and the leader of what some called at the time "a terrorist" organization all went to school together. Security heightened at the school during the war. Many of the parents occupied the world stage in various roles while their children interacted and lived in their own worlds.

We had moved to London the previous year as the Soviet Union was breaking apart. We witnessed up close the political shift as Eastern Europe turned to the West. My children and I knocked down the Berlin Wall together. I wanted to write a novel that encompassed this rich period as well as showed the currents that were not so benign running beneath the surface, out of the sight line of many who were focused on the fall of the Soviet empire. During this period, there were large-scale weapons sales to Iraq and others and sales of component parts that would allow the building of weapons of mass destruction. It seemed probable that these would haunt us going forward.

I began researching the complex weapons trade, reading extensively about the Middle East and the arms merchants. At the same time, the voice of a ten-year-old girl, Lizzy, who'd just lost her father in ambiguous circumstances in the Persian Gulf, started taking shape in my head. Before long I knew that she and her mother, a journalist and editor of a news magazine, and her two sisters moved to London in 1982 as the European Union was forming and that the three sisters enrolled in the American School.

And so the story of Lizzy and the West family began. The narrative added characters as Miriam West remarried to a British knight who had a son and daughter and as Lizzy met the soulful, mysterious soccer player Adil Hasan after an explosion in chemistry class. This young American girl and Palestinian/Lebanese boy—one who had lost a father, the other who had lost a mother—fell in love, unaware that their families' lives and histories were connected. Because of the work of Adil's father, however, Adil and Lizzy were separated.

The action in *Burning Distance* takes place in London and Washington, D.C., and spans over a decade—1981–1996. The writing of the book involved extensive research; I then needed to transform facts into fiction and into the language of literature. Sometimes I felt as if I were actually trying to digest intercontinental ballistic missiles, spinning lathes and centrifuges, chewing them, massaging them over and over, swallowing them, then doing so again and again to knead information into a narrative that began and ended with characters and with the workings of the human heart, which would then inform the power and politics of the story.

Fortunately, the characters helped and began to take over, opening the narrative to me as I weaved the story of a family who'd lost a father with the love story of Lizzy and Adil with a political intrigue dealing with arms merchants. Sometimes the book seemed larger than my experience and skill as a writer, and yet I couldn't put it down. Between drafts I wrote short stories, articles, drafts of two other books, then I came back again, fresh, ready to reenter the lives of my characters and live through another and then another draft.

The novel was in draft when the planes crashed into the Twin Towers on September 11. I was in New York City that day, about to go to a meeting. When I saw in real time on television what happened and couldn't get out of New York City, I took my manuscript and worked with a new sense of urgency. Yet it still took years of digesting, reading, writing other work before this manuscript was ready.

In that time, I interviewed and shared the manuscript with experts, including at the CIA, senior arms control experts in the State Department and National Security Council, at the National Defense University, Human Rights Watch, and the International Crisis Group to understand and confirm the arms sales and flows. The book is fiction. The characters and the plot are my invention, but the pattern of activity and the context is well researched and confirmed by these experts.

During the writing of the book, I took Arabic classes to understand the language, at least at a basic level. In my work with PEN, International Crisis Group, Human Rights Watch, and Save the Children, I've traveled numerous times to the Middle East, including to Lebanon, Egypt, Jordan, Israel, and Iraq. I was in Iraq two months after the second Gulf War ended, visiting Baghdad and Basra with Save the Children in a period just before the insurgency began.

My youngest son was a senior in college and head of an ROTC unit at Tufts/Harvard/MIT on 9/11. He went on to serve five tours of duty in Iraq and Afghanistan as a Marine, winning a Silver Star, Bronze Star for Valor, and Purple Heart. When he finished his service, he turned his pen to writing and is now an award-winning (finalist for National Book Award) novelist and journalist who has published seven books with more coming. My oldest son, a mathematician and wrestler, went on to wrestle in the Athens Olympics in 2004 and went to Harvard and got a PhD in mathematics at MIT and is a working mathematician.

As a novelist, I'm interested in the personal stories within global events and in seeing the ordinary within the extraordinary. I'm interested in how the events we call history impact individual lives and in how the human heart shapes both the personal and the political. *Burning Distance* is a story of history's trajectories into the lives of individuals; it is a love story and a political thriller.

BOOK CLUB
DISCUSSION QUESTIONS

1. Lizzy's father's words echo throughout Lizzy's story. Do you think they prove to be true? Can you site any examples?

2. Why do you think Lizzy and Adil fall in love? Are they a modern-day Romeo and Juliet?

3. What interrupts their love story?

4. What brings them together? Do they overcome the obstacles?

5. What is the effect of Lizzy's father's life and death on Lizzy's life and on her mother's and sisters' lives?

6. Why does Lizzy's mother say Lizzy is "racing into the darkness"? Is her mother right? Is Lizzy right? What is Miriam West afraid of? Why isn't Lizzy afraid?

7. Do you think Lizzy made the right decision as to whom she married? Why? Why not?

8. What are the effects of Gerald Wagner and his actions on the West family? On society at large?

9. What is Winston's emotional journey in the book?

10. Which of the four sisters do you most admire or identify with—Lizzy, Jane, Sophie, Pickles?

11. What path would you predict going forward for Lizzy? For Adil? For Ramsay?

12. How important are the world events around you in the living of your life? How does that compare with the West family?

13. What do you think happened to Gerald Wagner?

14. What does "burning distance" mean?

15. What event does *Burning Distance* foreshadow?